PRAISE FOR

BEAUFORT

"Evocative, heartbreaking and haunting . . . [Israel's] *Red Badge of Courage*. Because Leshem, like Stephen Crane, never saw combat, this is not a work of autobiography or observations but one of empathy and reconstruction—and all the stronger for that because the author has deployed both qualities without judgment. *Beaufort* is that rare thing, a novel of deep moral concern in which sympathetically drawn and beautifully realized characters are allowed to speak for themselves."

—*Los Angeles Times*

"Thirteen young soldiers spring to life with voices at once self-critical and brash, tender and darkly flippant. . . . Though firsthand accounts and combat memoirs line the shelves of bookstores, Leshem's fiction rivals them in the completeness of his cosmos of war."

—*San Francisco Chronicle*

"Stark and searing and stitched with black humor . . . *Beaufort* makes several statements: courage, yes; camaraderie, sure; but also the futility of war."

—*Milwaukee Journal Sentinel*

"Evocative . . . Leshem's novel captures the soldiers' pathos and the claustrophobia of an isolated outpost. As they approach withdrawal and the planned demolition of Beaufort, these emotions build to a shattering climax."

—*Dallas Morning News*

"An important novel . . . This is a picture of war from a soldier's point of view. Its language is crude, the body count rises, and yet the tenderness of the bonds among the men is extraordinary." —*Library Journal* (starred review)

"Told in a stream-of-consciousness diary style, [Leshem's] gripping first novel describes life for a group of adolescents who must quickly become battle-hardened soldiers. . . . By turns, [*Beaufort*] is tragic, funny, mordant, irate, shocking, and poignant. . . . A must-read." —*Booklist* (starred review)

"[*Beaufort*] is a candid and unsparing portrayal of one young army commander's service in Lebanon. . . . It's Leshem's intensely authentic mapping of the soldiers' volatile inner landscape that makes this novel so gripping and essential; how they deal with their fears and doubts, the depth of their mutual dependency and love for each other, the secret language they share, and the concealed longings and fantasies that sustain them in unimaginable conditions."
—*Montreal Gazette*

"[A] darkly comic yet realistic story . . . Leshem plunges the reader headfirst into the depths of the Beaufort fortress. . . . Haunting."
—*The Jerusalem Post*

"A book we couldn't put down." —*Penthouse*

"Surprisingly, Ron Leshem himself did not serve in the Israeli army. A journalist and television producer, he is appropriately modest about his inexperience compared to the men who inspired his novel, but it feels very, very real. This is a classic war story, with all the traditional

elements of heroism, danger and black humor, but the reader never loses sight of the futility of the war itself."
—BookReporter.com

"Breathtakingly intense . . . [*Beaufort*] is rich with layers of combat detail: the relationships, apprehensions, panic, humor, tension, tears, and battle fatigue. . . . Leshem's journalistic instincts lend the novel a gritty reality that is captivating and compelling—even if you don't normally read combat fiction. This is a fascinating piece of Israel's history and the history of war, told in a breathtaking way [with an] excellent, literate, often lyrical translation by Evan Fallenberg."
—*San Diego Jewish Journal*

"At once profane, violent, tragic and hilarious . . . army life and the labyrinthine Beaufort compound is so richly detailed."
—*J, the Jewish News Weekly of Northern California*

"Leshem's debut offers an antidote, perhaps, both to the romanticization of battle and to the 'shoot-and-cry' syndrome that afflicts Israeli society."
—*Zeek* magazine

"[*Beaufort*] is powerfully told . . . [and] goes deeper into the stories and characters of these young men of the IDF, their lives before and their dreams of after, their loves, their connections to each other, with intimate details about daily life. . . . [Leshem] gets readers with their 'nerve endings exposed' . . . [to] touch them in the deepest way."
—*Jewish Week*

"Gritty . . . the anxiety and fear are palpable throughout Leshem's vivid novel—you can practically feel the shells explode." —*Publishers Weekly*

"A gripping, viscerally powerful tale . . . An alternately grim and blackly comic war/coming-of-age novel."
—*Kirkus Reviews*

"Ron Leshem has succeeded in creating an entire world, simply through language."
—David Grossman, author of *The Yellow Wind*

BEAUFORT

RON LESHEM

TRANSLATED FROM THE HEBREW
BY EVAN FALLENBERG

DELTA TRADE PAPERBACKS

BEAUFORT
A Delta Book

PUBLISHING HISTORY
Delacorte Press hardcover edition published January 2008
Delta Trade Paperback edition / March 2009

Published by
Bantam Dell
A Division of Random House, Inc.
New York, New York

Book design by Glen Edelstein

Library of Congress Catalog Card Number: 2007030292

ISBN 978-0-553-38529-8

Printed in the United States of America
Published simultaneously in Canada

www.bantamdell.com

BVG 10 9 8 7 6 5 4 3 2 1

WHAT HE CAN'T DO ANYMORE

Yonatan can't see us growing ugly anymore. "We'll never be as handsome as we are today," he would always say, and I would ask if that was meant to make us feel better, because it didn't.

What? Are you totally out of it? How could you not know this game? No way you don't know it. It's called "What He Can't Do Anymore," and it's what everyone plays when a friend is killed. You toss his name into the air and whoever's there at the time has to say something about what he can't do anymore. Sometimes it goes on for hours. Like on the soccer field, in the middle of a penalty kick. Late at night, too, for no good reason, you wake everyone up about half a minute after they've dropped off to sleep. Or when you're at home, working on your girlfriend, not thinking about us at all, when the last thing in the world you want is to play the game, well, BAM! the phone rings and it's us on the line. "Yonatan can't..." we say, and you have to—everyone has to—reel off some association, that's the rule, and you can't repeat what's already been said. Here's what I'm talking about:

Yonatan can't take his little brother to a movie anymore. Yonatan can't watch Hapoel bring home the soccer trophy anymore. Yonatan can't listen to the latest disc by Zion Golan anymore. He can't see Tom with the ugliest slut in Nahariya anymore, and after he laughed at all of us, that little Mongoloid. He'll never know how fucked up it is when you can't get it up. He'll never know how great it is when your mother's proud of you for getting accepted to college. Even a community college. He won't be at his grandfather's funeral, he won't know if his sister gets married, he won't take a piss with us from the highest peak in South America, he won't ski in Chacaltaya, he won't screw the hottest Peruvian chick in Casa Fistuk.

Yonatan can't know anymore the feeling of renting an apartment with his girlfriend. Yonatan can't know anymore what it is to go with her to Castro clothes and come out with the new winter collection, or to Roladin Bakery in the middle of the night, when it's raining, because all of a sudden she wants a doughnut, and anyway you're a jerk, you never knew how to say no to her. And here I am thinking how lucky I am that I've already had the chance to run out for doughnuts in the rain.

He'll never cheat on her. He'll never know what it's like to fuck the living daylights out of the sexiest babe in the country, some whore from Haifa who lures you into a one-night stand and then you understand, too late, that it wasn't worth it, and the love of your life has left you. He'll never know how much that hurts. And he'll never know what it's like to sit on the grass with a kid that's his very own, telling him stories about how we were bigger than life in those ambushes in Lebanon, how we pulled off some magnificent stuff up there. There are lots of things Yonatan can't do anymore.

Yonatan won't know what song they played at his grave

when he died: "Shir Hamaalot," a psalm done Middle Eastern–style. It became his song. Everyone who was killed has a song that sticks with his friends from the time of the funeral. For months you listen and never get sick of it.

Yonatan will never know how River the medic cried over his body, how he wouldn't calm down, how he fell apart, to pieces. Wailed like a baby. Yonatan'll never know how Furman and I spent a whole day in the trenches and down the slopes looking for his missing head. When the missile hit the guard post his head blew off and rolled down to the Litani River. We didn't want to believe it had rolled all the way down, to the river, but that's exactly what happened, and in the end we gave up. Nothing we could do about it. I leaned over in that heavy smoke and grabbed his body with both hands, a body with no head. He'll never know. And how the fire kept burning all around and we kept shooting and shooting and shooting in every possible direction, like that was supposed to make us feel better. And how everyone was shattered from it. The day before, we'd danced the waltz in our freezing dugout. We lit candles, we were happy. And then it ended. He'll never ever know, there's no chance of it.

Yonatan can't sniff that sweet sweat mixed with the faint smell of shampoo during a long night of wild sex and cuddling, like the week we all had after we left Lebanon, when everything ended. Yonatan will never even know we left Lebanon.

1

A LOT OF PEOPLE HAVE LOST A LOT of people since we lost Yonatan. We've lost others since then, too, because another war broke out and everything got more savage. But more indifferent, too. And who's got enough time on his hands to deal with what happened back then? When it broke out we lost Barnoy. Then another eleven guys. And when the numbers stabilized at nine hundred and twenty and it looked like it was over, we lost Koka's brother, who'd followed in his footsteps and enlisted with us. We've made love a thousand times since then, it's not like we haven't, and we've laughed a thousand times. We went on to other places, we escaped and came back, we remembered. But quietly. We imagined how we'll return to the fortress, to our mountain. There'll be a hotel there, maybe. Or a place for lovers to park. Or maybe it will be deserted. There'll be peace. And I will lead her along the paths, we'll walk hand in hand. "Here, baby, this is exactly where it happened." And stone by stone I'll show her. She might even ask if that's the whole story. "How can that be the whole story? What made you cry so much, it's actually really beautiful and peaceful here, everything's green with trees, and quiet. This is the place where you broke down?"

Try to imagine that they stick you high up on a mountain cliff, higher than the roof of the Azrieli Building. How could you not have a breathtaking view? Here it's wide expanses of green countryside checkered with patches of brown and red, snowy mountains, frothing rivers, narrow, winding, deserted European roads, and the sweetest wind there is. Zitlawi used to say that air like this should be bottled and sold to rich people on the north side of Tel Aviv. Christ, what quality. So fucking pastoral you could cut the calm with a knife. Our sunsets, too, they're the most beautiful on the planet, and the sunrises are even more beautiful, glimmering serenity from the roof of the world. Bring a girl or two here when the sky is orange and you've got it made. And dawn, an amazing cocktail of deep blue and turquoise and wine red and thin strips of pink, like an oil painting on canvas. And the deep wadi that twists away from the big rock we're sitting on. Try to explain how this could be the place where you broke down.

But from that night I remember the lights of Kiryat Shmona, on the Israeli side of the border, as they recede on the horizon, and everyone's beating hearts—I swear it, I can hear them as we make our way up to the top that very first time. And from minute to minute it's getting colder. There's not a living soul around except for us, practically not a single village in our zone, either. The convoy crawls along, gets swallowed up in a thick fog, there's no seeing more than a hundred yards ahead. Tanks are spread along the road to provide cover for us. From a slit near the roof of the Safari I try to figure out how far along we've come, silently poring over the map of danger spots and racing through an abbreviated battle history, muttering because no talking is allowed.

Where will the evil flare out from? I suddenly have the urge to shout to the commanding officer that we've gone too far, but I bite my lip and remain silent. From this moment on nobody can tell me anymore "You haven't got a clue what Lebanon is, wait'll you get there." I'm there, finally, that's what's important. A long line, heavy traffic: a supply Safari, a GI Safari, a diesel Safari, behind these an ordnance truck with a big crane, an Abir truck carrying a doctor and a medic, another GI Safari, the commander's Hummer, the lieutenant's Hummer, and an Electronic Warfare Hummer. Oshri asks if I've brought my lucky underwear with me. I gesture to him that I'm wearing them. After all, our good fortune depends on my lucky underwear. I'm wearing them, even if that means thirty-two days without washing them.

And I remember how the gate of the outpost opens to let us in, how the Safari comes to a halt inside a cloud. Everyone grabs hold of whatever's lying around—bags, equipment, your own or someone else's—and runs like hell inside. The commanders curse under their breath—"Out of the vehicles, run, get a move on!"—and people go down, people come up, you're not allowed to stand in place, you have to grab some shelter. When the parking area fills up with dozens of soldiers the enemy fires salvoes of mortar shells. And I try, but I can't see anything, don't recognize anyone around me, grab hold of the shirt of some soldier I don't know and get pulled along after him. I'm thrown into a crowded maze, surrounded by thick concrete on all sides, long passageways with no entrance or exit, rooms leading to steep dead-end stairways, cul-de-sacs, and a collection of larger rooms lit up in red, with low ceilings and stretchers. Thirty seconds later I'm already in one of the bomb shelters, a long and narrow alcove, a kind of underground cavern with concave walls covered in rusting metal and cramped three-layer bunk beds hanging by heavy iron chains from the ceiling.

WELCOME TO DOWNTOWN someone has carved over the

doorway, and inside the air is stuffy, suffocating, a stench of sweat overwhelms you again and again, in waves. This pit, called "the submarine," is where my entire life will be taking place from now on. I consider a quick trip to the toilet. A seasoned sergeant tells me to follow the blue light to the end of the hall and take a right, but he informs me I'll need a battle vest and a helmet. I decide to hold it in. What's the matter, is there a war on or something? I'm really not in the mood to go up in smoke here right now. Back then it seemed like it was light-years away when all it was was thirty, forty feet, three green toilets with a graffiti welcome—I CAME, I SAW, I CONQUERED. JULIUS CAESAR—and an official military sign commanding users DO NOT LEAVE PIECES OF SHIT ON THE TOILET SEAT so there is never any chance of forgetting where you are living. And in the morning, with the first sunrise, as the view of Lebanon spreads out before us like an endless green ocean, our commanding officer makes his opening statement, which he has undoubtedly been rehearsing for weeks, maybe months, or maybe it has been handed down through the generations: "Welcome. If there is a heaven, this is what it looks like, and if there is a hell, this is how it feels. The Beaufort outpost."

Once, Lila asked me what exactly Beaufort is and I thought how difficult it is to explain in words. You have to be there to understand, and even that's not enough. Because Beaufort is a lot of things. Like any military outpost, Beaufort is backgammon, Turkish coffee, and cheese toasts. You play backgammon for cheese toasts, whoever loses makes them for everyone—killer cheese toasts with pesto. When things are really boring, you play poker for cigarettes. Beaufort is living without a single second of privacy, long weeks with the squad, one bed pushed up against the next, the ability to pick out the smell from every guy's boots in your sleep. With your eyes closed and at any given moment being able to name the guy who farted by the smell alone. This is how true friendship is measured. Beaufort is lying to your mother on the phone so she won't worry. You always say, "Everything's great, I just finished showering and I'm off to bed," when in fact you haven't showered for twenty-one days, the water in the tanks has been used up, and in another minute you're going up for guard duty. And not just any guard duty but the scariest position there is. When she asks when you're coming home you answer in code. "Mom, you know the name of the neighbor's dog? I'm out of here on the day that begins with the same letter." What's most important is to keep Hezbollah from listening in and figuring out when to bomb your convoy. You really want to tell her you love her, that you miss her, but you can't, because your entire squad is there. If you say it you'll be giving them ammunition for months, they'll tear you apart with humiliation. And then there's the worst situation of all: in the middle of a conversation with your mother the mortar shells start blowing up around you. She hears an explosion and then the line goes dead. She's over there shaking, certain her kid's been killed, waiting on the balcony for a visit from the army bereavement team. You can't stop thinking about her, feeling sorry for her, but it might be days before the phone line to the command post can be reconnected. Worry. That's the reason I preferred not to call at all. I told my mother I'd been transferred to a base right on the border, near the fence, Lebanon lite, not at all deep in—not way deep in Lebanon—so that she'd sleep at night. Gut feeling, you ask? She knew the truth the whole time, even if she won't admit it to this day.

Beaufort is the Southern Lebanese Army, local Christians, a crazy bunch of Phalangists. Cigarettes in their mouths all day long. Smelly, wild, funny. They come in every morning at eight o'clock and we put a guard on them. They build, renovate whatever's been destroyed by the air raids, do what they're told. They're not allowed inside the secure area, not even permitted near the dining room.

Beaufort is guard duty. Sixteen hours a day. How do you stay sane after thousands of dead hours? We're all fucked up in different ways, just do me a favor and don't choke it during guard duty. "Choke it" is our way of saying "jack off." It's not that there aren't guys who choke it; they choke it big time. You won't believe this but a lot of people get super horny from our green jungle atmosphere. I'm not kidding. Nature is totally romantic, sensual. You would lose control, too. And it's not only nature that makes us horny. The Sayas network at 67 MHz, used for open transmissions between the outposts, can also give you a hard-on sometimes. It's not an official network—it got its underground nickname from a radio broadcaster who specializes in melancholy late-night chats—but everyone knows it because everyone, at one stage of boredom or another, tunes the dial to Sayas, the guys' favorite, where they can talk bullshit all night long and melt from the female voices. That's because girls from the command post are on the other end, in the war room, hot as fire, no AC, no boys, no reason not to unbutton their shirts a little, let off some steam. They sprawl across their chairs—I'll bet on it—stretching their muscles, spreading their legs, dripping hormones, dying for someone to make them laugh and slowly flirt with them and in the end make a little date with them back in Israel. Why not? Give them what they really need. Sure, baby, I got lots of weapons. I got my short-barrel M16 flat top, a real beauty. And my Glock, a fantastic pistol. And I also have... my personal weapon. Measure it? You want me to? No problem, sure, I'm happy to measure it for you, actually forgot how long it is, apologies, baby. That's the way you talk, making it up as you go along, turning yourself on, and they giggle, toying and teasing on that very thin border, one step over the line, one step back, and you're dying to believe that maybe at the end of the night, when all the other guys drop out, the girls are left alone, poor things, to satisfy one another. What, you don't think so? A few strokes, great stuff, nobody's ever died of it. Just don't build any major expectations: the nicer her voice is over the airwaves, the more of a dog she is. I take full responsibility for that statement, I've been disappointed often enough in my life. A high squeaky voice, on the other hand, means you might want to invest a little time, because she's got mile-long tits. It's a fact, I'm not jerking you around.

Beaufort is going out on seventy-two-hour ambushes with a huge supply of beef jerky in your knapsack. You can't believe how much of that stuff you can eat in three days. Beef jerky with chocolate and beef jerky with strawberry jam. And how much you can talk and talk without really saying anything. Pretty soon you reach the stage where you know everything about everyone. Who did what, when, with who, why, in what position, and what he was thinking about while he was doing it. I can tell you about their parents, their brothers and sisters, their not-so-close friends, their darkest perversions. There's a lot of alone time, too, when you're fed up with all that talking. You think about yourself, your home. You wonder if your mother is hanging laundry just now, or maybe she's watching Dudu Topaz on television. Lila's probably showering now, too. Or maybe she's cheating on me.

Freezing cold—we call it "cold enough for foxes" up here, ice-cube cold, the nose is frozen and the extremities neutralized. The feet have been numb for ages. Fingers, too. That's Beaufort. You have cold burns all over but your belly is burning hot, dripping sweat even. At these times everyone starts thinking about some asshole drinking coffee on Sheinkin Street in Tel Aviv. And here's fucking me, smelling like diesel oil, sweating from fear, lying in the middle of nowhere and nobody's going to help me if I die. Not the guy in that café on Sheinkin Street, that's for sure. When I'm blown to pieces a few minutes from now he'll keep drinking from his mug, probably at the very moment it happens he'll tell some joke and everyone will fake a laugh and then he'll go screw his girlfriend, he won't even turn on the news, and as far as he is concerned, nothing will have happened this evening. Because it's business as usual for him. He drives to his desk job at army headquarters every morning in the car that Daddy bought him, finishes the army every afternoon at four o'clock, and drinks coffee with whipped cream all the time. Blond hair, five o'clock shadow, sort of ugly. Hate him? You bet, it helps sometimes. Hatred is an excellent solution to boredom.

Beaufort is Oshri. He rolls over in my direction, lies next to me, chews my ear off in whispers. Every time. "Tell me, Erez, please, man: how did I wind up here?" he asks. "What am I doing here dressed up like a bush? Why do I paint my face? What am I, a kid? What am I, in some Crusader fortress, you fucking little prick? What is this, are we living in the Bible? Am I some sort of retard, pissing in bottles? What am I doing here in subzero weather, in the snow, waiting to take down some Arab who decides to climb out of bed at three o'clock in the morning? Does this make sense to you? And then going back to that stinking trash can I sleep in up at the outpost? Does that seem logical? Tell me, have you seen where I sleep? It isn't good for me here, really not good. Grown-ups shouldn't have to live like this, sinking in black mud mixed with snow at night. It's a bad fucking trip is what it is. Open your eyes. People have been dying on this mountain for a thousand years, isn't it about time to close shop? I swear, it doesn't make sense that there's such a place as Beaufort. I'm telling you, there's no such place and we're all stuck in this nightmare for no good reason. It's a mistake."

He goads me, tries every time to shoot the matter to new heights on the scale of absurdity, astonishing himself, while I bust up laughing, out of control, but it's all inside so they won't see. I take care to hold it in. I know in a minute or two the guy will sober up. I know him. Everything will look normal again, logical. He chose to be here, and he has a good reason for it, the best, and he'll remember it. He loves the mountain, it's good for him. And I'm good for him, too. He's my soul mate, my good luck charm, my best friend since the first cigarette at the induction center. Friend? No way: brother! My brother, who knows what's best for me better than I ever will. He says, "Erez, draw a black sheep for me," and I draw him a whole flock. He says, "Erez, give me a hug, you pussy," and I climb into bed with him, squash his little body into the wall, fall asleep holding him. He says, "Erez," and I know it's for life.

And sometimes Beaufort is a one-night ambush. Even then we bring the beef jerky. Of course we do! One night, simple, like the one in December '97. I'm the squad sergeant, lying in a thorny bush just as dawn is breaking, lost in thought. Calm. Like I'm drugged. That calm. And my whole being is dying to run down that steep, rocky slope covered with undergrowth, run to the edge of the cliff and leap off. An incredible dive from the peak of the mountain to the sweetwater runoff in the deep valley below, a long, whistling plunge that thunders in my ears. I am dying to dip into those waters, to float on my back, get swept away by the current into the blue streams, lie in the shade of the soft, bold, wild vegetation that crowds around the water and snakes after it like a dream jungle. To warm up lying like barefoot nature children on rocks: naked, horny, carefree. Dying to smoke a joint, get high, laze around, snuggle. Oshri says you can hear the splash of the water from below if you really try, but the closer you are the more forbidden and dangerous it is. Beaufort is a cage of ugliness right at the center of heaven. You hardly move one hesitant camouflaged foot to the outskirts of our iron gate, groping, sniffing, then you come back and close yourself inside our little enclave again. If only I could fly along the rivers and by way of the mountains I would be home already.

"Cheetah to Deputy One. Testing transmission."

"Roger, affirmative," I respond into the two-way radio. "Functioning." I return to my long silence.

Bleary eyes, mountain air, a brown and green desert, orchards and gardens, small stone buildings in turquoise and orange, olive groves. Everything is spread out before us. Are you dozing off? Dozing off? No way! Hey, you see that? You catch that? Is it what I think it is? Yeah, yeah. Are they armed? Yes, absolutely. Armed.

"Cheetah, this is Deputy One," I report. "We've got three scumbags north of the Virlist road." Oshri's got one in his sights, Chaki another, and Bendori the third. They've entered killing range, they've got packs on their backs, it can't be anything else. "Deputy One to Cheetah, marksmen on targets. Do I have confirmation?" I wait.

"Deputy One, this is Cheetah. Negative, repeat: negative. No confirmation, Deputy One."

"Cheetah, this is Deputy One, we've got them covered. Scumbags. Awaiting confirmation."

"No confirmation, Deputy One. Negative, repeat: no confirmation for action."

"But they're moving forward. Fast. We shouldn't lose them. We've got them in our sights."

"Negative, Deputy One."

Negative? Why negative, you fucking assholes! Does it make sense to you that I should lie here like some goddamn faggot missing an opportunity like this? Does it really? No way. "Squad, on my count. Four, three, two, one, fire. Twenty-one, twenty-two, fire. Prepare to attack."

"Commander Cheetah to Deputy One, do not fire your weapons! No confirmation, stay in position."

"Squad, prepare to attack."

"Erez, you psycho! Stay where you are. That's an order! Erez, you're in violation of an order!"

"Squad, attack!"

2

BUT ANYWAY, MY NAME IS REALLY LIRAZ. In basic training, at the very first roll call, the platoon commander ran down the names and when he got to mine he stopped. He didn't like it, my name. "Wait, wait. What's that?" he asked. "What kind of a name is that? Liraz? That's a chick's name. From now on you're Erez, like the cedars of Lebanon. Congratulations." Erez. That's who I am to this day.

Was there ever anything I wanted more than to lead—on my own, as commander—a squad of fighters to the top of the Beaufort? You can be sure there wasn't. But when I came back from officers' academy I discovered that nobody had any intention of making my dream come true. My company commander said I was too testy, hot-tempered, aggressive, impulsive. That maybe on paper I was an excellent fighter who always looked for opportunities to engage the enemy and always demonstrated courage, but that I was a shithead of a person. Testy people, he told me, can't lead fighting squads. True, one time, I attacked a military policeman. The little pussy caught me with mud on my boots. I told him, "You piece of shit, I'm on my way back from thirty-five days in Lebanon, I haven't showered for weeks, and at six this morning we suddenly got clearance and my commanding officer shouted, 'Run, Erez, get out of here now or you're stuck here another week.' So what's the deal here, you going to fuck me up over a pair of muddy boots?" But this guy, he didn't give a shit. He wrote out a complaint. But that's not the whole story. That ass wipe knows me from the neighborhood, in Afula. I said to him, "Gonen, you're pretty full of yourself, aren't you? You put a uniform on and became a big shot, eh? You know what? I'm going to be generous with you. Take your report, rip it up, and get out of here now. We'll forget about the whole thing." He didn't understand the hint and fucked me over. I gave him forty-eight hours to let the earth swallow him up and then I beat the living daylights out of him. To this day, to tell the truth, I haven't gotten over the disgrace of it: a guy from Afula writing a complaint on a fellow Afulan.

Okay, it's also true that I was tried for willful desecration of military property when I was a platoon sergeant. I threw a two-way radio at somebody along with a few other small objects. And when someone accidentally mentioned my sister, Vicky, I would lose it. Lots of things would make me lose it. I even got sent to jail for insubordination in that ambush business, when they shouted, "Do not fire your weapons! No confirmation, you psycho!" Sure, it was a long time ago, but turn me into a training officer instead of a commander? No way I was going to deal with paper targets, no way I would train soldiers to shoot without first learning, through my own experience, what it felt like to lead them at the front. For weeks I stuck to the company commander like a leech. I begged, went crazy, shouted, cried, refused jobs. I even asked to be discharged from the brigade. They'd never seen anyone so fired up before. But it didn't impress them. Until the hand of fate intervened and one of the officers left unexpectedly when his father died. The position of squadron leader opened up and I filled it. In actual fact I became squadron leader on probation and under a magnifying glass.

At the time, the kids were on a survival navigation course at the brigade's training base. I showed up there one morning without insignias on my uniform and observed them from the side, the thirteen of them. I didn't introduce myself, I didn't approach them. They didn't have the slightest clue that I was their new commanding officer. For several weeks I spied on them, eavesdropped, heard things. Heard things and grew alarmed. For example, I heard Emilio shouting at Bayliss, "What were you touching my bag for?" Just like that, word for word. This is a squad here, you loser. Everyone touches everyone's bags, that's the whole idea. Being a squad means stealing Zitlawi's potato chips, taking underwear from River's bag, lifting socks from Spitzer—because his are cleanest, everyone knows his mother uses fabric softener. Being a squad means that you run to the shower, take off your towel, and get swatted on your butt. The weather's cold enough to freeze the balls off a brass monkey and you're dying to get under the nice hot water of the shower, but everyone pushes you out, slapping you around from every direction, and you just thank God you have friends like these.

But not these guys. I'd been handed a frigid bunch, not a drop of group spirit in them. They weren't connected to one another, they didn't put their all into what they were doing, they looked sloppy. I got rid of their sergeant on the very first day, a thickset asshole, too Ashkenazi. I replaced him with Oshri. In my opening talk I recommended they forget the rulebook. Six hours of sleep, an hour each for breakfast, lunch, and dinner, and an hour of rest after every three in the sun don't make a fighter ready for Lebanon. That's barely training for company clerks, a bunch of girls. I brought them down to three hours of light sleep a day, made them pull all-nighters more often than not. When I found a mess in one of the rooms I moved them out to sleep in tents. When I overheard Itamar shouting at his mother over the phone—"All right already, shut your mouth!"—I informed them that there would be no more phone calls. Anyone caught with a cell phone would be kicked out. To put it simply, I was on their tails day and night. They did push-ups on their fists on hot gravel until they bled. "Like in jail," I told them. "Like prisoners of war. You can shout about it but nobody's going to rescue you. On the other hand, you can just open your legs and enjoy yourselves." After a few days you could see a spark in their eyes, first signs of a common denominator. Not just any common denominator but the most toxic of them all: hatred. They hated my guts, all of them, to the very last man.

Well, maybe there was one exception. River, the medic. It started during a complicated week of field exercises. The soldiers crawled, trampled thorns, moved boulders, took out their aggressions on nature. The usual stuff. When they were scratched up from head to toe and Bayliss was dripping blood from his mouth I gave one last and final order: At nine o'clock from where I'm standing, two hundred and fifty feet from here, see that green tree? Bring it down! Within seconds they had scaled it, stormed it, were jumping on it, tearing at it, ripping away, a battalion of elephants assisted by a rodent commando unit. Look at this, I said to Oshri, they're actually taking the thing down. But before I could wipe the smile off my face I caught sight of River off to the left, leaning on a rock and glaring at me. While I was still contemplating what kind of punishment this unexplained loitering called for, River approached me—River, the quietest, most disciplined soldier of all of them—and said without hesitation, "This wasn't necessary. You should stop them." I swallowed. I felt so stupid. What had I turned into? A few seconds passed before I muttered that he was right. From that day on I made

River work harder than all of them. I tore his ass, I shredded his soul, I wanted to turn him into a fighting machine. Under me he became a stallion, every vein in his body throbbing. At night, when the squad would tuck into junk food and Coke and then a deep sleep, I would leave him outside for medic training and physical fitness sessions that sometimes lasted hours. At two in the morning he would join me for a run around the base with Itamar slung over his back, playing the wounded soldier. Itamar, who's built like a tank, like a D9 bulldozer. Even in hailstorms we went out. I turned River into a two-way radio and made him run from commander to commander for wake-up calls or to deliver messages. In the end, when he nearly broke, I gave him five minutes to recharge his batteries by leaning on an electricity pole. It's not easy being the soldier the squad commander likes best. River didn't bat an eye, didn't complain. One day, when I let him go back to his tent, I allowed myself to tell him I was happy with him. I think I said something stupid like "It would be my honor to be a wounded soldier in your care." He said nothing. Gave me that famous penetrating glare of his and I knew—don't ask me how, it can't be explained—that he was happy with me, too. There's no making sense of that.

My big brother Guy once told me that to be a squad commander is to love. Thirteen fragile soldiers are placed in your hands, you called them "the kids," you drag them in their diapers on a long, long journey through a dense forest of breaking points, and the whole time you just pray that nothing bad will happen to them. You worry about them, he told me, not about yourself, and when one of your soldiers tells you that his uncle died of a heart attack and you see the pain in the whites of his eyes, suddenly you hurt, too, way deep down inside. The truth is, I wanted to suffer from that kind of sick love. I swear it, I really tried. But it didn't work for me.

Sometimes I felt disrespect for them, sometimes even revulsion. Sometimes anger, and every once in a great while a little satisfaction. But most of the time I simply didn't feel anything at all. For a long time River was the only exception.

I wanted to love Emilio, for instance. He's a guy who came to Israel from Argentina without his parents, only with his twin sister, left all his friends and family on another planet just to enlist in the IDF. Wasn't he worthy of respect? Of course he was. But how can you not go crazy from a soldier who pukes nonstop, like some coffee machine gone berserk? On treks, during runs, when he gets shouted at. And how about Tom? The guy's on a jag: red eyes, sees snails flying in the air, people zoning, drifting, Muslims tripping out in Mecca, has no idea where he is, just goes with the flow, floats. And Spitzer? Too relaxed. Itamar: too fat. Bayliss, too religious and self-righteous. Boaz is too enthusiastic, Eldad too vain, certain that all the girls are hot for him. He's disgusting, a spoiled Tel Aviv rich kid, an intellectual pretending he's down-to-earth, one of the guys. And Pinchuk? Juvenile. Sleeps curled up with a teddy bear he calls Yaron, thinks that's really cool. Gets offended at nothing. And Barnoy's a bleeding heart and Zion's dense as a log and Koka's just plain boring. And we're actually on our way to war—as pompous as that sounds—and how am I, as commanding officer, supposed to love this squadron of weaklings and whiners who aren't capable of taking in what's about to happen to them? Two months at the training base seemed like an eternity.

3

AND MOST ESPECIALLY, I wanted to love Zitlawi. How could you not love the guy? Zitlawi is warm and funny and happy. He can charm the pants off you. You'll never hear him complaining. Zitlawi's a good friend—the best—and that's something I admire. I had a lot of reasons to love Zitlawi, I know, but with all the will and effort it just didn't work, because Zitlawi doesn't have an iota of discipline, no respect for his commanding officers, too scatterbrained, spacey, the kind who leaves his gun in the most irresponsible places possible. If you don't tie his hands and feet to his body he'll lose them in a matter of seconds. That drives me crazy.

Truth is, Zitlawi is a real arse, a small-time punk with a cigarette behind his ear and a way of talking that makes everything sound like a string of curses, even when it isn't (it usually is). A whole new language took root with us thanks to him, expressions and pearls of wisdom that spread through the entire northern zone in a matter of days. Back then, the IDF dictionary was putting out new volumes every month, thanks to him.

To "ram," for example. In our language it means sleep

deeply. The full term is "to pillow-ram." It can be conjugated, too: pillow-rammer, pillow-ramming, pillow-rammed. A "rusher" is a quick make-out with a girl. A "double-rusher" is a small rusher. A double can happen between two guys, but not a rusher. An "owl" is a guy who walks around with his cock in his hand, jacking off all the time. A "terror dick" is one that gets nonstop hard-ons, morning, noon, and night. During kitchen duty, watching *Schindler's List* on video. "Scud five" is a huge dick.

A "ticket-taker" is a guy who sleeps with all the girls. "Tevye the Milkman" also sleeps with all the girls, but he's a nerd with glasses. A "fortune-teller" is a girl who puts out (when you're with her you're "fortunate" because she "tells" you to screw her. See also: "ear-hole virgin," "boiler heater"). Then there's a "mezuzah," a girl that everyone kisses, and a "Pringle": once she's open, everyone wants a taste. A "Magic Marker" is a girl that gives blow jobs. "Hook up with a suck-baby" means go fuck yourself. A sexy tourist is called a "foreign fuck," "ironing board" is flat-chested, "mosquito-bitten" is a girl cursed with small breasts.

A "hummus" is a dumb soldier. A "flip-flop" is someone thickheaded, a "schnitzel" is even more thickheaded, and an "eggplant" is as thick as you get. A thickheaded girl is called a "booma." A brown-noser is a "tangerine-peeler," a soldier with no friends. A "Herzl" is a fighter who talks too much about the future, which comes from the guy who envisioned the founding of the State of Israel. "Zionist" is another nickname for a blabberer, or someone who sticks his nose into everyone's business. *"Kapod"* is a pet name for Sephardim, *"hardor"* for Ashkenazim, and "journalist" for Ashkenazim who tell lies. Zitlawi calls everyone a fox, a shark, a hammer, a sleaze. A "panther" is a fox that Zitlawi particularly likes. A "pink panther" is a gay fox.

A "flamer" is a homo. A "momo" is a homo, too. There are lots of ways to call someone gay: ass-checker, for example, and zipper-reader, and doorpost-wiggler. Bed-shaker, wall-scratcher, umbrella-opener, pot-opener, soap-dropper. Sheet-ripper, faucet-stealer, tile-chewer, tree-hugger, sink-gripper, ball-grabber, pickle-dicer, shoe-tier, tea-stirrer, thing-sucker, banana-straightener, horse-whisperer, pillow-biter, feather-cougher. A homo's a guy who cries at movies, disappoints his parents, rides a bike without a seat. He's a suckler, a limper, a bend-overer, an excavator, a nailer. A champagne-boy is a homo, too, and so's a sharpener, a flutist, a Scout leader, a thong-wearer, a closet-lover, a sit-pisser, an exhaust pipe, a bugler. "Omo" is homo. "Sensitive" is homo. In fact, say anything but "homo," because it's not nice to swear. And lesbian? Don't say that, either. "Carpet-nibbler" is okay, you can use that.

"Strawberry-pisser" is someone who's scared. An "orange soda" is someone scared shitless. "Toast" is a burnt-out soldier. A "draft dodger in uniform" is a soldier with a desk job somewhere near his home. "Fox-brained" is a code name for someone fucked up by drugs and "rabbit" for a light user. "Enchanted garden" is a hash den.

A "potato-chip-wetter" is a miser, someone who doesn't want you to hear him crunching. A "marble-shitter" is a monster, a weird soldier, a loner, so ugly he looks like he hasn't really evolved. A "sprinkler" is a bragger; the female version's a "Nile perch." A "futt" is a fat slut. A fox-scarer. A mud pie. A "kebab" is a fat guy. So's a "sumo," someone so big he blocks the view. A male soldier who sits around doing nothing is called a "semen-squanderer" while the female version is "wasting labor pains." A "yam-peeler" is someone lazy. A "rivet-pisser" is someone who gets too excited about things. "Siamese cat" is a spoiled brat. "*Chakhna*" means stinky and "*karkhana,*" a drugged-out mess. A "chocolate situation" is one where nobody's happy and a "honey situation" is where they are. And to Zitlawi I'm a "pinscher," someone who barks all the time but isn't really dangerous, just a moaner. That's what he thought of me. Sometimes he also called me "gremlin" behind my back, meaning someone with a nice face but whose soul is dark and evil. Zitlawi himself was known as "Psalms," someone with a saying for everything.

"Jakha" is a personal favor. Do a *jakha* for me, will you? *Jakha* me. He's *jakhad* and so forth, ad infinitum. To "drum" is to stir coffee. Turkish coffee, or Beaufort instant, with halva and walnut oil. Zitlawi would spend hours, days, with the *finjan* and the thermos. If he had his way he would pummel all the guys with blows and pummel all the girls in bed. There wasn't a single girl he wasn't prepared to mince, fry, spear, or devour, the horny bastard. No holds barred, no pickiness, if you could believe the words that came out of his mouth along with the drooling saliva.

And then there's the worst curse of all: May your prayer-on-paper be nicked from the crack in the Wailing Wall where you stuffed it.

Zitlawi's most frequent saying: "Are you making fun of the way I talk?" That's what he would ask, with a killer look, whenever one of the guys pointed out some mistake to him, corrected his Hebrew, or, worst of all, dared to smile, which naturally happened all the time. He was violent, but sometimes good-hearted, too, like when he forbade guys in the company from squashing the monsterlike grasshoppers that hung around near the lights of the outpost. And Zitlawi had this little box of tapes he would listen to, the collected songs of Hana Harman. Once I asked him where she was from, that singer, and he was really offended. "Hana Harman is not a she," he told me, "he's a he." And not just any old singer but an Arab singer. One of the good Arabs.

I had a head-on collision with him when I took over command of the squad, on the afternoon of the hottest day in history. The boys stood facing me in rows of three on the roll-call field, frightened, dripping sweat, waiting to hear the first new decrees. They were wearing sunglasses on the order of the brigade medical officer—all of them except Zitlawi, who observed me with smiling eyes. When I asked him why, he said, "What do I need sunglasses for? My mother told me I shouldn't hide my beautiful eyes." On the spot he got the first punishment, and then again that night in the tent camp, when he was caught after lights-out organizing "The Prettiest Goober Contest," a phlegm-spitting competition. From then on he never stopped getting punished. In my first personal interview with him he spoke briefly and dodged direct questions. He was a smart-mouth. The only thing I learned about him was that he came from Tiberias, had three brothers, and liked to listen to Yehuda Poliker's music while getting a blow job. There was nothing particular in his files from the Adjutant General HQ or his army social worker to raise my suspicions. Three weeks of insubordination passed before I discovered the tip of the iceberg.

It happened when Oshri took the initiative, pulling Zitlawi out of bed at three in the morning and dragging him without permission, without prior coordination, for a walking tour of the cypress forest just south of the eucalyptus grove near us, with a canteen filled with hot tea. For the first ten minutes, as they walked outside the base, Oshri didn't utter a word, which caused Zitlawi to fill the void with bullshit chatter. He tried to guess the meaning of this hike, he cursed, talked a little about squad matters and mostly about himself in an effort to hide the fact that—simply put—he was terrified of the situation. When they came to a clearing in the forest, Oshri sat at one of the three rickety picnic tables that had been placed on the dirt there. He waited a few seconds, then he asked, "Zitlawi, what's your story?" Yeah, what *was* his fucking story, what was happening with the guy, what was the source of all this damage he was doing to himself along the way? The kid played dumb, claimed this was what made him happy, he was used to entertaining people and if someone had a problem with it they should toss him out of the military framework. He said he wouldn't appeal to the IDF chief of staff if he were kicked out, he wouldn't rat to the radio about abuse or hazing or breaching central command orders, they had nothing to worry about, he would keep quiet, he said. Oshri pulled two thin Indian cigarettes out of a wrinkled pink paper bag, little ones made of dry rolled eucalyptus leaves. He lit them both. Zitlawi sniffed the cloud of sweet, spicy scent that filled the air—or maybe the smell was bitter, kind of hard to define, the odor of a campfire. "Why not?" he said. "But isn't there any *boof,* as long as we're at it?" Oshri didn't even know what boof was. A little cube of hash, Zitlawi explained. Everyone has a pothead friend who keeps some boof in the little condom pocket of his jeans for emergencies, don't they? Something nice for the guys at the right moment. Oshri kept silent, lay back on the damp wooden bench of the picnic table, and let the stars mesmerize him. And he smoked. He has this kind of face that always looks mesmerized, narrow and dark and closed, with especially tiny ears, only his lips big and thick, and he's all peace and serenity, a rascal who seems to know that everything's going to work out soon so there's no need to panic. Zitlawi remained standing, watching him from above. "What do you want to hear?" he asked. "That the crazy boy has unique qualities of his own? That he's special, different, like the kids in special needs classes?" Oshri didn't answer. "And what about you?" Zitlawi asked. "What's your story, Mr. Sergeant?" Oshri was preoccupied with the halo around the moon and didn't even bother turning to look at him. Zitlawi lay down on the table, too. They smoked three cigarettes one after the other. It wasn't until the third that they exchanged another word, and then Oshri took the initiative again, kind of faking it. "You got anybody to fix me up with?" he asked. He told him he didn't have a girlfriend—here, something about himself—and in fact had never had one, because before he ever had the chance to fall in love they always, every time, let him know there was no chance, and now, in the army, the situation was even worse, there wasn't even anybody to look at and it had been bothering him for some time now that everyone around him was screwing right and left and he wasn't. Oshri finished talking and prepared his defenses for attack, expecting a nasty comment. Zitlawi took a Snickers bar out of the pocket of his uniform and broke it in two. "Sir!" he said as he offered Oshri the bigger of the two pieces. "Now that's actually a matter I know something about. We'll work something out for you, you can count on me." He said this in a completely serious tone of voice, with compassion even. And this really was a matter Zitlawi knew something about, because girls of every kind threw themselves at him, insisting that he's sexy if not particularly good-looking. His face was coarse and his body massive, the manliest guy in the company. And he was funny. Girls love funny guys, especially during sex when you're getting turned on and talking, it gives them a mega-orgasm. Then Oshri let his head drop backward over the edge of the bench and said, "What's gonna be?" Bingo. That turned out to be an excellent question, even if it had been asked unintentionally. Zitlawi grabbed on to it and used it to open a peephole into himself. His mother was a fortune-teller, he told Oshri, surprising him. A real one, though, a member of the union, with diplomas and certificates and everything. The kind who knew how to answer questions like "What's gonna be?" quite accurately. She studied Kabala and read coffee grounds, did palm readings and tea leaves and oil, read tarot cards. She could interpret dreams and do someone's astrology chart and reverse curses. She could make a former lover come back, get rid of the evil eye, help with fertility and family matters and fears and anxieties and low self-confidence, too, and lead couples to better communication. She handed out charms for good luck and for failing businesses, she was an expert in numerology and astrology, she solved marital and financial troubles. She gave courses, appeared at bachelorette parties and at events in private homes. In short, she brought happiness to people. The only thing she didn't do was crystal-ball gazing. When people asked "What's gonna be?" she answered, in detail, and she was never wrong. And ever since she accurately predicted the results of the elections in Tiberias she'd become famous all over the north, and visits to her were scheduled two months in advance at the very least. Her name was Aliza, but people called her Solange and that was also her professional name, and at home you weren't allowed to use the term "fortune teller." Instead she was a spiritual advisor, that's what it was being called in those last few seconds before the new millennium.

It took a few long seconds for Oshri to realize that Zitlawi wasn't pulling his leg. The kid was serious. It seemed he actually had a fortune-teller for a mother, which is to say, a psychotic with an audience. But that wasn't the end of the story. "Truth is," Zitlawi continued, "even with her success in the elections and in business these past few months, things aren't too great at home. My father goes through money in places he shouldn't, and it gets harder every day to talk sense to him. He's not an easy man. And my mother's got cancer. Bad, even. It started with a cough and then she was spitting up blood and had trouble breathing, and then they found a tumor, two inches in diameter, in the top part of her left lung. They took it out but that didn't help because the cancer cells got into her bloodstream and now they're everywhere. In the liver, the bones. All of a sudden it's, like, life-threatening, even if the doctors aren't saying so very clearly. They're trying to make us be optimistic. Strong. Who's going to take care of my three brothers? There's Samson—we call him Sammy. He's only six. And Roy's ten, and Eli—Eliko—who's finishing high school next year. Who's going to take care of them?"

There, it had come out. The next morning Oshri told me. Together we went to our unit's social worker and for a couple of days we tried, the whole senior staff, to convince Zitlawi to leave. We told him he had to serve near home, but he wouldn't listen. We asked him again and again to go home to his mother. After all, the squad could spend weeks and weeks up at Beaufort, even months, and she needed him. What would happen if he wasn't there to say good-bye? Zitlawi paid a visit to Rabbi Pitusi in the Poriah neighborhood of Tiberias, presented the dilemma to him, explained what he felt in his heart, and asked the rabbi's blessings for his decision to stick with the group at Beaufort. The rabbi consented. Maybe it was an escape for Zitlawi, it's hard to know. But ever since that night in the cypress forest he's been one of us, and that's what counts. As for me, I search for sadness in his eyes every time I look at him, make an effort to locate a single glum twitch of muscles. But there's none. I haven't found it because he's smiling this never-quit smile, and there's no telling if good intentions lie behind it, or bad.

4

FEBRUARY 1999. Here's the picture at thirty-nine minutes to nightfall, five hours to departure for the target: River, stark naked, gasping for breath after a maniacal run, comes to a stop in the watermelon patch behind Rabbi Elipaz's abandoned cowshed and tries to convince a frightened religious girl—a minor—to loan him her bicycle. He fires off rounds of confused explanations, something about an ATV that took off with everyone's uniforms, apparently in the direction of the pasture. The uniforms aren't even the worst of it: the sun is setting and they have to reach Ha'egel immediately. The girl, who has never heard of the Ha'egel, has never seen this River before, has never laid eyes on a dick, and most of all doesn't understand what this whole mess has to do with the sun setting, loans him her bicycle at once. That is to say, she doesn't really loan it to him, she merely doesn't protest. And him, that little owl, he doesn't get anything from her—not her name, not her phone number, not a little kiss, just a long silence and a bicycle. He nabs it and takes off.

Half a mile away as the crow flies, at the entrance to a

grove of pear trees, Zitlawi and the ATV are sunk deep in mud. He grabs hold of the pile of uniforms and underwear and climbs onto the highest eucalyptus tree. Totally infantile, the guy doesn't know when to quit. After all, the goal had already been achieved: a first-rate clip for the end-of-training film starring River, Emilio, and Bayliss. Bitching landscape, a wide road in the Golan Heights where they were running naked, waving their arms like wounded animals, cursing like Palestinian policemen, and pleading with Zitlawi for their lost honor. Emilio even cried a little, the crazy jerk. Everything captured on film; what more could you ask? But now the time has really come to climb down from the tree, rescue the ATV, wipe the embarrassment from River's red face, return the bicycle to the blond girl, hook up with the other naked guys left shivering back at the Bajurya pool—it's the middle of winter—pick up Spitzer and the camera, get back to Bayliss's village, Nov, and hope that his father, Menahem, will take them over to Ha'egel, the Armored Corps base where they monitor convoy movements. Otherwise it was all up for them.

Truth be told, Emilio had had his doubts from the start. Back at the cookout they were having in the yard of the house at Nov he said it was very strange and unlike Zitlawi to be so eager to pass up on the food and miss an opportunity to sit around doing absolutely nothing. And for what? Nothing more than a boring old puddle of winter rainwater next to a main road? And what was suddenly so important about stripping naked? And what the fuck was so screwed up in their heads that made them risk being really, really late on the most critical day of their military service? It was a lost cause, though: Emilio's worn-out whining—which every guy in the squad had learned to tune out ages ago—didn't stand a chance against Zitlawi's powers of persuasion. Even Bayliss, who knew from the time he was still in diapers how to explain to guests that Bajurya was not fit for swimming—too shallow, home to otters, salamanders, rats, and black cockroaches—even he plunged headlong into the trap.

The chances of me hearing about this incident were slight. I gave this motley crew their punishment without even waiting to hear the whole story. I refused to hear it. With a record like theirs, being eighty minutes late justified being shut up in the outpost for forty-nine days, in other words, a two-week extension to the thirty-five days they were already scheduled for on their first tour of duty in Lebanon. Apart from Emilio, who always appeared to be on the verge of tears, nobody was surprised. Zitlawi even muttered something about it having been worth it. Truth is, they have a special mood for moments like these, a detached desperation, and they're already quite used to it. The chances of me knowing about the business at Bajurya would have been low if it hadn't been for this girl who was mixed up in it all. And not just any girl, but a sixteen-year-old student at the girls' religious school in Nov, an innocent lamb with bells, a super-babe if you believe what they say. Her name—Hodaya—Zitlawi got hold of with major effort when they returned the bike. Other than that they knew nothing about her, only that a real, live, sexy encounter with a religious girl wouldn't easily be forgotten in our company, would pursue its victim up and down the front lines of Lebanon. All the way to Beirut stories of Corporal Naor River's battle history would be told in exaggerated and embellished terms. It's one thing if some religious girl had fallen into the hands of Zitlawi or Spitzer, or anyone else for that matter. But River? Well, that could only have come from God. He was the baddest boy of them all, the one that drew the most fire, the one who'd been working on his abs since sixth grade, and his suntan, too, and horny like a fifteen-year-old virgin. And shy like you can't believe, the shiest ever when a girl's around. It could only end badly.

* * *

It was a Monday when we gathered on the whitetop, the asphalt courtyard where convoys get organized for dispatch to enemy territory. I was just waiting for the sun to finish its business and for the curtain to rise on a new winter at Beaufort. I really missed the pungent smell of it, of green nature and thick vegetation and crisp air, of grease and Lysol and gunpowder and sweat, and all of it together. I'm not kidding, I really missed it. And the old guys, the veterans, in the company, too: Twina a.k.a. Tuti and Tiran a.k.a. Kuti, Bodnik the rat and Neufeld the flea and Pizov, who we called Poza, and the triplets—the good, the bad, and the stuffed—Lubeck, Ezroni, and Boaron. We pounce on each other, hug like always and wait for the first appearance of the youngsters, my kids. They're so happy, the vets, and why not? When you're part of a sergeants' squad, to you Beaufort becomes a sleep research institute, lots of snoozing hours every day, all day, entire days, with little breaks in between for heroic operations. No distress, no assignments, no floor-mopping. It's no wonder that the kids at Beaufort spend a large part of their time plotting mutinies and composing official complaints "on the grounds of unfair distribution of workload," my ass, but it's also no wonder that they bury those complaints and cool down when they remember that one day not too far off in the future, they, too, will be entitled. So why get messed up with the best friends of the commander? Not a healthy idea.

This is the opportunity for the vets to play indifferent. The cooks, the sentinels, the Signal Corps soldiers—all the Beaufort regulars go out of their way to be nonchalant in wholesale quantities. Everything's cool, no big deal. The new guys can hardly contain their excitement, they're counting the seconds; I know that feeling. They're dying for action, certain all of Hezbollah is pissing its pants, no way that they're not, and if you ask them they'll tell you that Nasrallah's vacation is over because this killer company is on its way to take over the front, to make war, to get rid of the faggots and the white-bread boys currently manning the outpost.

We sat off to the side, waiting huddled on a mound of sand. A Yasur chopper crossed the red sky and disappeared over the other side of the border. Oshri said we might be making the return trip in one of those, on a stretcher or under a gray army blanket. He winked, and I shut him up with a hard slap on the neck, to make him pipe down, chill out. This gathering place was paved low, hidden from Lebanese observation points so that terrorists would not know when exactly convoys were being organized for entry into their territory. A small, sputtering generator spat a cloud of diesel into the air along with the exhaust pipes of the vehicles so that the air was choked with a kind of salty stench. The whitetop was unlit, the only light coming from the headlights of the Safari trucks parked all around. A small booklet produced by the IDF, with detailed information about what time the moon will shine each day of the month, and at what percent illumination determines the movement of the convoys. When the sky is light they stay put. By order. That night a late moonrise was in store for us, which meant clogged roads and long traffic jams of trucks filled with soldiers and supplies and equipment crossing the border in both directions. By the time the moon would be high in the sky, at two a.m., the roads would be clear of traffic again.

Another three hours and twenty minutes until that clutch would be put in gear. We lined up in threes in the courtyard, fighting against a winter wind. In tight tables we recorded names, military ID numbers, positions in vehicles. If something happened they'd know immediately which one of us was gone. "Com-ass" we call it, "combat assignation," and it was Oshri who passed from guy to guy and wrote his "iron number" on the back of his hand in thick black marker, which would remain there for days and days and raise negative associations among all the history buffs. They called it the "death number." That might be true, but it was the only way of making sure that during moments of panic nobody would forget his place and the commanders would know quickly who was missing. In rows nearby, the veteran soldiers were still fighting over lucky numbers. Seven, for example, was a number nobody was willing to take.

I gathered my squad around for some last-minute pointers and to give them a speech I had written in my head for months. What sounds today more or less like an embarrassing mix of Zionism and kitsch was, back then, absolutely true and straight from the heart, I swear: "We may not be an elite commando unit," I told them. "Not even the Israeli naval command. We don't run around with shiny insignias and we're not allowed to remove the elastic from our trouser cuffs and we don't spend our army service in state-of-the-art digital training facilities with the American army. There are no superstars here, and we're not looking for superstars. But in our unit we do the hardest work there is in the IDF, and that's something to be proud of. I don't know if this evening, on the way here, you had a chance to open your eyes. You would have seen kids having fun on wooden playgrounds in the northern kibbutzim, and on the main drag of Kiryat Shmona you would have seen women licking chocolate crepes with banana and sprinkles and trying on silk bathrobes in the shops. The skies are quiet here and not a single terrorist can get near the border fence. And why is that? It's because of the war we're on our way to, together, tonight. People like to forget what went on here twenty years ago, right in this very place. They also like to forget what could happen if the IDF doesn't do its job. Katyusha rockets, border infiltrations, terrorist cells that slaughter whole families: that's the alternative.

"When we're inside," I told them, "in the middle of no-man's-land teeming with murderous wild beasts, I want you to keep this goal in mind all the time. Look at your watches," I said. "From this moment on I want you to forget everything you knew till now, erase all the bullshit. Your lives are going to run according to a different script. From now on you stop calling me 'Platoon leader, sir.' Now I'm Erez, and it's for good reason. I'm not going to be any less strict with you—on the contrary, from this moment there are no more concessions whatsoever—but from this moment, and this is the difference, we're completely dependent on one another. At the level of life and death. I want to trust you people, so don't disappoint me. That's all. Now, iron numbers, count off!"

After that there was silence. The battalion commander of Ha'egel, the man who would lead the convoy, stood looking at our row. "You're playing with fire for the first time today," he said. Just at that very moment, only then, did the Bayliss family pickup truck come to a screeching halt in front of the guard outside the main gate. I was already hoping they wouldn't show up at all, but that band of jokers, in wrinkled uniforms splotched with mud, caused me the biggest embarrassment of my lifetime. Yeah, it was clear I would have to murder them. In my worst nightmares I hadn't imagined such an unprofessional, humiliating start to our first time on the way to the front. The lieutenant colonel stared at me and said nothing. He waited for one long moment, then continued his briefing.

"You still have no idea where you're headed," he said. "I'm warning you in advance: on this trip, every little thing, like lighting up your watch, could have tragic consequences."

Their ears were sharpened, they were absorbing every word, and still it seemed to me that they weren't really taking it all in. A forty-minute journey was all that separated us from the outpost, but the convoy briefing sounded like an order to head out to battle. "I'm going to review situations and responses," he informed them. "I'll explain them to you like retarded children so there will be no questions left in your mind.

"First situation: missiles. How will you know if the convoy's being fired on with missiles? You'll see a flying torch headed our way, an orange-red dot floating through the air, or a blinding flash followed by a whizzing sound. If it's a Sagger missile you'll hear the clatter of a motor, too. When we're on our way, each Safari will post a missile sentinel at the opening at the back. If the sentinel sees some sign, he breaks into the open transmitter and shouts, 'Missiles! Missiles!' If they're from the right he shouts, 'Missiles, right!' and if they're from the left he shouts, 'Missiles, left!' The drivers will stop immediately and all of you will get yourselves off the vehicle to the same side the missiles are coming from. Why? Because the shrapnel will fly to the opposite side. Now, imagine a situation where all of you jump off the vehicles in the middle of nowhere and Hezbollah's waiting for you in the bushes and abducts a soldier. What do you do? In order to prepare for such a situation, in a few minutes you're going to divide into pairs. The members of each pair stay together and guard each other's ass. Fighters, I'm expecting you to take responsibility for those guys who don't have adequate training. If we find ourselves with a cook running around alone in the middle of Lebanon, the bereavement team back home can already start making their way to his parents' house. And one more important comment, men: we're moving out today in old Safari trucks, as you can see for yourselves. This means that the drivers' doors are blocked off from the inside by improvised protective panels so that they can only be opened from the outside. This means that in the event of an emergency, whoever's sitting in the front passenger seat has to run around to the driver's side and help him get out of the vehicle. Don't forget any of them, please.

"Next situation: mortar shells. First guy who hears a champagne cork popping shouts, 'Launch! Launch!' Mortar shells never come alone, it could be seventy at one go. The vehicles will come to a stop, each pair will jump down and run as far as possible from the other pairs. Do not stand near one another, create distance between yourselves. Otherwise, we'll lose an entire squad thanks to one lousy shell. What do you do after that? Wait. Just stay where you are until the barrage lets up. Is that clear?

"Third situation: 'Code Hannibal.' If you've been abducted, what do you do? As far as the abducted soldier himself is concerned, fight as hard as you can, pop buttons off and let them drop onto the ground so we have a trail. The rest of you try to stop the terrorists at any cost. If they're making off with an abducted soldier and there's no other choice, you shoot. I repeat: you shoot. The abducted soldier as well. An abduction is worse than death. I hope you people understand that.

"Fourth situation: an explosives charge. The vehicles stop, you stay inside and wait. An intervention force, which I will name in just a few minutes, handles the rescue, scans the area to make sure we're not talking about a wider range of charges that might be awaiting us. You will stretch white marking tape around the area of the charge. A charge at the head of the convoy is the most common. In this situation, apart from the vehicle that's been hit, everyone travels backward. If the explosives hit the middle of the convoy, the vehicles in front move forward and the ones in back move backward. If the damage has hit at the back of the convoy, everyone moves forward. Take into account a situation where we hit a charge and seconds later we're attacked by mortar shells, all according to plan. Be prepared.

"Fifth situation: we find ourselves in a field of explosive charges, they're going off one after the other in every direction, and at the very same moment, BAM!—we're jumped by armed Hezbollah guerillas, face-to-face. What do you do? Does the intervention force attack the terrorists, or do they freeze in place out of fear they're going to set off additional charges hidden in the bushes and along the road? Listen, and listen good, I don't want any misunderstandings here, no fuckups, no messes, and this is an iron rule: explosive charge or not, you people go on the offensive. A face-to-face encounter trumps everything, even under attack of mortar shells, or missiles, or cloned aliens from Mars for that matter. It's holy. Engaging them, not letting them get away, is our highest value. Is that clear? Be ready, because when the intervention squad is engaging in hand-to-hand combat or busy rescuing the convoy, the terrorists will try to pump rounds of ammo into the last Safari with twenty soldiers stuffed inside who can't see a thing and can't shoot. That's why it's the responsibility of the missile sentinel on each Safari to man the back opening of the vehicle and watch what's happening.

"That's all for situations and responses. From this moment on I want your helmets on your heads, ammo cartridges locked into your weapons, and nobody sleeping along the way. The motto for everything I've just said is simple: if something happens we want to minimize the damage. I'm not hiding anything from you, there's no way to ensure no harm will come to this convoy, but if you use your brains the damage can be contained. Drivers, be aware: we're moving slowly, the roads are slippery, don't forget to kill all lights and headlights the minute we've passed the three-mile mark. The rest of the trip will be made with night-vision equipment on your eyes. Keep maximum distance between each Safari and the next, but don't lose each other. If there's someone here who forgot to leave his mobile phone at home, go now to your bag and separate the battery from the phone. In fifteen minutes, everyone in place and ready to move out. Good luck."

* * *

And that was all. At that moment everything fell silent, the shouting ended. Tasks were suddenly carried out with the volume turned all the way down, and they were technical and precise. The soldiers closed themselves off from one another, preoccupied with trying to digest the battalion commander's briefing, and slightly freaked out. I could see their eyes as they went over the procedures, picturing dangers. There were so many confused commands they had to remember from that moment, but then it was the time for a few drills—explosive-charge drill, face-to-face-encounter drill, dropping-shell drill—so we jumped in and out until the battalion commander was satisfied. Minutes later everyone was crammed into the back of the Safari, packed in and silent, waiting. In other times this truck would have been carrying eggs, or chickens to the slaughter, but now, done over in olive and looking like it had been saddled with a huge safe, it transported soldiers into fighting territory.

There were long hours of waiting ahead before we would receive the order to move out. It was enough for some sentinel in Taibe or Marjayoun or the Dlaat outpost to notice some suspicious movement on the roads for everything to be frozen in place, or a soldier at Beaufort with a pair of binoculars to imagine a wild boar limping toward the road for an additional thirty-minute postponement, at the very least. A whole day, even, if an alert was issued about some large explosive charge or if some doubt was raised about whether the electronic warning devices accompanying the convoy were in proper working order. The order to abort could come even in the last few seconds, with all of us already in place on the vehicles and waiting at the border gate. They won't take a chance with a mission like this, they'll send the soldiers to spend the night on comfortable beds at the Soldiers' Hotel in

Kiryat Shmona. The big celebrations that take place when this happens, when we storm the hotel, come with a price: it's hard to describe how bad the feeling is at Beaufort when soldiers who were supposed to be going home discover that the convoy has been cancelled.

At twenty-two forty-five that evening we were at border gate number 93 and it seemed that everything was in order. The intelligence officer gathered all the commanders and read an update to them. "Nothing special to report this evening," he said. "Alert 012 on Hezbollah intentions to carry out an immediate attack on a convoy on the Nikras road is still operative. We'll wait for final clearance and then we'll move out." The last minutes. The bolt is removed. This was the first time I had earned the right to mount the Safari as a commander, in the front seat, to observe the trip from the passenger's seat and not from some narrow slit in the sides of the back portion of the vehicle. The night-vision equipment colored the world in stark shades of green and black. "Tapuz stations, confirm. Over and out."

"Diesel, in order."

"Kfir, in order."

"Puma, in order."

"Venus, waiting for confirmation."

"Venus, in order."

The driver, a reservist, tried to light a last cigarette but I let loose with an angry response. "Put it out," I demanded. He tried to make a case for another half minute, what was the big deal? I grabbed his hand, yanked the cigarette away from him, stubbed it out on the dashboard, and threw it out the window. From that moment on we didn't exchange a word. A long silence. Nights in the north always make you feel this loneliness; here, I can feel it now. Then from the transmitter we heard "Mission confirmed," and it happened.

On the first leg of the journey you hit 55 mph, that's what the regulations state. After that you crawl along, barely at twenty. The endless trip takes you through climbs, descents, twists. This is the tensest time of my life. I go over past threats, recall a sixteen-year-old Lebanese boy waiting for an IDF convoy with an explosive charge strapped to his body. The soldiers were suspicious, even fired warning shots in the air, and then suddenly the kid saluted. They stopped shooting. Seconds later he blew himself up on them, just a few yards from the convoy. Go figure where it's going to come from and how you'll respond. I think about Bayliss, who's positioned as missile sentinel now at the back of the Safari, completely exposed, surely shivering from cold and looking for the first time at this view of Switzerland. You can't miss the thin halo of pale blue light floating above Beaufort, carried high in the middle of the sky in the center of the black forest ahead. And how beautiful the ancient fortress that stands next to the outpost is in the moonlight. I wonder how long it will be before I can make out the huge flag flying on the top of our hill.

"Get the fuck out, already! Everything out, out!" Always the same huge ruckus in the parking area. Guys jumping down, stepping on each other, everyone throwing bags on everyone. Where are the sleeping bags? Where're the personal bags? Everyone's just thinking about his own stuff, worried something will get left behind on one of the trucks and wind up making its way back to Israel with the outgoing troops. As for me, I run amok, this way and back again. "Oshri, count them now!" I see the looks in their eyes, they are glazed, each lost in his own thoughts, looking around in every direction trying to take in as much as possible. They have no idea what to do. They sit down on the floor of the secure area and wait.

The guys in the company we are replacing were not willing to put on their dress fatigues or clear out of their rooms or beds in advance. They insisted on waiting for the moment that our convoy was visible to the naked eye from the guard positions as it climbed the hill. It brings bad luck to pack in advance. And when they packed it was done like a hurricane, in total madness that left behind destruction: a dismantled outpost in chaos.

When I went down to the senior staff submarine to get myself settled in, Oshri was already there, sprawled across the rusty iron bed. A tropical island was hanging in a direct angle from his pillow, stuck with Scotch tape to the metal walls of the stifling trench we lived in, along with a lone, improvised coconut tree and a green sea and a floating raft carrying a small black man with a cup and a straw, bobbing on the waves. A countdown chart, too, showing the number of days we had left at Beaufort. When the hell did he have time to hang it all? The chart, with eighty-eight days just begging to be wiped out, had been inaugurated a few hours earlier with an X over the first day. Yes, eighty-eight. That's less than ninety, that's three months minus one day, Oshri announced while lying on his back, the bum. I polished my boots and asked him what was so terrible about being with me. "What's with you, are you attention deprived?" he asked by way of response, his soft, round Yemenite face all happy and jokey. "You've got to give me advance warning for that sort of thing." He wouldn't stay on, I knew that. Even if I begged and pleaded he wouldn't postpone his discharge, his head was totally there, on the outside. As for me, just the thought of the replacements that could land on me—some pale-face pussy platoon sergeant, for example, who might show up here, or a homo, even, who knows—could make me crazy. "Where would they find you one like that?" Oshri would ask every time the subject came up, trying to cool me off. "Sergeants are wild asses, everywhere you look. Don't worry, they'll send you someone lousy, like me." I always answered that I could rely on Furman, the company commander; just to screw me he'd bring a female sergeant. But Oshri sank into his sleeping bag, rolled up inside his faded green sheet printed with a fake, subversive Middle Eastern version of the Care Bears. He's leaving me, that little son of a bitch. Just like that, while we're on the front, he'll go off and start a different life. I was even angry—somewhere deep inside I felt like he was cheating on me. In the name of our friendship, in the name of our mission, in the name of the knowledge that at the end of the day we had it good up there, and we were good there, really, really good and professional, better than anywhere else we'd be. I didn't know how I would pass the time up there on the hill and in the infiltration operations and training exercises without Oshri. He's the only one who understands me. When my engine's gone out he revs me up again. When I'm on fire he cools me down. When I'm cold he's the only one who knows how to warm my soul and when I'm hot he takes care to stop me one minute before my childish mood lands me in military prison. Because only Oshri knows how to signal me when I'm being a jerk, when I'm shooting off, out of control, knows how to toss it right in my face without pissing me off or hurting my feelings. He says, "Report to me for a heart-to-heart," and I know I've been an asshole. He's modest, an introvert, warm. He's the only person who knows everything about me and still—it's hard to believe—loves me. And I know everything about him, too. Only me. About the tattoo on his right arm, for example, which is always covered with a patch to hide the embarrassment. It was supposed to have been a gesture to a tourist from Japan he'd met in Eilat. Her name was Mika but the tattoo read "Mike." I'd warned him in advance but Oshri, drunk, only noticed in the morning. When he worked out in the fitness room in a white T-shirt everyone shouted at him, "Come on already, take that stupid thing off," trying to draw him out, get him to expose himself. "What's he hiding there?" they would ask, pressing me for information. But I never sold him out. Just like I never told anybody that that little Yemenite has a cat at home. He looks like somebody who'd have some scary attack dog—an Amstaff or Rottweiler at the very least. Never a Chihuahua or a cat. And yet it turns out that he goes home and pets a little creature with a mustache, the kind females like. And he's really strong-willed. Disciplined. A good boy. Doesn't touch drugs, hasn't ever even tried them. Me, I got friends in the neighborhood whose faces should be on Colombian postage stamps. Back in ninth grade they were minor potheads, making up all kinds of stories and telling me, "It develops your brain, this stuff. It's been researched!" In tenth grade they'd gotten me used to having to set off at a sprint whenever a squad car drove up, and by eleventh grade they were doing time, overnight lockups. I had no idea where they were in twelfth grade. They got in trouble on every occasion, again and again, and I was their nerd. Hard to believe, but there, in our neighborhood gang, it was me who was known as the good boy. Then along comes Oshri and steals my crown, big-time. Next to him I'm a criminal. But he's going to be gone for a year. He says he'll send me e-mails, but I don't even have a computer. And if I did, how exactly does it work trying to send your thoughts, get your aggressions out, get advice? So who am I left with? Lila. Other than her, I'm all alone. But she can't understand the things that happen to me, there's no way. She can't understand anything about the army. How could she? "Start writing her letters," Oshri advised me. "But only optimistic ones."

In eighth grade, when I went over to Lila's house in the rich neighborhood on the other side of Afula for the first time, her father said, "You're going to marry this guy." Just like that, in my face, in front of the aunts who were drinking coffee in the living room, the ugly bitches from down south. Lila nearly passed out from embarrassment. "Listen to what I'm telling you. I see how you look at him and I know it's for life," he insisted. And who would believe it, but we're still together, not going anywhere, and it really is for life. Before my first tour of duty in Lebanon I thought I would keep things from her. I made something up about a nice, quiet posting near the border by some farming village. At the last minute I realized the truth was preferable, because if something happened to me, God forbid, it would catch her by surprise, explode in her face, and that would be much harder for her. I'd already seen girlfriends whose lives had caved in on them suddenly, in one swoop, without any advance preparation. So I told her, "Look, there's a chance I'll get killed. That's the way it is in Lebanon. There's no plastering over the truth, no sense in jerking you around about this." With the sincerest words I knew I told her it was better for her to be prepared. She asked why I was doing it. I answered that it was an enormous personal challenge for me, that's why I wanted to be there. On the last night, before crossing the border, we did it twice. When I was completely wasted she put my dog tags around my neck and slipped a little piece of paper with something she'd written inside the pouch. She made me promise not to read it until the day of my release from the army. And I promised. But what if I die without knowing? Curiosity tempts you in situations like these to peek, because the feeling of having missed something will turn heaven into hell if you go up there without knowing what she wrote. And still, I don't look. Sometimes, when I'm bored, I nearly give in, but then I close my eyes and see her lying on my bed in purple panties (thong panties, if possible), slowly stroking her breasts, her head dangling backward over the bed and her hair falling to the floor until I'm dying to run my hands through it, and over her hot belly, her soft skin, smooth as a baby's, and like a magnet to continue down, to sneak in under the cloth and squeeze, to feel how wet it is there because of me, and to hope that in a few more seconds she'll beg to feel me there. I think about her trembling, and that's how I forget about that little piece of paper.

Furman, the company commander, cut into the scene when he appeared in the doorway. "Come," he said, all aggressive-like. Last time we mixed it up, him and me, was sitting on the couch in his office. Just us, face-to-face, trying to dismantle the land mines between us until the middle of the night and managing for a few days or even a few weeks to get us both to back down from the heavy artillery we'd been aiming at one another. "Turning over a new leaf," he'd said. "It's all only temporary," I'd answered. "For the sake of the soldiers," he'd said. "For the sake of the operations," I'd countered. And then we had a cease-fire. He hates my guts, which is fine, legitimate, not everyone has to be crazy about everyone else. They stuck him with me, that's clear, he took me because he had no choice, he was forced into it, but now we're at the front, our first time together, and everyone has to be a little mature about this, since I'm part of the senior staff. So at two-thirty in the morning Furman dragged me out for another round of couples therapy. We went out into the darkness like we were doing a sector briefing. Which I guess it actually was. At first anyway—the warm-ups—and there sure was plenty to brief on, because the next day I had to pass on the battalion positions and the call signals and signposts to my squad and the others as well, as duty officer.

"The Ali Taher mountain range battalion oversees six outposts, remember? Beaufort and Dlaat belong to the IDF while Brosh, Gamba, Hadar, and Valencia belong to our Christian partners, the SLA. We each watch out for the other's ass, take care of overlapping zones. By air we're six or seven miles from the Israeli border at Metullah, our elevation is 2,460 feet above sea level, and we're responsible for Marjayoun and the Litani River, which means this place for years has been the eyes of southern Lebanon and one of the most important strategic points in Israeli control of the entire northern region. Before we raised the flag here in June 1982, the Palestinians were bombarding the northern Galilee from

Beaufort. Look here, keep alert, down over there are the tobacco factories, past them is the town of Nabatiye, then Tibnit and Arb Salim and Jabel Zafi just beyond." Furman went through the map of targets at lightning speed and I stood there tense and confused, looking but seeing nothing, absorbing nothing. "The region is practically unpopulated," he continued, "and on principle citizens don't just walk around the sector, certainly not at night. If somebody approaches, you can be sure he's no innocent, so he's dead on the spot."

"Automatically," I answered. "No hesitation."

"I don't remember it being so quiet here," I muttered, and Furman reminded me that at Beaufort there's no shouting, no talking loud, no switching on lights, no walking around in light-colored clothes. "You'll get used to it," he said. "A hundred soldiers are stationed here: Armored Corps, Ordnance Corps, Signal Corps, medics, and of course us, the infantry, who usually total about seventy guns. The outpost sits on less than two acres of land. Under usual nighttime circumstances we man four guard positions: we call them White, Red, Blue, and Green. But when there's fog or high alert we set up additional posts. Apart from soldiers manning the guard positions, no one goes out in the light of day, no one goes out under the night sky, no one dares step out from under the ten-foot-thick cement overhang. We live in darkness. Even the toilets are more or less off limits. The architect who planned the toilets and showers separated them from the living quarters and guard posts. They say he was totally fucking drunk. Or maybe he wanted to keep the germs and infections and diseases and stench away from the small, airtight main building. A matter of hygiene. But we've found a reasonable solution to the problem: we piss into empty plastic bottles and try to allow trips to the toilets only for getting rid of the heavy loads, and during quiet interludes. As for the heavy loads, they have been reduced here to record lows and require the permission of an officer or one of the guys on war-room duty."

"During the time I served here," I said, "we sat on the can reading the newspaper first thing in the morning for as long as we wanted."

"Times are different here now," he said. "Next: Dawn Alert. Remember what that is?"

Sure, I remember. It's part of standard procedures. You wake up in a good mood, like a morning fuck. Every morning, between five and six-thirty, the entire outpost is on its feet, high alert, fully equipped. The danger hours: Hezbollah loves the glow of sunrise, the ideal time for attacking the outpost, the kind of attack that starts with combined hellfire: RPGs, grenades, mortar shells, light weaponry, everything all at once with an intense opening blow, then the foot soldiers, somebody trying to storm the place, wipe us out. All the recent attacks on the outpost have taken place in the hours between the end of night and morning, when there's still no light, but on the other hand the night-vision equipment is no longer effective, when everything's in this sort of in-between state and it's hard for us to pinpoint where they're shooting from and it's hard for us to return their fire and it's hard for us to function because it's hard to stay on your feet at those hours. And the fighters are *milfed.*

I tried to break the ice by asking Furman where the hell that word—*milfed, milfered, milfistic,* in all its mutations—had come from. You were suddenly hearing it in every second sentence in the army. "Jesus, what a fucking stupid word," I said, laughing. "Who's the asshole who made it up?"

"It's an abbreviation," he said without hesitation, "for 'military fatigue.' "

"Whoa, Furman, I am seriously impressed. With that kind of general-knowledge smarts I'd have gone and made a bundle on TV ages ago," I said. "You know, the *Bible Quiz,* we'll set you up with some hostess from *Wheel of Fortune.*" Furman gave me a long, drawn-out pissed-off look. All right, so it wasn't funny, I admit it. I came out the asshole. But give me a little slack just to be polite, you fucking shithead prick: Smile, I thought, so I don't stand here like some kind of smiley-face jerk. I wound up as frozen as the ice I was trying to break.

"Early wake-up, Erez, which means being completely awake during these critical hours, not just some artificial opening of the eyes, not a bunch of worn-out soldiers sloppily organized"—he took us right back to the matter at hand in that patronizing, sour tone of his that hits me in the spleen like a fist—"and it will be your responsibility to make sure that everyone internalizes this way down deep in their consciousness," he said. At some other time this kind of snub would have totally knocked me off course and provoked me into a massive fight. But not tonight.

After that there came a long silence that exposed the sharp hush that existed there without us, a hush that numbs you and is familiar only to those who have had the privilege of standing high above the thick ring of clouds on that isolated, barren peak at an hour when even the birds are catching Z's in their sleeping bags, enjoying their El Al business-class eye masks. There is no such silence in all of Israel.

This was during the season of swampy mud, and Furman and I crossed the open and covered trenches, dragging our feet from guard post to guard post, exchanging the air in our lungs that we'd brought from home with this new air that was as purified as undiluted laughing gas, leaving frozen droplets of water on your tongue and the insides of your mouth when you drew a whistling breath. It's totally addictive and so completely refreshing. When you're dying to be angry you can't, when your body wants to be tense you're relaxed. A kind of nirvana. I waited for Furman to be the first to squeeze the trigger, break the silence.

"You know that you make one single mistake and you're out of here, don't you?" he said as we passed the tank facing the main gate, just before the final turn that would bring us back to the building.

"Don't get your hopes up, there's not going to be a mistake," I replied.

"This is beyond your capabilities, Erez, you're not made out for this. Everyone here knows you well enough to know you're going to screw it up for yourself. It's just a matter of time," he said.

"What's your problem?" I asked, getting mad. "Really. I'm asking you: What's your problem? You think I don't know you did everything in your power to keep me from advancing? I actually do know. And now you're probably putting in overtime in front of the mirror practicing your 'I told you so' speech for Amos and the brigade commander. So you'd better start getting used to this idea: you're going to be disappointed. I'm staying put here."

"I don't know what kind of fairy tales you've been living in your head," Furman said, "but I can tell you that I plan to be completely professional with you, as professional and businesslike as possible. I'm just warning you in advance that all that is going to end with your first fuckup. The ball's in your court. You're welcome to surprise me."

"You're afraid I'll surprise you, that's exactly your problem. Amos put me here because he knows the truth, he knows I can bring in operational results and not just sit back and take the blows all the time. That I can inject some courage into those guys and pursue encounters with terrorists. That I'll send a few of those assholes to Israel in black bags, like back in the glory days of this place."

That was the first time I'd seen the King of Apathy turn red, and even the cold air and the quiet couldn't calm him down. He pushed me hard in the chest against the tank. "You've totally got the wrong idea," he said. "Nobody wants terrorists from you, nobody wants assassinations, nobody wants confrontations with the enemy. You have only one mission: you came up here with thirteen soldiers and I want you to leave here with thirteen soldiers without a scratch on them. That's all."

"What are you trying to tell me?" I asked.

"I'm trying to tell you that I know your problematic record," he said, "and you haven't changed or matured by even a single day since the time you spent in jail for disobeying orders in that ambush. Believe me," he continued, on the offensive, "and Amos and the brigade commander and the head of Northern Command and the chief of general staff and God Himself will tell you exactly what I'm about to: the IDF is not looking for complications now, and certainly not the kind that are the initiative of some gung-ho officer playing war. Just keep cool."

In those days I loved to say that a white-bread commander like this guy could never have come from the units I'd passed through, that the blond in his hair had seeped through his skull and mucked up his clearheadedness for operational planning so that his mouth fired off whole rounds of statements of fear without shame. Captain Ofir Furman had come to us from the commando babes, which, at the time, was for me the explanation for all our troubles. The months of training under his command had signaled to me that this was going to be painful and filled with friction. I knew all this, but now that we'd come to the heart of it for the first time it was clear to me that the situation was much worse than I'd thought. This guy was going to try to turn me into a potted plant. And he was making a mistake, big-time. His irritating and threatening tone was still echoing in my brain when he started walking ahead toward the company with me lagging a few steps behind, trying to digest it all.

At three in the morning we all jammed into the briefing room for our welcome speech. Furman supplied us with an hour and a half of theories and speeches, maps, exercises, and combat standing orders. Everyone dozed off. After that the kids were sent off to sleep, but just when you finally get a chance to sleep is when you're most awake, because of the fear, trying to piece together what you're supposed to do if a barrage of mortar bombs rains down on you suddenly, and if the whole mess starts up right when you're dozing. Even God can't help you then, when your head's in shambles. You're tossed into your pint-sized quarters where the beds are stacked three high and with so little space between them that there's no real room for you to move around. You can't sit on them, you can only lie down. They sway, they creak, when somebody climbs them they all rock and nearly break. The kids were too tired to argue over who was going to get which bed, and Spitzer even dared to ask if they were allowed to undress. The senior staff members laughed. "What a stupid question. It's going to be a long time before you can take off your uniform, kid. All right, that's enough, shut your mouths and your eyes." It's really hard to sleep in the fighters' quarters, located deep inside the building, where you can hear radio static and people dragging heavy things down the hallways and running and shouting, and in the nearby kitchen, pots are being hurled to the floor and there's a clanging of metal as squads return from overnight ambushes at quarter to five in the morning and raid the dining room for a lavish meal. All these sounds jumble up in your brain. In the rooms near the building exits, where we sleep—the senior staff and veterans—the lights are very dim because the bulbs have been scribbled over with a layer of red or blue markers designed to darken as much as possible the halo of light that flickers over the outpost. But where the kids sleep, in the inner rooms, the light is on all the time, and it blinds you and is really strong and it produces unnatural colors, totally psychedelic. Staring directly into the bulbs mesmerizes you for a few minutes, then you feel dizzy and want to puke. The guys crawled into their sleeping bags in stunned desperation, then thirty minutes later the loudspeakers announced wake-up. Dawn Alert. Everyone tumbled out of the barracks for an hour and a half, during which they sat dumbstruck and nodding off on chairs made of broken wood and rusting metal in the entrance to the security area, waiting for the hourglass to set them free. Everyone was sitting except for my youngsters, who I told to stand, with full gear on their backs, facing the green and white sign posted over the western wall and proclaiming our super-goal. THE AIM: TO DEFEND ISRAEL'S NORTHERN BORDER, FROM MOUNT DOV IN THE EAST TO ROSH HANIKRA IN THE WEST. Flags were draped across the walls of the room, and the boys' faces were serious as they internalized the place, the outpost, the situation. They were excited. Only Zitlawi's eyes drifted northward, to a wall filled with girls posing nude or in bikinis.

5

WHEN YOU'RE YOUNG, Beaufort is a big, bustling diner where you're not even the Arab guy who chops vegetables; you're the migrant worker who scrapes the scum that the oil splatters on the utensils, the plates, the stainless steel. And guard duty? An hour and a half at a time followed by three hours of "rest," then another ninety minutes over and over again for the entire day. "Rest" means back in the kitchen and, for a little variety, outpost chores. The company sergeant major takes you every once in a while to pour diesel fuel into the generator, which stands at the remotest edge of the outpost (a spot that is supposed to guarantee that if the fuel tanks are hit by mortar shells we won't get blasted into the sky in little bits and pieces). When he takes you for a walk you're elated, you take a stolen glance at the world, say hello to the tanks, kick stones down the path, and it's all a real pleasure except that you come back splattered with oil, aware that there may be two weeks between you and your next shower.

The Beaufort kitchen was unlike any kitchen you'll find in

the IDF today, mainly because it had no running water. The washing of the dishes took place in laundry tubs, one with soap for scraping and the other for rinsing. There were no hoses. Twice a week, on Mondays and Thursdays, a water truck driven by an SLA guy made its way up to us, complete with iron chains and a coded lock that prevented the water tank it carried from being broken into along the way. At the entrance to Beaufort, the outpost doctor would remove the lock and check the water quality with a special poison-testing kit. The lack of water also regulated showering, so that a single shower pass was allocated to every soldier for each period of two and a half to three weeks, subject, of course, to the severity of warnings against mortar shells that might catch soldiers unprepared and unarmed. At least the food at Beaufort was excellent, better than any fighter could dream up in his feverish brain. On that the opinions were unanimous. The very best rations in the entire IDF were sent to Beaufort; everything that Chili, our kitchen's master sergeant, could possibly think to ask for was provided by the heads of nutrition back in Israel. They sent every kind of cheese—hard cheeses, feta, Swiss, Roquefort, mozzarella—and banana-flavored milk and Rich's non-dairy cream and all kinds of puddings in all the best flavors, and grainy French mustard and fantastic salads and schnitzel and Lebanese kebab and cartonloads of curly fries and first-class spreads. Real gourmet meals. We had everything there, except for chicken. Chicken was never sent to Beaufort because it spoils too quickly. No more than twenty or so soldiers would show up for breakfast and about forty for lunch (the sergeants were sleeping then), but every evening, when the sun went down, the outpost went into party mode. Nobody dared miss the massive meat meals that were the centerpiece of our days and around which everything turned. For the youngsters it was also the cause of their nightmares, the

Great Wall of Dishes piled on the floor of the back kitchen for washing. A mere three soldiers on kitchen duty were meant to tackle the whole thing, struggling with it right through to morning, but even before the first meal, River and Bayliss held a democratic vote (at my command) that determined that all thirteen soldiers would give a hand every night to the three on duty. If they worked together like a well-oiled conveyor belt, I explained, they would be faster to discover original methods for washing and drying and storing the copious quantities of pots and cutlery than other groups of soldiers sent there in the past.

On their very first day of kitchen duty under Master Sergeant Chili they totally screwed up. That's what happens when you don't know the legend or the man. They gathered around the dishwashing tubs for a training session after breakfast had been put away, and Zitlawi opened his mouth. He started talking and didn't notice that Chili was listening.

"What do you mean you didn't get an erection?" Zitlawi asked, attacking River. "How could you not get an erection? There's no way. Are you taking the shit out of me? Damn, please tell me you're shitting me. What, are you a homo, man? Hey, it's fine, baby, really, I don't have a problem with that, just warn us so we can set you up with a great job in the air force. All kinds of perks there. But listen to your old pal for a minute: where I come from, when some sweet little sixteen-year-old checks out your M-16, it moves automatic-like to the firing position of an Iraqi supermissile in count-down mode. And no cold weather or birds or cows or ATVs should have fucked up your sensors. You have tarnished the reputation of the entire company, man. I hope you understand the hugeness of your fuckup."

"She wasn't my type," River said. "With me these things are very specific." The squad demanded an explanation on the matter of the specifics. "First of all, athletic," he announced without hesitation, "plus cream-colored skin is a must, ditto green or blue eyes. South American origin, long, flowing, curly hair, the right-sized tits. She's got to love sports and hiking, and if she isn't crazy about the beach, then she's out of the running right at the start. She should have the name of a real quality babe, something like Avishag, let's say." Over the soaping tub Zitlawi wanted more specifics about the tits. "Be a pro about this. Give us size range, bra cups." River, who was already red-faced and hunched as a result of everyone's expectant silence, their attention all on him, refused politely. If you ask me, he had already realized that Hodaya was simmering somewhere inside him and that he would go out looking for her, whether or not he had a good chance of succeeding. Oshri and I laughed quietly, because there's no such thing as a babe whose name begins with an *H*, every old-timer knows that. That is to say, any girl whose name begins with an *H*—or any vowel, for that matter—can never be a total babe. Ever. A tested truth. No Avishag, no Hodaya. I don't even need to see the objects of this kid's fantasies to know I'm right. Babes are Sharon Stone, Sigal Simchon. Too bad for the guy, he's going to take a bad fall.

"Tell me, Bayliss," Zitlawi said, repositioning the spotlight. "Sixteen-year-old religious girls: what do they know about the facts of life? No, really, I'm asking. I'm totally serious. It's an important question, don't you think? Philosophical. Psychological. Ideological. Does someone at least teach them things that are worth knowing? Does someone, let's say, spread their legs gently and make nice to them? Because the truth is, I stood there facing that holy virgin of yours there in the cowshed and I felt real compassion for her knowing how much good I could do for her. How I could set that girl on fire. But she'll never know."

This is where they tripped up. Chili is not the kind of guy

to take a pedophilic monologue lying down. He's got a gentle soul, and morals. He's religiously traditional. When someone messes around with the sanctity of women he goes nuts. He came over, restrained, to check on the progress of their work close-up, see how well they were carrying it out. He spotted a grain of rice on an orange plastic drinking cup, then he brought down a totally inhumane punishment on the squad: the blanching of all the kitchen's utensils, which would take an entire day, right up until the loudspeakers announced Dawn Alert again.

In the meantime, Oshri and I took them out in threes for a tour of the guard posts, their first look around in the light of day between pots and pans. They dashed from the entrance of the security area to Green, the northern post, the most isolated and distant of the four. They wore helmets and camouflage vests topped with warm coats and gloves, not yet accustomed to the cold. They peered into what was about to become their lives, into the enormous ancient fortress—known as The Rock—and at the tattered and dusty flag flying at the top of the pole, the rips and tears of which are clearly visible from below. You don't replace a flag with a history and a certain pride and honor, I told them.

In passing from the breathtaking fortress to the ugly outpost alongside, the eye catches, off to the left, a low whitewashed wall with a metal plaque hanging from it by chains. The date on the plaque has faded, the text is missing in places, but the last line is deeply engraved:

THE BEAUFORT WAS CAPTURED BY THE SOLDIERS AND COMMANDERS OF THE GOLANI RECONNAISSANCE UNIT. THE BATTLE TOOK THE LIVES OF GONI HARNICK, YOSSI ELIEL, GIL BEN-AKIVA, RAZ GUTERMAN, YARON ZAMIR, AVIKAM SHERF. WHERE DO YOU FIND MEN LIKE THE ONE WHO WAS AS A WEEPING WILLOW, AND LIKE AN ANCIENT FORTRESS, AT THE END OF HIS ROAD?

Those guys back in the eighties had a real literary streak. I showed my boys the targets. The closest populated settlement, a mere six hundred and fifty feet down the hill, was Arnoun. The new Arnoun, a village of about one hundred buildings, well paved and fairly progressive, and to its right, the old, abandoned Arnoun, which had served as a stronghold for terrorists until the IDF removed them. The constant presence of terrorists at the foot of the Beaufort, at the point where the access road to our outpost split off from the main road, was intolerable. An old woman, living alone, according to the intelligence officers, was the sole person there now, heavy concrete barriers blocking the entrance to cars and guests.

From Green you can see everything. Yukhmur is in plain view, straight ahead. A little to its left is the Nikras road, which connects all the outposts, from Dlaat through Beaufort to Gamba and on. Green was made up of a battery of three guard posts, two of which were protected by domes and concrete roofs in the hopes of minimizing damage by the frequent fall of mortar shells in this direction. I explained to them honestly that there was no way of coming out alive from a direct hit. The line of vision from inside the protected position was quite narrow, enabling clear observation for only about thirty feet, not much more, so that during daylight it had been decided to man the exposed post as well, allowing greater flexibility and broader visibility. One soldier stood inside while the other stood outside. In the outside posts the concrete barriers protected only the lower body; from the chest up, the body was exposed. What more was there to know? At the guard post there was a MAG heavy machine gun, always loaded and ready to shoot, its belt feed permanently in place. In back there were two emergency backup posts so that the soldiers could take shelter there if need be.

We continued our tour. It was pitch-black in the trenches

and they were lined with long Day-Glo strips in orange, yellow, and green to keep you from stumbling. Outside, everything was olive color as camouflage, along with the occasional black netting, and there was an endless number of stairways, everything hidden from view by walls of sandbags. A big old shipping container sitting in the parking area and riddled with holes on every side from shrapnel was our storeroom. Once upon a time they played soccer here, in the carefree eighties, and caught a tan lying in their underpants on the front of a tank. These days we stayed in uniform even inside our sleeping bags.

We reached Red, the eastern guard post, which commanded a view of the rest of the outpost and of the access road. There's a 60mm mortar shell there, two covered guard posts, and an exposed backup post for escape under hand-to-hand combat attack. White, our southern post, is closer to deserted Arnoun. It has one manned covered post and two exposed posts that are usually not in use. The field of vision is limited here and only marginally effective; mainly you can see the Litani River, but if they try to storm us on foot it will probably come from here because White is where the hill is least steep. From here you can see Manzurieh, an SLA outpost with batteries of cannons. Israel, too: you can see Metullah, and Kiryat Shmona.

After that I introduced them to the guys from the Combat Intelligence Corps, the soldiers who listen around the clock to static that comes from the screen of a broken computer. Every once in a while you hear a click and they say, "There, a car just drove down the road," or "There, a car is braking." Go figure. I guess it helps, maybe when there's fog, but those guys, what can I say? Have pity on them. They work and sleep in that same little room with grating metallic noises and yelps and brakes and chirps, 24-7. After two years at Beaufort is there any chance of them coming out anything but totally insane? In any event they seemed a little weird to us, cut off, new immigrants with glasses the size of television screens. We continued our tour. The wild chirping and the soft whisper of the transmitters accompanied us the whole way, and on occasion the rumble of armored personnel carrier engines shook the earth. "So, River," I asked, "what have you got to say?"

"Exotic," he answered. "Fucking exotic."

By the time the sun rose on the next day they were deep into the silent, grinding boredom that is outpost routine, from guard duty to kitchen duty to maintenance duty. They gather up the piss bottles and spent shells from the guard posts, which after a night of guard duty look like the remains of a fourth world war. They polish the MAG machine guns, and if we're lucky and the skies are quiet, they're also sent on lightning missions to disinfect the toilets—three toilets for one hundred men means nuclear holocaust; they make the public restrooms at the Rafiah border crossing into Gaza look like the King David Deluxe. They sweep and wash down the secure area again and again in an ongoing attempt that is doomed to failure at keeping up with the pileup of clinging mud the men bring back with them from the cold to the linoleum floors and concrete courtyard. "Where have they dumped us?" I heard Bayliss asking rhetorically, teeming with despair. "This was supposed to be a war, they promised us war, and suddenly it turns out there isn't one. Not even a feeling of danger. Yeah, I know, we went on this scary convoy but that was the end of it. Since then it's been nothing but talk, and if you ask the sergeants when there's no officer around, they'll tell you that the threats are completely detached from the reality, and any connection is totally coincidental. All we have is hard labor here. Donkey work. Where's the real thing?"

6

ON OUR SIXTH NIGHT ON THE HILL, Mickey Bayliss stopped wearing his kippa. He waited for me to leave the officers' quarters and went in to inform Oshri. After that he went to tell the guys, who were at the time already buried deep in their beds. He tossed out his announcement, picked up his bulletproof vest, and went off to guard duty. The squad was paralyzed, that's the only way to describe it. The whole thing seemed completely illogical. They fell silent. When he returned in the middle of the night they were waiting for him, awake and curious, and they asked questions: Which sins had he already managed to commit and which were still in the planning stages? And with whom? Zitlawi offered hearty congratulations to the new member of the jack-off club, to the league of the heavy abusers. Spitzer promised to fix him up with his first secular girl, Emilio described in great detail the juicy slab of pork he would season specially and grill for him. Truth is, we love surprises, but not a single fake smile managed to cover up the inexplicable feeling of sadness that pervaded the barracks just then. Even before that I knew it wasn't easy to stay religious, keeping the commandments and all that, in our company. I'd seen enough of them, lots of them, one after another: good guys cutting corners. Like on the Sabbath, smoking a cigarette they claimed had been lit by someone else. Like on a holy day, keeping an eye on the television they claimed had been turned on by someone else. In the end, even they join in to watch porn videos. And when Dave from the war room, a bearded redheaded guy with the black kippa of the seriously religious, would run around like crazy every morning in desperation looking for men for a prayer quorum, they'd all dodge him. All of them but Bayliss. Because Bayliss never once missed the morning prayers, the afternoon prayers, the evening prayers. He always talked about the obligation, the calling, the "personal fortitude." He was no fanatic, not close-minded or blind to other opinions and lifestyles, but everyone thought of him as a star of the religious Zionist world, their hope and pride. And here he was suddenly looking them straight in the eye and telling them he'd decided to take a timeout. Maybe for a year, he said, maybe ten, maybe for his whole life. He said he didn't have the spiritual willpower, that he didn't feel strong enough, that he wasn't worthy of representing them. And if he wasn't worthy, then there was no need for him to continue wearing a kippa. On the contrary, he said he would be putting the religious Zionists to shame if he kept it on.

In our brigade—in fact, in all the infantry brigades—the crocheted-kippa guys of the religious Zionist camp had become the backbone. They were the best fighters and were growing in numbers and power. They were a new generation, not like their settler fathers, not like anything that the state religious education system had produced in the past. Ours were a different breed: no more ragged parkas or tattered sandals; no more heavy beards of Diaspora Jews. They'd done away with a look that set them apart and now they resembled us. They dressed like us and wore their hair like us, they talked like us, liked the same films, the same music. They knew how to party like the best of us. You won't always see them with a kippa on their heads. They don't want you to prejudge them, making excuses that they're not good enough or that they don't keep the commandments strictly enough to call themselves card-carrying members of the religious Zionist club. Maybe one day they'll mend their ways and study and put their kippas back on their heads, they say. They call themselves "pocket-kippa guys," and some of them screw as many girls as we do. Really, I swear it, this generation actually fucks, because they know how to bend the religious obligations since religious obligations are not, to them, the center of their world. But with anything connected to loving the Land of Israel and patriotism, to sacrifice, even to friendship, they're the best, the most "religious" of us all, and a lot of times the most extreme. With bodybuilding, too, nobody can compete with their enthusiasm and their determination to succeed. These guys are achievers, go-getters, they dream of a kippa-wearing chief of staff and they believe they'll endear themselves to the people of Israel at the point of greatest consensus: battle and sacrifice. They've already filled the ranks of the battalions, the reconnaissance units, the officers' courses. Just before enlisting they stock up on answers to all the questions. Tools. When a secular friend on duty with them says, "Prove to me that there's a God," or in bed, during late-night talks, he'll come up with something really tough like "What possible reason is there for me not to jerk off?" these guys will never be caught tongue-tied or hesitant. Sometimes it seemed that being one of them, part of that perfect world, was the sexiest thing in our day, nothing less than the most popular brand name. I'd actually been handed a secular squad, which was rare, unusual, but I had Bayliss. And Bayliss was one of their leaders, ethical and strong-willed, the poster child, the one everyone everywhere knew and loved, the one who knew everything about everyone like only a religious person with aunts and uncles and cousins in every settlement and outpost can know, and he still hung on to his fortitude. When he announced that he'd decided to stop wearing his kippa, we all knew it wasn't really the kippa that bothered us. It was the way Bayliss had decided to give it up, just like that, when all around these guys were doing so well and put forward such a solid front.

At midnight I joined him at his guard post. He was surprised, even a bit taken aback, and didn't say hello. I asked him why but he just muttered a dejected "That's that." I continued to hang around there, waiting for something to come out of his mouth. Bayliss didn't say a word. When I understood I would have to take the initiative I tried to find the right thing to say that would break the ice. "So," I asked, "what happened? All of a sudden there's no God?"

"It's all over," he answered. He explained that he'd had enough, that he was wasted in terms of being religious. I kept asking again and again what he meant by "wasted," but he didn't respond. I tried pissing him off, I asked him what his parents would say, what kind of personal example this would set for everyone who looked up to him. A few long minutes passed before he finally cracked.

Bayliss told me he'd never met any secular people until the ninth grade. He encountered them for the first time when Rabbi Schwartz arranged to take the kids in his village to a demonstration in Rabin Square in Tel Aviv, which was called the Kings of Israel Square back then. Another demonstration followed that one, and then another. The struggle against withdrawal from the Golan Heights had punctured the first hole in the well-insulated bubble. In a little religious village like theirs there was no chance some secular chick would walk across the grass waving temptations in front of your eyes. Everyone you know, everyone you've ever met in your short life, is part of the world of faith. The girls study in a girls' school in Tiberias, the boys in a religious boarding school. At six in the morning they're already at prayer, then they study religious subjects until noon and secular subjects like computers and literature in the afternoon. At six in the evening they start up with the faith lessons and finish the day with Talmud. No movies, no going to the cinema, there was no television at the yeshiva. Cigarettes were forbidden, buses only came twice a week and the one and only pub (for people in their twenties and up) always served the same stuff for the same price. There was a once-a-year visit to Tel Aviv with your parents. And above all in school there was politics, where you wouldn't find a single leftist. He remembered himself, before Prime Minister Rabin was assassinated, wishing time and again for exactly that to happen. It was in their thoughts, and when it took place nobody shed too many tears. When they were told to send a representative to the funeral they were hard-pressed to find a volunteer. Was it a fuckup of the state religious education system? Maybe, but Rabin had made an about-face on his promises, Bayliss told me.

"We weren't superhuman," he said, "just human. A little more restrained, but living with all the same urges, jerking off, everyone jerks off, if not at thirteen like the secular kids, then three years later for sure. And just like other horny sixteen-year-olds, we talked in private about girls. But we didn't say, 'I screwed her,' or 'I touched her breasts.'

"I've never in my life talked to anybody about a woman's breasts," he was careful to point out. But there were substitute ways of saying things. Instead of "I got her all hot and horny," you say, "I had some business with her," and everyone understands what you're talking about. And when some rude guy asks, "How far did the business go?" and you answer "Far" or "A little" or "Almost all the way," the most important thing is not to say anything specific. They'd made up a slang of their own, and they substituted letters for all kinds of expletives, like "trick" instead of "prick," or a "son of a witch." To this very day they still say "loobs" instead of "boobs." It's a matter of holiness. They don't have sex ed classes in the schools, either. Bayliss met his first girlfriend thanks to a mix-up in telephone numbers. A completely secular girl. They nearly had sex on their first date. It was when he was in the eleventh grade, on the Lag BaOmer holiday. She was from the south—Kiryat Gat—and he was from way up in the Golan Heights. His parents were certain he was at boarding school. He left home at one in the afternoon and hitchhiked to Kiryat Gat, where he arrived at six. She was waiting for him in her room. They went to the beach. She asked if he'd already done stuff and he said he had, tried to play it cool. But he didn't know where to touch her, what to do; he didn't even know how to kiss her, so how in hell was he supposed to know how to take her bra off? How would he even know he was *supposed* to take it off? She dropped hints, he screwed up. What a jerk he was! They sat talking for a while. She moved in with her hands. In his wildest dreams he'd never imagined anything like this, hadn't gone looking for it, it just came to him suddenly from heaven. They stayed together, horny, all night. At two o'clock she asked him if he had a condom. He didn't know exactly what she was talking about. He'd heard the word on some TV program but he didn't really know what it was for. And he certainly didn't have one. On the way home he thought about how his life as he knew it was shattering. He'd done what he'd done and the sky hadn't fallen. He'd even enjoyed himself.

It was on the morning of that holiday that all his doubts began. By eleven he was back at school, late for a class given by Rabbi Uri, a super-secular guy raised on a kibbutz who had become religious and was now a teacher. During the break he locked himself in the bathroom with his best friend and told him he'd had some business. Business? his friend asked. They weren't even supposed to touch girls, let alone screw them, which would put his whole life in danger. But even there, in the heartland of the religious Zionist faithful, a guy who traveled all the way to the city to fool around with a girl was a stud, a superstar, and anyone who began to open up to the secular world got bit by the bug and became ambitious to learn more and more about it, totally famished for a taste of what lay behind the forbidden mountain. Bayliss would sneak out—his parents thought he was at boarding school, at school they thought he was at home—and sometimes he would bring his friend along and they would tear up the city. Their classes on faith didn't fortify them, he started sleeping in and missing the morning prayers. Three weeks later he went for the real thing, catching rides. On the way he stopped at a pharmacy, at her urging. At the entrance to her house he took off his kippa. If he was going to have sex without getting married, if he was going to desecrate God's name, then at least it should be without a kippa on his head. It was of the utmost importance not to represent religious Zionism in such a bad light. That's the way they are, Bayliss explained to me: even if they're going to vandalize a bus stop or spray graffiti on the walls of a school or break into a soccer field, they'll take the kippas off their heads. It's an important statement.

All of a sudden the girl says, "I'm going to take a shower. Want to join me?" Nothing comes out of his mouth for a full five minutes, then he goes in. They only had three condoms, but they managed. It was a totally wild Sabbath for them, his first time. And outside, the rivers kept on flowing at their pace. Haim, his neighbor, for example, had been going out with Tzurit for three years. He'd call her "sweetie pie" sometimes and maybe even declared his love for her, but he never dared touch her. And if sometimes his hand would brush against her shoulder, by accident, he'd apologize immediately: "Sorry, I didn't mean to!" In the late spring the guys would go out in their underwear during breaks to a local reservoir for a swim. When their rabbi came by to check up on them they would duck under the water and stay there for a minute or more. Then one day, when a cow entered the water and couldn't get out, slowly sinking and then drowning, they stopped going there out of fear. But there, at the edge of the water, he also smoked for the first time and had his first look at a *Playboy* magazine that was keeping the entire class occupied, passed from hand to hand.

He'd thought that in the army he would mend his ways, leave behind the foolishness. But the army, according to Bayliss, was even worse. After all those descriptions of lust and adolescence, he explained that it was the army, the army itself, that was ruining religious boys, exposing them to temptations and testing them in impossible situations. "I don't feel like being a phony anymore," he said. "At home, safe in my environment, I could handle it. But here, what options do I have? I could become more religious, improve myself, be less despicable, strengthen my willpower. But I don't have the spiritual fortitude to start on some quest to find myself, spend time doing it, figure out what's really happening to me. I can't even get up for prayers in the morning anymore. Some secular person stealing a look at me would see a disgrace and he'd hold the religious world in contempt, on my account. What can I say? I take off my hat to anyone who manages to survive his army service as a religious person. Not me, I'm not strong enough, not up to the challenge. I set myself a mission and failed."

"And what about God?" I asked.

"I don't know," he answered. "Maybe there's such a thing as personal providence. I'm not sure. Who knows?"

Over the next few months, on furloughs home, he would put the kippa back in place as the bus climbed upward toward the Golan Heights. There, in Nov, he continued to attend prayer services and lived in two worlds. No one could know that Menahem Bayliss's son was no longer religious, that he'd broken ranks. He had one very religious, very observant sister who had completed her national service for religious women and was now studying at the nation's Orthodox university, Bar-Ilan. Another sister had already been living for years in a West Bank settlement. He, too, was well-thought-of, a nice young man who said hello in the street, and at Nov they were convinced he'd go far. He couldn't break the soul and spirit and image of his family just to earn a few more hours of sleep for himself on Saturday mornings. Most important of all, his father could continue to believe he was one of them while his mother, who knew the truth, could believe with all her heart that this was only a passing phase.

When a guard from the next shift came to replace Bayliss, I walked him back to the security area. I searched the lines of his face for signs of weakness or emotion but he was indifferent.

I brought a boiling cup of black coffee with three sugars in it to Oshri, in bed. "What's the matter, don't you love me anymore, you shithead?" I asked, trying to draw fire. "Truth is," he said, "if you'd grow a pair of big tits I'd marry you. Really." How could you not marry someone who brings you coffee like this, the best in southern Lebanon? "So, what'll it take, man?" I continued, acting like the juvenile that I am. "A sex-change operation? And what if I come out of it dog-faced ugly? What then? I'll be left with nothing." He made another X on the chart on his wall like he'd been waiting all day to do it so he could make my eyes burn. Couldn't he have found a moment to do it when I wasn't around? I grimaced. "Oh come on, are you going to start moaning to me about it again?" he asked. "We'll warm up the girls for you in Colombia. What's wrong with that? You should say thank you."

At seven in the morning, when the kids were mopping the floors, Furman called us in for an officers' meeting to hear the intelligence reports. He said there was a good chance something was going to happen, that we shouldn't be fooled by the silence. A massing of terrorists in a ring around the tobacco factories was putting Hezbollah in a more advantageous position to fire rockets and mortar shells at us. We all leaned over the aerial photos of the mountain range and Furman drew a red ellipse on the shiny lamination and told us about how in less than forty-eight hours five enemy supply trucks had been spotted arriving at the site and large wooden crates had been unloaded. After that he read an encrypted message from Command Intelligence, something about an aerial convoy of weaponry being brought from Tehran to Hezbollah via Damascus. The two were perhaps connected, he said. I asked why we weren't bombing them. After all, we know they're there, right? Furman ignored me, didn't even glance at me, like he hadn't even heard me, and he kept on briefing us, something about Wadi Zirin, which actually had been quiet the past few days.

"Was that a stupid question?" I persisted. "No, really, tell me if that was a stupid question, because I don't think it was. I'm trying to understand the logic of sitting here like bimbos in the outpost and letting Hezbollah gain a stronghold in their attack position."

"When Command Center tells us to attack," Furman responded, "we'll attack."

I assumed we weren't making any recommendations. "Why the hell aren't we at least making any recommendations?" I asked.

"Hey, Erez," Furman said, mocking me, "you're even more useful than I'd thought! Until I'm asked to attend a cabinet meeting, do me a favor and stick to your job." And my job, at that time, was to prepare the squad for their first operational mission: a one-night ambush on the access road. Yeah, that sounded pretty depressing and totally lame—lying like a fossil in the bushes some sixty or seventy feet from the gate of the outpost—but that was our mission. "Really, I'm very sorry we're not sending you to set up ambushes in Beirut," Furman continued, holding me in clear contempt. "In the meantime you'll have to make do with the menial task of preventing terrorists from getting near us in the outpost."

It wasn't even a real ambush, just what was known as a "patrol." Fifteen fighters hiding along the edges of a windy stretch of the path that ascends the Beaufort, a blind spot to the guard posts above. So, from seven in the evening until four-thirty in the morning you pray for a terrorist to leave the comfort of his warm bed on a winter night in order to make a heroic attempt at infiltration and drive away your boredom. Past events in the sector had taught us that Hezbollah operatives had managed to come within ten yards or so of the outpost in order to plant bombs. If our access road were to be mined we'd be cut off for days without food or fuel, not to mention the chance that one of our vehicles would be blown sky high. And of course the outpost would be in danger of being stormed. For two years already the enemy had been using every means possible to try to raid Beaufort and get inside the fortified fortress, mow down a few soldiers, and plant a yellow flag while a TV crew from Al-Manar captures the victory on film, to be used for boosting morale, of course.

A patrol on the access road reduces the chance of just such a fiasco because it gives us the advantage of surprise in the ensuing battle. Reduces, but doesn't remove it; on a foggy night, for example, even a whole cluster of ambushes won't help. On thick gray nights like those, a terrorist with balls could come in through the gate, sleep with us in the submarine, wake up in the morning before the rest of the outpost, and kill everyone before going back home all happy and content with one of Chili's schnitzels and a carton of chocolate milk in hand. Because when there's a thick fog everything shuts down. You can't see two feet in front of you. The guards shake in their boots, they hear the sound of martens and weasels running around freely in the undergrowth and sometimes jumping on us. Is that an animal or a bearded terrorist about to slit your throat from behind? You're welcome to guess. In this kind of situation you hold on tightly to your MAG, tenser than ever, but there's nothing you can do. And there are lots of foggy nights on this mountain. So why the hell do we let ourselves sit around waiting for this evil to come get us instead of striking first and neutralizing the threat in advance with a concentrated attack on the secret hiding place where they're polishing their swords and preparing to storm us?

At seven-twenty-five I gathered the squad for a talk about the sector and had them line up near the "gapcow," the gathering point for company wounded, where stretchers were always open and ready. I had to be tough with them, I didn't have a choice. "The terrorists are watching us," I told them. "They're checking out every IDF outpost one by one and weighing which is the best to attack. If they notice that we're a mess they'll be right on us. If, on the other hand, they can see we're totally prepared and in shape, they'll prefer to go for it somewhere else. You'll be surprised to learn that Hezbollah guys are no fools, they want to make it home safely, too. So they'll always prefer to take on the units where the combat readiness is less than perfect. For example, weeds on dirt embankments are a sign that things aren't in order, which could put us right in their sights. It's a matter of life and death." I couldn't risk failing so I decreed that wearing gloves was off limits in spite of the miserable cold since, as I explained, wearing gloves on duty made it hard to squeeze the trigger, lengthened reaction time, and hampered accuracy. True, the other squads were allowed to keep warm at night and they had left all kinds of accessories in the storage area, but that wouldn't pass muster with me; my squad would have to get used to the cold. After that I gave them a daily workout schedule in the exercise room (practically a closet, in fact, with dust-gathering exercise bicycles, five barbells, and a treadmill that the company had won on the brigade sport day. Nobody but us ever visited the exercise room, maybe because sweat suits or shorts were forbidden from use at the outpost and working out in uniform was a particularly stinky affair, made worse by the fact that the chances of a shower following a workout were almost nil. I also made it clear that there was no going to the bathroom without my permission, even if that meant waking me up in the middle of the night. I had to know where every one of them was at all times. As for the one phone at the outpost in those days—an ancient, black, faulty army telephone—I let them use it from nineteen hundred hours to twenty hundred hours only, a time when the long queue made making a phone call virtually impossible. The entire battalion fought over that one wretched line, with conversations from other outposts and operations rooms crossing lines and messing up the connection. And if by some miracle you managed to work your way up to the receiver, you'd get jabbed from behind and people would gesture to their watches. Two conversations, one with your mother and one with your girlfriend? Are you out of your mind? That's out of the question! You have to make a choice. Long personal calls from Beaufort were only possible in the depths of night when you came off guard duty, for example. Everyone did that; only my squad was forbidden. "How are you supposed to keep in touch with your girlfriend?" Zitlawi asked me. "First get yourself a girlfriend," I told him, "and then we'll teach you how to write letters." And to finish up, another test: What's "Caesar"? Caesar is the code name for the outpost. And what's "Two"? "Three" means operations in Israel, but what the hell is "Two"? And where's the "Dump"? And what's the code name for the computerized observation post in Marjayoun? Wake up! "Emilio, what's the code name for Manzurieh?"

"Milano," he answered.

"Congratulations," I said, attacking him, "you've just used up your whole quota of stupidity for the entire time we're at the front! I'm adding another week until your first leave."

"Are you out of your mind?" Zitlawi let fly in a kind of conditioned reflex, and he was put on confinement as well. Altogether, including the punishment they'd gotten in the saga of the convoy, the two wouldn't be seeing home for fifty-six days.

7

POTATO CHIPS MAKE NOISE. Pretzels make noise. Chocolate Kif Kef bars don't, provided that you take off the wrapper first. Wrappers make noise. So do sucking candies. When you're on a mission you give a lot of thought to the food that goes out with you. In enemy territory a bag of Ruffles could cost you your life. Make a rustling noise and you've exposed yourself. Hezbollah is listening. Drop a wrapper and expect to be bombarded.

Just before zero hour you enter the kitchen and organize provisions. The IDF provides an allotment of sliced beef jerky and chocolate bars—the good kind, Elite chocolate with nuts, the one with the red cow on the wrapper, to make you feel like they're really investing in you. There are the house rolls, too, which you squeeze and knead until they're about as thick and compressed as a broomstick so that they take up as little room in your bag as possible. You fill them with sliced cheese and jam, which is an Ethiopian dish that caught on in combat units in the last few years. In the end you add a large helping of gummy bears and chocolate-covered wafers that you buy on your own in advance, back in Israel. And of course there are the sickheads who pack dates and raisins (dominant mothers, I guess, or troubled childhoods). All this you shove into your treat pack, cramming in everything you can. Twenty minutes later it's all one big sticky mess. Bits of beef jerky on top of chocolate, chocolate on top of the gummy bears. Tastes like shit, but everybody gets hooked on it.

The treat pack is a brilliant invention, part of every fighter's required equipment. Basically a lunch bag made out of khaki-colored Cordura that's been refitted with black rope and plastic fasteners and attached to your backpack or vest, it's specially suited to operations that require camouflage and complete silence. You can run, jump, roll on the ground, and nothing will cause that treat pack to make noise. It won't fall off, either. Just don't forget, no wrappers inside.

Ninety minutes to sunset and Oshri instructs the squad to start preps. They take off their army boots and smear them with oil to prevent water from getting in, then they pile on the heavy clothes: long underwear, Thermax pants and shirts, combat uniform, a layer of fleece-lined clothes, and, to top it all off, a storm suit and combat vest. They wear Nomex gloves and three pairs of heavy socks one on top of the other and a pair of overboots, too. On their heads they wear a Madonna set, a black cloth headband with a microphone and earphone. Each fighter puts eight full rifle magazines into his backpack along with two hand grenades, two flashlights (one regular, one red), and a shiny red stick-light. You add a probe, too, which is a long, sharp rod for testing suspicious objects: you strike the stone to see if it isn't a fake one made from fiberglass and manufactured in Iran, its hollow insides hiding, say, a deadly claymore mine. And four personal heat packs, which can reach a temperature of about 120°F (just don't let them touch your skin). A compass, too, and personal night-vision equipment and a pair of binoculars. And the treat pack, of course: Every item that goes out with a fighter on a mission like this, even the piss bottle and the canteen and the helmet, are roped to the side of the backpack to ensure that nothing will be left behind or fall when it's time to retreat. Oshri adds spare transmitters and replacement batteries to the backpacks. River slips in a shit pack, a hermetically sealed bag that fits into your helmet and is designed for taking a dump while in enemy territory. When the bag is full, the squad seals it carefully and brings it back to the outpost for proper burial. If we leave our droppings in nature, in places the IDF has selected for staging ambushes, we'll expose our hiding places to the terrorists. If we're talking about an overnight ambush it's fair to demand that a sane and healthy soldier hold it in, and anyway, when we go out for a day or more we take "Stop-It" pills, which make us constipated for at least seventy-two hours. Don't even try it. Release, when it finally comes, rips you to shreds. And yet, in spite of it all, there's never been a single ambush that some soldier didn't stink up. It's worth being prepared.

They pop off one after the other for a final shit while Bayliss mans the sewing machine, manufacturing a few last treat packs and cloth pockets for anyone who doesn't have. River checks out everyone's veins, prodding them and trying to commit them to memory, forcing himself to believe he'll be able to administer an IV with his eyes closed, in the dark, if need be. It's also the time to take everyone's temperature and record the data in a chart. "They promised us a rectal thermometer," Zitlawi complains, to which Oshri replies that everyone should keep his perversions to himself. Truth is, the cold spell that hit Beaufort in the winter of '98 and led to the hospitalization of a bunch of soldiers gave birth to a whole folklore in the company about issues of rectal virginity. A "virgin" is someone who hasn't been rectally penetrated yet.

By a thermometer, that is. I'm one of them, luckily: after all those years in the field I haven't lost my virginity yet. Not Oshri, though, he lost his big-time. One winter, during a snowy ambush we both took part in as soldiers, the commander passed around an oral thermometer for all of us to take our temps. When it came to Oshri's turn, the thermometer read 95°F. That got the medic worried, and he made it clear that the poor fuck had no choice but to open up his butt and do a more accurate check. Those are the orders, no way around it. Oshri stubbornly refused, claimed he wasn't capable of removing eight layers of clothing in such conditions. But the commander and the medic insisted. In the end, he gave in. At first he tried administering it himself, kept at it for a while. When that didn't work the medic lost patience, grabbed him, spread his cheeks, and shoved it in in one go. If it had been a thin thermometer—a revolutionary development now found in the kit of every medic serving in low-temp areas—we would have forgotten about it a long time ago. But that night, with the thickest rod of glass you'll find anywhere in any Medical Corps storerooms, that little punk's screams could be heard all the way to Damascus. And there we were, surrounding him, watching him writhe in pain and laughing our heads off. Oshri likes to tell how at first it was scary and caused him to tighten up but after that it was relaxing, addictive, even pleasurable. I can only think how lucky it is that the kids haven't heard this particular battle story yet. If they had, they'd never stop bugging him about it. What's for sure is that they wouldn't be able to look him in the eye with respect and take orders from him.

Twenty-five minutes until we move out. When the outfitting of the packs has been completed, tradition has it that the squad takes advantage of a few spare minutes for some quick bargaining: "You got any extra heat packs? Give me two and you'll get a gummy bear." "What, all you've got is cherry flavor? Here, take grape." Oshri is always the last one to get in gear, when the squad is already in formation. They've all got short-barrel M-16s hanging from their shoulders with cutting-edge laser locators that make it easy to shoot from the hip instead of raising the gun to your shoulder. "Let's go," he announces. "Equipment lists." "Equipment lists, equipment lists," they repeat after him. This means they check each other's vests, their packs, make sure nothing's been forgotten and that everything's been recorded in the log that stays behind, at the outpost. If we get blown up they'll know in the war room and the storeroom what exactly is missing, what sensitive equipment has fallen into enemy hands. After that each guy steps onto the digital scale, one after the other, with all his equipment on his back and his vest and his gun in order to make sure that nobody's over the limit. The data are recorded in a chart. Another chart. Each backpack weighs anywhere from sixty-five to eighty-five pounds, a fighter's vest is another forty-five, and when you add combat equipment like the sharpshooter's case or the surveillance post display screens, it works out that sometimes a soldier has to carry on his back, for the duration of a long, operational march, a load of one hundred and fifty pounds. In the meantime, I'm in the aerial photograph room trying to absorb all the details of the operation. You have to memorize them: at which pile of rocks I cut to the right, next to which boulder I head left, where gaps may open up between the soldiers, at which spots there are possibilities for transmission or surveillance, when we can stop for the first time and at what point each man settles in. Amos, the battalion commander, is talking to me on the red phone, the hotline. "Don't sweat it, but tonight you're coming under fire," he says, dropping his bomb.

"What does that mean, Amos?"

"Don't ask me, I have no idea. Intelligence says they're on their way. I don't know how, I don't know how many, but it looks like you'll finally get to meet up with that terrorist cell that's been operating in the area recently."

"How can you throw this at me a minute before we move out?" I ask. "And without detailed information."

"Focus, Erez. Once you're out there you've got to remember we're here for our country. Everything you've gone through up to now has been preparation for this actual moment. So the time has come for you to do your best and show us what you guys are made of. Good luck."

Where the fuck was he pulling these clichés from all of a sudden? Battalion commanders don't really talk that way. Not on a day-to-day basis, anyway, maybe at funerals. While I'm still hanging on to the receiver trying to make sense of it, Oshri walks in. I cast around looking for the right words to tell him tonight's the night, but he beats me to it. "I don't think we should go out tonight," he says, out of character, surprising me. "The moon's at ninety-eight percent full, it's too dangerous. Like daylight. They'll see us all the way to Beirut." I chuckle. If our own General Spineless, little Furman, is finally sending us on a mission, who are we to refuse? Trust me, there's no danger at all. "Come on, buddy," I say, "we're already ten minutes behind schedule, let's give them some rousing commanding officer's speech and get the hell out of here." Oshri stands there for a few long seconds, staring into my eyes while I stare back at him, looking into his pupils for what suddenly comes next: I circle his neck with both hands and say, "What's wrong, little girl? Are you afraid?" "I'm not afraid," he answers, realizing it's too late to back down now, there's no recourse. I open the door and push him out. "Let me paint your face so we can get going before you start sweating all over the place in here," I say. In the courtyard Emilio has pulled out a video cam. "Come on," he says, "show Mom what nice warm clothes you're wearing, make her happy," to which Zitlawi responds, "Too bad, baby, filming us like that before an ambush. You're not giving us much of a chance." He tries to block the lens with the palms of his large paws. "We're fried now, anyone you filmed is toast. All over the papers tomorrow." But River enters the frame. "Cut it out, all those superstitions," he shouts, all worked up. "We'll set out of here, knock off a couple of terrorists with pleasure, confirm they're dead, and drink champagne for dessert. The ultimate." Bayliss, too, "God willing" like in the old days, promises everything will be fine.

Now's the time to get their adrenaline flowing, scare some life into them. And how do you get soldiers worked up? By putting pressure on, spooking them, that's the tactic. In most cases, a guy in a state of panic is a guy who reacts faster, so there's no choice but to mess with their brains a little. Oshri and I join them outside, where a mug of coffee is waiting for us, according to procedure. When the air is swimming with tension and the stomach with butterflies, you need no less than five and a half spoonfuls of Turkish coffee mixed with a single spoonful of sugar (it seems to me that the coffee that night was the bitterest I've ever tasted in my life). Everyone falls silent and I start to speak. "Kids, it's going to happen. Tonight we're drawing fire. This time it's for sure, not just some gut feeling of mine, not some prediction based on information from Intelligence, but an absolutely certain clash. And if that isn't enough, Hezbollah isn't our only enemy in this ambush but also level-one, ball-busting cold, which is waiting for us out there. You guys know the job, you're familiar with the procedures, make sure you follow the rules of marching, don't pull any sharp moves, flow with the landscape. We're going to be walking it slow, in complete silence. Your night-vision equipment stays on at all times. Does everyone remember the shelter points we set up in case of emergency? Emilio, have you got the hydrogen balloon catheters in your left pocket? Okay. Once we're in place we take turns on guard duty. If someone spots suspicious figures, usually the kind walking in columns with large packs on their backs, you whisper 'Sighted' and then we wait until they're within shooting range, we count four, three, two, one, fire, according to the way we've done it in training exercises. If someone's hit and bleeding he'll feel a sudden strong gushing through his body. Don't panic. Shout 'I've been hit!' according to procedure, then wait patiently. Tonight you're not only holding your own life in your hands but those of another seventy soldiers at Beaufort and, no less important, the prestige of the entire company. I'm counting on you."

They paint each other's faces, squeezing two thick lines of black and green from tubes of camouflage paint. It makes your skin itch like crazy and causes you to break out afterward. You smear up the neck, too, and then spread it around in circles. Standing in front of tiny cracked shaving mirrors hanging on the wall, they try to make sure there's not a single spot of shiny white skin that will expose them to some Shiite marksman. Emilio! You're shining! What's this pathetic cover-up of yours? Are we going on an ambush in Sweden? Squeeze that tube, get some paint on you! Moments before we cock our weapons and slip out the gate I announce six minutes, time for a last cigarette—that's in the rulebooks. They light whatever there is as long as it's not "lite." (No one would dare bring lite cigarettes to Beaufort.) The last-cig ceremony is a final leftover from the glory days, back when the IDF always had the upper hand around here, when the festive tradition before every ambush was a group shower with wild music, lots of slapping under the water, shouting in unison the order "Piss toward the drains!" followed by a mass smoke-in. In those days, Beaufort soldiers left for an ambush with puffy hair and a well-combed forelock, a look that would fit right in to the Tel Aviv nightlife scene. It's only in the last few years that everyone here looks dusty and gray.

Now is the time for a few laughs, pre-ambush laughs. I am

friendlier toward them than usual, try to cut the tension a little, let them joke about me, call me "midget." "Do you still wear boys' sizes?" they tease. "You look like a kid inside that storm suit."

"Yeah, I'm a midget with spiky hair," I answer. "That's why they say I look like a model." They calm down a bit, start punching each other. Then the moment arrives. "Okay, girls, we've got to move out," Oshri announces. They raise their guns. "Three, two, one, cock your weapons!" They ready their guns in one single, coordinated motion so that anyone listening in from outside the outpost would not be able to count how many of us there are. "Iron numbers, count off," he says in a whisper. One, two, three, up to fifteen. I'm number fifteen. We're off.

Nineteen hundred hours. Winter and rain, but I am so hot. My foot sinks into stinking mud—disgusting black mud, Lebanese mud—and I work hard to lift it out, again and again. I'm sticky all over. And the packs on my back are pulling me down toward the earth. The point we're headed to is only about six hundred and fifty feet outside the gate but it's hidden from view by twists in the road and you can't see it from the guard posts up above. Our mission: a patrol, an overnight ambush. The goals: to repel terrorist attacks from the outside, prevent Hezbollah from approaching the outpost, foil attempts at placing explosives in our sector, lie in wait for the enemy at a place he's not expecting you. A six-hundred-and-fifty-foot march takes forty minutes when you're trying to make your way along an overgrown path that may be littered with bombs. Your movements are delicate and gentle, the kind that are indiscernible from a distance. If someone slips and falls he'll not only split his head open or break his arm; he'll expose all of us. I march at the front with Zitlawi at my side carrying an IMI Negev light machine gun, the rest of the guys behind us. We're a long, silent column, twenty yards separating one man from the next, and we stop each time something suspicious crops up, then we kneel (in order to lower our shadows) and look around before continuing. Everything is hushed. Peaceful and tense. We're moving along smoothly, at a good pace. I approach the target spot, signal to everyone to stop, open up my infrared, and peer through it to make sure there are no enemies lurking about in the vicinity. I put all the technology to work, observing, and then I proceed to the spot with only Zitlawi and his Negev in order to make a thorough sweep before everyone else joins us. We've set up lots of ambushes here in the past so there's a chance the spot's been discovered and booby-trapped. Maybe somebody's even lying there in the bushes, about to pop up and pump a round of ammunition into us. So if we draw fire at least the whole squad won't be mowed down. The others take cover at a distance. At every ambush you're careful not to tread on a few prominent stalks so next time you can see if they've been trampled since then, if some unwanted guest has paid a visit. I check to see if the access paths to the spot have been exposed, if someone has cut back branches or made a pass from another direction. I check the earth—maybe it's been dug up—taking mental pictures of every stone. I move ahead on my own. Is there anything suspicious? This goes on for a quarter of an hour, the scariest goddamned time of your life, and I think to myself, Shit, just don't blow up now, because I feel completely alone, I miss the sound of my soldiers' breathing. Those are fourteen guys who won't let you die, I whisper to myself, there's no chance they're going to let you die, and if you don't believe that, then what have you got in life? If I ever get killed it'll be alone, at a moment like now, so better the bomb should blow up in another ten minutes when River's nearby. He'll know how to revive me.

When I see that everything's okay I signal behind me with my hands like a bird. That's how they know the coast is clear, they can approach. And they do, with nearly blind faith.

They live under the illusion that I would never lead them into an observation point they'd get blown up in. I'm surprised how they always follow after me without asking any questions. They're such children, really and truly innocents, they don't get that I'm their age, all in all a year older, that's it. I get instructions from my mother, ask my father to borrow the car, I'm just a little more experienced than the guys, but not much. They form a banana-shaped line and begin observing Wadi Zirin and the road that leads to the Beaufort. Congratulations, we're in, we've made it. Now all we have to do is wait for the enemy to arrive.

"The Silence" is what we call the first ten minutes of an ambush, during which no one dares cough, breathe, scratch, or even think. Even the equipment stays on the fighters during The Silence. Dropped your weapon? Leave it there, don't pick it up, whatever you do, don't make any more noise. If a terrorist is hiding out in your spot, let him be the first to make a noise; let him move a bush aside, make some incautious movement that will expose him. That's why these are the most critical moments of them all. Sometimes, because of gut feelings, The Silence stretches to twenty minutes; this time I pull it out to thirty. I want to be absolutely certain there's no other noise in our vicinity. And then I whisper, "Basic maneuvers," which they pass on from one to the other: "Basic maneuvers, basic maneuvers." This means they remove their helmets, placing them carefully on their backs. They rearrange their packs, lay mattresses on the ground, and, if thirsty, they put the tube that connects to the water pouch on their vests into their mouths. Spitzer and Koka attach missile launchers to their weapons. Zitlawi adds an eighty-bullet belt feed to his Negev and then another, bringing the total to two hundred and forty bullets in the drum. Bayliss loads a bullet into the M24 sniper rifle and locks the bolt, which gives him five bullets in the magazine and one in the chamber. Emilio is responsible for the thermal video camera used while in motion, which he places in his pack, and takes out a stationary thermal imaging system, a small television that is placed on a tripod and enables surveillance at a distance of two to three miles. Since he is weaponless he remains near me. For night vision we use the Aquila weapon sight, which magnifies everything to three times larger than actual size, and a device we call the "one-eyed rabbit." I am at the center of the banana, my gun stuck to my shoulder. Oshri has his back to me facing the less threatening side. Zion is in charge of the crew to my left, Eldad of the crew to my right. Boaz is the signal operator, Tom the marksman, River the medic, Itamar and Pinchuk the lookouts along with Barnoy, watching behind us and to the sides. Now it's okay to talk, preferable even, just so they don't fall asleep on me. When you think someone is drifting off, the procedure is to pinch him, slap him, punch him even. Jab him with an elbow, a blow to the head, whatever it takes to keep him awake. As a squad commander I dish out blows liberally, of course, really smack them around. And then I say, real innocent-like, "Oh, sorry, I thought you were sleeping." They actually like it. I hear someone whisper "Vicky" in the background. They're talking about my sister again. "There's no way you guys would actually dare..." I say, to which River responds in a low voice, "No, no, she's no one you know. He's talking about some hooker." Everyone laughs. They know I can't get up now to register a complaint. So I go along with it, for their sake, to entertain them. That's how it is: when you're out there the most difficult task of all is keeping yourself preoccupied. During the first few hours you talk, mostly light conversation. Zion tells about how it's uncomfortable for him to be screwing Eldad's sister when Eldad's sleeping in the next room. It happened that he was a guest in their home once and he and Eldad's sister clicked and they've been a couple ever since. And there's Eldad, inside a bush in the middle of Lebanon, listening to stories about his sister's fucking in great detail, how his friend hammers her, butt-fucks her, even—and there's nothing he can do about it. What can he do, punch the guy? He whispers, "Zion, enough." Zion says, "What? Your sister's really great. I want everyone to know. Come on, let me tell Zitlawi." The squad is spread around, listening, chuckling quietly. Because the fun of it is that you don't have to act grown up in the squad, we're all made of the same stuff. When we've finished the topic of screwing, the conversation turns to plans for the future. After all, this guerilla camp will come to an end one day. For all practical purposes we're really, really close right up until we start talking about life outside the army and you realize that in fact we are so different that it's not to be believed. Then, in the middle of the night, you get the surrealistic conversations. Like this friend of mine from one of the West Bank settlements who would tell about this strong desire of his to make Arabs disappear. Neatly, simply. Just get his hands on them and make them go away without anyone ever knowing they'd been abducted. He explained that this was his dream. He would get carried away describing it in realistic detail, exactly how he'd carry it out and what he would do when, trying to convince us it was a feasible plan, even easy. Just stop near some Arab in the street, get him into the car, bury him somewhere, and leave no tracks. One night he told us about a friend from the settlement, a guy who thinks the same way he does, who was prepared to go ahead with it together with him, to go all the way. I said, "Jesus, you are one stupid fuck. Pass the gummy bears, will you? All this talk of yours is wasting good eating time." After that there was quiet and we ate rolls with hummus and pastrami. I wonder if in the end he carried out his plans.

We are supposed to stay here until thirty minutes to sunrise. You have to complete the trek back to the outpost while the sky is still dark; if you screw up and the sky is already growing light you'll be forced to stay in ambush position for an entire day, and that is truly fucked. I call over to Oshri in the coded ambush language we've established as a way of referring to what's around us. So, for example, the goat path on the horizon that looks like the Hebrew letter *lamed* we call "Lila," which naturally leads to all kinds of digressions: "When are we going to open Lila up, man? I actually recommended to Furman that we bring in reinforcements and push that baby wide open, go all the way, but the Intelligence officer says she's not ready yet, too dry." Those are the kinds of things that fly around in an ambush, totally childish. But what can you do? That's the way we like it, there's no point in getting worked up about it. And on that night, while I'm pretending to be engrossed in studying the code map, which is dangling by a piece of string from my backpack, they're ragging on Emilio's grandmother, and saying that River is allergic to condoms, that he starts sneezing like crazy every time he . . . and how religious guys fuck like rabbits and how the apostate rabbi Bayliss's little sister is one bitching babe. Yup, these guys are crazy about religious girls. Zitlawi tries to understand why Spitzer hasn't introduced his Russian girlfriend to them, and how it is that Spitzer got hooked up with a Russian, of all things, because Russian girls like the sleazy guys, the arses, and the arses like Russian girls and Spitzer's a good little white boy, as good and white as they come. Is it possible that he's embarrassed by her? The squad investigates.

"Is she a *bliad* Russian, man?" Zitlawi asks.

Spitzer can't for the life of him figure out what Zitlawi means by a "*bliad* Russian." "You know," Zitlawi persists, "a '*bliad* Russian,' the kind with a heavy accent like those Russian guys who get wasted on vodka and then *bliad* becomes every other word that comes out of their mouths. Don't take it hard, pal, those girls have their advantages: they moan like hell and they take you ballroom dancing." The thirsty audience laps up every word of it. "It's like the blacks in America," Zitlawi continues, "just like the ones in the movies who can't stop saying 'you know' all the time. Or the assholes right here in Israel who keep saying *'k'ilu'* even when they don't mean 'like.' How could you not know any *bliad* Russians? Sure you do. But between us, man," Zitlawi advises Spitzer, "why not go for some upper-class Russian chick from the north side of Moscow?"

"No," Spitzer answers, "she's not a *bliad* Russian." His puppy eyes look hurt.

"Aw, come off it," Zitlawi whispers, "you're just a jerk, getting all emotional. I should take a plastic hammer to your brain. I was just asking, as a friend. Why do you take it all serious-like?" and he throws a stone at him.

"I answered you," Spitzer says. "She's not a *bliad* Russian and she's not hot for sleazebags." She actually wants to meet the squad after all the stories she's heard, but he's not willing to take the risk where unpredictable childish outbursts are concerned. They could cost him his relationship. "She's the sensitive type," he explains. "She came to Israel on her own: think about what kind of courage that takes. She's a volunteer at Kibbutz Kinneret, works in the fields. When she talks about going to study medicine at university, you'd better believe she's going to do it." Beaufort intrigues her, she questions him about it for hours. She keeps trying to understand but doesn't get it. In the meantime, Zitlawi is busy downing a chocolate bar, stuck one step behind everybody else trying to figure out why Russian girls like the dark guys, because it's common knowledge that Moroccans have little pricks. Iraqis have big ones, he says, but the Moroccans—tiny. But shapely. Tiny but shapely. Now he's on a roll, and even though someone says, "Damn, the remote's not working," which means they're trying to turn the TV off, which is like saying, "Time for a commercial break, man," which is like saying, "Flush already," or "Shut your mouth," or "Change the subject." But he is oblivious to them.

As for me, I stifle a smile while Oshri, as usual, is in shock. He's always in shock at times like these when we're out in the field, asking himself how the hell he wound up in such a surrealistic life. He brings his lips close, intending, like usual, to whisper in my ear, but this time I beat him to it. "Aren't you going to miss all this shit?" I ask him quietly, but Zitlawi manages to intercept my whispering, demanding to know to where the honorable sergeant will be making his escape. "Ladies," Oshri announces to them, "in the near future you will find me sprawled drunk and high on some nudist beach in South America." Suddenly there is a dull sound from far off, a kind of a pop, really strong. It's a missile being fired. "Helmets on!" I cry in a serious tone to make it clear that the laughs are over. They're startled and drop all their food on the ground. A few seconds later there are two gigantic explosions about a hundred yards away from us. A huge flash and then a mushroom cloud. Now it's okay to shout because you've been exposed. You're being fired at. I call into the transmitter: "Cheetah, this is One. Squad under attack." I shout, "Open fire to rescue!" hoping that the outpost will dispatch tanks and artillery quickly to the source of the fire, that they'll launch combat choppers and anything else they've got. There are more and more explosions, it doesn't let up. Pits open up around us, craters, there are fires burning in every direction, my eyes see red—one minute light, one minute dark. They seem to be firing from Mazraat Al-Hamra, from below the abandoned farm there, a distance of four or five miles from us. These are rockets, not mortar shells. They are falling very close to each other so you can't escape them. Not far from where we are, near the J-curve on the access road up to Beaufort, there are a few huge antitank slabs of concrete we call *dabeshim,* which we can hide behind. I shout, "Retreat!" to get us out of there. "My crew in twos!" I holler, and they are supposed to get to safety in small groups not too close to each other. I run first, then after me they come in pairs, three pairs in all. Then Oshri shouts, "Forget crews, everyone run now!" and the rest of them charge, all in a group. He stays back alone for another twenty seconds in our ambush position, to make sure no sensitive equipment has been left behind. I have already reached the concrete slabs. Two huge explosions shake the earth and crack it open. I've never in my life heard anything so loud, or seen that blinding a light. A ton of mud flies at me, covers me. Twenty yards away a fire is raging. During a split second of silence between bombs and whistles I can hear the siren up at the outpost, which means they're getting into their vests and helmets and the intervention force is already cocking their weapons and the rescue team is loading stretchers and pretty soon they'll be on their way to pull us out of this. After all, they can see what's happening on their thermal surveillance equipment. But eight of my men haven't reached me yet, goddamn it, I can't even see them. Oshri and the fighters, where are they? Another explosion. It's right on top of them, for sure, and here I am with nothing to do, helpless, telling myself they may all be dead. I'm already picturing it, that's it, it's all over, I'm going to be picking up eight dead bodies. What did we do in our training exercises? Are we supposed to wait for the bombing to stop or not? Should I run over there now, dodging the bombs and hoping my luck holds out? I start racing through their names like I'm taking stock—who's over there, who isn't, maybe they're wounded, writhing in pain. And Oshri! Shit. Oshri. I love that kid so much, I've got to run back there right now, fuck the training exercises. The air is thick with smoke. I don't know how long—maybe seconds, maybe minutes, maybe longer—I'm alone, a little boy's thoughts clogging up my brain, just waiting for something to happen, something to keep me busy. The waiting is killing me. And then I hear this long shriek and I can see them running for their lives, and they are alive, emerging from the screen of smoke. "Lie down behind the concrete!" I shout. "Hang on tight to each other!" The kids lie down close together, burrowing down, their hands cupped over their ears. Oshri and I lie down, too, on top of them, crosswise, on their heads. They're shaking, God, how they're shaking. "Everyone here?" I ask. They're not even capable of talking, they're paralyzed. "Snap out of it!" I yell. But they're silent. Then suddenly everything goes quiet except for the sound of the bonfires all around us, and our own heavy breathing. It's a real silence that grows and grows, even the transmitter isn't chirping, and all around the night returns and we can feel the waves of cold cooling off the pools of sweat on our faces. We are tense. No one talks. Silence. Then suddenly the silence ends, all at once. Another huge barrage of Katyusha rockets, but I mean huge. They're falling ten yards away from us. I hear them whistling and say to myself, That's it, what are the chances of them not falling on us this time, finishing us off? BOOM! BOOM! BOOM! They're getting closer, they're falling on the J-curve. I can't breathe, can't do anything but stay hidden and hope to God we don't get hit. Between explosions I hear the kids screaming from behind the *dabeshim,* their voices choppy. "Let's get out of here already!" I see River and Oshri hanging on to each other, hiding inside each other, River trying to dig himself right into the ground. Even if he manages to cover himself with dirt it won't help if a shell falls on him. I call request after request into the transmitter for them to open fire and give us cover, but nothing happens. There's no one on the other end. The explosions that a minute ago were detonating in front of us are now suddenly behind us as well, at our backs. I take a gamble and shout to everyone to move to the other side of the cement slabs. The bombs keep on falling, four to a launch. The battalion commander is suddenly talking to me on the encrypted transmitter. "Everything okay, One?" he asks. Before I can answer there are four more explosions. The concrete wall has taken a direct hit and half of it breaks off and falls right above us, smashing my encrypted transmitter, breaking the antenna. Our connection is cut off. Sure, we've still got the open wireless line but we can't use it since Hezbollah will be listening in. If we say "Squad under fire" they'll understand they are firing exactly in the right spot and they won't stop until we're dust.

Oshri says, "Let's evacuate to the outpost." I say, "No." He argues with me, gets hysterical. "You're wrong!" he persists. I've never seen him question my authority like this before. "We've got to get out of here," he screams. "We're fried if we don't get out now!" I'm considering it, and if so, where to. Maybe back to the outpost, maybe it's better to run down to the home of the collaborator who lives a quarter mile below us, and the path that leads there seems for the moment less exposed, and fewer bombs have fallen there. In the end, I give in. "Get on the open transmission and have them send a Nakpadon." That's a huge Israeli-made tank that's perfect for rescue missions because every part of it closes inward, nothing's exposed to attack. "Cheetah, this is Deputy One," Oshri shouts into the transmitter. "Requesting a Nakpadon for evacuation."

"Deputy One, this is Cheetah," Furman answers. "Good to hear you! Give us a report."

"Requesting a Nakpadon for evacuation," Oshri answers, insistent.

"Negative. That's negative."

Oshri and I look at one another. Negative? What the hell is that motherfucker talking about? Negative? Do they have any idea what our situation is? "Deputy to Cheetah, Number One is next to me, asks me to relay request for immediate evacuation."

"There's no way to send anything out to you right now. Hold tight."

"Too dangerous, Cheetah," Oshri pleads.

"Get off the transmitter, Deputy. You'll have to manage without it for a while."

Oshri takes it in, gives up. Through the smoke that separates us I try—unsuccessfully—to see if he's in shock or wounded, what exactly is going on with him. Maybe he's just nervous. The bombs are still falling, minutes are passing—who knows how many?—and Furman asks again for a report. "Everything in order, Deputy One?" Oshri doesn't answer. "Is everything in order, Deputy One?"

"Answer them calmly," I tell him. "Say everything's in order."

"I can't," he says.

"Is everything in order, Deputy One?" they ask again from the war room.

I shout, "Oshri, tell them that everything's okay already, and that we're far from the line of fire. Hezbollah's listening in on this, damn it, tell them we're not in the line of fire anymore!"

His hands shaking, he answers. "Roger, affirmative, everything in order. We're out of the line of fire."

After thirty seconds or so we can feel the missiles gradually moving away from us toward the outpost. Maybe the terrorists have come to the conclusion that they're firing in the wrong place. My soldiers' weapons are still shaking, they're banging against the rocks. "What, you're not going to get scared on me, are you?" I ask Zitlawi, who's below me. "Don't choke up on me now." I only want them to move, I think, to laugh. I've got to find a way to keep them busy in the meantime. The situation is getting worse.

Just then, when it seems it's all over, the transmitter crackles with a cry from the war room: "Scumbags approaching White!" Which means, a Hezbollah terrorist cell is approaching on foot, trying to infiltrate the guard post on the north side of Beaufort. Suddenly it becomes clear that the rocket fire was intended to draw our attention away while a cell crept in. The outpost opens fire with shells and anti-tank missiles and machine guns. It's called "Firebox," when all posts fire in every direction without discretion, surrounding the mountain with a deadly ring. The only place they're not firing is at us, behind the cement slabs. Again, long, scary minutes pass. I'm lying under concrete with fourteen people in the middle of nowhere and not a single commander is saying a thing to me and I have no idea what's happening. It's an inferno all around us, tanks are firing nonstop, rocket tails are slicing through the skies over our heads, flares, it's clear something dangerous is going down. Oshri is holding River's head, forcing him to lift his gaze and watch the glowing rockets, it's Independence Day up in the sky. But the kid insists on sticking to the earth. Emilio asks if the outpost is in danger, Zitlawi wonders if they've forgotten about us, and we simply wait.

Long months will pass before River writes the following lines about that night (I'll read them only years later, which is to say only recently): "Lying there, I was most of all curious. Curious to know whether I would get out alive or not, if I'd survive, if the next bomb would blow off my leg or my whole body, if shrapnel would pierce my hand or crush me completely. Curious to know if it would hurt. The tension kills you in these situations, gets into your bloodstream. It's the uncertainty. As far as I'm concerned, let something happen already, whatever it is, just so I know what it's going to be. That's what I was thinking about. Because at those moments you don't think about home, or your parents, you only think about whether you're going to live or not and you pray that something you've been trained to handle will happen already, that some terrorist will come along, that some battle will begin, because you have no tools to cope with the situation. You pray to God, to Allah, even to Muhammad or Jesus, or all of them together, because there's no way of describing how scary it is when it closes in on you, makes your heart pound at a rate of four hundred beats to the minute and there's nowhere to run away to. That night, for the first time, I felt death. I heard how close by the bombs were whistling, and the rockets, and I watched them up there and then saw as they exploded near me and I told myself as far as I'm concerned, it's all over for me. Fear, they always reassure you, is only part of the preparations; when you set out on your mission it dissipates. When they open fire on you it will disappear completely. Well, it turns out that isn't quite true. Try to imagine your very first bungee jump, multiply that by a hundred or a thousand, then cut the rope and you'll begin to know the feeling.

"As for me, ever since that huge rocket ambush I don't feel good about myself at night. All the time, until today in fact, I don't like nighttime. Because every night after that experience my heart skipped a beat when night fell at the outpost. My eyes would race around looking for flashes and launches in every direction. I'd close them and see explosions. Even today sometimes, especially when I'm outside the city, I suddenly get hit by the smell of the night at the J-curve toward the bottom of the Beaufort and the feelings and the quick beating of my heart remind me what my heart felt like back then. I'm always more tense and less sure of myself. But those were the moments of our first memories together, our first black humor, our first pride. And sometimes, when it's really quiet and someone asks, 'You guys remember the rockets at J?' we all answer, 'Holy shit, do we ever,' because on that night, for the first time, I understood where I was. We would never again ask where that war was that everyone was talking about." That's what River wrote.

That was the first time we lay there together under fire. Three terrorists were killed that night outside the outpost, and it was only after they went down that things started to quiet down a little. Furman came up on the transmitter. "Start to evacuate," he ordered. "Back to the outpost in pairs," I called out, and we all began to run up the steep slope pulling one another along. We were our own rescue team. In the video taken on our arrival you see us, pale, each one of us whiter than the next, coming in with glazed looks on our faces through the "gapcow" and crumpling there. We didn't even disarm our weapons. When we entered, everyone was standing around applauding us like crazy. They told us they were certain for a while that we were all dead. Finished. They were watching from the war room by way of a video camera on the fence of the outpost and saw the heavy clouds of smoke over our heads. In the recording, which today is stored on the base at Elyakim, in the Lebanon War Archives, you can hear Furman saying, "Prepare eight stretchers, we've got eight 'poppies.'" Eight bodies. They say there was crying in the halls, and how.

In the middle of all the madness and joy I tried to count my soldiers, face by face, to make sure everyone had made it back. But it was impossible. They were mixed in with piles of guys hugging each other. That's the way it is: from all that pressure the tears flow even though you're not exactly crying, and you kiss everything that moves. I held Oshri in my arms and wouldn't let go. I kept thinking how good it was to have him with me. Then Furman showed up. "That's the last time in your life," he whispered, "that you give your soldiers an order to improve their positions en masse. You do it in pairs or by crew. Were you sleeping when they taught you that at the officers' academy? You were crowded together, Erez, one mortar shell would've taken the whole bunch of you out." What? A few seconds passed before I was able to respond. "What are you talking about?" I asked. "What crews? The bombs were dropping right on our position. If the eight guys who got out of there last hadn't run out together, they'd be dead right now." Furman ignored my answer, turned his back to me, and started to walk away. "Why didn't you evacuate us?" I shouted after him. But he kept walking, getting farther away. "You were sure I had eight poppies and you didn't come to get us!" I hollered. That made him stop. He asked me to meet him in his office.

"Screw the office, you tell me how it is that you didn't come rescue us. What the hell were you people thinking?"

"It wasn't the right thing to do tactically. It would have caused more casualties."

I felt a volcano rising inside me, boiling and bubbling, which in another second was going to explode. I could almost have cocked my gun at him, right there in front of all the guys at the outpost, who were watching us, stunned. I tried biting my lips but it didn't work. "Do you get it?" I asked him. "Do you get what you did? You sent us out there without knowing if you'd be able to rescue us, if you had the balls to do it! Isn't the safety of the men our highest principle, our supreme goal? Bringing your soldiers back, wounded, at any price? Do you have any idea what kind of hits we were taking out there?" He didn't say a word. His face was red but he stood there like he didn't care, which made me even madder. "And how is it that you sent us out in ninety-eight percent moonlight?" I continued. "Hezbollah could see us with a plain old pair of binoculars."

"Erez, what's important now is that your soldiers are scared shitless. You're taking them out there again tonight to rip that fear out of them. Get yourselves organized."

"No way. No way. No chance we're going out there now."

"Yes, you are. And I don't want any arguments about it."

I pushed him aside, into a wall. All around us nobody dared to breathe. I shouted that he'd better forget about it, that I wasn't taking them back out there. If he wanted to he could send another squad. "Is that the way you're going to be about it?" he said in a cold and mocking tone. "You want to go back to being a private? What are you, some new recruit who thinks he can get whatever he wants? No problem, go ahead and refuse to follow an order. Don't go out. I'll go out in place of you. With your squad."

"How can you talk to me like that, Furman? A second ago I was nearly killed. You people forget where you are."

"So what do you want?"

"That my soldiers won't go out tonight."

We didn't go out that night. Furman consulted with whoever he needed to consult with back in Israel and decided to leave us alone, which I figured would cost me buckets of sweat in the near future. I went to the public phone and dialed. Lila didn't answer. "Hi, what's up, where are you? I guess you're probably sleeping, so I won't disturb you. I just wanted to say that I'm fine, because maybe they'll say something on the radio. Things got a little wild up here. Nothing happened, so don't worry. I'll try to catch you again sometime."

Sometime before daybreak the squad met in the dining room and sat around a table full of treats, the fantastic meal that traditionally awaits fighters after every return from an ambush or operation. Little cartons of banana milk shake, cookies and pastries, schnitzel and French fries, exactly in that order. It's called an "operational spread." I wasn't there. I sat thinking alone in the briefing room, trying to recall it all, and asking myself whether I'd passed the test, if I'd been brave enough, if I'd been a disappointment. Zitlawi came to find me. "You coming for coffee in the security room?" he asked. My soldiers had never asked me to join them for coffee before. Now they were sitting next to me, talking with me; suddenly there was a kind of a click between us, something that said, "We've accepted you, man, you're one of us. Okay, it'll take a little while to get used to this, but you're one of us." A lot of things changed after the night of the huge rocket ambush. Even me. Until that night I couldn't give a fuck if, let's say, Zion's girl was cheating on him. Now all of a sudden it mattered a lot, because I cared about him. I depended on him and he depended on me. I know I was shitty toward them, they hated me. Now I guess everything had shifted, priorities and shit. "No, thanks, some other time," I told Zitlawi that night. "There's something I have to do." In a strange way I was even kind of embarrassed, ashamed. The only thing that would calm me down was some solo time with Oshri. We lay on the beds not saying anything. I thought, What exactly am I supposed to be feeling right now? Relief? Maybe fear? Maybe it should be hitting me how close we'd been? Or that I should love them more than I already do? Could it be that apart from anger, plain old anger, I'm not feeling anything? Maybe because of the confusion. "They were shaking," I told Oshri. "Shaking and quivering. I don't want to think what would have been if we'd had to go on the offensive out there, engage in hand-to-hand combat."

"What, and we weren't shaking?" Oshri asked.

I didn't answer. He hesitated for a moment, then said he actually felt certain we would have been fine in combat because it was the helplessness and the indecision and the lack of opportunity to react that neutralized our will to do battle. Lying there in the fetal position in the dirt, no enemy in sight, no way of putting a face to him—that was the problem. They'd been taught to fight, all of us had, hadn't we? If there'd been anyone to charge at they would have charged with us, every last one of them. "How can you be so sure?" I asked. "I don't know," he responded. "I can sense it."

So much research has been done by the IDF and foreign armies in an attempt at unraveling that mystery, which has never been solved: What is it that makes a man rise up and charge? What causes him to stand exposed and face the fire when he's behind a rock, protected and comfortable? It's so involuntary, so illogical, so unnatural. Our survival instinct is supposed to be stronger than anything, right? And still we rise up, when the time comes, we switch on the autopilot without thinking about it, we take the chance and we charge, risking it all. Studies say that friendship is the driving force, along with social pressure. Yes, feeling humiliated in front of your friends is a bigger deal than the mission itself. "These people and this country," I would chant whenever asked why, knowing I would always be the first to charge. But maybe I just love action. We stopped talking, fell silent. "I'm sorry," Oshri said suddenly. I should have answered, What, are you crazy? and then leaned over his bed, taken hold of his hand, and with my other hand caressed his face and said, Man, you are one sorry dude. What's there to be sorry about? You were a god out there, bro, you saved their lives. What? The argument? Forget about it, it's all bullshit, you *need* to argue with me during such situations. Truth is, you were right. Instead, I said nothing. I thought I saw him gazing at his countdown chart, but I didn't ask. That seemed preferable.

8

DAYS PASSED. Storms of mortar shells fell on the Beaufort during the nights. We called it "purple rain." It was a kind of concert that started with the loudspeakers suddenly announcing, "Launch! Launch!" and then there'd be a second or two of silent tension, sometimes three, when we'd all freeze in place and wait. And then a terrifying, shattering explosion. Two, on occasion. The earth shakes, things move around in the room. The loudspeaker closes the circle by announcing, "Hit! Hit!" and then, even before there's time to turn it off, there comes another announcement of "Launch! Launch!" and more explosions. More bombs. Launches and explosions and bombs. Sometimes it lasts for long minutes, dozens of thundering booms one after another, and hits. The more time passed, the more the announcements sounded drowsy, jaded, and serene, like the beat of some natural sound track. The floor would vibrate, the walls would groan, but the outpost remained calm, particularly when the attacks would begin. These were little breaks from everyday life, when our daily routine—maintenance jobs, running around, arguments—would stop, and we would grab an easy chair or, whenever possible, throw ourselves on our beds, shut our eyes, and listen to the sound, thriving on it, enjoying it. BOOM! BOOM! BOOM! Shattered slabs of concrete rained down in every direction. Antennas fell crushed to the roof, water reservoirs took direct hits and sprayed water everywhere, flooding the parking area in a puddle of infuriating mud. Whoever chose to continue doing what he was doing at those times slackened his pace and kept time with the explosions and even added original musical accompaniment. The symphony of our routine, which was composed there, plays in my head to this very day. Spitzer pounding bread rolls with a meat hammer before an ambush, rolling them out to the thickness of a broom handle, squishing them one after the other like an assembly line. Chili the cook, ladling dollops of soft cheese on creamed potatoes, kept time, too, as he added fried onions to each one. BOOM! BOOM! Hit, hit. Bayliss scrubbing his face in circular motions with a rag and laundry detergent, no running water to be had, trying to remove the last of the old camouflage paint stains. Launch, launch to the strains of the music from *The Lion King,* which we loved watching as it jerked along on the screen of a small television set that skipped and almost never showed a clear picture. And the endless corny old Israeli films we could watch twenty-four hours a day. And horror movies and trips to outer space and Bruce Willis storming terrorists who'd taken over a building; we lay there reciting every line again and again. BOOM! BOOM! And the chirping of the transmitters and the bobbin on the sewing machine, and the sipping of tea, and the stirring of coffee and a quick round of dramatic pounding on the *darbuka* drums. And Dave from the war room, who wants us to believe he's a celebrity hairstylist, shaves everyone's heads with the electric razor. And the phone calls. And the calls to dinner: "Come and get it, soldiers! Come and get it, vets!"—accompanied by banging metal on a large pot. And the loud footsteps in the hallways, and the flag fluttering above the fortress on a flagpole. It's keeping time, too, with the wind. Launch, launch, hit, hit. And the morning prayer service of a quorum of men at sunrise. BOOM! Everything keeps time. It's actually at those times when there's no rain of mortar shells that I totally tensed up.

If I told Lila about this, if she saw it, what would she say? I never tried to describe the experience to her. She would think I was exaggerating, that's for sure. And even if she didn't think I was exaggerating, there's no chance she would understand. My fault, not hers. How can words make it real? Anyway, is it even worth it to me for her to know, for her to be a little afraid? Would fear like this—the fear of losing me—make her love stronger? Or maybe weaker? Would the animal passion in the kiss I get every time I return to Israel, where she waits for me by the door and pounces, continue to make her suck every drop from me, sniffing my body from top to bottom and never letting up, as if it's her last chance? Or maybe it would put her guard up, distance her, a stubborn inner voice shrieking at her from within: "You jerk, don't stick with him, don't devote yourself to him, you'll only get hurt." And it really would hurt her. Maybe it would make her drive me crazy, this fear, cause her to give me an ultimatum about getting out, leaving the army. When I'm levelheaded about it I think it's better for me to keep my mouth shut.

Each time an attack began I'd imagine her: she's probably just back from a trek, where she rode a gushing waterfall into a natural spring, giggling, screaming, singing, telling stories about each and every plant, everybody touching her, hugging her. Her shirt is wet, stretched out, torn, her bra is showing. Maybe she was actually wearing a bikini, a blue and red one, and now, in her room, she's taken it off and she's free, with her friends, and here she is falling asleep for long seconds under the shower. I manage to hear those little breaths of hers that I love. A steaming flow of water caresses her, her eyes are completely blinded, there's steam everywhere. At the field school where she's doing her army service, each new group of soldiers stays for a week. High school students go there, too, in large numbers, and she takes them out on treks. They get horny as hell in this atmosphere of freedom, I know that feeling. Running around in their underwear all night between rooms, a beer in their hands, cigarettes behind their ears. They lie on the grass getting high and look around for somewhere hot and wet to stick their hormones. They're happy. And how does she handle it? Is there a chance that she loses control on occasion? Let's say she's wet right now, maybe even a little drunk. What would I be willing for her to do? Maybe, for the sake of argument, it wouldn't bother me if she let a girlfriend undress her, stroke her a little, maybe even kiss her. If she closed her eyes and thought about me while it was happening, while one of those nymphomaniac lesbians who serve in the field schools turned her on, rubbed her nipples and her soft belly, maybe I would go along with it. It's clear that not one of those lesbos would miss an opportunity to tempt her into mutual masturbation, at the very least. Would that bother me? In fact it would, absolutely. Very much. I'm getting mad just thinking about it. I've got to figure out with her what she does and what she almost does and what she wants to do and how she resists temptation. But there's no chance we'll talk about that, in the open, even after all the time we've been together. That's really cheap and whorish, to hold a conversation like that with your girlfriend, and while I'm cheap and whorish, she's not. She's true quality, a lot smarter than me. We're like heaven and earth. It doesn't matter how many times she tells me she loves me, that it's the real thing, that I can let my guard down. She'll say it, and I'll even believe her, and I'll still keep trying to impress her, I'll think eight times about every stupid word before I let it out of my mouth. I am totally childish compared with her. She's already grown up, a real woman.

"Why do you love me, baby?" I'm dying to ask her when we're pressed up against one another. "After all, I'm a complete asshole, a fucked-up little arse. You could find so many guys better than me." But I don't ask her, I'm afraid of putting ideas in her head. With all her maturity, she's pure and innocent, looks at life with a naïve outlook that drives me nuts. She always believes in everyone's goodwill, never listens to me when I warn her. God, how I love her. And the mortar shells keep falling. And Bitter, my dog, is probably relaxing right now on the windowsill of the room he and I share, looking out into the darkened park where a few punks are closing off their night with a last cigarette before heading off to their beds. His white belly is on the sill and his black legs are dangling out the window, and for sure he's missing me. He's waiting for me to join him, behind the curtain, where I'll light a cigarette. The wind strokes my chest and Bitter licks my face for a few seconds. He'll look to the left and I will, too. He'll look to the right, and I'll do the same. He'll wag his tail. When his tail stands up straight, does it mean he's horny or what? In the end he'll get bored first and make for the blanket and the pillow. He'll signal me to join him. When he was a puppy I liked to put him on my stomach, all folded up, right on the muscles around my navel. He'd climb upward toward my heart, sit right on my chest, and fall asleep there. I would push him back down to my stomach and he'd inch forward again to my heart and fall asleep. He'd do it again and again, he only wanted my heart, to fall asleep to the heartbeats like a baby bonded to its mother. His love for me was unconditional. And the mortar shells are falling, they're bombarding us whole nights on end and my eyes are red, burning from fatigue. The guys are in the next room, Spitzer sprawled on his belly playing a small electric organ. He sings, "Over by Marjayoun I became a buffoon," and together they mangle a few popular songs. When they get to Chava Alberstein I've had enough. It's sacrilegious to make fun of Memorial Day songs. I get up from my bed and kick their door. "What's an organ doing at Beaufort? Next thing you'll be bringing me the Afula Junior Singers," I shout at them. Another hit, another launch. They try to sleep, I can hear them being quiet from my bed. Only Zitlawi is his usual energetic self and he's trying to find someone to pester. He jumps into Spitzer's bed, smashes up against him. "It's 'cause I love you," he says by way of apology. "Forget trying to sleep now. I'm going to help you make a film, *The Guide for Spitzer's Russian Girlfriend.* Great idea, no? I mean, she hasn't got a clue, right? About war, I mean. And you can't tell her in words, that's for sure. So why don't we prepare something fucking great and real for her so she doesn't miss all the action?" Spitzer loves the idea. That human aquarium doesn't know how to conceal his smile when he gets excited about something, and really, it is a good idea, even I have to admit it. What's wrong with a little romance? They wait for a little quiet, for the explosions to let up, and when the sun is high in the sky and the only bombs on the sound track are the dull echoes of explosions coming from every direction—a typical Lebanese afternoon—they go on duty together to the White guard post with Emilio's Argentine video camera. Against Emilio's will, because he is certain it will end badly. But what can he do? Moan a little, like usual. Spitzer stands inside the walled trench with his back to the view of Lebanon, tense and uncomfortable, to inaugurate the filmed guide. Zitlawi takes a few steps backward to get a good angle, presses the red button, then zooms in for a close-up in order to capture the little of Spitzer that peers out between his vest and his helmet, barely a pair of eyes and a mouth.

"From here we are able to keep watch over Nabatiye, which is actually a city. Over there is Tibnit, then Arb Salim and Jabel Zafi," Spitzer announces to the camera stiffly, barely even pointing out the places he is talking about. "Whoa, whoa," Zitlawi says, stopping him, "do you really think that's what you want to send her? What are you, totally fucked? It's terrible, man. This isn't the fucking news. Put a little emotion into it." He places the camera on top of one of the sandbags lining the trench, sets it on automatic, and joins Spitzer inside the frame, slinging his arm over his shoulders. "Shit, what's her name?" he asks in a whisper. "All of a sudden I forgot. Is it Nicole?" Nicole, you idiot? It's Lana. "Okay, Lana, baby," Zitlawi says, "our little Spitzer is making a video for you so you won't miss anything that's going on. As you can see, we're sunk deep in the shit while you're probably screwing some guy at a beach on the Sea of Galilee, sucking lemonade up a straw, maybe cheating on Spitzer with a surfer boy with gel in his hair, a cool guy who thinks he's something special, a suntanned hunk in a pair of thongs, the asshole. But we love you, you sweet thing, we're crazy about you, so here it is, *A Guide for Lana,* take one. Fun stuff, specials, goodies, the bodies of dead terrorists. We're going to make a world war for you! Just get the Vaseline ready, this is going to hurt."

Launch, launch. Purple rain.

9

WHEN EXACTLY DID IT HAPPEN? I swore I'd never forget the date, but suddenly now I can't remember. A total disgrace. Seems to me it was the eve of Holocaust Remembrance Day that Ziv was killed. Five days before his discharge. He'd already bought a ticket to South America, he had a girlfriend, owned a car—a Beetle he'd purchased two months earlier; the good life. He'd promised everyone that this would be his last trip into Lebanon. He called me "Chong," which is army slang for someone really green, a new recruit. I would say to him, "Shut up already."

When Ziv sat facing me at the Sabbath evening meal—held out his hand and said, "Nice to meet you, I'm Ziv Farran"—I didn't even reply. I was waiting for Dave, the guy from the war room, to finish collecting the prayer books, then I started eating. There was a holy ark, housing the Torah scrolls, in the corner of the dining room. It was army green and made of metal so thin that it dented if you kicked it. Layers of paint applied over the years thickened the ark by maybe a quarter of an inch, and rust covered its small metal legs. It was unsteady, it wobbled, and it was propped up by pieces of cardboard that would dissolve with every ten or twelve floor moppings. Next to it stood another, shorter supply cabinet in which were stored dozens of prayer books, all banged up and stained. On Friday afternoons Dave would pull them out and place them on the wooden table covered in light blue Formica that, to us, looked new and was reserved for special occasions, the cleanest there was at the outpost. You weren't allowed to eat on it, so of course sitting on it or standing on it or jumping on it or playing Ping-Pong on it or flipping it on its back and using it to skate across the wet floor were all totally out of the question. Dave made sure of it. He was still religious and respectful and all that, even though his ultra-Orthodox family and community had booted him out for joining the army, it's a big stain on them. So Beaufort was basically his home. Anyway, when the Sabbath started, the dining room was made over into a synagogue. Around thirty soldiers would sing and mumble the prayers, but quickly, making it up as they went along, because the rest of us—the wild beasts—were waiting outside for the royal feast, the one we spent the whole week waiting for, salivating. We never managed to hold out till the end of the service. We'd lose patience way before it ended and we'd burst into the room shouting, "People are hungry here, enough with all that wailing!" And there, on the tables, we'd find all the stuff the army pencil pushers could only dream about: steaks, hamburgers, fish, *bourekas,* five-star cakes. A real fucking restaurant. But by that Sabbath, when Ziv arrived, the storerooms were empty. Chili's fridges, too. We had a light meal that night, on little plates. Creamed potatoes and homemade *matbukha,* and a tomato salad seasoned with onions and egg. And our famous test—soft white cheese with fried onions and a sauce that's spicy as fire—the company specialty, the ultimate measure of stamina; whoever didn't survive this dish (and sometimes even officers failed) wasn't ready to take part in an ambush against Hezbollah. But there was no meat that night. And when all of us burst into the room to put an end to the prayers, I dragged Oshri quickly over to our usual seats, trying to make sure none of the white-bread guests that had landed at the outpost that evening would accidentally breach custom and mess up our seating arrangements. It didn't help. Before we even had a chance to pour hot tea into our blue plastic cups and signal to the guys from the Ordnance Corps or the Signal Corps or the Army Administration or the kennels to come sit with us and fill up our table, Ziv appeared and sat right in front of me. The pretty boy looked like he'd been parachuted in from some commercial for low-cal sour cream, minus the gorgeous babe. One of these TV soldiers with a pair of the most Italian sunglasses you've ever seen in your life and a perfect, even tan, the kind you can only get from a tanning salon. Real fighters don't shine like that, and what's all that happiness doing smeared across his face like that? What the fuck! I'm thinking that if that little white boy really knows something about bomb removal, I'll cut my dick off. "Am I imagining it or is that gel in Mr. Sunshine's hair, right here in the middle of the Beaufort?" I asked Oshri, out loud. "That's some styling job," Oshri answered. Even Ziv was smiling—he hadn't stopped smiling from the minute he'd arrived on the hill—and then he asked if the rumor was true that we'd be going out on the operation together. The word "Negative" was sitting on the tip of my tongue but just then Amos, the battalion commander, came over to update us and it turned out Ziv was right. We'd be going out together, me and Ziv, on command. I was to stick close by him—that's what was decided—introduce him to the sector, entertain him, then lead him and the squad inside, to the target. He'd be the commander for bomb removal while I'd be the commander of the security force giving him backup. Was that clear? I nodded, not giving a damn.

It had all started a week and two days earlier, when a large supply convoy was supposed to make the climb to Beaufort. If on a normal day we made do with surveillance and patrolling, where we'd circle the outpost on foot in the morning fog looking for any unusual markings—on that morning, with a convoy due, we wanted to make sure that the roads leading to us were free of traps and explosions. I took the squad out to open the road, which for generations of Beaufort soldiers has been the most despised job there is. It's a slow and exhausting march along the four-mile hilly path that leads from the outpost, crosses the J-curve, enters the village of Arnoun, winds through country lanes, draws near the Dlaat outpost, and reaches the Parah landing strip, an abandoned airfield on the way to Manzurieh. According to custom we would give a female name to every road opening, and this time it was Hodaya who got the honors. We're on our way to open up Hodaya, Oshri announced, and stuck Bayliss with the job of wire-searcher. The wire-searcher walks next to the tracker at the head of the column looking for trip wires, the kind that you step on and they set off explosions that send you to heaven so fast you don't even have time for the "Hear O Israel" prayer. All the others were strung out in a line behind us wearing vests and heavy ceramic flak jackets. Several of the guys were carrying dozens of pounds of electronic equipment on their backs with two-yard-long antennas sticking out above them. They were having trouble breathing, and sweating like pigs, trying to carry out the mission with precision, a mission that's supposed to be an ongoing series of quick glances in search of suspicious signs, but which very quickly turns into the dragging of feet coupled with a closed-off and exhausted look. Anyway, there is a certain logic to this procedure: with a road-opening the fighters march at a distance from each other, either alone or in pairs—the fewer together, the better. Better to expose a long, broken line of foot soldiers like this one to a potential threat than endanger a convoy of Safari jeeps crammed full with soldiers. And of course you've got trackers along while you're marching. We liked to believe back then that trackers, all native Arabic speakers, had some extrasensory inborn ability to locate every land mine buried along the way. We followed after them feeling assured, full of admiration, trying to deny the obvious conclusion that it was all a load of bullshit, since even the skill and experience and genes that had been honed over thousands of years on this land wouldn't enable any man to find a single thing in the kind of groundcover we were marching through. You could have hidden a tank right there in the bushes that surrounded us and we wouldn't have seen it. Really, God's honest truth. But apparently the commanders actually knew that very well, since high-alert, well-documented intelligence warnings were piling up, and they preferred to keep our road closed. On those occasions they would bring in the gigantic D9 bulldozers, the ones as big as three-storey buildings, a real fortress on wheels. Driven by SLA men, they were maneuvered back and forth over the roads. Huge numbers of mines and explosives hit them yet they came out of every attack without a scratch.

That morning, when we set out to open Hodaya, we never guessed how short the trip would be. We'd barely gone four hundred yards, we'd passed the J-curve, hit the Virlist road, and there, a few steps away from us and only seconds later there was an explosion. We shouted, "Bomb!" and we all froze in our tracks, waiting for an assessment of the damage and the rear-rescue exercise. It was the most fatal mix there was: an advanced claymore fragmentation mine filled with standard-issue explosives fortified with bits of metal and nails and activated by an infrared sensor triggered by movement. It was well hidden by a sort of artificial rock that acted as camouflage. Everything necessary to bring disaster to our troops was there. However, the Shiite jackass who, I admit, was clever enough and deserving of praise to slip onto a closed military road under the noses of the guards above had made two embarrassing mistakes: he placed the explosive device facedown so that it was pointed at the ground, and he forgot one of the wires most crucial in connecting the whole apparatus. The explosion was weak, almost unnoticeable—a kind of fireworks. No flames, no columns of smoke, not a single scratch or scrape sustained by the troops. And still, since this was the first explosion any force in our company had encountered in fifteen months, it was only natural that there would be quite an uproar back at the outpost. Real excitement, a day or two of heroic stories and the royal treatment for everyone involved. We actually thought like that back then, that it was the royal treatment. But was it likely that a terrorist had made his long way up the hill, nearly to the top, and made do with placing a single claymore mine? That's it? The whole shebang? He hadn't left behind a whole array of explosives, the kind meant to hit rescue teams, for example? He hadn't set traps still waiting for us on the road? What were the chances? Very low. That's experience talking. So, that morning, right after the incident, it was decided to seal off the road to all traffic, on foot or otherwise. No one coming in or going out, no mail, no packages filled with snacks from home, no supply convoys, and no SLA soldiers to come to the outpost to fix the damage from nightly purple rain attacks. Until it could be determined that no other explosive devices had been placed in the vicinity, we were cut off.

The days crawled by, the storerooms emptied out. There was no more meat, no more schnitzels or beef jerky, and everything in the canteen fridge had disappeared. We were waiting for a D9 bulldozer to plow the road and absorb any explosions, but Command had a more creative idea. On Friday afternoon, just before sunset, a Bell 206 chopper landed in our back lot. Amos jumped out of it into a sandstorm, followed by three shiny, perfumed fighters from the bomb removal unit. We stood facing them, Oshri and me, about ten yards from the outpost fence. Together we stood watching the new guests. It was Ziv we spotted first. "Looks like we've got ourselves a few more stuck-up pricks," I said. "That's just what we're missing around here." From there we went to the Sabbath evening meal and Ziv held out his hand and said, "Nice to meet you, I'm Ziv Farran," with crinkly, shining eyes. That fair hair, the thick, red lips. I didn't even bother answering. I made do with a quick, feeble handshake that made it clear how little patience I had for being friendly, and looked away. That's when Amos came over to pair us up. We'd be going out on an operation together, him and me, a two-headed command. I don't think I really understood, even then, the logic behind such a decision. They called it an "Admiral Procedure": we would lead a squad on foot into the pit left by the explosion on the Virlist road, in order to investigate it (what did that mean, anyway, to investigate a pit?) and patrol the area for the purpose of locating and neutralizing any additional explosives. It all sounded too dangerous. Bizarre. What about the bulldozers, what happened to them? This was a classic job for the bulldozers. But there you had it, Command had decided, and in fact it sounded like a chance for some action, and apparently it was important to investigate the pit, the apparatus, to gather intelligence, so this group of guys who looked like they'd stepped out of an American movie came to join us, with their shiny black parachute bags and cutting-edge vests and electronic equipment and binders, and their styled hair. They stood out in our dusty human landscape, leaving no doubt whatsoever that they did not have any connection at all to us, to our brigade. And yet suddenly we were assigned to be together. I nodded.

I had a good excuse for the long silence that followed: Spitzer and Zitlawi took advantage of the quiet and began playing two old and partially destringed guitars some kibbutz had donated to Beaufort back in the eighties. They moved from one generation to the next, right up to the most recent songs. Spitzer played, Zitlawi thumped the wooden guitar, and the whole room joined in for the singing of "Flowers in the Gun Barrel and Girls in the Turret." Everyone was beating the rhythm on the tables and singing with amazing precision, even the most recent verses about the sunshine over Gaza and Rafiah, which suddenly seemed about the most relevant thing in the world. Before I heard him singing I would have sworn that Zitlawi had never even heard such fancy, flowery language in his life. Amos seemed to be pretty pleased with the excitement and the feeling of togetherness. In the spirit of Moshe Dayan in a military parade, he scrutinized us all from the head table. He whispered to Furman, all happy and content. Ziv swallowed some of the cheese with the deadly fried onion and survived it in style. Didn't give a single sign of suffering. I motioned my surprise to Oshri. Chili entered with cups of chocolate mousse, one per pair. That was one great Sabbath evening meal we had there.

When it was over I was summoned to a three-way meeting in Furman's office. Before I'd even shut the door behind me, Amos pulled the trigger. "You never learn, do you?" he asked, on the attack. Then he fell silent and waited for me to respond. I really was surprised. What? What had I done? My brain was bombarded with bits and pieces of thought until I cracked it: the night of the rocket launchers, the argument that followed it. That was the matter. I was in shock. I couldn't believe that a senior officer like Amos could fall victim to a childish trap set by a whining company commander and was planning on holding, that very minute, a meaningless discussion about Furman and his wounded honor, lost as it were when I shouted what I shouted after the ambush. Was it logical to be dealing with this kind of bullshit instead of talking about what was really important, in other words, crucifying whoever should be crucified for the operational and moral failure that had occurred when we were lying there, drawing fire, and no rescue team was organized to save us? Since when had the IDF stopped considering the rescue of wounded soldiers to be a supreme value? They'd abandoned us out there. But Amos insisted on opening with his own agenda, or rather, with Furman's. He sank deep into the torn black imitation-leather company-commander's armchair. Furman was sitting on a small wooden chair on the other side of the desk, hunched into himself. I quickly took a chair for myself and sat down, pulling myself as close as possible to Amos. This was no field trial here. "Yes, it's true," I admitted, "sure as shit true. I went nuts, which is why I shouted in front of everyone. But I had good reason to, because how the fuck could I be expected to endanger the lives of my soldiers on enemy soil? They've been living since that night with the feeling that they don't have backup. I swear it, they tell themselves that nobody's watching their asses, that you can't trust anyone." I think I sounded pretty aggressive. Furman butted in. "That's what I'm talking about. That's exactly what I'm talking about. I can't command the outpost like that." I was about to attack him but Amos—impatient, kind of bored—cut us off. He had no intention of listening to the details and his ride home could already be heard in the distance, circling and preparing to land. "One more outburst like that, Erez," he said in a deep voice that was nearly a whisper, "and you'll land up back in prison. But this time it'll be for a long stretch." He stood up, grabbed his weapon, and left. I bit my lip and followed him out without a word; all I cared about was not being left alone in the room with Furman. For some strange reason, at that painful and humiliating moment, I felt a kind of relief. Was that what a reprimand sounded like? In fact it seemed more like an attempt at projecting forgiveness, like he was just going through the motions in order to keep Furman happy while at the same time subtly signaling that on the personal, moral level he could understand what it was that had set me on fire. My company commander, on the other hand, did not want me at the outpost; that was perfectly clear. As far as he was concerned it would be better for me to be dismissed. What was keeping me there, at Beaufort, was the fact that the brigade apparently had no one readily available they could replace me with. And maybe also because the brigade commander believed in me, seemed to understand that while I still had a lot to improve in myself—especially my impulsiveness—I was a devoted player with good intentions, a decent fighter who would grow into a decent commander. Better than Furman, that's for sure.

At sometime past twenty-two hundred hours I went off to the showers. In a lot of cases, officers preferred to give up that pleasure completely—sometimes they wouldn't shower for four weeks at a time so they wouldn't be caught with their pants down when the outpost was suddenly under attack. I tried to manage once in two and a half weeks. That Sabbath I took a chance because it really was calm. There was a special scent to that peace and quiet, hard to explain, and when it surfaced in the Lebanese air you filled up with tranquility and your level of tension lowered. It surfaced that evening, so I went to rinse the dust off myself for a minute under the flow of the water (the supply of water in the tanks was low, you had to keep from getting carried away). That brief moment in time was worth everything. First, the cloth that has been strangling your body is removed: the shirts that have been sticking to you are taken off, the socks. A winter wind strokes your skin, it's orgasmic. You die from happiness, even if you're frozen to the bone. Your naked feet turn into blocks of ice when they touch the ground. You take a few seconds longer to perform each action; the point is to steal a few moments while naked. You shiver, your whole being is drugged with cold and you're about to be drugged with heat. You step under the boiling hot water (hoping there will be no hitches). Your diaphragm fills up with steam. Holy shit, what a luxury.

But then Ziv showed up. He burst in, stripped, jumped under the water. Fact is that in those few short seconds when I lose touch with reality under the water, I need total quiet around me. It's part of the procedure. There's no talking to me. That's what I'm accustomed to and everyone can go fuck themselves. It's my escape, my refuge, my only private fortress. I shut my eyes and think of nothing whatsoever. I'm hollow. Just don't mess with me now, I whispered to myself. Let him save his energy for the upcoming evening in the submarine, for the rowdy late-night snack. Shit, anything but right now.

"I was warned in advance not to bother you," he said.

"Hmmmm," I answered, in despair.

"People talk, man. You know."

"Okay, what have your girlfriends been telling you about me?" I asked him, full of scorn.

And then, without a moment of hesitation, Ziv whips out the Abu-Jabai episode. "The battalion commander shouted to you five times over the transmitter: 'Erez, no confirmation.' But you wouldn't listen. Landed in jail for that, huh, big guy? You see, I'm up-to-date." That's what he said, not in the least shy about it.

"So, we're going to play *This Is Your Life*?" I answered. I shut off the water and went to get dressed. The peacefulness had been sapped anyway. I considered explaining that while it was true there was this matter of prison because I'd been charged with disobeying an order—which gave them no choice—I'd also received positive feedback, praise for engaging in combat. Mixed messages, that's the way it worked in this army. And the operational results had been excellent, all the officers had patted me on the shoulder and whispered that I'd done great. But I kept quiet. "In the officers' academy

I learned about it, about you," Ziv said, amused by the situation. "Would you believe it? The young criminal." I wondered whether it was good or bad—probably more good than bad—that my incident was being discussed at the academy. I had nothing to be ashamed of, I'd been a sergeant back then when I'd stormed without permission, and in the meantime I'd become an officer myself, which said something. I got dressed. On the bench, next to my decrepit toiletries kit, which had been in Lebanon with both of my brothers and had seen combat, was Ziv's, which looked like it belonged to a battalion commander. Draped over it was a white, short-sleeved T-shirt. I thought I wasn't seeing right. It couldn't be, couldn't be true, but there it was, in big blue and red letters printed right on the shirt: OUT OF LEBANON IN PEACE. I swear it, the motto of the Four Mothers movement plastered on his shirt. That band of females, those hysterical women that stir up trouble at intersections, wailing and moaning and threatening to wear us all down. Trying to convince anyone willing to listen that we, the fighters, are nothing but cannon fodder for a meaningless war, expendable tools. And the IDF, they claim, is blind and deaf and inciting to war, sending young men into the crossfire. We are those young men.

Try to imagine the feeling. In those days you'd make your way home after a month and a half, and it was like that damned Lebanon was chasing after you. It was everywhere: on the radio, on television, in the street. Talk, talk, talk, no end to it. A whole country full of people who don't know shit about the army but they know better than anyone what needs to be done. At least they think they know. And then along come the commentators: get out, stay in, escalate, soften, change, leave it, left, right—each one of them smarter than the next, each one of them adding his own contribution to boosting the enemy's morale, to his honor, to the wide smile you'd see on Nasrallah's face on TV. And helpless mothers who can't sleep at night, and people worried about their friends, and frightened girls in love: only Lebanon, all day long. They'd stir up doubts, when all you wanted was a little peace and quiet, that's all. I'd learned a long time before that there was no chance of finding any peace and quiet when you went home. You came down from the snowy mountain, from our bubble, cut off from the world and floating somewhere up there above the clouds and the chatter, and you'd land on muddy ground, where you'd find a wounded, confused nation of yakkers. The Four Mothers shrieked and everyone listened. That's how it is in Israel, I can understand it. But up at Beaufort? You asshole! Stirring up doubts up here? Spreading defeatist mottos and political messages? We don't need any cracks right now, anything that's going to seep in with the kids, that'll take their minds off the goal, that'll break the supreme concentration you need when you go out on a mission. Cracks like those endanger your faith, the willingness to give your all to this place. Up at Beaufort we'd succeeded, for the time being, in keeping out of those debates. And the kids? Thank God they were fired up, full of morale, hoping for encounters with the enemy, eager for action, as many ambushes as possible and for as long as possible. They wanted to return to Israel with *X*'s on their weapons, an *X* for each terrorist they'd downed. We were fighters; that's what we had enlisted to be. We'd chosen to be at the outpost, surrounded by the best friends you can ever have, partners in everything. Friendships that need no interpretation and in which there were no cracks. Telling a soldier at Beaufort that he was not needed was certainly not a healthy idea, and sure wouldn't motivate anybody. It was a lie, too. A complete and total lie. Anyone who didn't understand that, anyone who didn't see that the alternative was dead children all along the northern border, was an ass, a fool.

That was the first time I'd seen—in Lebanon, at Beaufort—the war that was raging at home and should have stayed there.

I debated whether to say something or not. You know the feeling where you're so stunned that there's no chance you'll be able to butt in? Well, that's how it was. "What's with you?" I asked, restrained.

"Don't know," he answered. "Kind of curious, I guess, that's all." He still hadn't caught on to my anger.

"Here's a piece of free advice, you pansy piece of shit. If you don't want this entire outpost to fuck your little ass to pieces you'd better not play the PEACE NOW activist up here."

Silence followed. For the first time his smile disappeared and his eyes lost their light. In a single moment it seemed the structure of his face had shifted, was one big grimace. Apparently, I'd hit home. I glared into his eyes another few seconds, then took my toiletries and got out of there. He just stood there.

That night I went back to him. I'm not sure why. It's out of character for me. But I went back to him on my own initiative at around two-thirty in the morning. I told myself we needed to show our professionalism, our maturity, because we had a mission to lead. A complicated one. And when you're leading an operation together—soldiers, that is—there's got to be communication between you, chemistry even, as much as possible. We didn't have the privilege of fighting among ourselves. Maybe that was the reason for the sharp change in his expression in the showers, which was now etched in my brain and making me so restless. He'd looked despondent. He was pretty much alone up here. I tried to think back to the tone of my voice, how deadly I'd spoken to him. Had I shouted? Or did I just come across as nasty? I couldn't exactly remember. I tortured myself over this for about two hours while Oshri slept facing me and I was alone with myself, thinking, lying wide awake and scrunched up, uncovered, like some deadbeat loser. I was thinking maybe it was Ziv who should make the first move, or maybe that I should report the extreme-left activist in the withdrawal movement who was unfit to command an engineering squad. Why should I even agree to go into the field with him? After that, the temporary insanity wore off and I understood I wouldn't be able to fall asleep without talking to him. I gave in. Maybe it had something to do with Amos's reprimand, or maybe because of plain old curiosity. I went to the room where the guests slept and I leaned over him. He lay there dozing, maybe even actually sleeping. I shook him gently awake and asked in the most matter-of-fact tone possible if he wanted to join me for a late-night observation of the sector. Let him learn, why not? It took him a few seconds to restart himself, get a grip, then he grinned like a kid and sat up. He had this look on his face of someone who's just made up. Seemed to be a good guy in spite of it all, a guy who likes people. Strange, I thought, that he didn't despise me. He didn't look at me like some fuckup inferior punk from Afula who likes to play with guns, someone too immature to get that the leftists had the answers. Maybe he even respected me. Because here he was, happy I was holding out my hand to him, and even after I said what I'd said he wanted to connect with me. Surprising. We went out into the darkness together.

We walked along without exchanging a word. It was so quiet there. Only the wind whistling, and every two or three minutes a short series of dull explosions from a faraway sector. The yellow flames and the orange mushroom clouds looked tiny on the horizon. Up above was a thick carpet of thousands of glowing stars. That's how it was at Beaufort: the darker it was on the ground, the brighter it was in the sky. When we got close to the Red guard post, Ziv stopped me with a touch to the shoulder. He said it was amazing here, and he left his hand there a few seconds longer, holding me gently. I told him that the explosive devices were supposed to be coming from a slope near the Musicali road. He asked from where Hezbollah would be able to observe us when we'd be out there. Mainly from Arnoun, I said, pointing out the village. Then there were another few minutes of silence and we stood gazing at the flickering lights coming from the border, off in the distance. He asked if I'd been offended by that business with the Abu-Jabai cell. "Don't flatter yourself," I said. He didn't let me off the hook. He was quick to choke off the silence and announce dramatically that he only had a week to go in uniform until his discharge. Wow, I said, some finale you arranged for yourself up here. After that he was leaving for South America. "Don't you want to join me?" he asked.

"Are you trying to pick me up?"

"Don't worry," he said, "I come equipped with a girlfriend."

He asked where I lived. Afula, I told him. I asked him back and he told me Holon. Holon? I was surprised, expected something fancier. "We're going to have a barbecue in my backyard, you and me, after we get this road open," he announced. "You don't give up, do you?" I said with a smile. We continued our stroll. He talked about his specialty, explosives. He told me how, at the beginning of the explosives war, nine years earlier, the terrorists were primarily using wireless systems detonated from a distance by laser, or infrared, or ultra-something, with the most advanced technologies available, thanks to the Iranians. The more they advanced, the more the IDF advanced, providing solutions and creating electronic warfare equipment and learning to locate and neutralize. But then the terrorists caught on and suddenly went back to their roots, to the most primitive means and most ancient methods. Now that they were simple again they were more difficult to detect, the biggest problem being metal wires buried in the dirt. All this green earth was covered in dozens of such traps: explosive devices and mines. The cat-and-mouse game was lost from the start, because there was no way of catching up with the enemy. Everything here was one big inferno. Years would pass and still we would have no chance of roaming around in this jungle freely. A pity. We would jet off to South America, maybe South Africa, to the rain forests. "I have to have Oshri on this operation with me," I told him. "I don't move an inch without him." He nodded. I said, "I'm bringing two marksmen, one guy with a Negev light machine gun, one Nakpadon driver." We argued over the need for one more tracker, one more medic. Silence again. That's how we walked around, breaking the ice. Somewhere near the Green guard post I remembered the T-shirt, I even got worked up about it for a minute. It really was a disgrace, what was he—a total jerk? But I held off. I reminded myself to stay focused, not to break down barriers, but it was impossible not to break down barriers with the guy. He was so stubborn, with those warm hands and that smile of his and that winking, charming tone that left you no chance of staying pissed off at him for any length of time. So the barriers fell. Beats me if I know how that happened, but the more time we spent together during those six days, the closer we got. We stood at the surveillance posts together, we learned the signposts together, agreed on codes, pored over old aerial photographs, briefed the squad, conducted exercises, dress rehearsals. Ziv wanted to know everything, rummage through everything, do everything. We put the kids through every surprise imaginable: Wounded soldier at the back of the squad! Wounded soldier in the middle of the squad! Wounded soldier at the front of the squad! For three nights we had them running around the outpost so they'd be totally calibrated for this operation. In the end, I think, we felt pretty ready.

Every morning before sunrise he would come to the submarine and sit on the knapsacks near me, on the floor, and keep me from sleeping. He would get me laughing, talking about life, trying to figure out whether he should study history or not, whether his girlfriend would wait for him to come back from the big trip he was planning. He loved trekking more than anything. He couldn't understand how I wasn't familiar with this cave or that around Israel and promised to take me in his white VW to the sea, to sit in his special spot on the white rock, drink until the middle of the night, and whistle songs. He told me he'd take me to Puerto Rico, too, to fish. And the Amazon. We'd fly there. It was a must. How could I not have heard of the Amazon? He laughed at me. Peru, Ecuador, those places were just for me, he said. To lie on a beach with *ayahuasca*, well, yes, it sure did sound like a blast. But what exactly was *ayahuasca*? Some drink from a holy plant that made you hallucinate. Hallucinations? Not for me, I told him. But those rain forests, with a shiny red and yellow toucan sitting on your shoulder and a blue-green butterfly fluttering nearby and drunken swans crossing clear blue rivers? That actually sounded great. Why not? He'd watched too many hours of *National Geographic,* I guess. What was that clown always going on about those rain forests for? I didn't miss them here in Israel—not the forests or the rain. That's how we passed the time. And Ziv would photograph us together in every position and every situation, and he would hug me and smack me hard in the head. And imitate me. And train me how to be this stuck-up barman—well, he tried anyway, because there was no alcohol anywhere to be found at the outpost. He told me he had a secret hiding place for booze back at his base. What a jerk I was. I'm trying to remember. We played cards—Speed and Whist—betting on beers. He lost. By the third night he'd already moved his sleeping bag to our room and by the fourth, his knapsack. He'd say to me, "Shut your mouth, Chong." And I'd say, "Okay, Granddad, get a move on, put those false teeth in place." Zitlawi would show up and join in, give Ziv language lessons. "A '*bourekas*-grinder' is an officer who doesn't have a clue what to do in a war,"

Zitlawi explained. " 'Souvlaki' is an officer who comes up to Beaufort just to waste some of our high-quality food. 'Butt-tasty' is gourmet food. When someone farts we say 'Saddam is coming for a visit.' 'Wetting the edge' means fucking, the same as 'flipping a girl's grapefruits.' A 'piercer' is a new name for a babe. A 'bambi' is a childish soldier, a *'jaalul'* is an irritating one. 'Safari' is when we act like crazy kids on a field trip. 'Self-conflicted' is a soldier with complexes, a 'family terrorist attack' is when your extended family comes to your house for a visit when you've just come back from Lebanon and you need a little peace and quiet, you're dying for sleep. 'They turned over your chair' means you've been screwed, like when they send you to carry out an operation in Lebanon a week before your discharge." Ziv and I pretended to be totally serious, listening, arguing, finally kicking the kid out of the room, with a hug—Come on, Zitlawi baby, curtail your presence, take a running leap into the wall, turn the wheel, go bring some pickles—and then we'd burst out laughing. We'd spend hours horsing around like that. And then we'd "re-rout" together: that is, return to routine. Sleep. Make Z's.

I don't know what it was I liked about Ziv, but there was something that attracted me. Maybe it was the fact that he was the big guy on campus among the bomb-removal guys. The other two called him Number One: that was his nick-name and the definition of his job. Two and Three totally revered him. He'd actually started out training to be a pilot, then he was top of the new recruits for the Engineering Corps commando unit. Good-looking, athletic but not muscle-bound. Modest. Hyperactive, too, always on the move, al-ways wanting to wrestle with me, giving me massages. Sounds stupid but I hadn't ever really had any Ashkenazi friends until then. Until him. He would laugh at everything I said, look at me with this great look, didn't make fun of me even when I said something stupid. He wasn't patronizing.

The last night, too, we spent talking bullshit. Mostly about my Lila. Oshri was always saying I was weak in the romance department. Ziv, on the other hand, seemed like a professor of romance so I asked him for an original idea for our sixth anniversary (we celebrated from the first kiss). I had to come up with something significant this time, something, like, sensitive, otherwise it'd be all over for me with her. And there wasn't much time to prepare, barely a month. "Do you know anything about hotels?" I asked him. He laughed at me. "Hotels are passé," he explained. "Have you heard of the Vanishing Valley?" he asked. When I shrugged he repeated it, excited now, "Yes, the Vanishing Valley." No, I hadn't heard of it. He ripped out a page from a military notebook and handed it to me, along with a pen. Golden desert, a purple-black volcanic mountain, red horizon, Red Sea, big blue stars, and a silence that would quiet your soul until you went crazy. I wrote it all down, the road to Eilat, the ancient camel track near Uziah. Down to the palms at Racham. Craters there, a narrow crevice, a stream. We would lay out our sleeping bags at Mitzpeh Amram facing the Bay of Eilat and a sea of boulders, above the waterfalls and canyon and colored stones that wind and water had sculpted into strange shapes, and there we would sleep. And the Vanishing Valley, that's where it was. Even quieter than Beaufort. The next morning we would tackle the Sahara dunes of the Kasui riverbed and the cliffs and dirt paths at Maaleh Shaharut, and we'd climb Mount Argaman and hover over the abyss. "It's paradise," Ziv said. "Bring thirty-foot ropes for rock-climbing." I wrote everything down. She loves trekking, my little girl. What a man: I would surprise her.

I asked him if I could make one request. "Shoot," he said. "That T-shirt of yours," I said, "the white one from those Arab-lovers: don't go out wearing it tomorrow. It'll bring us bad luck. It'll make me lose my concentration. Take it off and I'll keep it for you until you're out of here. A favor I'm asking, for your bro." He laughed, told me I was sick in the head, and agreed. He took off his shirt and threw it to me.

A few hours earlier we had gathered in Furman's office for a final briefing, to present deployment for the Admiral Procedure, as it was called. A discussion of situations and responses that deteriorated into haggling, proof that not a single one of the officers knew exactly what he was supposed to be doing. I go that way, you move over there, no, wait, you go that way, nobody's over there. We changed the plans at least ten times until I was completely confused. Ziv's number three man suddenly insisted on being Number Two, and Number Two claimed he was qualified to be Number One so they should really give him the chance because Ziv was being discharged anyway. They couldn't come to a decision about where we should march—on the road, near the road, maybe as far as possible from the road. And where we would stand and wait—on the path or in the undergrowth. Nothing was agreed upon. Ziv was afraid of the road because it was a target, so it stood to reason that explosive devices would be aimed at it. I was afraid of the undergrowth at the side of the road, at that time full of chest-high bushes (later they would be chopped down). The trackers were of the same opinion as me. And then there was the matter of approaching an explosive device. It was decided we would first send a dog back and forth. When he returned we would move out and encircle the pit, three hundred and sixty degrees—half a circle from the south side, then half a circle from the north. If we came across another device we would shoot a rocket at it, blow it up. And where would we situate the Nakpadon, the huge tank perfect for rescue missions? Should it cross the pit with the explosive charge and continue downward to wait for us at the bottom? Or should we leave it parked above, behind us? I presented the security plan and Furman asked questions. After that we reviewed the alerts listed in the intelligence reports and the tracker expressed his reservations; Furman deflected them. For some reason, nothing was actually clear. Then an argument broke out between Ziv and me about how we would move: he demanded to march first, followed by Number Two, and then a medic with a stretcher. I refused. What was the idea of sending a medic up front? A medic had to be in the back, as far back as possible, that was the IDF way. Medics don't come near the action, they need to be protected in case they're needed in an emergency. Ziv insisted that the medic be close. I gave in. "Behind Number Three is the closest I'm willing to allow him," I said.

When the briefing had ended Ziv went up to River. "You're the medic, right?" he asked. "Nice to meet you, Farran." Chitchat, small talk, and then he gets to the point: "I want to explain to you what happens if I get hit," he said. He lifted his flak jacket, a special number created by the Engineering Corps with a ceramic coating and lots of pockets for explosive materials. "If I get hit," Ziv explained, "you'll have to open all the Velcro bands and the snaps and then cut the flak jacket and get it off me. Do it as fast as possible, and get it as far away as you can. It could blow up and then the whole squad would vaporize." That's how he said it, brief and to the point, with a short demo. River said okay, no problem, open, cut, remove, toss. We parted. Number Three, a redhead, went with Bayliss to the Nakpadon to install an electronic scrambler that helps prevent charges from exploding. One of the green lights that was supposed to indicate if the scrambler was working wouldn't go on. They asked the officer from the Signal Corps, but he said there was no way of knowing: "There's never any indication whether those instruments are working or not. Maybe it's just the light that's burnt out." Ziv, in the meantime, had gone back up to Red for a last look around. Alone.

In theory, we had carried out all the preps. But something

still didn't feel right. That's how the night ended, even before it began.

Emilio, film me a minute, bro. Come on, come here a second. What are you making a big deal about it? Shit, man, film me already. Is it filming? Good. Excellent. Come in for a close-up. Nice. Hello? Army Radio? Razi Barkai's morning program? Good, yes, good morning, Razi. How are you? This is Zitlawi speaking. Yeah, man, we feel like we're securing the northern border. Sure we are. In fact, I want to tell all the people of this country that we're here for you, at any cost, keeping you safe. Believe me, the most important thing to us is that you can sleep well at night. Fact is, Razi, you're dealing with a bunch of sharks here, that's what we are. Each one of us a killer. Even Emilio the nerd. So what if he looks totally white-bread? He's actually real combat material. You want to know what combat is, just look at him. The guy's never afraid, doesn't act like an Ashkenazi at all. Aw, come on, you shit-head, what are you taking it so hard for? If you cover up the lens I'll bust your gut up, so chill out. Shall we continue? Very good, my man. Yes, Razi, the kid is one hell of an assas-sin, and it's all for you people. Mmmmm, yes, it's true, we keep narghiles at the guard posts. Sure, why not? You've got to have a little fun, there's no choice. But we want you all to feel safe, to keep on enjoying yourselves all the time. Sorry, I've got to run, Channel Two is waiting to talk to me. Yeah, the *Good Morning, Israel* show.

Still filming, bro? Okay, back to *A Guide for Lana, Spitzer's Russian Girlfriend*. Take two. Hey, Lana, sweetheart: travel-ogue, it's two o'clock in the morning now. See my face? Look close. This is the face of a person who's forgotten what home looks like. After fifty-six days in this shithole he was sup-posed to go see his mother and already had his bag on his back waiting for the convoy, and all of a sudden they say there isn't one. Cancelled. Now he's stuck here another couple of days, maybe a week. Or two. And our officer, Erez, is one whacked-out psycho case. I'm totally sick of the guy, had it up to here with him. Makes us eat shit the whole day long, you have no idea: hell on earth, a nightmare. Barks at us all the time. I don't know how we ended up with this prick. My grandmother would say, "If you go through a little hell now you'll enjoy heaven that much more." So here we are, preparing for the enjoyment. Working our asses off on guard duty and kitchen duty all day long. You think the guys in the top commando units do kitchen duty? No way! Their food's catered. Come, come with us for a minute, cutie-pie, we'll show you our toilets. It's a bit of a walk, but no big deal, right? You see? Without a doubt the most exclusive model there is. Nasrallah's wife would be happy to come drop her pile of shit here, you can be sure of that. A fucking nuclear holocaust. Let's keep going. This is the door to the outpost. If it falls on your foot, you die. Left here. Have patience, please. Go with the flow. This is our war room. Meet Dave. Brother, tell us about the job of the guys in the war room. Don't worry, buddy, it's approved by the army-censor's office. Our pal Mofaz himself gave his permission. Let it roll. The outpost is divided into three parts: Carmel One, Carmel Two, Carmel Three. If the outpost is hit it's my job to alert everyone to go on the attack. Wow, Davey, thank you. We learned a lot. Hey, here's Bayliss, down on the floor talking on the phone. What a cutie. Let's sneak up behind him, eavesdrop a little. Hey, Mom, how are you? Dangerous? No way! Believe me, Ma, it's like summer camp here. If something happens to me up here it'll be from boredom, so don't worry. How's Dad? Okay, enough, this Bayliss is fucking boring! We'll continue our tour. Here we are, back in the room again. You see, sweetheart? Here's Spitzer, your little bunny rabbit, like a blob on the mattress, sleeping, the little angel. Angel? What angel? A devil! But just so you know, he's faithful to you all the way.

No hanky-panky, even though the place is full of awesome chicks. And if anyone tries to say something bad about you—you know, like "that Russky," that sort of thing—Spitzer whomps him, beats the shit out of him on the spot. Hey, look, the kid's waking up. Good morning, sweetie. What a beautiful smile! Say something to your whore. Talk to her. What do you mean, you don't want to? What? What's wrong with you? Hey, no violence. Chill out.

That's how the night ended, and at five o'clock in the morning we got up as usual, spent an hour and a half on the equipment, prepped for an attack on the outpost. After that I went back to sleep. At seven-thirty Furman slapped me awake. "Get up, on the double," he said. "What are you doing sleeping on the day of an Admiral Procedure?" I went to the briefing room, half asleep. Ziv was already there, working at full throttle on preparations. A quick, final briefing to tie up loose ends. I went back to the submarine to bring the equipment. Ziv's T-shirt was rolled up on a corner of my bed and I threw it behind the small cabinet so we'd all forget about it. I didn't want the kids to catch sight of it by accident. We were off.

Oshri climbed onto the Nakpadon. Bayliss was driving. River was with me on foot and Emilio was serving as missile observer, on the lookout for launches from the direction of Nabatiye and Tibnit. Anyway, it was just an ass-saving job; you'd never spot a launch from a mile and a half away. You'd really only notice it at about the time it fell on you. Zitlawi was marching with us, too, carrying on his back the portable scrambler—the kind that fries your balls—with Spitzer, Boaz, and Tom serving as the security force. Then there was the dog-handler, and Ziv, and his two backups. We were all completely silent. About a hundred yards before the pit I signaled to everyone to go down on one knee. With two fingers

I indicated to Ziv that he should look straight ahead, that's where the pit was.

We started to send the dog ahead, send the dog ahead, send the dog ahead—three times. Dogs don't get what you want from them on the first try. They don't always know what to look for or what to find. He didn't really get close to the pit, came back too quick, wasn't concentrating. It wasn't working. So, according to the plan, we carried out a comprehensive search, circled the place to determine whether terrorists had beaten a path in through the undergrowth, and which route they'd chosen to booby-trap the target. We unrolled white marking tape wherever we walked in order to know where we'd already been. It was hot and sticky out. The sun had come up too fast. It took us half an hour to complete the first half-circle.

Oshri peered out from the Nakpadon, which had stopped along the road, past the curve. He shouted, "River, River, come get the stretcher." River didn't think twice and began to run through the field. I shouted like I've never shouted in my life: "Don't move! No way! Don't move!" River stopped, came back. He trusts Oshri and me without giving it a thought, it amazes me every time. The stretcher remained on the Nakpadon. I looked down, saw Oshri standing up, exposed, the top half of his body sticking out of the vehicle. "Get back inside!" I shouted at him, too.

An argument broke out over how to continue. The tracker insisted he couldn't lead us through the bushes, it wasn't safe; we'd have to proceed on the road. The bomb removal crew, on the other hand, protested in unison that the road was the least safe option. In the end it was decided to stay close to the road but not on it, pressed up to the slabs of concrete we call *dabeshim,* on the dirt road that runs the length of the curve. My soldiers positioned themselves behind the *dabeshim* and maintained surveillance. Ziv began descending the slope. "Bring me the medic and the signal operator, I'm going into the pit," he said. I told him to forget about it, "None of my kids is moving," I told him. "*I'll* come with you." I would be his medic and his signal operator. That pissed Ziv off. "You're going to be surprised to hear this," he said, "but the medic and the signal operator come with me. That's what was decided up at the outpost." But I refused. Can't say exactly why, but I did. I felt like I couldn't rely on anyone. I didn't want to involve them in this because something didn't feel right about it. Another argument. "It's too bad we're standing here exposed in a place they can see us," I said in the end. "You either take me or I'm climbing inside the Nakpadon and leaving with my soldiers." He gave in and we formed a line. Ziv was first, I was a few yards behind him, then his two men and the tracker. "Just so you know," Ziv said, already moving toward the pit, "this is not according to procedure. You're not supposed to be in charge here, you're supposed to be providing security." He took another few steps forward, maybe ten, no more than that, and I was behind him. He turned his head back toward me and said, "Kid, keep your distance," with that broad smile of his. He was always so quick to cool down and make up. "Kid, keep your distance." That's what he said, and I answered, "Go on already, you wuss."

And suddenly, an explosion. A huge boom. Ziv fell. Clouds of earth and mud and dust covered us in waves. Everything stopped, fell silent. That's according to procedure: you freeze in place. The explosion caused a ringing in my ears. Everything was muffled.

When Ziv fell I could still hear his voice echoing in the air: "Kid, keep your distance." He lifted himself on his side for a moment, then fell again. Black smoke began to swallow us up and I lost sight of him. A second passed, maybe two or three, and Ziv's buddies ran toward the pit, ignoring what had been discussed in the briefing and in complete contempt of procedure. "Stop, stop!" I shrieked. You were supposed to cut a path, slowly, with the help of the dog-handler. If a bomb could explode on us like that, who knew how many more were lying in wait for us. Ten? Maybe more? Someone had his eye on us, maybe in Arnoun, and was just pressing the button, making sure we'd get wiped out one by one. The two of them looked at me for a moment, then continued. They didn't care. They disappeared into a screen of dust, completely out of sight. "Cheetah, One here. We found a present! A present! One flower down, the rest intact. Start rescue." Silence. I waited for something to happen. I transmitted again. "Head of Admiral took a hit. I repeat, head of Admiral took a hit. Unclear how bad. Requesting chopper for rescue. Requesting chopper for rescue. Over and out." A few more seconds passed, then I heard Ziv's deputies shouting: "Medic, medic, come quick!" That was forbidden, too, according to our training. You have to drag the wounded soldier out. But they were shouting and River went running—occupational instincts. "Stop! Stop, River!" I shouted. When he didn't, I began to run, too. Where was Ziv? Where was he? You couldn't see anything because of all the smoke. I never thought for a second that he was dead, the possibility didn't even cross my mind. I didn't know anything, didn't think anything, didn't take anything in.

River found him lying in a thick fog. He bent down, tried rousing him. Was he conscious? No. He asked Number Two to take Ziv's helmet off and Number Three to strip his clothes. They opened his flak jacket, ripped open his shirt. They didn't cry. River checked his breathing. There was none. These were maneuvers that weren't supposed to be carried out in the vicinity of the explosion, but that's what they did. It seemed too complicated to move him. River tried resuscitating him, tried forcing air into his body, without success. We could hear the liquids blocking his breathing tube. Ziv was perfectly whole, all his limbs attached, but his neck was swollen, bulging, and his nose was bleeding, his ears, too, and his mouth even more. Blood was coming out of every hole. He was covered in bits of shrapnel, his eyes were wide open and red. And everything smelled like plastic going up in flames. It was hard to breathe. "River," I said, "what's going on?" He didn't answer me, just kept on trying to resuscitate Ziv. I asked again and again: What's going on? What's going on? What's going on? He said nothing. I shouted, "Tell me what's happening with him!" and I pulled River's face in my direction. It was covered in blood. He said, "Nothing." Nothing what? Nothing what! River kept trying with all his strength, drained liquids, huge quantities of blood from his mouth. It kept coming. Come on, already, get some air in there. But the blood never stopped flowing. I could hear myself shouting in my head: "How long is this going to take? Get him breathing, for God's sake get him breathing, I'll do anything, anything! I'll stop smoking, just let him breathe." Then River starts going nuts, pounding with all his strength on Ziv's body in desperation. It went on forever. And there's Ziv, lying in a pair of short, dark underpants, wasted. River knew he was gone, the blast had killed him, all his internal organs and his blood vessels had imploded like a diver whose lungs have shriveled and along comes a little pressurization and he's done for. But out in the field there's no pronouncing someone dead. That can only be done by the outpost doctor. I looked behind me, the smoke was beginning to blow off. I could see how my soldiers were starting to lose it, how their body movements made it clear they were under stress. I shouted, "Emilio, look at me now! Everyone, look at me!" I figured I'd better remain in their line of vision; if they didn't see me for a minute they'd go mental. "At this stage don't panic," Furman said over the transmitter. Don't panic, you asshole. He gave us rescue commands to make sure we'd make it back up to the outpost without incident.

I remember how the minutes passed and Ziv was lying there, unconscious, not breathing, his body limp as rubber, his head bloated, hot all over from the pooling blood, and there I was, standing next to him, waiting, feeling so alone while the thoughts got all mixed up in my head: one part of me was thinking about what needed to be done, like reporting to the outpost, having them aim artillery, requesting that the doctor be put on standby, getting them to alert the "gapcow," the gathering point for company wounded, talking to the soldiers about what needed to be done operationally. And the other part wasn't thinking about anything at all. It was trying to think about what I needed to think about, but nothing was happening.

Bayliss started the engine of the Nakpadon and headed back toward us. He was driving backward and stopped thirty yards away. The entire chassis was full of holes. It was supposed to be a secure vehicle, the Nakpadon, but it had been pummeled with so many pellets that some of them had gotten stuck in the chassis and others had actually penetrated inward. Oshri and Bayliss brought the stretcher. Number Two and Number Three helped River load Ziv onto it and then we repositioned ourselves, moving him for further treatment to the foot of the Nakpadon. Still dangerous, but less so. River tried resuscitating him again, a last effort. Tried removing fluids again, too. It's called "logging," when you turn the wounded guy carefully onto his side, careful not to break his neck—in these situations gentle treatment is really important so the head and the body move together—then you stick a finger in and remove liquids from the mouth. River even succeeded, managed to get some air in for a second and Ziv's chest inflated for a breath or two. But that's all. We refused to accept that it was over, but every push on his chest brought more blood to the surface. Hell, let's get him up to the outpost already, to the doctor. In a couple of seconds we had the stretcher hoisted onto the

Nakpadon, and River climbed on, too. Bayliss, at the wheel, was trying to navigate, but the periscope was damaged and of course there are no windows so he was forced to drive without seeing the way. He was just hoping not to plunge into the chasm. Oshri peered out of the slit at the top and guided him the best he could—a little to the left, a little to the right. At the outer gate to the base they drove onto a speed bump and nearly ran over three guys doing maintenance. River, in the meantime, was like a robot in the belly of the Nakpadon, caring for Ziv even though there was nothing for him to take care of because there were no external injuries. He tried giving Ziv an infusion. Why? The guy wasn't breathing, had no pulse. Why would he try to give him an infusion? I ran like a madman on the road, alongside the vehicle.

We reached the outpost. Oshri took charge of unloading. A few soldiers came out to help, grabbed hold of the stretcher and ran it inside to the army-reserve doctor and the two medics all waiting for his arrival. River dragged in after them. They started intubation, which is when you insert a tube that's attached to an oxygen pump down the throat, almost all the way to the lungs. The tube went in easy the first time. That's lucky, because sometimes it goes crooked and punctures the esophagus. "Doctor, Doctor, his throat is all bloated. Full of blood. Don't miss!" River was shouting, getting in their way. I tried to get close, too, but the medics forced us out, pushed us backward. After that they kept themselves busy, taking care of an injury to Ziv's leg, something small and unimportant that nobody had noticed. They wrapped an elastic bandage around it. Furman crowded the squad into the briefing room so they wouldn't see. The doctor pronounced Ziv dead. Oshri started to cry. I ripped the Madonna headband with the microphone and earphone off my head and entered the room. I went to the farthest corner, stood against the wall, alone, while they leaned over the body, finishing matters up.

River stepped aside, too, went to the dining room on his own, leaned backward over the blue table reserved for holy books, took off his vest and his equipment. He stood there taking air in. I went up to him and said, "It'll be okay. You performed well. It'll be okay." I wanted him to talk to me. The door to the room was nearly shut, just a crack open, and through that small opening we watched as they placed a wool blanket over Ziv. The doctor shut his eyes and then they covered his head, too. They lifted the stretcher, carried him to the storeroom until the rescue chopper could come. River fell apart. It happened in a second, just burst out of him. All his reservoirs started flowing, he cried like a baby, then he went crazy on a couple pieces of furniture: picked up a chair and hurled it at the wall, upended a table. I stood facing him, trying to figure out what to say. His face was covered in blood. His hands, too. He took a long look at them, absorbing what had happened to him in the past few hours. "They did everything they could, River," I said, putting my hand on his shoulder. "You did. The doctor did. He's dead. There's nothing we can do about it." He cried even harder. "I have to take a shower," he shrieked, "I've got to shower!" I asked him to wait a bit, till things had calmed down some. Outside they were still on alert. "I don't give a fuck!" he shouted. "I need a shower!" I took hold of him, grabbed his waist, sat him down. He was mad at the whole world: at Hezbollah, at the IDF, at God. "What is this? What are we doing here? What is this fucking goddamned bullshit?" He went wild, was all wet with tears. "Fuck everyone! Give me one good reason why he died. For what?" Those few minutes, when River collapsed in my arms, I remember only in a kind of fog. I know I said all kinds of things to him, trying to get him to calm down. But I didn't cry. I waited for him to get hold of himself, let it all out. I sat on the floor next to him with my back to the wall. All the images ran through my mind. And the smell of gunpowder. And Ziv, may he rest in peace. I could see him starting down toward the J-curve and disappearing all of a sudden, falling. And the explosion, I kept feeling it again and again, seeing black. And how I'd run inside. And the first sight of him, wounded, full of blood. I was going over it all. How we'd cared for him, how we'd functioned, what I'd done right and what I hadn't. Everything was racing through my head. The stretcher, the wool blanket. And what a dead man looks like—the blank look, like something is missing. River cried while I sat thinking.

Even when he calmed down we remained silent, for a long time, I don't know how long. "My first injured soldier," he said finally. I didn't know how to answer that. "The first time I take care of a wounded soldier, and he dies. I made mistakes, you saw for yourself."

"Listen to me," I said, resolutely. "Ziv was gone from the first minute."

River started to cry again, this time quietly, subdued, but at length. Then he lay down on the floor and curled up. "You were great, River," I said. "You didn't go into shock, not even for a minute." I moved over to him, grabbed hold of his neck, pulled him close. "It'll be okay," I reassured him. "We'll look out for one another. You're here, I'm here. It'll be okay." He lowered his gaze. I asked him, "Do you trust me?" Our eyes were as near to each other as possible. "Do you trust me?" I persisted. "I want you to tell me if you trust me." He looked up at me again. And that's when it happened. "I'm ready to die for you," he said. He was right there in front of me, as close as can be, and says, "I'm ready to die for you." Just like that, straight at me. Think about what kind of a thing that is to say: "I'm ready to die for you." What can you answer to that? Anything you could say gets dwarfed, becomes meaningless. I thought about what to answer, maybe that I'd be prepared to die for him in the next life, but that would sound stupid. So what do you do in a situation like this? Just give a hug, a kiss, say, "I love you." What a disgrace that I can't remember the date. His eyes were wet, sparkling, they pierced my soul. Suddenly he was a little kid lying there in front of me. I lay the palms of my hands on his cheeks and stroked him. We were so weak and resigned when Ziv fell, but now my strength was returning. We crushed each other in a long embrace, then I stood up, extended my hand to him, and pulled him over to the water pails so he could clean himself up a little.

He asked permission to go back to Israel to attend the funeral, but I declined. I told him it wasn't possible, that we would send him home in the near future. I couldn't let him get away from us, from the squad, from me; I thought that after such a traumatic event the best thing for him would be to get back to routine.

We left the dining room. River crossed the security area quickly, locked deep inside himself. Everyone watched him, a few tried talking to him, but River ignored them, kept silent. He went into the submarine and lay down on his bed. The guys were on edge, in shock—every last one of them—but River had lost Ziv in his own hands. He pulled a box of goodies sent to him by friends back in Israel from under his bed and told the guys to help themselves, he wasn't capable of touching any of it. I went to rest, too. On the way I saw Number Two and Number Three sitting in a dark corner of the security area near a row of open stretchers—drained, dead tired, sobbing, broken. I'd never seen tears at Beaufort before, not until that day. And they looked so alone and out of their element there, in our place. I didn't look directly at them, just checked them out from the corner of my eye. I didn't know what to say. Nothing could be done. All the while the knowledge that the body lay nearby, in the storeroom, permeated the air.

That night, Ziv's body was covered with a second blanket, he was wrapped up according to procedure, and the Kaddish prayer for the dead was recited. I was asked to carry the stretcher. I stood twenty yards from the helicopter pad, one hand on the body, the other on my weapon. Ziv's bag was on me, on my back. We waited. For a moment I exposed his face, I had this strong urge to see it one last time. I gazed at him: Who says that death has no face? In fact, it does. A Yasur chopper landed then and we ran forward against the wind into the dust, inside the darkness. On one side of the chopper we loaded the body while on the other a few high-ranking officers got out for an update on the situation. They didn't even notice Ziv while we were loading him in, they marched ahead without even a passing glance at the blanket, or at us. I tossed the bag that had been sitting on my back inside the helicopter. ZIV FARRAN. IDF #5154182, BOMB REMOVAL SQUAD: it was all written there. Dave handed me his flak jacket and helmet. There was a hole in it made by a big pellet from a claymore mine. I handed them up to the flight mechanic, who placed them on the floor of the chopper. Thirty seconds later he was in the air. I stood in place, watching him grow distant until he disappeared into the horizon. In the background, mortars fired by the terrorists in every sector reinforced the feeling that something was going down. I went back to Oshri. He was lying in bed staring at the television screen intermittently broadcasting from Hezbollah's Al-Manar station. "Look at the Jews," they were singing in broken Hebrew with a Shiite accent. "The Jews are in deep mourning. The Jews have a big problem. They love life, those Jews. We, on the other hand, love death. We love death, that's why we'll win." A man impersonating Prime Minister Ehud Barak walked into a room set up to look like the Tel Aviv office of the IDF chief of staff but painted in colors from the flags of Arab states. He shouted, "What is this fear in the ranks of our soldiers? Why are they running away? What is this madness, this pressure? Why aren't our soldiers prepared to serve in Lebanon?" The screen showed rows of coffins, our own. Real footage from different military cemeteries. We watched in silence. Every once in a while the ground shook. "This is the valley of death here, not the security zone," Oshri said. Everyone was in a poetic mood. I handed him a garbage bag, asked him to go around and collect all the uniforms and things that had been spattered with blood. River's gun, too— I went to the junior soldiers' submarine to get it, for a thorough cleaning. I found Spitzer dozing there, his head on Zitlawi's chest and his arms around him. Zitlawi was staring at a naked bulb. But River wasn't there. I raced to the dining room, the briefing room, the line for the telephone in the hallway filled with stretchers. I looked everywhere for him. Outside, too. I went to the showers, the connecting trenches, the guard posts: from White to Blue to Red. On the way up to Green I saw his skinny shadow. He was crouched there by a steep stairway, frozen, his face pointed in the direction of the slope. He was holding an open book, one of our tattered prayer books. Strange reaction this kid was having. I was worried. "What are you doing?" I asked him. "I don't know," he answered. He was looking for the words, I guess. "You should say the 'Thanksgiving Blessing' if anything," I told him. "I don't know it," he said. I pulled the prayer book out of his hands, closed it, and put it on top of one of the sandbags nearby. "Okay, man, let's do it together," I said. "Repeat after me: 'Blessed are You, God, King of the Universe, who bestows good things upon the guilty, who has bestowed every goodness upon me. Amen. May He who has bestowed goodness upon you continue to bestow every goodness upon you forever.' " That's what I recited, the prayer for someone who's been saved from disaster and the response of those listening, and he repeated it, at first quietly, a kind of mumble, and then aloud, almost shouting. I asked him, "Has anyone ever told you that you look like Marco from that TV show about the kid who goes looking for his mother for the whole summer vacation? You look like him. Same face." He smiled, and sang part of the theme song. "When we were kids," he said, "my grandfather would take us to synagogue. He's religious, my grandfather. Son of a rabbi. But I haven't set foot inside a synagogue since my bar mitzvah. I'm a real infidel, a pork-eater and all that." I told him that my parents are observant, but just like him I've grown away from it. "So what's this all about?" I asked him. "Death? Is that what's going to make us change our ways? Suddenly we'll become believers? Come on, man, it doesn't make sense. It's childish."

"We did not take that bomb seriously," he said. "Not at all. The same way we behave with mortar shells and rockets. We laugh, we sing, we whistle, everything's a big joke. And then they hit us, explode bombs in our faces, and suddenly a guy dies for no good reason right in our arms."

"Yes," I said, "but what does that mean?"

"That maybe we should be a little afraid," River answered.

"No, kiddo," I said. "We don't have that luxury. It's the privilege of people who aren't here to be afraid and to ask theoretical questions. To be afraid you have to think too much, you have to be a regular citizen, not a soldier." He nodded.

That evening, at the Reichan outpost not far from us, eight paratroopers were wounded. "Moderately": they lost arms, legs, eyes. But no one counts those. Only the dead are counted.

The next day, as the sun set and the Sabbath began—exactly one week since Ziv had landed—it became clear that even the people furthest from religion were discovering some spiritual side of themselves. Everyone came with makeshift kippas, everyone suddenly knew how to pray—or at least pretended to. Even the most in-your-face secular guys, the ones who can't stay away from Chili's fridge through the whole day of Yom Kippur fasting, apparently felt a need to say thank you for having survived the week. Each in his own way, at his own pace, in motions he'd brought from home. You could hear the singing from every corner of Beaufort, and the "amens" that came in waves. Only the guards on duty were absent from the jam-packed service. And Bayliss.

You go on, that's the way it is. No shortcuts, no special treatment. No shrinks, no mind-fucking. Nights, I would stay awake, going from guard post to guard post, walking around and listening. I looked into their eyes, all of them, to see that they were getting back to routine. I would test River from time to time to make sure the kid wasn't turning into a six-pack. "Six-pack" is our code word for someone deeply fucked up, someone with a screw loose. I'd say, "Kid, Ziv will never..." and he would fill in the blank, what it was he wouldn't be able to do anymore. It was a kind of a test, a sanity test. The crazier the answer, the healthier the player was—and the less you needed to worry about him. Ziv won't be able to sing "A Sea of Cornstalks" anymore in the middle of a plowed wheat field during a training exercise using live ammo. Ziv won't be able to tattoo a portrait of Hanan Ashrawi on his ass anymore. Come on, bitch, let's see you mess with us boys. Ziv won't be able to get hornier than hell from the spring 1967 Delta underwear catalog anymore and he'll never eat a flower or drink a leaf and he'll never say, "Tomorrow it'll all be over."

But River blamed himself. He barely opened his mouth. The guy was shell-shocked, withdrawn. He was stuck in this illusion that Ziv had been alive after the explosion, that some other treatment would have saved his life. I shouted at him. "Forget about that, you jerk. He was dead." But River wouldn't listen. "You've been through a trauma," I would say to him. "You held someone in your hands and he died, and there are consequences to that. You've got to rest, chill out. After all, we've agreed: we're together to the end." On the third night, when I thought he'd calmed down, River caught hold of me during one of my tours of the guard posts. In what sounded like an angry sort of voice he said, "Erez, I just wanted you to know that when I asked what the fuck we're doing here, I really meant it." I thought, That's the pain talking. I didn't pay too much attention to it, but I played along according to the script, as expected. "You have your doubts about our mission here, River?" I asked, certain of a negative response. "Don't the towns and villages along our northern border interest you anymore?" But River didn't even take a breath or miss a beat before answering. "It has nothing to do with the northern border. We're just looking out for our own asses, that's all. We sit up here at Beaufort, disconnected from everything, drawing rockets and mortar shells and explosive devices, endangering our lives, just so we can continue sitting at Beaufort. That's the entire mission. What a shitty feeling. What on earth were we doing in that fucked-up operation, anyway? All we wanted to do was open up some goddamned road, the goddamned road that leads back and forth to Israel, nothing more than that. You tell me, Erez, as an officer. What are we doing here?"

"What do you prefer?" I recited. "For Hezbollah to move freely right up to the fence and settle in there? You're talking bullshit, River. Chill out. If we weren't here, if we didn't have a string of outposts deep in Lebanese territory, the enemy would be pushed up against the border fence with their weapons drawn and ready to shoot at Metullah and Nurit and Manara." How could you argue with such a claim? River didn't even try. He tucked his tail between his legs and went back inside. I thought he'd just gone a little nuts, that was all. He was blaming himself, which was understandable. Me, too. For months I blamed myself. After all, I was the commander of the security force when Ziv fell. Even if Ziv was senior to me and on his way out of the army in another few days, he was no guerilla fighter, and not at home on the roads of this sector. It was my responsibility to keep him from entering the spot, my responsibility to locate the hitches in advance, to refuse point-blank to set out on the mission. No way we should have gone out in those conditions! And how the hell did Hezbollah place that mine anyway, just a few feet from the J-curve? My team watched that spot all night. Could they have snuck that device in under their noses? The noses of my own soldiers? Had one of them fallen asleep on duty? And why hadn't the scrambler made the mechanism go haywire? Why hadn't it even beeped?

When River returned to the submarine he found the guys crowded around a helmet with Zitlawi ripping pieces of paper with names on them. It was a lottery to determine who would be the first one killed, he explained. He asked Emilio to draw, but he refused. Spitzer did, too. In the end he himself drew out a slip of paper. River's name was on it. A low grumble rose from the group gathered there, but River didn't react. He squeezed past them to his bed and lay down with his face to the wall. He didn't utter a word until lunchtime. Bayliss kicked the helmet, sent it flying, and shouted that they'd all lost their minds, that it wasn't funny, and then he went to lie down, too. They all lay down and shut their eyes.

The following Monday it was decided to send us for a home visit. This was an impossible mission, given that the roads were still closed to traffic and the air force refused to bring in choppers due to an alert on possible antiaircraft missile launchings. And yet, there was no way the guys could be kept at the outpost any longer. I'd had an eye on my soldiers and saw they were worn out, wasted, and missing home real bad. For some of them—the ones who'd been punished and given extra time at Beaufort when we'd first arrived—this should have been their first furlough, and even that had come after a long delay. Twenty-two days earlier, River, Bayliss, and Spitzer had already been packed, their knapsacks on their backs, when their convoy was cancelled at the last minute—as usual, thanks to Intelligence—as were two more the following week. Time dragged on and the three stayed in their same smelly underpants and filthy mood for another week. On the twenty-eighth of March they were certain that was it, they were on their way home. Zitlawi and Emilio were supposed to leave with them, having completed their record-breaking punishment. But bad luck had it that twelve hours before they were due to set out a bomb exploded for the first time on the Virlist road and as a result the roads were sealed off. Another week and two days passed, a real siege, and then Ziv came with Number Two and the redhead and six more days crawled by, and then Ziv was killed. They needed to get home, these kids.

When I told them they were heading home on Monday they didn't believe me. They refused to prepare or get their equipment together—it was a kind of superstition. Nobody knew how we were supposed to get back to Israel. Then in the afternoon a cryptic message came over the teleprinter in the war room. The message was called "Exodus" and the mission was to leave the outpost on foot—not in vehicles or choppers—by the White guard post at the back of Beaufort, marching in a line through the undergrowth that covered a steep and rocky slope on a path that had never been used. From there, on a long trek through village fields, we would proceed to the Parah landing strip and from there another three miles along a winding dirt road. Then, at an improvised parking area, perfectly timed, just when we arrived, Safari vehicles would come out of nowhere to bring us to the border. That would be the first time we would carry out this plan, and the last. Hezbollah, they believed, would be totally caught by surprise. They probably wouldn't even notice us at all. A line of soldiers did not glow in the dark, didn't go back and forth like a convoy of trucks or a chopper. And even if they did catch sight of somebody marching in the dark they wouldn't have a chance to get organized in time to strike a serious blow. Still, when the rumor about Exodus spread around the outpost, there wasn't a single person who believed it. It was insane, marching like that through a battle zone with cooks and soldiers from the Signal Corps and the Ordnance Corps. Between you and me, those guys are pencil pushers. We kept saying there was no way, we laughed, and still it happened. At two o'clock in the morning we found ourselves in the middle of an olive grove at the edge of the hill.

It's freezing cold out but your belly's burning up as usual, drops of sweat are trickling down your forehead and cheeks. Your legs are tired from crossing wadis, slopes, stone walls, wire fences—it's never-ending. After falling a couple of times you understand you shouldn't step on the white rocks. And like always, you can hear the dull sound of shooting in the distance, pinching the frozen silence. Your fear vanishes as you start moving; if we come under fire it will disappear completely. At two-thirty the roosters of Arnoun begin their loud crowing, which reaches the entire sector. Dogs, too, suddenly start barking. Could it be that they smell us? Are the residents here able to sleep with this kind of noise? Or are they awake already? In the distance, from the villages, in the midst of clusters of weak lights, occasionally you glimpse a dark green fluorescent light coming from the mosques. A few more minutes pass and we are sucked into a little forest, no more than a grove of trees. A few yards away we encounter a bonfire between the trees, the smell of smoke thick in the air. What the hell is some Arab doing barbecuing at three in the morning? Emilio moans that it is too dangerous, utter insanity. "Who would dare come near us, kid?" Zitlawi whispers. "Believe me, when I'm surrounded by all these shitheads from our squad I feel safer than I do at home." I stop, tap

Oshri on the shoulder, and say under my breath, "Number Two, distance yourself from the next guy and keep quiet. Pass it on." Oshri runs to River, the next in line. "Three," he says, "distance yourself. Pass it on." We walk carefully, we lower our shadows, we can't see three feet ahead. Suddenly the calls of the muezzin pierce the air. *"Muhammad rasul Allah, Muhammad rasul Allah,"* comes the cry again and again in that thick, coarse voice for a long while. Gradually, other voices join his from different directions. I order everyone to drink, and they take sips from the tubes coming out of their packs. Every once in a while we see some suspicious movement and everyone goes down on one knee. Oshri and I check to see the coast is clear and then we signal to them that it's okay to proceed. As a gesture to the non-combat guys, we stop occasionally for a rest. You fall backward all at once, lose your balance, fall on your pack, which stops you—it's the best feeling for a fighter, that letting loose. You let your heavy pack hit the ground, but quietly. It feels like falling onto a soft king-size bed with satin sheets. You lie there staring up at the sky. The moon mesmerizes you. I hear River whispering with Bayliss, mentioning—on his own initiative for the first time—the girl from Nov, Bayliss's village. He pretends not to remember her name. Says he just wanted to know she was okay, that she didn't have some kind of trauma—my ass!—because really, what happened to her wasn't very nice. He is mumbling, confused. "Do you know her?" he asks. "Not really. She lives at boarding school," Bayliss answers, where the problem girls are sent, the ones who didn't manage in other learning environments. The good girls are sent to school in Tiberias, he explains. But if River is interested he can fix him up with someone from the girls' yeshiva. They are eighteen to twenty-three years old, more suitable. And legal. The only problem is the kippa. After all, these are traditional girls. River cuts him off, reassures him he isn't interested, he only wanted to know about the girl's welfare, was feeling a little guilty or something—nothing more than that. "But what do you mean by 'problem girls'?" No, Bayliss tells him sharply, these are not easy lays. River decides to let it go. We pass along the message to start moving again and the rest period comes to an end. Your gaze drops once again from the moon to reality: the ground. That's the way it is, you're booted out of your dream and you're surprised to find you're still there in the middle of this otherworldly green-black darkness, in a landscape that surprises you.

A house, straight ahead of us. I don't remember that we are supposed to find a house along the route. There wasn't one in the aerial photos or on the maps. Candlelight flickers in the kitchen window. We pass by crouched down, proceeding very quietly, praying that no one will go to the refrigerator for a midnight snack. I steal a glance inside. I think about how normal life goes on here, with a pleasant family dining table and a rocking chair in the living room, and the drawings of a small child on the fridge. Where is the television? Interesting. Four o'clock in the morning and the wind has kicked up, the temps are down to their coldest, piercing your bones; there is no way not to shiver, your teeth chatter. Finally, we reach the meeting point, where the Safaris pick us up. Our shivering turns to goose bumps of excitement that Israel is drawing closer, along with a feeling of relief that this insane thing is ending without incident. By the time the border gate opens and we cross through, and bolt from the vehicles on the whitetop at Ha'egel base, we can see the first light in the sky. Take in a deep breath of air, I gesture to River. Look at the sky and calm yourself. There's nothing like entering Israel at that hour, when everyone's waking up along with you, a new day. They have no idea where you're coming from and no clue what you've been through. Milk trucks unload their wares at Itzik Zagouri's grocery in Kiryat Shmona and the bakery puts out its first tray of croissants and the paperboys deliver their newspapers and the roosters are having a field day—Jewish roosters, kosher ones—and people are out jogging, waving hello to you. It's a different planet. Such sweet moments, like from a movie, and at first glance everything seems so innocent. Just a village filled with calm people smiling at one another, unaware of what's happening a few feet away from their lives, right under their noses. We cross their main street like zombies, after being up all night, covered in dust. We don't talk, not even with one another. We try to recover, reduce the level of adrenaline, get used to a new environment. And then we have to part. Bye, bro, take care of yourself, man. That's all, just a short, quiet good-bye, then each guy heads in a different direction. Suddenly, how weird it is in the first moment, even scary, to be without them, to walk along completely alone or with people you don't know. You feel so strange. You're sorry you didn't give a few hugs before splitting up. But it would be stupid to run back now just for that. And soon you'll be in your own small bed, back to being a spoiled mama's boy between colored sheets. Life up on the hill will seem senseless, like a bad dream. You'll wait, tense, to get back into uniform and up there again if only to satisfy your curiosity, to verify that it really happened, that it exists, that you're not hallucinating.

For the kids, too, this sudden switch to being alone isn't simple. That's a fact. River and Zitlawi decided, completely spontaneously, to join Bayliss for a two-day trip around the Golan Heights before returning home to their parents. Anyway they'd have a weeklong vacation at home, they said, and their good friends from high school would only be back from their army bases on the weekend, if at all. So Bayliss asked his father, Menahem, to pick them up, and the three of them stood waiting for him at the gas station near the shopping mall. Oshri caught a ride with an Armored Corps officer heading toward the Tel Aviv area, while I had been summoned to a debriefing in the office of the commander of the IDF Northern Division about what had happened to Ziv and the Admiral Procedure. All of a sudden I wasn't so eager to get out of uniform. On the contrary, I felt glad to have the excuse to wear it a little longer, to keep myself busy in the brief moment before home would smack me in the face and I would turn into one giant ball of sleep, ramming my pillow sixteen straight hours a day if they'd only let me. Israel makes a person tired.

I walked through a deserted public garden just before reaching the central bus station. A little Pekinese followed me, wouldn't leave me alone. The last thing I needed was the smell of some strange dog on me to drive Bitter crazy. He'd feel betrayed, it's only natural. He's all alone without me, he'll never learn to keep himself busy without me. I knew I should find a public phone to call Lila, so she'd know I was on my way. I wondered if her commanding officers would let her off, and how fast it would happen. Today? Tomorrow? I hoped I wouldn't sit rotting at home without her until Friday, and my heart starting pounding. The uncertainty drove me crazy. Fuck it if they don't let her go! Who are they anyway, the bunch of eager assholes, nothing more than a pack of tour guides at a field school. All at once the truest, strongest longing you could ever imagine settled on me. I spend weeks trying to feel like I miss her but I manage without her just fine. Fantasize about her a little, sometimes when my dick is hard, but no more than that. And here I am suddenly, without warning, practically with tears in my eyes from all this thinking about her. Really, truly, it's like my heart is going to explode, I'm dying to smell her neck. I want her to hold me, stroke my ears, put her hand on my hair, plow it with her fingernails. I want to lie naked with her—no blanket—and stare off into space, listen to the music of Rami Kleinstein or Arik Einstein. Put some strawberries, bananas, and milk into the blender, make her a shake. Take Bitter for a walk in the park.

I say out loud: If I don't get to look at her today I'll go crazy, for real. Engines are revving in the bus station, first runs of the day. Nothing's been renovated since the seventies: the rusted red and white poles, the overhangs, the *bourekas* stand. Eccentric old people talk to themselves. I buy a phone card, go to the public phone. No answer. How come there's nobody in the room this early in the morning? Maybe they're off on a trek? And what'll I do if it's a long one, a few days? I catch a bus to Safed.

The debriefing only began at three o'clock in the afternoon. They had plenty of time at the Northern Command. In the meantime I wasted a day sitting on the benches at this rear base, enjoying the view toward the Hula Valley and the neatly pressed desk jockeys running through the flowerbeds, lying on the grass to catch the rays and the girls. I didn't know a soul. A secretary caught sight of me, came out with a newspaper. Two days old, she said. I flipped through it. There was a gigantic photo of Number Two throwing himself on the grave at the funeral. And one of Ziv, from his soldier's ID. And another of him with his girlfriend on vacation in Greece. A real beauty. There was an article that was supposed to be an investigation into the event, splashed over two pages, all of it total bullshit. So much crap was written in that newspaper that I was in pain, I swear; I could have murdered the reporter. I thought about the family: if they'd read it, and believed it, what would they think of us? It said we'd left him there for four hours to die. That we hadn't managed to get him back to the outpost for treatment, that he'd suffered in agony for hours until his soul finally expired. By the time he'd reached the outpost, the newspaper said, it was too late. What would happen if River read this now? A disgrace. Every fifteen minutes or so I would try the public phone. Lila's room was deserted. A little before one o'clock I closed my eyes under a tree near the commander's office, until a long row of army vehicles filled up the parking area and woke me up. The head honchos had arrived.

They all grabbed places around the conference table in the office: the brigadier general himself, the brigade commanders, the vice-brigade commanders, the regiment commander, the heads of the commando units. Debriefing Number 105, Combat-Corps Headquarters, Chief Infantry and Paratroops Officer Headquarters, Department of Routine Security Matters. Re: Detonation of Explosive Device Against Engineering Corps Squad. Operation in Sector: 91st Division, Hiram Territorial Brigade, Ali Taher Mountain Range Battalion—Beaufort. Results: One IDF casualty. In turn, each man present explained why he bore no responsibility. The first said, "I okayed the operation because I thought Hanan had spoken with Ehud." Then Hanan said, "I gave my okay because I understood that the commander of the bomb removal unit had talked to someone." That's the way it went, one after another. I couldn't keep up. I stood up and said I didn't understand what we were doing there, because if they wanted to point the finger at me, then they should go ahead and do it and save everyone time. I mean, who could they really blame? The dog's nose? The tracker's eyes? The batteries in the scrambler? The brigadier general motioned to me to calm down. "We're not looking to put the blame on anyone. We just want to know what happened," he said, trying to sound paternal. I answered that if that was the case, then the questions were not, in my opinion, being asked the right way. Then, when I figured out it was stupid to get into this kind of wrangling with them, I shut my mouth. It was all too much, too big, for me. He asked what I'd done during the event. I told him in two sentences or less and fell silent again. I sat myself behind one of the officers and hid there. I'm just a nothing of a second lieutenant, I shouldn't even have been there at all. The brigade commander gave a summary of the main errors and failures and requested that a bomb-dismantling robot be appended to future outpost operations. The guys from the Engineering Corps explained that robots couldn't maneuver that mountainous topography. And then the brigadier general summed up. "Our basic assumption," he said, "is that explosive devices are going to continue to be our main threat. Some forty of them have been placed in the vicinity of our outposts recently. We must treat the entire length of the access road leading to Beaufort as an area under suspicion to be traversed only when there is no other option and only after the procedure for opening roads has been carried out, with a tracker and dog at the lead. Concurrently, our offensive assault activity in the Ali Taher sector is insufficient. We need to plan operations that will bring greater damage to the terrorist cells that are placing the explosive devices. The necessary manpower and battle equipment will be requisitioned according to need."

The IDF never again carried out the Admiral Procedure in Lebanon. Ziv was its last casualty.

I got up and left, couldn't hold out to the end. At the gate to the base I caught a ride down to Rosh Pina. There was soft music in the car and I looked out the window, motionless as if dozing, but inside I was in a kind of delirium, shaking, counting the seconds, barely breathing. I was trying to plan my time so that it wouldn't get away from me in the blink of an eye so that I'd find myself too quickly back inside a Safari crossing the border. I thought how I should get to the home of Ziv's parents one evening, to tell them the truth about what had happened, so they wouldn't buy into all those lies. I swear I wanted to visit them. But I didn't. Mainly I was afraid. I was sure the family, the friends, they'd blame me. What would I tell his mother? That I had been the head of security on the operation? That mine was the last ugly face Ziv saw before he fell? That I was the last person to look at his own face before we loaded the body into the chopper? I didn't go visit them. Not then and not on the first anniversary of his death. I read in the paper that his grandmother died ten days after he got killed. She'd refused to eat or drink. Said she didn't want to live in a country where grandmothers bury their grandchildren. Those were tough, sad words, but kind of kitschy. We've heard them too many times, so we don't get too worked up about them. And his mother told reporters how she'd begged him not to go into Lebanon again, and he would always answer, "What do you want from me? You brought me up to think big, and not just about myself, didn't you?" That's what she said. Turns out that she and her husband, Aharon, had been active in the Four Mothers organization from the time it was established, and his older brother, who'd served years earlier in Lebanon, had started a protest movement of army reservists who served in combat units: "Bring My Brother Back from Lebanon" they called themselves. That was even before he'd lost Ziv. I really actually wanted to meet them, to explain. And every day I'd tell myself again that I had to do it, but I never did. Never visited the family, never visited the grave.

When I got home that Tuesday, after the debriefing at command headquarters, I told my parents about it. They didn't get too worked up. Asked a few questions, took an interest, but only briefly. Twenty minutes later we sat down to eat, we went on with our life. I decided not to tell Lila, or my friends, either. I didn't want to get into it. I preferred to forget.

By this time Bayliss, River, and Zitlawi had already finished a long round of showers and huge meals at Bayliss's house in Nov. They put a couple of mattresses on the floor in Bayliss's cramped bedroom, sealed off the small porch window, and tried to make themselves sleep. It took a while for them to realize it wasn't going to work. Their bodies wouldn't let them waste the first few hours of their furlough, especially when they were together. Even after an exhausting night's journey without a minute of sleep they had too much energy that needed to be burned up. They sat in their boxer shorts and T-shirts on the front porch overlooking Menahem's horse ranch. It was fairly cool out, but there was an atmosphere of spring that had to be taken advantage of. Zitlawi tried to grab and jump onto a colt. He even fell a few times from the back of an old horse named Jehoshaphat. After that he lay in the hammock, challenging himself to get it to swing to new heights. Bayliss's mother, Rivka, poured them apple juice, served strawberry cake with whipped cream. His younger siblings brought a soccer ball and dragged River onto a makeshift playing field, where River wrestled with them in the sand. Bayliss, wearing the kippa he'd placed there while waiting for his father to pick them up in Kiryat Shmona, pored over maps, trying to come up with an original trek on some out-of-the-way path for them to take the following morning. It was calm and peaceful there until Zitlawi was the first to spot a girl riding a bicycle on the lane leading from the synagogue. Gazing at her long, straight, fair hair, he wondered for a moment if it was her or not. A few seconds later he jumped onto a small blue bicycle that belonged to one of the kids and raced after her. He dashed off without saying a word. It took a couple of minutes until River, who'd been busy playing ball, figured out what was going on. It was Hodaya, with a small knapsack on her back; he'd seen her disappearing behind a row of trees leading out of the village. He felt a pain in his stomach, a fist, at seeing her, and seeing that arse chasing after her. It killed him. Bayliss caught sight of River watching them even after they'd vanished, while the children tried pulling him back to the game. Bayliss came up to River. "Believe me, she is one fucked-up girl," he said. It didn't help. "Ignore Zitlawi, that maniac," Bayliss told him. "And ignore her, too. You only laid eyes on her for two minutes once. What's gotten into you?" It was when River failed to deny it that Bayliss understood the situation was pretty bad. Zitlawi, in the meantime, had nearly managed to catch up to her, was just a few feet behind her. By the Bajurya pool he left the road and turned onto a path that led to Elipaz's cowshed, exactly where he'd seen her that other time. He whistled to her. She ignored him. When he caught up to her, rode alongside her, she turned her gaze to him for the first time and kept on riding. She was in fucking good shape, even he was starting to breathe heavy. "You know, we haven't been in Israel since that last time you saw us," he told her. She ignored him. "We came back from Lebanon today. Will you allow me to apologize? I can explain the whole thing," he said. She still hadn't said a word. She picked up the pace, as if she was trying to make it harder on him, compete with him, prove herself. But she didn't seem frightened, not at all. At least that's what Zitlawi claimed. He says he was even surprised. When they reached the field behind the cowshed she braked and got off her bicycle, took a large pad of white drawing paper, a pencil box with crayons, and a small blanket from her knapsack, while he stood watching from the side. From time to time he'd toss out a question, ask something about her without getting an answer, try to find the right button to press that would get her to cooperate. "What's wrong? Are you mad?" he asked in the end, with the tone of someone who's lost patience. "It really seems like you're mad."

"You think so?" she answered. "No reason to be. I just like quiet when I'm drawing. I didn't come out here to chat."

"Okay, I'll shut up," he replied, happy that at least he'd gotten an answer. He was a little surprised at the uncharacteristic self-confidence. After all, she was only a girl of sixteen. Where did she learn to talk like that? he wondered. He smiled to himself.

She lay on the blanket, on her stomach, with the pad of drawing paper on the dirt in front of her. Zitlawi sat on a rock off to the side, not daring to get too close. But he refused to give up, enjoying the challenge too much. He caught sight of a thick book and two sandwiches in a plastic bag peeking out of Hodaya's knapsack. She wasn't drawing anything at all. Even after fifteen minutes the page was blank. All she did was scan the surrounding groves, and the distant cliff, and the bored cows, with slow glances. Sometimes she would turn over onto her back and gaze up at the clouds, mesmerized, then flip onto her stomach once again. Zitlawi, restless, searched desperately for some new way to get the conversation going again. The lines he used in the clubs wouldn't help with this little girl. He couldn't call her by the pet names he used for the others, he'd never manage to break the ice that way. He couldn't even ask her why she wasn't drawing. It might hurt her feelings, he thought, make her even more distant. So he kept silent until he could find something to say or until she broke down first. When he told us about it afterward he couldn't remember how long it had taken, but finally she spoke. "Is that friend of yours all right?" she asked. "Did he get over it?"

"Who? River?" Zitlawi answered. "The guy you saw naked?"

She nodded. He shrugged it off, tried to explain that with them, the secular boys, it was no big deal getting caught naked. It meant nothing, he said, happened all the time, nobody even got embarrassed. And she had nothing to worry about, River had forgotten all about it in a matter of hours, maybe even minutes. But where she was concerned they'd felt really bad, because maybe she'd been traumatized by it. He said he was sure she'd been scared. If she were only secular, she'd understand how much fun it was to be so free, naked. But because she was a religious girl they'd been worried. By this point in the conversation, Zitlawi's prick was already in launch position—you can be sure of that—it was fucking with his mind and making him talk dirty. He calls it "eight inches of steel wrapped in hot flesh." He prayed for some response, just a tiny bit of cooperation on her part. But she kept quiet. "Tell the truth, Hodaya, don't you get the urge to go running naked in the fields here sometimes?" he asked her, crossing boundaries without flinching. "It's so peaceful here, and private." Did he really see a little smile between her thin lips, or was it the product of his warped imagination? There's no way of knowing. Still, she said nothing. His heart was bursting from the tension. In his mind she'd already taken off the thin, dark red sweater wrapped around her long, graceful neck. And her black skirt. She was standing there in front of him in bra and panties. He would have killed to know what kind of panties she was wearing under her clothes. What kind of panties did religious girls wear, anyway? "Am I right?" he asked, continuing to lead her on. "Boy, do you talk a lot of nonsense," she answered. What? Nonsense? What are you talking about? He tried to get it out of her which part of his nonsense she was referring to. He wouldn't let up. "What do you mean, nonsense? Tell me." She smiled—this time it was definitely a smile, absolutely—and lay on her back. He took a deep breath and then tossed a grenade. "Should I prove it to you?" he asked. "If you think I'm talking nonsense I'll just have to prove it to you." He stood up and started undressing. He took off his white undershirt and threw it onto the rock. He checked to gauge her reaction, but the girl wasn't even looking in his direction. She was looking up at the sky. He felt cold. He took off his shorts, was left standing in a pair of red briefs. "It seems to me you need something to draw today," he told her in a half-shaking voice. "Draw me." She rolled over onto her side, looked him over without embarrassment, her gaze direct. She didn't take her eyes off him, tried to show him she had no problems with her self-confidence. She wanted to break him. And he stood staring at her, too. They waited to see who would lower their eyes first. Zitlawi drew in another breath and pulled his briefs clear in one go. "Go on, draw me," he said. "I'll run through the fields if you tell me to." She laughed. Really laughed. She had this sheepish gaze—at least that's the way Zitlawi described it—a sweet, innocent look, really cute. If you can believe him, he saw a twinkle deep down in the whites of her eyes. But she got up, gathered her belongings, and mounted her bike. "Get a life," she told him, and rode off. He shouted after her—"Hey, wait up!"—put on his underpants and his shorts, hung the shirt around his neck, and set off after her on this kiddy cycle. "I was just trying to make you laugh," he said. "Talk to me a little." She rode faster, and so did he. They rode like crazy on the deserted road, competing, cutting each other off, spinning in circles. She really had laughed, that little witch. Near the entrance to the village he ran into her—not too hard—and blocked her path. He said, "Listen, sweetheart, it's not fair this way. Give me a chance. Just once. Come take a hike or something with me tomorrow, or the day after. I'll be a good boy." She was so beautiful.

"You're staying with Menahem and Rivka?" she asked.

"Yes," he replied.

"So we'll see each other," she said, and she raced off into the village.

"Those were the purest moments of my life." That is how Zitlawi, the arse, the pervert, described those few minutes of his story. And every time he tells it he turns red all over, then he's quick to try and erase the romantic glow from his face and return to descriptions of his rising prick, in order to overcome his embarrassment. But on that day, when he returned to the house, he refused to tell them a word of what had happened. He sat in front of the computer and competed against Bayliss's little brothers in a car race, while River lay on the couch in the living room, gloomy and blank-faced, letting the television keep him occupied. Fatigue was a convincing excuse, which is why Zitlawi didn't even feel that something was wrong between them. And when Bayliss finished working alone on the plans for their trek and suggested the two of them join him for a short ride on the ATV to catch the sunset over the Sea of Galilee, River declined. They tried in vain to persuade him, but it was a lost cause. He went up to the second floor, threw himself down on the mattress, alone, heard them revving the engine, having fun, and he tried falling asleep. The sun was already orange. The ATV raced across the fields to a position on the winding dirt road behind the southernmost homes of the Bnei Yehuda settlement. Among the thistles on the cliff you could see everything. Darkening red water, the hills. No drug in the world could compare to this serenity. Bayliss debated whether to say something about Hodaya, but he decided against it. He didn't have the energy to get into a conversation like that. And mainly he just didn't want to know. They sat in silence, waiting for the sky to turn black, and then they returned to Nov, skipped dinner, and went straight to bed, early. River heard them come in but he kept his eyes shut. Zitlawi lay down on his mattress next to River's. They fell asleep together in the hopes that the energy they would gather in the course of the night would make the next day happier and more fun.

But after midnight the inconceivable happened, a moment that will apparently forever be engraved in the annals of our company. River was the first to wake up from the sound of someone climbing up the drainpipe, and when the porch door opened the other two opened their eyes. Zitlawi, who was closer to the window, immediately recognized Hodaya inside the blue parka, and he jumped up to greet her. She looked into the room and whispered, "I came," with a self-satisfied smile, glowing from the courage she'd mustered. He placed a finger over her mouth to keep her quiet. "The guys are sleeping," he said, and then he walked outside and pulled her after him. They closed the glass door. Hodaya leaned against a low stone railing. Bayliss turned his back to them at once, stayed all night with his face to the wall. River, on the other hand, insisted on torturing himself and watched them bleary-eyed in the dark. "Don't think I'm just a little girl," Hodaya said. "I'm not shy, either." Really, that's exactly what she said. They heard her inside the room, there are witnesses. Because if River hadn't been there, if Bayliss hadn't been there, not one of us would have believed Zitlawi's story. She opened her parka, then took it off, threw it to the ground. She stood facing him in a white sweatshirt and green skirt. He watched her as if he were dreaming, didn't even react. Next she removed her skirt and dropped it to her feet, and in seconds she had removed her tights, too. She was left wearing only a pair of soft, tight, white underpants and a sweatshirt on the back porch of the house, which, luckily, faced a small grove of trees and not the neighbors' houses, even though the two of them could still be seen by anyone passing by on the path below. A lot of rabbis walked around down there, it wasn't worth taking a chance. Hodaya seemed to be waiting for Zitlawi to give her the signal to keep stripping, but he wasn't capable of batting an eyelid. He didn't even blink. It's strange he didn't hug her, didn't grab her ass, didn't shove his hands under her shirt. The kid was in shock. When she took the initiative and began removing her sweatshirt, he understood that the girl was a lost cause and had no limits—she was crazed, a nymphomaniac—so he opened the door and pushed her inside, into the room. What else could he do? She sat down on his mattress and in seconds was wearing nothing but the thin white T-shirt, no bra. She has perfect breasts—everyone agrees on that—and that night they were hot and erect. Zitlawi, totally in shock, all wrapped up in questions of how to proceed, which is to say, how to deal with the fact that two guys were stuck there in the room with him, pretending to sleep, lay on his back, fairly exhausted, confused, and hoping she would embrace him. She drew close, took hold of his underpants and pulled them right off, stripped him, not a bit shy. What a crazy girl! Then she lay down next to him, shivering with cold, or excitement, and covered herself. They began to kiss, Zitlawi stuck his tongue as far in as it would go. He held her breasts through her T-shirt, mashed them. River watched. He heard the tiny sighs, the stifled giggles. For a second Hodaya's white backside flashed in front of his eyes with Zitlawi's large paw thrashing it. He saw her—quivering, drugged. Her soft hair was wild, her sweet lips calling out, thirsty for as much contact as possible, biting Zitlawi's nipples, her hands kneading his arms, his face. And his hands, under the blanket, gripping her small, round ass. God, what was going on there? This girl was crazed for him, that much was clear. And above them, on the shelf, three volumes of holy writings by Rabbi Kook shone in the moonbeams filtering in from outside.

Early in the morning River took off. He caught a bus home, passed up on the trek.

10

THAT SAME EVENING I HAD A FIGHT with Lila. She told me about a friend of hers, an army social worker, who had a boyfriend fighting with a Nahal unit in Lebanon and was wounded. He'd stepped on an explosive device and lost a foot and his left eye. She stayed with him, held out for half a year, but in private she would tell Lila how hard it was for her. "I just want to go out and have a good time, but I can't," she would tell her. "If he came with me, what exactly would he do? Watch from the side? He used to love dancing but now he's too embarrassed. And it kills him when I dance, you can see by his body language how bad it is for him." Like an idiot, Lila asked her how their sex life was since the accident. Her friend told her it was nonexistent. It had been six months since they'd done it. "There have been a few kisses," she said, "but no heavy stuff." Could you blame her? Of course not. It put her off, it was scary. The guy probably looks like a monster: he's missing an eye, walks around with a black eye patch. When he's at home and isn't feeling ashamed he takes off the patch and goes around with a glass eye. She admitted that he didn't really attract her anymore.

Then one day, after half a year, the guy tells her—on his own initiative—that they'd better split up. She pretended to be sad about it, told him that she'd actually be happy to stay together with him, but she didn't really insist. Way down deep everybody knew she wanted to breathe, to get away. She wanted someone to go to the beach with, not some gimp. She wanted to walk down the street with her nose in the clouds thinking that everyone's talking about her and the stud she'd caught, the hunk, the male model. She was sick and tired of feeling embarrassed, sick and tired of that whole long period of crying and troubles. She wanted to goof around, be happy, smile. Smell a new body. She wanted someone to tear her to pieces so that she'd enjoy it. Lila told me the story and I said, "That guy comes out of this a real man, a total stud. It's clear the bitch wouldn't have stayed with him in the long run, he beat her to the punch." Lila was all over me right away, pissed off. "I would stay with you," she said. No way, I told her. You all pick up and leave. In the history of our company, in all of the neighboring outposts, in every story I'd ever heard, they always left, sooner or later. "You would, too," I told her. "No doubt about it. But don't worry, I've already thought about it and if it happens I'm bailing out. I'm jumping out of the rescue chopper on the way to the hospital, maybe even shoot myself. For sure." She started to cry, then she screamed at me that I was being childish and stupid and that the army had screwed up my head. We had a serious fight. That night we didn't even sleep together.

Lila had gone to the junior high for nerds. I'd gone to the junior high for punks. A high-class girl and a slum boy, that's us. But I'd had long, straight hair and a baby face and I was up to no good and went around with different girls and hit all the parties and barely even pissed in her direction. I guess that's why, in the eighth grade, she decided I'd be her husband. The first year we were on and off, the second we were together, fucking each other's minds but nothing else.

In the third year we kissed for the first time, at night we'd run off and mess around in the woods near her house, or in her mother's Beetle, or on the roof of her grandmother's cottage. In the fourth year she would sit on her little bed, half nude, and play the guitar for me while I went nuts, drooled. We slept together. Any time she wanted to set me on fire she'd play the guitar like that in her underpants. I would pounce on her, sniff her scent. Everyone's got a scent, and hers I like best. It's a matter of taste. If I don't like a girl's scent it doesn't mean she smells bad, it only means she's not for me. And if I love it so much that sometimes I go mental when I'm alone, that I can't concentrate on anything but trying to recapture that scent, it means that she's the girl most right for me in the whole world. She graduated with honors, while I didn't even finish my matriculation exams. Her father would say, "The game's up. Another guy doesn't stand a chance, Lila. Listen to what I'm telling you, I see it in the look on your face." That's what he said from the first day, and she would deny it, but she always knew he was right. And in the fifth year, for the first time, I lay my head on her instead of hers on me. That said it all, especially that for me, too, it was us for life. I would come back from the army and curl up with her, spend whole days spooning with her, wrap myself around her looking for ways to expand the area of contact of our two bodies to the maximum. At night we would fall asleep embracing and I would think that it was impossible I'd become that kind of guy, the kind who keeps on holding his girl instead of setting boundaries in the middle of the bed and going off to his own side, where it was peaceful, about six seconds after the loving was over and the girl closed her eyes. I wasn't shy around her, either, almost never. I said nearly everything that came to my mind instead of filtering it first.

On Thursday, a week after Ziv was killed, when Lila came back from lunch at her parents' house and opened the door to my room, I was still sleeping. Bitter, who was hiding between my legs, jumped on her, yelping, and licked her face from every angle and direction. The two of them sat next to me on the bed and she took hold of my hand. I woke up and told her I was breaking up with her. Just like that. Boom. I was totally dazed, my brain was on slow motion, my eyes were nearly shut, but I knew what I was doing. There was no turning back. I took one look at her and I knew it was over. I sat up, stroked her cheek for a second, gave her a quick kiss, and went to take a shower. She didn't cry, which was strange. She didn't shout at me. When I came out of the bathroom she was gone. Maybe I'd hurt her too much, or maybe she just remembered that I'm too much of a dumb fuck for her, finally figured out what a jerk she'd been running around with, a boring asshole with no future, so why should she make an effort? Maybe. Well, she could go fuck herself because there was no place for her in my life. I needed to concentrate on carrying out my job without the burden of a girlfriend. She was so preoccupied with totally unimportant things. She could spend ages trying to pick out the colors of sheets and blankets, or where to hang pictures. She'd organize her winter and summer clothes and expect me to give my opinion on pairs of socks that she doesn't like anymore, or on desserts in the fridge—which were good, which were fattening—or she'd spend hours telling me all about the plot of some television show. And about her friends, how she was mad at them. What a lot of thought she put into being mad! But I was fed up with taking part in those petty thoughts about the simple life and making meaningless decisions. In another place, at that very second, someone was torturing himself with a life-or-death decision, and I could be there. She would laugh, all happy with that bullshit, wouldn't lay off when I needed to be alone sometimes. She didn't understand that I had to. But how could she? How could she reach out and talk to me in my own language when she wasn't up there with me to know how it felt? From the window of my room I could see her walking away—slowly, but not looking back. Maybe this would be my last glimpse of her for the rest of my life, or maybe it was only for a while—who knew how long? I thought there was no way she understood, she probably thought I was a complete asshole. But what choice did I have?

On Saturday night we got ready to return to Beaufort. We gathered at the meeting point—training grounds near Kiryat Shmona—where we carried out a counter-ambush exercise. Forty minutes before we were due to set out we got an update from Command cancelling the convoy. We were told there were red alerts from Intelligence. "We're setting out tomorrow," I told the squad. "In the meantime we'll take over a few rooms at the Soldiers' Hotel. Anyone who wants to visit wounded soldiers at Rambam Hospital in Haifa is welcome to." A lot of guys did, and so did I.

Almost every time we went into or out of Lebanon we'd spend some time at the Soldiers' Hotel. It's an old building, six beds or more to a room with thin and sorry-looking green and white sheets like a hospital, but for our purposes it was a full-service, high-quality hotel. Sometimes we managed to get our girlfriends up there and they'd lie in our arms and sleep with us. Other times we'd just watch cable TV and take hot showers that lasted an hour or two. That's part of the experience: to sit nursing a cappuccino in the lobby surrounded by shelves of stained and faded books that have been donated, and an old television facing the long army benches, and a small pool table and metal armchairs with thin foam cushions. We could sprawl out, relax, and shoot the breeze on the beds in our underwear or naked, no flak jackets or boots, without worrying about the possibility of incoming attacks. When we got there that evening, I sent the kids to bed and Oshri and I sat down over a couple of pints of beer and a bucket of black coffee in a makeshift pub sponsored by the servicemen's welfare association in the basement of the hotel. We sat alone in a corner, trying to take it all in: we only had six days left together. This was our last stay together at the Soldiers' Hotel, the last convoy into Lebanon, the first day of our last week. And that would be it. On Saturday night he'd catch a lift home and plunge into his discharge furlough, while I'd continue with routine, barely able to pick up the phone and talk to him. And soon he'd have a completely different life. New friends. How would I manage? He was the silent king of the company, that Oshri, the number one administrator: he knew better than anyone how to get his hands on food, gasoline, clothing, ammunition. Number one fighter, too: reserved, patient, fearless. A real man. And of course, number one friend: modest, concerned about everyone being happy, never thinking about his own needs. Someone really and truly unique. When he asked you "What's up?" it wasn't just any old "What's up?" with a fake smile like everyone else. It was a true "What's up?" Like, "Tell me what's happening with you, brother, I really want to know." Oshri's skin is super dark and his heart is hot as fire. I'm crazy about him, love him to pieces. So then we toasted each other *"L'haim"* and shared some company gossip and I brought him up to date on the crisis with Lila. He was pissed off with me. "You'll regret it your whole life," he said. I couldn't believe how angry he was. "You are one crazy asshole. She's the only person who can make something out of you. You think you're going to spend your whole life in the army, in this stinking mud hole? What are you going to do without her, when it's all over up here? You're a jerk. That's what you are."

"I can't think about that right now. Who am I, you? Off to fuck babes in South America two days from now? I'm stuck here in the mud, and that's that. Nothing I can do about it."

"Aren't you afraid," he asked, "at being on your own? If your arm gets blown off you'll never find anybody who'll fall in love with you and look after you. You'll die all by yourself, a disgusting, miserable old man. Aren't you afraid of being alone?" What? Where did that come from? Fucking unbelievable! God must have put him up to it. I mean, only two days earlier we'd been fighting about this and now here we were when suddenly out of nowhere he explodes this question on me and looks at me all strange. How could this have happened?

Truth is, this wasn't new. A long time before, we'd agreed, Oshri and me, that losing a limb was worse than anything, worse than death. We weren't the only ones who thought that way, either. All the guys in the brigade said so, it's a known fact. When you lose a limb no girl wants you anymore. And you can't play soccer anymore, or swim. No treks. You're just going to get bumped around like that your whole life, so it's better to die, no doubt about it. When I finished officers' academy I said to Oshri, "If I get blown up and lose a part of my body, just shoot me. Kill me on the spot." He asked if I was sure about it, and I answered that I was. I made him swear he'd do it. When you die, I explained to him, you have maybe two or three seconds of pain and then you lose consciousness and you're in the world to come. The people who die don't go through long-term suffering. On the other hand, when you lose a limb you're assured of lifelong misery. Decades of it. Oshri thought for a few minutes and told me I was right and suggested we should promise the same for each other, that if one of us lost a part of his body the other would finish him off, shoot a bullet into him. Ever since then, before each time we went into Lebanon, we would promise each other again and swear an oath. That night, too, just before his discharge, I demanded it again. I didn't care if he had to come from the other side of the world to do it: I wanted him to grab a weapon, sneak into my hospital room without leaving tracks or traces, and do the job. He swore to it and then we went to sleep.

Before I fell asleep I thought about how lonely I'd be in another week when Oshri turned into a regular citizen and forgot it all, and also about that guy from the Nahal unit who doesn't have a clue how to find another girlfriend. Best he could do would be a girl in a wheelchair. Or worse. Probably better off not finding anyone. And why didn't I feel anything when I thought about Lila? Only a big relief.

The next day we entered Lebanon.

Oshri's farewell party was scheduled for Wednesday. That's part of procedure when a member of the command staff leaves: you take his soldiers out for a morning of fun in the ancient fortress that sits next to our outpost. The Arabs call it Qalaat A-Shakif. It's three stories high with seven more built downward into the hill, or maybe more. Legend has it that the fortress reaches all the way down to the Litani River, to the place where they would draw water, like some endless underground high-command bunker. But we stop two floors below ground level since if you go any lower the fortress is apparently booby-trapped—by terrorists, Palestinians, from back in the time of the Lebanon War eighteen years earlier. No point in taking chances. We leave our secure area, climb the rusty metal ladder at the back of the outpost, step over the ruins of the outer stone wall, and find ourselves in the courtyard of the Crusader castle. Thistles reach as high as your chest and scratch the shit out of you. We squeeze through the narrow opening one by one, sucked inside, crawl through tunnels, descend with ropes, cram into a dark and narrow stairwell to a wide hall that looks like a place where kings might have paced back and forth at night when they couldn't fall asleep. What an empire they set themselves up with here: suddenly huge arched windows come into sight and long, tall firing slits that cast narrow sunbeams. Whoever planned the lighting for this place was a genius. If you look outside you catch sight of the clear water flowing down below at an angle you can't see from anywhere else on the hill. Trees with thick, green crowns send branches into the water, and there are dark, slippery stones. These are my favorite places, the kind where you can see how everything was here, once: in the time of the Bible and the Middle Ages and the world wars and the Lebanese civil war. No matter when you were to pass through here—on a caravan of elephants, on camelback, on a French tank, or in a group of warplanes that drops you from the sky—no surprise would greet you here. Everything's as it was, nature. Same view. The only change is the flag—blue and white at the moment. It's time for the Argentine video camera.

Is that thing filming, brother? Come on, already, push the button! Pay attention, folks, this is Zitlawi, your announcer. Good morning, brothers. Beautiful, eh? Most romantic place in the country. We're here like tourists. Like tourists. That guy—what's his name?—the one who does those travel shows all around the world?—he'd kill to be here, yeah? But he can't. Not allowed. Too bad six million Israelis can't make it up here. On second thought, maybe it's not too bad. They don't deserve it. Let them keep on drinking cappuccinos with whipped cream. Now to the point: Erez, fucking hell, buddy, they've got to get a couple of girls up here to us fast. Even Lebanese babes, I don't care. Sixteen years old. Tell me the truth, you'd go for it, wouldn't you? Sure you would. This place makes me totally horny. Perfect place for asking a girl to marry you, believe me. River, man, you bring a girl up here at sunset, and whoa! You can already start ordering the catering. What is that? What did you find over there? Holy shit, something really fine: an indoor garden. Check this out, what kind of defense system they built themselves here. These firing slits are much more professional than what we got. I'm going to blow this guy away! RATATAT, RATATAT! And what's with the size of these rocks? How'd they get them up here a thousand years ago, can you tell me that? I'm starting to get tired, I'm not shitting you, they've got so many fucking rooms. Emilio, baby, why don't you trip and fall and we'll get on *Candid Camera* and you'll win a car for sure. Hey, get a load of this. You filming? These must be their torture chambers, right? What do you think, Bayliss? Look at the graffiti. Terrorists. Wonder what's written. They've destroyed the walls. Let's put our names up there, too. What do you say, man? The Ugly Israeli, the Ugly Arab, it's all the same. Come on, you fat ass Itamar, get a move on down already, we're trying to move forward here. What are you waiting for, someone to massage your butt? Move! Bloody hell, it must have been a fucking nightmare to conquer this place. I can't even imagine it. All the shit we've been through up here in Lebanon has been worth it to get into this place. See the sheep down in the field? Man, wouldn't you like to ride the shit out of one of those babies? A flying sheep; now, why haven't they invented one of those yet? You know, this place is the best for tossing people out. Yeah, like that, from this window. Just pitch them out. Go on, throw me out. I'd really like to. Come on, let's go down another level. It's like Rome here, man. So what if I've never been to Rome?

We ran around the passageways for a while and then made our way down to the main hall. There was an indoor swimming pool, about a fourth of an Olympic-size pool, no water, with carved stone pillars surrounding it. Zitlawi pulled out the gas burner and the lemon-flavored wafers. Oshri lit a small campfire and I skewered marshmallows on sticks for roasting. We brought out the cigarettes—even the guys who don't smoke, it's part of procedure. We threw our uniforms off to the side, lay naked in the sand. And we were silent. It's not every day you see the kids all quiet, but in the cold, moldy, compressed air there was something stronger than all of us that makes you go kind of fuzzy, wears you out, causes you to focus on yourself, to whisper. To be quiet. We lay our heads on our flak jackets and helmets, we sank into the drugged-out atmosphere. We were safe there, no terrorist would blow up the fortress. And if they did, they wouldn't hit us way down deep inside. Maybe we were allowed to be there, maybe not—probably not, we didn't check the rule-books on this one—but it was tradition, and company tradition is more important than all kinds of commands that change all the time. This was the way we took leave of a friend, with honor. I sat next to River. "What's wrong?" I asked him. "Why the long face?" But he brushed me off. "Nothing," he whispered. "Liar," I said. His face looked sad, I wasn't making this up. He was trying hard to toss the hot potato somewhere else, kept trying hard to find a new topic of conversation, but the wheels in our brains work slow underground. "The minute there's peace with Lebanon I'm coming up here for some rock climbing," he said. "Right from the bottom, from the wadi, up the steepest part of the hill, stone by stone up to the cliff. I'm dying to do it." Then he pretended to fall asleep, turned his back to me. The others drowsed, too. I lit a cigarette. Lila would kill me if she saw me smoking, she doesn't allow it, worries. She keeps me on a short leash. Then again, she doesn't anymore. Another half year until the millennium, I thought. Big, round number. Weird. When it happens, on the first day of January in the year 2000, at zero-zero hours and zero-zero minutes, when the dials all go to zero at the zero second, we may still be up here on the hill. What kind of a moment is that going to be? Quiet and regular, like now? Disappointing? Just a moment like any other moment? Will we lie there in the submarine munching, say, sunflower seeds and pistachios, and looking at our watches? Or maybe it will be one of those unforgettable moments. We'll go crazy, throw a party the likes of which Lebanon has never seen before. Or maybe Hezbollah will decide to shake up the world at that very moment, zero hour, and light the skies up with orange? They can if they want to, and we'll run and hide like mice in their holes with our mouths hanging open, in shock, until we get our act together and fire back at them. Because maybe it will be a real war, maybe even a world war if someone wants it, the kind that starts at zero hour. No way can we be drunk that night, we've got to remember to be sober. And in another seven hundred years or so someone is going to stand here and ask, imagining, Who was here right at the new millennium at the historic moment? They'll be thinking about us. Or not. Maybe I'll be on a furlough right then, who knows? I'll hook up with Lila again, maybe, and we'll go to Tel Aviv. At the biggest square, hundreds of thousands of people will count backward watching huge screens and they'll kiss and the skies will be full of color from all the fireworks. Maybe. I'm not sure where I'd rather be on the first of January. With all the doomsday prophesies and disasters people are predicting, and God making a big-time comeback, and legends and mysticism and miracle workers, the tension will be a killer. I mean, our curiosity—even if in the end nothing happens and if we all believe nothing's going to happen—our curiosity is what will get us. If I could hug Lila and keep her safe in the millennium but spend it with Oshri and everybody here, that would be the best. Not with the city jerks, the slick crowd, the ones stinking of pollution and asphalt, that bunch of fucking sheep, the atheist pacifists who look down their noses at anyone who doesn't worship their perverted sex and drugs and art. I'd rather be here, these kind of Bible-y moments suit me best. When my grandkids ask me, "Where were you, Grandpa, at that moment?" I'll have a good answer for them: "At war," I'll say. "At war." The millennium is almost here. Probably billions of people have been imagining it: spaceships, star wars, robots. And I'll be hiding out in a Crusader fortress. How weird. I fell asleep.

Rare footage. Our squad commander is sleeping like a puppy dog. Hey, man, that thing's running, right? Look, Lana sweetheart, don't let the guy's dwarflike height throw you off, we're talking about a well-oiled war machine here. He's a Rottweiler with the balls of a hippopotamus. The most gung-ho soldier in the Israeli army. He knows what he's doing, he knows what he's fighting for, he's as cool as a lemon Popsicle. You can always count on him to draw first. And here's River, our little play toy. Tell us, River, you little monkey, what haven't you managed to do yet in life? Yes, Lana's dying to hear, brother. Imagine that you get wasted here: what would be the worst thing you'd miss, that you didn't get a chance to do? In that last moment before you pop off to heaven, or hell, what have you got to do? I'm asking you for real. What's with this "don't want to talk about death" business, huh? Cut the bullshit, we're family. Toss something out, everyone's got something. Me, for example. I've never seen Tzvika Pick sing in Caesarea, something I've planned on for a long time. Yeah, I guess it's pretty easy to make me happy, isn't it? Another thing: I've never killed anybody. Yet. What? What are you guys looking at me like that for? I'm talking about a terrorist. Come on, River, your turn. Good. Yes. You haven't screwed a Brazilian girl yet. Excellent answer. Here's a tip from your big brother, Zitlawi: there's one on Ben Yehuda Street in Tel Aviv. Chez Jasmine. Know the place?

What? What do you mean that doesn't cut it? It's got to be at Carnaval? Okay, got it. Oh yeah, and you wouldn't mind trouncing your older brother in tennis, either. We'll try and set something up for you. Bayliss, what about you? Shoot. Really? You've never been overseas? That's a real fuckup. Next. Spitzer. Spitz. How about you, my man? Here, buddy, talk into the microphone. It's your girlfriend we're talking to here, not mine. Give her some drama, don't be afraid to show off a little, we all love you here, you sweet little bonbon. Make it something from your heart, that's the best. What? You've never really made your parents proud? Come on, man, I'm going to barf in a minute. What's with you?

And here's Oshri, our sergeant, the hero. The one who's leaving us. Say good-bye to him. Say something nice about modesty. You'll never get a word out of this quiet guy. He's a real introvert. Notice how he's always got this peaceful look splashed across his face. Mister Cool. And dark as he is, he's got the taste of an Ashkenazi, listens to worn-out recordings of Israeli classics all day long on his Walkman. Teaches horseback riding, too, at this ranch for rich bitches. I'll bet you didn't pick up on that at first glance, did you? No way. He'll arrange some riding lessons for you if you want. But when there are no girls around and he isn't shy, then the punk inside him comes out, the vampire, the kind who picks fights for kicks—friendly fights, for fun, and he beats the shit out of all our sorry asses. He head-butts you, bites you, bear-hugs you. Loves a good fight, that's his favorite thing. Tell me, Sergeant, sir, what made you join a combat unit? What? What do you mean, the induction officer? You mean they just put you here? No, you're supposed to say that you had some sort of role model, some guy from the neighborhood, older than you, someone you looked up to that got killed in some accident, and his death gave you the drive for revenge, or that your father was a commander and he brought you up on continuity and excellence and the pioneering spirit and Zionism. What? No? How could that be? None of it? So why'd you stay on? You've been here so long.

A heavy fog descended on the hill without warning. Zero visibility. I remember Oshri waking me up, suggesting we get out of there fast and back into the secure area. A thick white cloud surrounded us from the outside like a ring around the fortress, and then it started to penetrate through the firing slits in waves. It's not a good idea to walk around outside in weather like that. Terrorists love it, they come out of their holes and move around under the protection of fog. The loudspeakers were already warning against potential incoming launches while we were climbing up to the exit. Up there, on the highest point of the whole mountain range, the sky was clear and blue. We looked down, to the ring of clouds that seemed like a white ocean flowing to the horizon, a heavy block of clouds that only we and the ruined fortress were sticking out of and floating above. In the midst of all that euphoria, that pastoral landscape, our ears were already attuned to the sound of the first shots that would be fired. We had no choice but to get down to the outpost inside the cloud. We felt our way to the ladder, dove down. I was first, Oshri was last, and the kids were in the middle. Like blind men we felt our way.

The first explosion hit just as my feet touched ground. It was a mortar shell. Seconds later there was another one. The loudspeakers didn't announce launches, the sirens weren't wailing. The bombs just fell. BOOM! Then silence. I shouted, "Move it!" and the kids sped up, came down one after the other and ran like hell, disappeared into the white whirlpool trying to find their way to the buildings. I stood next to the ladder, catching them as they hit the ground and pushing them in the right direction. Until I got hold of Oshri. "It's me, that's it," he said. "Last one." I grabbed his hand and we started running together. We couldn't see a thing. Another hit, right in the outpost. Another, closest yet. A yellow flash and thick gray smoke. I lost Oshri's hand for a minute, then a second later I heard him screaming. But I couldn't see him. I went looking, started shouting, "Where are you?" I could hear his voice but I couldn't figure out where he was. I mean, it didn't make any sense—he was a few feet away from me, no more than that. For sure. "Oshri! Talk to me!" Then I heard him moaning, saw him running in the opposite direction. I figured he didn't know what to do, got confused. "Where are you going?" I shouted. "Oshri, talk to me. You're going the wrong way!" I kept shouting. A strong arm took hold of me. It was Furman. "Get inside," he hollered, pulling me in. "Not without Oshri," I said. He pulled me in hard, shoved me. "Settle down, we're bringing him in, too," he said.

Even inside we were in a kind of fog. The kids were standing around, we were all waiting. River dashed in covered in blood—Oshri's blood. He was pulling him by his left arm, dragging him inside. "Wounded soldier, I've got a wounded soldier!" he shouted. The smell of gunpowder trailed in after them. Oshri was conscious but stunned, completely unfocused. And his arm was shredded. It was totally shredded. He was holding it tight. He'd taken a direct hit from a big piece of shrapnel and his right arm had been sliced, one of his bones was fractured and hanging out. Another piece of shrapnel had hit his leg and he was limping. He stood facing me and began to cry. He came close to me, his arm had been ripped out of place, mangled. He looked me in the eye and shouted, "Help me! Help me!" I froze up. "Help me, Erez!" he pleaded. He stood in front of me, terrified, waiting, but I had frozen up. I didn't do anything. Zero functioning. We'd practiced for this kind of situation so many times but I just stood there while time passed and kept on moving. "What do you want me to do?" I asked, like I was angry with him;

that's the way it came out. "There's nothing I can do." I stood there looking at him, powerless, and then I lowered my gaze. I couldn't understand why he wasn't running to someone else for help, but then his legs gave way and he dropped to a sitting position. River tried laying him out flat but he put up a fight. Why fight? And then he passed out. Everyone just stood there watching. Dave stood at the door to make sure nobody went nuts and ran outside to get hit. It happens. Furman went back outside to make sure there were no other wounded out there. Why? Why did I freeze up?

It wasn't some lightbulb that lit up in my head all of a sudden, it was a blinding explosion in my brain. That's when I started to cry, too. Without meaning to. It was the first time I cried. When Ziv got hit I didn't cry. And Ziv's was fatal, he was stone-dead. Oshri was lying there on the cold floor. When I pulled myself together I held him for a while in my arms, I tried pushing his flesh back inside so it wouldn't spill out, but I didn't really know what I was doing. I felt like it was eating me up, I was crashing, all my limbs were collapsing, and under my skin there was nothing but tiny slivers of glass. What skin, what am I talking about? I didn't have any skin, I was suddenly just a big bundle of exposed nerves without a bit of skin for cover, burned up and burning with every touch and every word. I was in pain, horrified, everything was sharp, knocking me off my feet. My muscles were constricting, I was having trouble breathing, trying to draw air into my lungs, as much air as possible, but I couldn't manage it. And I felt so embarrassed. Then the doctor showed up with his equipment and he started setting the arm, gave Oshri morphine. Pressure dressings to stop the bleeding, an infusion, all that stuff—he didn't feel a thing. The morphine was flowing through his blood, he sort of woke up and shouted, "Erez, come here!" I guess he didn't notice I was already right there next to him, sitting by the stretcher. "Light a

Marlboro for me," he said. We stared at him, stunned. Didn't he know what had happened to him? Didn't he understand? Or maybe they'd drugged him up too much. It didn't make sense for him to be talking like that. I asked the doctor what was going on and he told me, "Keep him busy, that's good, we don't want him to lose consciousness again."

"Light a Marlboro for me," Oshri said again.

"Forget about cigarettes for the time being, it's not good for you," I told him.

"Why, what's going on? Did I give up smoking?" he asked, his eyes closed.

We didn't know what more to say, what to talk about. "Hang on," Zitlawi said, jumping in from the side, "you nicked my lighter, didn't you, Oshri?" Oshri said yes and stuck his left hand into the pocket of his pants and pulled out Zitlawi's lighter. It was scary. "Keep him busy!" the doctor commanded us, agitated. But how? River noticed the patch that had fallen off his mutilated right arm and the tattoo that was now exposed for the first time. "Hey, look," he said. "You got rid of the tattoo, and without some painful operation." He looked at Zitlawi. If Zitlawi wouldn't talk, who would? "I met a girl once who had a tattoo of a mouse running away from her ass," he recounted, feeling his way. "Yup, for real. And another one with a tattoo of a hand holding her tits. I even heard about some chick that had the name of her boyfriend tattooed on her pussy. I swear it. And then they broke up."

We strapped Oshri onto the stretcher. I stepped aside because I'd started crying again. Everyone stood there staring at me, no less than they were staring at the mangled arm and the pool of blood. Oshri looked dazed, but he kept talking. "What are you crying for?" he asked me. "What? Am I dead or something?" There was a long silence. Then the medical evacuation team landed and loaded him into the chopper.

"That's it, Lebanon's all over for me," Oshri said, and we were separated. He took off. I didn't put a bullet in his head, he didn't jump off the helicopter.

What a world this is. Just a week earlier, on our furlough, we'd gone together to Rambam Hospital in Haifa to visit Gulo, the sniper from the Dlaat outpost. In the middle of a battle he was hit by friendly fire, a bullet fired at close range from an IMI Negev light machine gun (the guy was apparently shooting too wide. It happens. A real mess there—fire, grenades). While we were at the hospital Oshri came out with something really weird. He said, "Don't worry, pretty soon I'll be joining you. I'll be lying right there in the bed next to you." And now, a week later, he'd be lying right there—maybe in the next bed. Could it be? Yeah, I know, you don't believe it when someone tries to sell you tales about weird fate and tragic coincidences. It always sounds too made-up to be believed. Like the soldier who tells his mother which song he wants played at his funeral if he dies, and then the next day he gets killed. Or the mother who jumps out of bed in the middle of the night feeling like something terrible has happened. It reaches her through nightmares or a revelation, until she finally goes out onto the porch to wait for the car bringing army personnel to deliver the news. And they come. What are the chances? Almost nil. Or the friend who talks to you about his fear of losing an arm and then loses it four days later. Believe it, brother, believe it. I swear it. If that had been part of a movie I wouldn't have bought into the string of coincidences, either. But that's reality. I swear it on my mother's life.

Even today, when I'm alone, sometimes I can picture Oshri coming through the door in slow motion. His arm is hanging there, behind him everything's smoke, and he's screaming, "Help me!" They lay him out on the floor trying to reattach the severed arm, there's blood everywhere. All in slow motion. I close my eyes and I can see him. When people talk to me about "Cursed Lebanon" that's the picture that comes to mind, those are the horrors. Me pushing his flesh back inside like some animal, trying not to lose any pieces, the doctor wrapping him with a stomach bandage and River with a sterilized field dressing, the chopper arriving ... that's Lebanon, you're totally smeared with blood and the guy lying there is your best friend. So how is it that you don't stop for a minute to think? And what about that last Saturday night we spent together before going back into Lebanon—I see that, too, when I close my eyes. To this very day. We traveled from his village, Arugot, down to the Besor district, to the huge reservoir between Re'im and Be'eri. There in the darkness, on the edge of the water, we made plans over ripe bananas and mandarin oranges. We promised ourselves we'd be the best commanders the Beaufort had ever seen. We decided to make it through alive, in one piece. We swore it. We'd go in and out of Lebanon without a scratch—not on us, not on the kids. We swore it. And when you take an oath on something, we thought, there's no chance God will let it get screwed up.

I swear on my mother's life, every word of this story is true.

11

DEPRESSING LETTERS ALWAYS BEGIN with "Dear Sweetie," which is usually followed by a line or two from some song by Shlomo Artzi. And then the real stuff pours out.

Dear Sweetie, how are you? *These days are full of rage, that's what they say. These days are of an age*... How am I? I don't know who to rage at first: you, my parents, my commanders, the soldiers. God, for putting me in this shitty situation. Most of all, myself. At the worst moments I think I don't even have any anger left inside me, and that makes me even sadder.

This isn't just another letter about how much I miss you, this time it's bottom-of-the-barrel stuff, total demoralization. Read it and try to understand. Just try. I've had it. I know that's a stupid statement to make these days, so banal and unoriginal, but I swear it: I've had it. I don't know what to do with myself. Oshri's been my friend for three years, the best friend a guy can have. For three years we've been dealing with all kinds of bullshit, asking each other for help with dumb things. Stuff like carrying a jerry can from one place to another. I always gave a hand, I was sure I was the perfect friend, the best there is. That's what I know how to do—be a friend—I'm really good at that. But then, when the moment of truth came, when he came running in with his arm hanging in the air and shouting and crying, "Help me, Erez!"—when he really and truly needed me—that's when I didn't. I stood there like some pencil-pushing asshole. I saw he needed me and I choked. It's not that I didn't know where to apply pressure and take care of his injury. I did. I've done tons of training exercises, it should have been completely natural to me, without even thinking. But when it actually happened I just stood there paralyzed. Why? If someone else hadn't taken charge Oshri might not even be with us anymore, he might have lost too much blood and wasted on us. "Wasted," sweetie, that's our way of saying "died."

Something held me back there, and I didn't even have the balls to tell myself, "You loser! Why aren't you helping?" Maybe I didn't want it enough. No, that's not it. I knew the reason. I was scared shitless. He didn't deserve that, Oshri. He didn't deserve for me to be scared shitless. Me, neither. I shouldn't even be saying these things, shouldn't even be thinking them. I can't allow myself to be afraid, or soft, or overly sensitive. This is a cruel place and you've got to be tough. And no, there's apparently no room for love up here, and *All love comes to an end. It's just that this end seems cursed to me.*

I hope you'll miss me.

Love, Erez

I started writing depressing letters when Ziv was killed. Short ones, every night. Lila was the logical—and only—candidate for receiving these outpourings from me. When all is said and done, a woman's a woman. She may be totally idiotic when it comes to army matters, doesn't understand a single thing, but she cares about me. And even though she was always trying to get me to turn in my uniform, never understood what the hell it was I was doing up at Beaufort, why I was looking for trouble, she would listen to me with this really cute look on her face and react warmly, between one scolding and the next. When I broke up with her I had to find a new address for my letters. I was actually happy about it, at last it was a chance to find someone who could really understand. I made a thorough study of everyone who knows me—parents, brothers, friends—and gave some thought to who would want to hear it all. I couldn't come up with anyone. There was no replacement for Lila. Then Oshri was wounded and the letters got longer. I would go back to bed, find once again that he wasn't there, and I wouldn't be able to fall asleep. So I wrote. To her, for the time being, floating there at the top of every page. Maybe I'm crazier about her than somebody should be allowed to be, and maybe I'll go back to her when it's all over, like nothing happened, pick up right where we left off, on the roof of her grandmother's cottage during our third year together. We'd be great together when I came back, if I came back. That's also the reason that some of the letters, the toughest of them, she's never seen. They're between me and God. I tore them up later, or shoved them way down deep in my knapsack. That happens sometimes, after you've written the first four lines or so you realize that you can't send this letter. That if your girlfriend reads it you'll lose her, she'll stop loving you. It's too depressing, too horrible, too extreme, too scary. A letter that exposes you to be someone other than the guy she knows from home. You're more cruel, for example, and a lot less funny. It's while you write a letter like that that you discover who you really are. And then you write that you've had enough. Enough of shooting, enough of soldiering, enough of yourself. You write that you're worn out, exhausted, that you've discovered they're all a bunch of liars. Me, too, I'm a liar, because I'm not really here to protect the residents of northern Israel but because I have this urge to kill. I enjoy it. And my commander is a liar because he stands beside me and says he's there for me, but the minute the bullets start flying he's out of there, looking out for his own ass—anyway, that's the way it seems to me. In the end, we're all liars. Everything here is a matter of chance. That's all, only chance: nothing else. If you die or not, it's just your fate. Doesn't matter how many exercises you've taken part in, what a good fighter you are, how careful and alert you are: if you're standing at the wrong place at the wrong time you're wasted. And the enemy? We have one, but I've never ever seen his face. Every explosive device is just a ball of fire that soars through the air and falls on you. They drop from the sky, launched from places you can't see, but they've got your name on them. Have the blood and filth and noise made me indifferent? Coarser? I don't know.

Here and there I see a few other guys with notepads scribbling lines and looking around all the time to make sure no one sees them. I wonder—I really do—if their letters look saner than mine. Once I yanked a letter out of Itamar's hands, just out of curiosity. He shouted and begged me to give it back but I just had to. "I feel like I can't go on," he'd written to his girlfriend. "I dream at night about lox on toast or a good steak, but here at the outpost they've got me on a dog's diet. The cook decided I'm too fat and keeps stuffing me with salads all the time. I'm shattered, falling apart, don't feel well. They can all go fuck themselves." That's what his letter said.

Those were the last days of our winter stay at Beaufort in 1999, the first days of hot sun; the snow on the surrounding mountain peaks had melted long before. These were joyless days, days without the security of knowing Lila was waiting for me. Soon, on the third of June, we would take leave of the outpost and go down to a training base in the Golan Heights. We'd be getting back into shape, going home from time to time—that's what was awaiting us. There'd be girls, too: army secretaries and social workers and personnel managers and course leaders. The kids would blossom. In the meantime, our sector was quiet. No purple rain had fallen on us for the last few days, and in the mornings we'd go out feeling free and relaxed to open roads because our gut instincts inexplicably told us there were no ambushes waiting for us along the road. And it was true. There was a kind of cease-fire—maybe we'd paid enough of a price already. Most of the time I was quiet and businesslike. Sometimes I was sad, sometimes just spacey. All the time closed up, introverted. I'd think about Lila mostly in the mornings. I'd wake up with a hard-on like the barrel of a Merkava tank, only thicker. I'd rub myself a little, gently rock the bed, imagine her scents. But then after a minute or two I'd be overcome with fatigue, and by thinking about the missions ahead, and the understanding that it was best not to remember. At other times, only during really bad bouts, I'd catch myself thinking about her with someone else, maybe a soldier—even a non-combat guy, a pencil pusher—who might be with her at that very minute. Maybe I even knew the guy. I'd torture myself with all kinds of insights teeming with lifelike descriptions, then I'd pull myself together, focus, convince myself she couldn't possibly make out with anyone else since we'd been together for a million years already. She'd only ever made out with me. So there was no way. She didn't know how to kiss other guys. I'd put it out of my mind and keep on working.

The kids were fine, I think. But as far as I was concerned this was the end. I decided I wouldn't be coming back to Beaufort. It was time to put an end to it, to get out. I was determined: I had nothing more to do there. My parents were pushing me, too. They managed to bring up at every opportunity, even during short phone calls, the fact that my brother had been wounded in Lebanon and that they weren't up to dealing with that again emotionally. They liked to say that our family had contributed enough. That was the end of Beaufort for me.

SECOND TOUR OF DUTY

12

NEXT YEAR THEY WON'T BE CALLING ME RIVER. Naor, either.

Maybe Shanti, Master Shanti. Or Santosh or Yogi. Or Dharma, Rajesh, Rakesh, Asao, Bhajan, Ashutosh. Who knows what they'll call me, there's no end to the possibilities. Maybe they'll make up a completely new name for me. They'll find one for you, too, Lana. Something from nature. That is, if you'll come with us, you and Spitzer. They're Israelis there—Kothumi and Kareem—all of them, Israelis, but they've had enough of Israel so they took off for a while. That's okay. Why not? They're happy now.

Have you heard about Pacha Mama? That's "Mother Earth," a commune—the most famous one. That suits me, a commune. Heard of Costa Rica? Sure you have: the "rich coast." And how about Kundalini yoga? Means "twisted." It's a kind of a serpent that lies dormant at the base of your spine and you have to wake it up. If it wakes up inside you, then you bring on liberation—I'm not shitting you: you nourish the soul, merge with the flow of creative energy, invigorate the psyche, and BOOM! You've reached enlightenment. I swear it. It calms your soul, puts the pieces of your heart back together. A totally spiritual life. Okay, I'm going to show you. First stage: stand with your knees bent and move your body around, easy, earth to sky, shake it out, breathe deep, flow slowly. Second stage: dance, put on some good music—Spitzer will play something for you—close your eyes, let the dance come from inside you, be natural. Don't force it, just let yourself get caught up in it, carried away. Third stage: sit down, your eyes still closed, then, when you're ready to chill out, lie down on your back—that's the fourth stage already—completely peaceful. In a minute or two the Kundalini serpent will wake up. You'll see. "Snake" and "Messiah" have the same numerological value in Hebrew, I'm not kidding you: 358. You think that's a coincidence? Not if you ask the guru who came up with this Kundalini thing, a Jewish guy from New York called Swami Rudrananda, who everybody called Rudi. He lived like a king until his plane crashed into a hill on a flight from New Jersey. Poor guy.

No? What do you mean, no? You didn't like it? Well, there are lots of options: Kundalini yoga, Bikram yoga, Hatha yoga, a workshop in spiritual cleansing; whatever anybody's into. We'll be happy, and aware—awareness, that's the most important thing. And there'll be workshops on the dimension of time, and on the creation of worlds according to Kabala. Yeah, even in Costa Rica people are crazy about Kabala. About channeling, too. And reincarnation, and healing. And of course intimacy, because everything is connected to intimacy in a commune. So how could we not be happy?

December 1999. While an entire nation was demanding we get out of Lebanon that winter, all I wanted to do was get in. Well, at first I didn't. I'd decided to become a regular citizen. I went to Tel Aviv to breathe a little. I sat alone, watching from the side, trying to figure out how I could connect to it all, to life outside the army, in the Tel Aviv bubble, on the beachfront promenade, in the cafés. At home. An entire nation was there, drinking mango and banana milk shakes, having a great time. I really hoped to feel part of it, to flow with the new rules, play along, get used to it. But it didn't happen. I know, I know, those army pencil pushers have a different babe every night—that's what I was thinking—but they don't have a clue what friendship is, what it is to feel so close to somebody. I watched them come into a pub together, arguing with each other about money. In our company all the money belonged to everybody. That's what I was used to, that's how I liked it. Those superficial non-combat guys didn't know what a red laser sighting is, or a Madonna headset, or the guard booths we call "hedgehogs," or what it feels like to complete a fifty-five-mile beret march. They didn't know what it is to go on the attack, to take a bullet, to apply pressure to a part of your best friend's body while he's lying there half dead. They disgusted me.

Maybe the truth is that I had a lot more fun going on deadly missions than drinking mango shakes. A lot. So who exactly was I kidding? What was I moaning about? I liked it. I liked painting my face up and crawling in the fog. I liked the darkness, the cold nights, the sweat on my forehead from so much stress, and how the drops trickled to my cheeks. A person who hasn't been there will never get it. And when I had really bad frostbite I liked to discover every time all over again that I still hadn't gone too far, that I still hadn't reached the height of pain. I was curious to get there, see how much further I could push my luck and prove to myself that I could stand to absorb new intensities—a lot of pain, a lot of fun. I believed that if I gave in to myself I would keep giving in my whole life. I'd marry some dull woman and have dull friends. I'd give in to my kid when he did bad in English class. Everything in my life would be mediocre, and mediocrity is scary. It's shitty. I decided not to give in. My soldiers—I was prepared to die for them, I swear it: I really was ready to die for them. That's not just some slogan; I felt good about it. Seems to me they were willing to die for me, too, and that's an incredible feeling.

On the way north the roads were full of homemade signs: BRING OUR BOYS HOME. The car I was catching a ride in barely made it through the Golani junction because of a small group of women trying to block traffic. It happened again farther north, at the Mahanaim junction, where people made a human chain. They were holding torches, and policemen were standing by, restrained; instead of whipping out their clubs and knocking a few of those females on the head, they seemed to be asleep on their feet. One big Ashkenazi broad stuck her face up against the window of the car. Her eyes looked right into mine for a few seconds, just inches away. She pressed her hands to the windshield and screamed, "Cannon fodder!" Totally hysterical. Too bad they couldn't see the whole picture the way we do. Up there, in Lebanon, the war looked a whole lot better.

On the door of the sergeants' room at our training base there was a sign that said WAKE IN CASE OF WAR, and nobody ever dared to wake them up. On the door of the staff sergeants' room a sign read IN CASE OF WAR WAKE THE SERGEANTS: WE WON'T WAKE UP ANYWAY, and over the entrance to the showers was bloodred graffiti: ENTRY FORBIDDEN TO DOGS AND INFORMERS. The guy who wrote that—and I'm not naming names here—was talking about soldiers who run crying to Carmela Menashe, the Israel Radio correspondent for army affairs, whenever we try to make men out of them. That's a problem. During the months we spent in training, back near civilization, there was suddenly access to cell phones and news and newspapers. When those broadcasters started wailing about soldiers afraid to cross the border, and the whole country was flooded with protest marches by women in black, then the guys started asking questions; it was only natural.

Zitlawi was the first of them. Something in the guy's wiring got screwed up. He sat down next to me in the canteen about a month before our second round of duty at the front and starting raising doubts. "Ehud Barak is prime minister, right?" he asked. "And he says he's pulling the IDF out of Lebanon, right? What do you mean, you don't know? He said so on television and ever since then everyone's talking about it."

"Okay, let's say that's true," I said.

"So what are we going up there for now? Explain it to me."

"What's that supposed to mean?" I asked, and I fixed a threatening look on Zitlawi. It didn't throw him off a bit. He kept at it. Zitlawi, the last guy I'd expect it from. "If the prime minister promised to pull the IDF out of Lebanon in another eight months," he continued, "then why not do it now? Yeah, right now. This morning. Because we're just going to draw fire up there for nothing. We'll be targets. Next week River'll take a hit and get wasted, two days later it'll be Zion and Boaz, a week after that I'll wind up in a wheelchair and then everybody will say, 'Wow, that's right, we should've gotten out of there a long time ago, before this big wave of killings.' I'm telling you straight: I don't get the logic of it."

That blew my fuse. I roared, "Nobody's getting out of anywhere!" because I couldn't think of anything better. "Do you really believe they're going to abandon the security zone? Forget it. Who would let Hezbollah get that close, pressed up against the Good Fence, making mincemeat out of the little kids in the kibbutzim along the border? The IDF is not pulling out of Lebanon in defeat, you can bet this army wouldn't dare to. Beaufort is the army's eyes. You'd better get that into your head."

What else could I have said?

In discussions with the officers, Furman would tell us that Barak was no fool, that the guy was leading our nation strategically, that there'd been no fatalities in Lebanon for several months and that the annual number of IDF casualties had fallen by nearly half. Now they were just trying to hang on to that achievement, stall for time, make the other side understand it was losing, and then come out with a political agreement in which Israel had the upper hand. Army Intelligence and the Mossad would know exactly when we should pull out—that's what Furman said, expecting us to agree. "Shit, why doesn't Barak stick his daughter up there with us on Beaufort?" I would say to piss him off. "Let all the government ministers put their stinking kids up there, if that's their strategy, and explain to them that it's a lofty goal to sacrifice your own life in order to stall for time. If they trust us so well, let them leave their kids in our hands and then they're welcome to stall for as much time as they want."

Furman's explanation didn't make sense to me. I figured if it was true that there was such a strategy and we were there for the time being as pawns in a political game, part of the tactics, and that they would be pulling us out anyway, then our situation was much worse than I'd thought. I couldn't believe it.

That night, when I went to the officers' showers, River ducked inside and sat down on the bench. "Do you have answers?" he asked. "Real answers, I'm only interested in real answers," he said. I shouted at him to get out of there.

"I think it's important, you should have answers," he said, not budging. "It sounds bad, like the government has no emotional involvement, like they couldn't care less. Zitlawi's right: our guys are going to get knocked off one after the other and it'll be for nothing, because they're pulling us out in the end. That much is clear. Some of us will leave Lebanon in coffins, and it would be a shame to die without understanding the logic. That's sad."

River. What a disappointment. That's what he said. I'd never heard a soldier get carried away in such a dangerous direction. "Someone's been brainwashing you," I told him. "Soldiers shouldn't be asking questions like those, shouldn't even be talking like that at all. If those kinds of ideas seep into your brain you'll be a lousy fighter. Doubt is the thing that'll kill you, the only thing, and it'll kill your friends, too. You'd better bury those doubts and chill out, fast."

He did. The next afternoon he announced that he'd decided not to go to officers' academy. He passed up the position that had been allotted to him that month and signed a waiver. He was the second to do that, after Bayliss, who'd turned down the academy when there were tangible signs in the air that Israel would be pulling out of the Golan Heights and evacuating settlements there in an agreement with Syria. That hurt, but I accepted it, tried to understand. River, on the other hand, the soldier closest to me in our squad—well, there was just no way this guy wasn't going to be an officer. River, who'd saved Oshri; River, who dashed into the cloud of fire that had consumed Ziv, while I was still hesitating; River, who knew no boundaries: how could he not be an officer? He refused to explain. I tried threatening him, bribing him, appealing to him personally. Nothing helped. I was powerless.

In the evening I gathered the squad on the parade grounds and put it as plainly as possible: "Anyone who doesn't want to go back into Lebanon, raise your hand, now." There was total silence. I waited a minute, then another, and another. They looked from one to the other, each waiting to see how their friends would react. "Whoever wants out, let him go now or keep quiet until discharge." No one came forward, no one left. "From this moment on," I announced, "anyone who dares question our mission will be booted out, sent home, with a stopover in military prison."

That was our situation when we returned to the Land of

Cedars, to a different Beaufort, with cracks in our faith and a strong echo sounding at our necks telling us, "You don't even need to be fighting now." You hear it, and you have to put that heavy pack on your back and march into the cold, and you're asking yourself, "Why should I?" And the nation was divided: some were carrying the burden, others were disinterested, others were chasing after your very soul, hounding you, not giving up, shouting, "END THE OCCUPATION," and how it's sheer madness. And you as a commander try to live in peace with the understanding that you will end a tour of duty like this with casualties, or at the very least with wounded men. Those are realistic scenarios you can't help playing in your head, along with the guys' names. There were rumors floating around at the time, too, they were coming at us from everywhere. For example, that fighters had been caught in outposts in the security zone smoking dope on duty. It was bad enough they were jerking off on duty, I'd already heard that one. More than once there had been guys who had bragged about it or been caught, and even that was too much for me, to think about them lowering their guns and jerking off during such a volatile period, right while they're on guard duty and the lives of all their friends depend on them and all around mortar shells are exploding and terrorists are trying to make their way in. When I had my suspicions I would make my way through the trenches to pay a visit, sneaking up on them in the middle of the night. I even forbade them from taking a piss during guard duty to make sure there were no misunderstandings, no excuses, no temptations. If you stick a dish of cream under a hungry cat's nose, don't be surprised if it eats the plate along with the cream. If I don't rub my dick for thirty-five days, even after watching Sharon Stone open her legs in *Basic Instinct,* then the kids can hold off for a little while, at least until they're in their sleeping bags at night. But drugs? Drugs at the guard posts? No way. "I personally promise to fire a bullet in the head of whoever I catch smoking," I told them when the first stories hit us. I had friends who lit up at home, on their free time. But at the outpost? I couldn't even imagine it. What a disgrace. I forced myself to believe that in my squad this had never happened.

That was another time Zitlawi the debater defused the tension. He agreed that was pretty serious, but said the blame shouldn't be placed on the soldiers. "If something like that happens," he explained, "it's because somebody pushed those soldiers into a corner, put them in shitty conditions, and they fall apart. Drugs become their only way out, their only way to forget all their troubles for a few hours." Bayliss said that was bullshit, that ours was just a lousy generation. "That's the face we present to the world, every home has somebody smoking dope. I've heard of parents who light up with their kids around, and kids who smoke with their parents." But Zitlawi wasn't giving up. He stood on a chair. "If we had some minimal, basic conditions here," he said, "for example, if we didn't have to walk through sewage to go brush our teeth every morning and every evening, maybe morale among the soldiers would be a little higher." What do you want? That's the IDF, that's what we have to offer. "And how is it that they know how to get us up here any way possible," he asked, "but the packages that people send from home they don't know how to get here? They can't send a chopper or a convoy for that? We get lousy treatment here." It was all coming out now. I thought, This is going to be one lousy tour of duty.

If the business with the drugs wasn't enough to depress us and put a damper on our happiness about returning to the front, along came Amos the battalion commander a few hours before we set out, to make our misery complete. He announced that from that moment on there would be no more ambushes staged from Beaufort. Amos noted that while it was true we'd been going out on ambushes every night for years, now a new division commander had been appointed, and he had come to a few innovative conclusions with regards to the situation. Ambushes were unnecessary, he said. Ineffectual. The outpost could be secured from within, there was no need to lie in a bush a half-mile away for that, he said, and there was no need for opening roads, or for "grass widow" operations, or for playing cat-and-mouse games between villages. There was no need to endanger soldiers in self-initiated operational activity outside the secure areas of the outpost except in urgent cases in which there was some clear intelligence imperative. That was what the division commander had decreed and what would be policy until the IDF pulled out of Lebanon. "You've decided to ruin us!" I shouted, crazed. I was pissed as hell. "There are terrorists out there and we need them dead. Let us go into some village and fuck them over, give us something, just don't let us sit there in the outpost scratching our balls on guard duty day and night. The soldiers have to get outside the gates now and again, they need to walk, feel the territory under their feet. You people are going to bleed us dry, you'll destroy the unit. It's like bringing in the most elite unit to do kitchen duty all day long."

At the time Oshri and I finished the training course, our company commander told us that the best part of serving at Beaufort was the knowledge that maybe tonight, maybe tomorrow night, and certainly by the night after that you would take down the terrorists that had hurt your friend, you'd wipe out that specific cell. That was the big dream we all shared, a fantasy of sorts that started off with a face-to-face encounter, the kind that comes off perfect, the best there is: I sight suspicious activity in the distance, coming closer, about seventy yards away, a body facing me straight on but not seeing me at all, and I pump a good number of bullets into him and then I storm, come closer, I'm on top of him, I perform a death verification right in his face. After that I open River's stretcher and bring the body up to the outpost. And when he's lying there dead, a stinking terrorist, a pile of shit, in the exact spot where all our dead and wounded have been brought in at their worst moments, I wrap him in our company flag, sit him upright, spit a giant glob of phlegm into his face, and have my picture taken with my arm around him. Maybe even put a beret on the corpse and give a smile for another photo. Then a last round of pictures with the entire squad before I announce a long furlough, at the very least, for everyone. I would spend time imagining the moment—after all, your imagination is the key survival tool during a tour of duty in Lebanon. You linger over every second of the story. And not just me, everybody was like that, taking part in the special ambiance, an entire folklore of revenge. That's the food chain, the chain of life.

In those years, at every opportunity that presented itself, they would send us out on real missions, the kind that made a fighter feel he hadn't been stuck on the hill for no good reason. He was there to carry out a "grass widow" operation on the home of the collaborator, for example. Anyone who served at Beaufort knows the house, the fanciest building in the village of Arnoun: five stories, who knows how many levels, full of leather couches, terraced gardens with fountains, luxury windows, expensive paintings on all the walls: Hollywood. It wasn't the collaborator himself who lived there, it was his brother; the brother of a collaborator deserves to live like a king. For example, he was the only resident of the village given permission by the IDF to bring his car inside the village, while everyone else had to park outside at a distance and walk in. That's the way it was until one day, back when I was still pretty new at Beaufort, something went wrong. A soldier lying in ambush under the house caught sight of a pair of eyes peering out from a shuttered window every few minutes, keeping watch on him. It aroused the suspicions of the squad commander, set off his alarm bells. He reported the information to the outpost. In the morning a force entered the house and conducted a search. They found maps, binoculars, and mobile phones. The stash was sent to Command Intelligence and from there to the Shin Bet and after a few days we were informed that the confiscated items indeed raised questions about the man. They said that the number of a suspected Hezbollah operative was stored in the memory of his mobile phone. It turned out that the brother was collaborating with the terrorists. He'd double-crossed us. The IDF announced that from then on the collaborator's house was to be sealed off. The residents of the house were expelled that same day, the contents of the house were parceled out to SLA soldiers in the area, and an IDF force showed up with a D9 bulldozer to knock down a few walls and neutralize the target. Shortly after that we began to use what was left of the mansion as a starting point for ambushes. Sometimes we would hide inside it during daylight hours, leaving only at night on operational activities, and sometimes we would spend days there, using the house as an observation point from which we would see the approach roads.

"Grass widow" was the code name used for ambushes carried out from inside a house. When we got intelligence information about terrorists who were going to be using a certain access road, we'd set out on a grass-widow operation, finding a house that abuts the road—preferably abandoned, of course, but that wasn't essential—with good visibility, the kind that overlooks intersecting roads or problem points that can't be seen from the outpost guard posts, and we occupied it. The problem with grass widows is that they burn easy: if you had mud on your boots when you entered the house, or you sprayed a little when you took a leak on the floor, the whole squad was in danger. One of the locals could come in later, notice that the IDF had left tracks, and run to report to Hezbollah. The next time you came back there'd be an explosive device waiting for you.

And then there were the lying-down ambushes. When I was a young soldier we were out there every night in one of those. A "banana ambush" was the regular on-your-stomach kind. On a more interesting day there'd be a "warn and strike" ambush, where the forces were divided into two: one carried out an observation with marksmen while the other carried out an attack, wherever necessary. Then there was the "thermometer ambush," which involved the use of an anti-tank grenade launcher for mass destruction. Use of a tank made it an "artichoke ambush." And then there was the "assimilation ambush," which was really fun: you'd put on a disguise and blend in with the landscape. One day you were a rock, another day you were a bush, the third you were a tree. You reached the site of the operation with a large camouflage kit—latex covered with rubber—which had been perfectly adapted to disappear into the surroundings. Getting ready for an assimilation ambush took a long time. First you made a quick trip out to the site and took pictures from every angle, and you collected rock samples and sent all the material back to Israel. A little while later this perfect kit was sent to the outpost, and all you needed to do was slip into it and hide. For example, three fighters could fit into every fake rock. In an average ambush there would be five such rocks, one next to the other. The last guy in covered the whole set of rocks with mud and a few branches, secured them to the ground, got inside, and sealed up the entrance. Anyone passing by wouldn't have a clue what was going on. You'd lie in there for seventy-two hours, sometimes even a lot longer. Every once in a while you opened the zipper of the firing slit, took in some air, and went back inside your hole, where you hummed the top hits from the army Entertainment Corps, the ones everyone loved. On a mission like this you totally felt like you were James Bond.

But now it was all over. Our operational activities schedule had been wiped out. The battalion commander made his announcement and it spread quickly among the squads as they hung out killing time waiting for the green light to enter Lebanon. Most of them, like me, went nuts. These fighters, my kids, were not made for sitting around with nothing to do. They weren't afraid, they weren't looking to run away from the battlefield. They wanted to do their part, contribute something to the nation. They went to Amos and asked him straight out if what they were hearing was true. He understood that the situation was explosive and called them together, in formation, lined up in threes, to explain that there was no choice, that the IDF guidelines had changed and the operational activities were no longer effective.

"What exactly are you saying?" they asked him. "That everything we worked for and endangered our lives for till today is worth shit? Unimportant?"

"No," he answered, "but we've been enlightened with regard to the operational aspect. We've come to the realization that there is no point at the moment in taking unnecessary chances." They asked him what was going to happen with the approach roads to Beaufort—after all, Hezbollah would be planting mines and explosive devices. Amos told them there was no choice, that it was indeed a risk, that we would have to be on the lookout from the outpost, that we'd be stopping convoys and making use of choppers instead. I think he even let slip the following, without meaning to: "The IDF can't afford any more casualties right now."

Maybe the army heads were right, maybe we'd been operating stupidly. On ambushes we would draw fire for no good reason, for no benefit and without any operational logic.

Lying out there, at the foot of the outpost, for nights on end in the rain when there was a tank parked inside the outpost anyway with a night-vision attachment that could enable observation at a distance of three miles, and a grenade launcher and a tube-launched missile and ten MAG 58s—with all that it was senseless to lie outside exposed and in danger of getting hit. But if that was the case, then what the fuck had we been doing there? In fact, at the time, without operational activity our whole army service seemed meaningless. I'd gone into Lebanon like Rambo, urging my soldiers to be "murderers." I told them the story of the early Zionist Joseph Trumpeldor, how he took a bullet and fell to the ground and still had the strength to push his guts back inside his stomach and say, "It's good to die for our country." With that pioneering spirit I wanted to push forward. And now, suddenly, what?

We returned to a different Lebanon. The intelligence officer reported on a new addition to the Hezbollah death arsenal: the TOW, a tube-launched, optically tracked, wire-guided antitank missile that had been airlifted into Damascus from Tehran and from there smuggled by convoy in vegetable trucks and cement mixers into our battlegrounds. This missile was particularly efficient, and deadly. It could be fired at a distance of 2.3 miles, had a warhead of about thirteen pounds, was capable of penetrating two and a half feet of armor, and was characterized by its precision. It could be fired from a collapsible tripod or even from a vehicle. Up until then, the officer told us, the terrorists had been equipped solely with old Russian-made missiles. Now these new state-of-the-art models—originally American—had fallen into their hands from Iranian stockpiles. "They're going to try to set our sector ablaze," Amos said, reinforcing the intelligence briefing. "They're going to make a bigger effort than ever before in order to make sure that Israel's last year in Lebanon will go down in the history books as one big bloodbath, and so that we'll be portrayed as having retreated under fire, in panic and in tears."

Half an hour before midnight a fat Yasur chopper dropped down from the darkness to pick us up. At the time, there were no convoys going in or out of southern Lebanon because of alerts on explosive devices planted on the roads. A few minutes before liftoff, an embarrassed but determined River took out a small laminated card he'd brought from home and read "The Traveler's Prayer" over the receiver of the transmitter. His voice boomed to every corner and from the vehicles parked in the area, surrounding us and silencing the squads gathered near the liftoff point. My kids stood around listening to him: " 'May it be Your will, our God and God of our forefathers, that You head us toward peace, guide our feet toward peace, lead us to peace, and bring us . . .' "

" '. . . make us reach,' " Bayliss interrupted, correcting him.

"What?" River asked, confused.

" 'Make us reach,' you reject, not 'bring us . . .' "

" '. . . make us reach,' " he continued, " 'our desired destination for life, gladness, and peace. May You rescue us from the hand of every foe, ambush, bandit, and evil animal along the way, and from all manner of punishments that gather on earth. May You send blessings to all our handiwork and grant us grace, kindness, and mercy in Your eyes and in the eyes of all who look upon us. May You hear the sound of our supplications, because You are God, who hears prayer and supplications. Blessed are You, God, who hears prayer.' "

"Amen!" they answered, and the chopper took off, rising sharply. We crumpled bits of yellow sponge and shoved them into our ears for plugs, which did nothing to stop the high-pitched whistle and the rumble of the engines from piercing our eardrums and causing each of us to turn inward for a few last moments of quality time with himself. I was actually feeling pretty good with myself, surprisingly. I felt wicked good, strong, excited. I was thinking that my bed was already waiting there for me, half a year later, and I'd missed it. I'd nearly forgotten it all: the long, narrow corridors, the scary darkness, the dim red and blue lighting, the view, the feel of the wind up there, the taste of the schnitzel, and the smell of Lysol and piss and five-foot-tall wet thistles that bury you, and all of it together. And no, I wasn't afraid anymore that I would die curious, without knowing what was written on that little scrap of paper that Lila had shoved inside the cloth pouch that held my dog tags. I would read it at the Induction Center on the day of my discharge and not a second sooner. And I wouldn't think about her. For half a year I hadn't breathed her smell, hadn't put my head on her small belly. More than once I'd considered it, nearly broke down and went to her to see about getting back together—one time I even talked to her sister—but I knew that the time wasn't right yet. It was also a test of resolve and stamina. In times likes these, my happiness couldn't be dependent on love or physical contact. My concerns couldn't be with the little woman back home: if she was worried, that was bad and painful; if she wasn't, that was far worse and meant I would have to live in fear that she'd be out the door in a minute. Even if it was written somewhere that we were meant for each other, I knew I still needed to be focused at this point, precise. In spite of all the regulations and bad news and tough decisions, this was, for me, a welcome return to Lebanon.

Fifty-nine seconds and no more: that was the amount of time permitted to the pilot to stay on the landing pad. We had to hold our packs tight and jump to the ground in record time, before he lifted off again. Whoever got off was off. Whoever got on was on. And whoever didn't manage—it was his tough luck. It didn't matter if you were hanging from the landing skids, the chopper would hurry to disappear into the horizon. Every additional second added danger. A direct hit on a stationary target like that—by missile or shell—would be Hezbollah's biggest achievement of all time.

That night, six minutes elapsed from the time our feet touched the dirt and when the first salvoes of mortar shells sprayed the concrete roofs and the parking area and the guard posts. The enemy had taken note of the soldier rotation and wanted to catch us in those moments of disorganization. It was a way of letting us know what to expect on this tour of duty. Launch! Launch! Helmets in place on our heads, vests, too. It lasted thirty minutes, and when it was over we—the officers—ran the length of the trenches to make sure we hadn't been attacked on foot and that none of our soldiers had been taken hostage under cover of the barrage. After that I got myself set up in the senior staff submarine. Oshri's bed was now occupied by Levanoni, the new sergeant. That's right: the Turks had expelled his grandfather from Palestine and sent him to Lebanon, thinking he'd spied for the British. The grandfather lived for a few years near Beirut, which is how he got the nickname that later became his family name, a kind of commemoration of the incident. Some of the family had even stayed on there. One cousin had been rescued by the Mossad and smuggled into Israel in 1982, at the time of the invasion. Two others had refused to leave, and there was practically no contact with them. They were living well there among the Muslims, they owned a luxury suit factory and went once a month to the presidential palace in Damascus to custom-tailor suits for Assad. This Levanoni who was now serving with us was no less crazy than his family stories, a frustrated kibbutznik from the Jordan Valley, a real loner who never smiled. Every once in a while he'd glare at you, skewer you without warning or reason with this killer look. Even I was afraid of the guy and knew it wasn't a good idea to piss him off. He was the serial-killer type. Within seconds he would shut down, close off the outside world. Kind of robot-like. He'd give himself Israeli history lessons while we'd be watching *Die Hard* on video. What a weirdo! I mean, I'm pretty into what's good for the country and all that stuff, but why go to extremes? And he didn't put me to sleep with all kinds of bullshit talk, or heart-to-hearts, either. He'd say, "Good night," acting like he was polite or something. Who at the outpost ever said, "Good night"? This was going to be tough.

We came back to Beaufort in style: Eldad, that man of rosy dreams, brought seedlings from mini citrus trees and stuck them in a makeshift planter at the entrance to the submarine, promising the guys a private garden. River installed a metal bar across the doorway for pull-ups. He would hang there and everyone would punch his stomach muscles to strengthen his abs. Spitzer brought an electric keyboard. It was small and junky but it worked. A new toaster oven, too. Him and Zitlawi set up a little baking corner on the small cabinet. They would burn some *malawakh* dough, then smear it with a red concoction made from four different sauces and add slices of hard cheese. There was always a bowl of cherry tomatoes on hand as well. Emilio got a onetime appointment to collect all the care packages that had been trickling in for the Hanukkah holiday. They were sergeants now, so these rare treats made their way to them. Boxes of different sizes with colorful wrapping buried the dusty knapsacks in the narrow spaces between the beds. Emilio gathered them between his legs, pulled out a letter, and read it out loud to the guys: "Tami, age seven, from Bnei Zion." Zitlawi asked if seven was considered a minor. "To the soldier guarding us," she wrote, "Happy Hanukkah. I really hope you won't die in Lebanon and a missile won't fall on you." She didn't leave a phone number or include a photo. Just some junk food and a pair of underpants and a package of licorice made to look like snakes. And beef jerky, like there was no beef jerky in Lebanon. No Marlboros, though. Stingy.

That week we inaugurated our own movie theater, called

"Cinema Miriam and Shushu" in honor of Pinchuk's mother, who donated the equipment—she sent it from Chicago—and his parrot, who was killed by a mortar shell when we forgot him next to the doghouse outside. There's a chance it wasn't actually a mortar shell that got him but one of the dogs, who went crazy from the explosions and swallowed him. Bottom line is, he got wasted, so we honored him. Why not? Getting your name on that cinema was one fucking excellent honor because we had it running all day long, always some full-length flick showing. *Independence Day,* for example, was a blockbuster hit, a damn good movie about aliens who try to take over the earth. Afternoons were for episodes of *Xena: Warrior Princess,* and last of all, every night, at three in the morning, the big finale, the most popular showing that nobody missed: romance films. We had some good ones, lots of them, and we'd sit there watching, and there'd be refreshments and cocktails. The homemade house special was a concoction of mint leaves, verbena, and lemongrass with milk and honey and a chocolate-covered wafer all mixed together. It was out of this world.

For spiritual balance and purification of negative energy, Zitlawi brought incense and a candle from home. He was quick to set foot in the Signal Corps Company Club, Beaufort's improvised fighters' club, now that he was a sergeant and allowed to enter. The club was a dark and gloomy concrete shelter for the veterans of Beaufort, three walls of which were painted gray and the fourth light-colored with white splotches and a wobbly Golani Brigade Signal Corps insignia painted in watercolors. The center of the wall read: IN MEMORY OF OUR FRIENDS IN THE ALON SQUAD—THE BEST AND BRIGHTEST—WHO FELL IN THE HELICOPTER TRAGEDY, FEBRUARY 1997. Twenty names were inscribed there, the guys who had been on their way to Beaufort. On the opposite wall was the face of Sephardic chief rabbi Ovadiah Yosef pasted onto the body of a babe with tits the size of Cadillacs, and another of the miracle-working Rabbi Baba Barukh surrounded by twenty-five hot chicks each with a speech bubble coming out of her mouth with some wisecrack or saying stuck up there over the years by different squads. There was a Ping-Pong table, too, and a few Indian cloths to give the place the feeling of an ashram, and, lying on the floor, a guide to making cocktails. In that little kingdom, shirts weren't tucked into pants and there were no commanders to worry about. Everything was laid-back, people sprawled out on the floor on shabby pillows, smoking cigarettes. They called it the Council Room, home of the alternative leadership, the guys who got things done at the outpost. They would gather around a portable burner where Bayliss boiled spicy, bitter coffee and Zitlawi would crush ice cubes in plastic bags, hurling them over and over again at the list of names on the wall, with apologies to the Signal Corps. In those days we shitted coffee and our blood ran black from it.

On the fifth night after we'd arrived back at Beaufort, Zitlawi taught them how to hold a séance. He made everyone sit cross-legged, had them meditate, lit four scented candles on the floor—yellow, blue, green, red—and pulled out cloves and rosemary from a cloth army satchel. "Cloves are a good luck charm," he explained. "They evoke positive spirits." In the middle of the room he set down a rectangular board made of white plywood with letters of the alphabet burnt into it in a circle, and little symbols and numbers and the words "yes" and "no" and four stars in the corners, and on top of the board he placed a thin piece of wood carved in the shape of a heart with a hole in the center. "You should know that there's nothing simpler than getting advice from the souls of relatives and friends," he informed the room, then demonstrated how it worked by placing the three middle fingers of each hand on the wooden heart so that the dead could move his fingers to form words. He wasn't, in fact, a licensed medium, but he was experienced. "Is someone there?" he called out. "I am summoning the pure souls." You weren't allowed to be rude or insistent with a ghost, you had to say "thank you" and "excuse me" so they wouldn't get mad. "One little mistake and something terrible will happen here," he warned everyone, then asked Emilio to dribble lemon juice onto the candles in order to ward off evil guests. The guys thumped *darbuka* drums, then got to work. "Who do you want to call?" Zitlawi asked. Spitzer suggested Maimon. Who the hell was that? Maimon was a guy he'd been together with in training who'd gotten killed at the Reichan outpost. "What's Maimon going to be able to do for you? Who's interested in Maimon?" Eldad retorted. "How about Zohar?" Yes, yes, everyone agreed that Zohar was a great idea. "Which Zohar?" Emilio asked. "Which Zohar?! Which Zohar?! Zohar Argov, you retard! The king! The greatest Israeli singer of all times." However, Zitlawi put a damper on their excitement: "You're not allowed to summon suicides," he said.

"When did you make that one up?" Eldad and Pinchuk demanded to know.

"Are you calling me an amateur?" Zitlawi asked, clearly pissed off.

Bayliss suggested asking for Menachem Begin. "You jerk, Begin's still alive!" Zitlawi exclaimed, and everyone cracked up. What are you talking about, still alive? He's been dead for at least twenty years. What about Ziv? Ziv Farran? River vetoed the idea, said they should just go for Maimon and that's it. They concentrated, closed their eyes, positioned their hands, but Maimon did not show up that evening.

Shortly after midnight they came back to the submarine. Zitlawi asked Spitzer to play a lullaby on his electric piano, an old favorite like "Ammunition Hill." Spitzer refused. They started without him—Zitlawi on the drums, Boaz and River banging the metal beds, and even Bayliss sang along under his breath: *We descended to the trenches, returning to our holes/ Back to certain death, awaiting us like trolls.* Spitzer pulled out a wad of photocopied papers, which turned out to be the play *Henry V.* The curious among them took note, sat up, demanded answers. He explained he was going for an audition at the Beit Zvi Acting School, which surprised everyone. He would be performing in front of five judges, which was scary as hell, and only a choice few got in. He would have to do a piece from classical theater and then a song of his choice.

"Want a tip from your brother?" Zitlawi asked. "Only homos get in. Take that into consideration."

"What are you going to sing?" Emilio asked Spitzer.

"Homo songs," Zitlawi interjected.

"What the fuck, will you give him a little credit here?" River butted in. "The guy's making a stab at his dreams and his aspirations."

"Listen, bitch," Zitlawi said, clearly offended, "what are you trying to tell me? That I don't aspire to anything?"

"I'm not worried about the song," Spitzer said. "Shakespeare's my problem right now."

River grabbed the pages and started reading aloud, hesitant and unsure of himself. *"You have witchcraft in your lips, Kate: there is more eloquence in a sugar touch of them than in the tongues of the French council."*

"And they should sooner persuade Harry of England," Spitzer continued, having memorized the words, *"than a general petition of monarchs."*

"Come," River continued, getting carried away, *"your answer in broken music; for thy voice is music and thy English broken; therefore, queen of all, Katharine, break thy mind to me in broken English; wilt thou have me?"*

"What is this crap, for crying out loud?" Zitlawi wailed. "You guys have to cut it out now!" Spitzer suggested war, there was war in the play, too. He knelt in the narrow space between the beds, took hold of a broom, and, leaning on it, declaimed, full of pathos, *"O God of battles! Steel my soldiers' hearts; possess them not with fear."*

"It's a prayer," Bayliss said, cutting him off. "Make it softer."

River asked, "Does he win in the end?"

"And take from them now the sense of reckoning, if the opposed numbers pluck their hearts from them. Not to-day, O Lord, O, not to-day!" Spitzer carried on while everyone watched, at first amused, then gradually more curious. *"In peace there's nothing so becomes a man as modest stillness and humility: but when the blast of war blows in our ears, then imitate the action of the tiger; stiffen the sinews, summon up the blood, disguise fair nature with hard-favour'd rage; then lend the eye a terrible aspect; let pry through the portage of the head like the brass cannon; let the brow o'erwhelm it as fearfully as doth a galled rock o'erhang and jutty his confounded base, swill'd with the wild and wasteful ocean. Now set the teeth and stretch the nostril wide, hold hard the breath and bend up every spirit to his full height."* Spitzer paused, breathing heavily, then concluded. *"Fathers that, like so many Alexanders, have in these parts from morn till even fought and sheathed their swords for lack of argument: Dishonour not your mothers; now attest that those whom you call'd fathers did beget you!"*

"Wow!" Zitlawi shouted. "The guy took the prayer right out of my mouth! A war like that wouldn't be bad for us right now, a real good one to wake us all up. The old kind of war they used to have when people really knew how to make war. Why shouldn't we? If old English fairies in wigs could do it, then why wouldn't we be able to? Lions, tigers, foxes—a reason to wake up in the morning. Bring it on, I swear that's what I want. Freeze my blood. If I'm wounded in battle, just leave me there to fall into enemy hands. That's an order. Don't come back to get me, be men, for God's sake, all of you, be more manly than that. A little cruelty will only do us good around here. It'll give people hope. They don't give us a chance to fight, they don't give us any targets. They don't let us see the enemy. Anybody seen an enemy around here lately? I've never seen a single one. What's the matter, we don't have enough courage? We're not gung ho enough? Come on, Kate, do a little witchcraft on me and I'll free the Western Wall for you."

They all applauded him and whistled until they'd had enough of it and got ready for bed.

During that period of increased tension a new rule came into effect: half of the fighters at the outpost would sleep each night with their army boots on. The squads were divided into pairs so that every fighter could sleep one out of two nights barefoot. That Thursday night Bayliss and River, the two best friends in the unit, twin souls, nearly killed each other when they couldn't agree whose turn it would be to sleep without boots, giving their feet the chance to breathe the fresh mountain air. Before they even had the chance to count the days backward and make the simple calculation, civil war had broken out between them, their basest impulses exposed. Neither one was willing to get into bed with weights on his feet. "What's going on with you two?" Spitzer shouted at them, trying to separate them. "You think you're in the Holocaust or something? Look what you're arguing about! How low can you get?" But it was too late. They stopped speaking to each other.

At three in the morning, River and Zitlawi reported for duty at the Green guard post. River went off to be on his own, to settle in to the external post in the trench, the one farther away. He leaned on the sandbags and used his night-vision equipment to look for cats and boar in the bush. Martens and weasels were all over the place, too. When he got tired of that he started counting the girls he'd messed around with—anything not to fall asleep, or, worse yet, to get into a conversation with Zitlawi. The two hadn't spoken since the boot incident and there was no reason for them to that night. Because even River's innocence had its limits. He felt that everyone was trying to hide Zitlawi's regular meetings with Hodaya from him, which had gone on all through the months they were in training in the Golan Heights. Everyone avoided mentioning it to him; they all knew how Zitlawi would take almost every opportunity, even weeknights, to slip out of the base and hitch a ride—once he went as far as stealing an army van; that is to say, he borrowed one—to spend a few hours visiting her. On weekends they would take hikes together, falling asleep in the farmlands overlooking the Sea of Galilee or at the Umm-el-Kanatier lookout point or above Eagle Falls. Everyone knew and no one said a word so that River understood, convinced himself he was disgusted. Mostly, he refused to forgive.

Zitlawi moved the transmission dial to the Sayas network. "Good evening to the girls at Command headquarters. Allow me to entertain you," he said to Corporal Julie in the war room, "with a joke about the guy who meets a blonde in a bar and fucks her brains out without a condom. Have you heard this one? No? Well, the next day she phones him up, asks him if he has AIDS. 'No,' he says. 'Why?' 'Because I already got it once,' she tells him, 'and I don't want it again.' What? You don't think that's funny? Okay, how about this one: An ant is walking through the woods when she comes to a river. She thinks and thinks about how she's going to cross it when suddenly she sees an elephant. 'Elephant, elephant,' she says to him, 'be a man and get me across this river.' So he does. When they get to the other side she gets off his back and says, 'Thank you very much, elephant.' So the elephant says, 'What do you mean "thank you"? Take your clothes off.' What, that's not funny, either? You're just bullshitting me now, making fun of me. Who says ants can't talk? It's called personification. Anyway, this ant is from Tiberias, you've never seen the ants we got there."

Christ, what an arse, that Zitlawi. After that he tried drawing her into a conversation about drugs. That's right, he didn't understand that those transmissions are all recorded. "No, sweetheart, not me. I don't do drugs. Maybe just poppers. You know what poppers are? Let's say you're having fun with a guy and then you're getting close to orgasm and you take a whiff, it enhances the orgasm. Comes in a little bottle you get at sex shops. It's not a drug drug, just a kind of a drug. It's legal, I think. I use it mostly when I get high from tabs. I put the poppers on the tabs, you get it? What, you don't know about LSD tabs? Shit, you really missed the most important lectures at school, didn't you? It's this thing that makes you hallucinate, like, makes you laugh, smile. You'll be looking at the view and it'll start coming at you in waves, like *Matrix* or something, and you'll be trying to focus and it'll spaz up on you, these mini video games. It's great, really. And then there's ecstasy. You know what ecstasy does to you? They call it the love drug because it puts all your emotions in action; like, let's say we're sitting there, alone, feeling good, and I take one, then we feel like we're in love, I swear it, and we've got to touch each other and stuff, and it's such a great feeling that you can't understand, like someone loves you. It lasts for maybe two and a half hours, when you feel like you're loved. Want to try? You're not going to report me to the police or anything, are you?

"Holy shit, Julie, I've been staring at the same thing for an hour and a half already. Makes you crazy. Fucking hell, if they don't change channels soon I'm going to do something totally fucked up."

At thirty-four minutes past four their replacements still hadn't climbed the stairwell from the submarine. There's nothing more demoralizing than the feeling that your replacement on guard duty isn't going to show up. Someone may have woken the guy up but he's still asleep. Or, it happens that the war-room runner, who goes around every night with long guard-duty lists and shakes the next shift awake, thinks the guy is on his way but doesn't notice he isn't. There you are at your post, counting the minutes, understanding you've been had and realizing you won't have time to catch a short sleep before morning duty, and that throws you off for the whole day.

Four-thirty-five. Zion and Tom emerged from the secure area walking in a sleepy daze. They crossed the lot where the armored personnel carriers were parked, and the doghouse, where our predators were still sleeping. It was the silence of that seam between night and day. The only sound was the soft click of the generator. They approached the stairs, and then there was this popping noise, dull, from far off, followed by the sound of flight along with a slight whistling. It wasn't a mortar shell; they knew the sound of mortar shells. It was a missile, you could tell by the sound it made as it soared. But not a Sagger missile, either. Strange. The loudspeakers didn't announce a launch, or incoming missiles. Not even a siren. Zion and Tom froze in place because there was no way of knowing where it was going to hit and whether it was better to run forward or backward. And anyway, who could possibly run at all at four-thirty-five in the morning? A few more seconds passed, and then an enormous blast shook the hill, and earth flew into the air and sandbags burst open and sprayed in every direction. A gigantic flame burned fast and bright a few yards away from the hedgehog guard post at Green and turned quickly into thick smoke that covered everything. River, who had been thrown backward by the blast, picked himself up and marched right into the gray cloud, as usual without hesitation. Zitlawi's cries of pain led him through the trench, and when Zitlawi shouted, "I'm hit!" Tom and Zion followed on his trail, grabbing fire extinguishers and spraying like mad. I had just jumped out of bed and was putting on my helmet and vest. I raced outside.

We got down on our knees in the soot-covered guard post, choking on the smoke. He was lying there, wounded. Pieces of the destroyed transmitter, binoculars, and gun were lying nearby. Furman showed up with the doctor and two medics, who brought their equipment and a stretcher. They started an infusion and we pulled him out of there carefully. They stopped the blood flow, bandaged him up. I asked who was supposed to replace him at Green. Bayliss? Wake him up, get him up here, and have him bring a MAG 58 and two crates of ammo. We had to have a guard there. What was Zitlawi's condition? Bleeding like crazy, shrapnel in his gut. Maybe his lung was punctured, or his intestines. The doctor was consulting with himself, aloud. What was his condition, damn it? Just don't let him go into shock. He was okay. Furman got the battalion commander on the transmitter, explained what was happening—kind of hysterical, only faking a cool act—how there were hits, shit going down, even a "poppy." "I'm not a 'poppy,'" Zitlawi said, correcting him. What a man! He tried to shout so that Furman would hear. "I'm not a 'poppy,' I'm a 'flower,'" he said. Not a dead body but a live one, just wounded. Even the doctor said he was okay. He'd be all right, he just had to keep breathing. The smoke was starting to clear. Zitlawi tried to call me, I think, to tell me something. I came near. He seemed to get a syllable or two out but he was having trouble. I patted his forehead, held his hand. You're okay, man. We all worked like soldiers, real professionals.

The rescue chopper landed thirty minutes later. Levanoni ordered the kids to phone home, reassure the folks that everything was fine, no problem, let them know they're alive and well and that the bad news their folks would be hearing had nothing to do with our company. There was no reason to worry them and get a round of rumors started. The kids all stood in line for the phone. It was a weird sight: their eyes were full of tears but they'd altered their voices to sound happy. They told their parents there was no trouble and all was well. When asked why they sounded strange they answered that they'd been shouting more than usual, singing, and now they were hoarse. The report from the operating room in Haifa came an hour later. The doctors were encouraged. The kid was suffering from internal bleeding, but he was strong. Two hours later we were already back to routine, even ate lunch. Spitzer packed Zitlawi's belongings in his knapsack, folded his clothes and sheets, his towel. He tried to squeeze in Zitlawi's *darbuka* drum and his flip-flops. And his half-eaten bag of potato chips. Then the SLA guys came to repair the guard post. They mixed cement, poured concrete, added another layer of protection. Only Zitlawi's blood remained on the walls as it was, blackening the post. When the sun went down it was the first night of Hanukkah, but we didn't light candles. How the hell were we supposed to recite "Blessed are You who has kept us in life, sustained us, and enabled us to reach this joyous occasion," giving thanks for miracles and wonders at a time like that, only hours after he'd been wounded?

At eight-fifteen we gathered in the briefing room to watch the news. The reception was lousy, noisy. I was leaning on the wall, off to the side. The correspondent for military affairs was going on about something to do with army intelligence and how Hezbollah's strategy was to portray the Israeli army as fleeing, hurt, and trounced. Suddenly the newscaster cut in. "We are now authorized to release for publication," she said, "the name of another casualty of the Hezbollah attack today. He is Sergeant Tomer Zitlawi, nineteen years old, from Tiberias, an IDF fighter serving at Beaufort. May his memory be blessed." For a moment we all thought there was no connection to our Zitlawi. How could there be? We stood watching the screen, nobody could believe it. We'd sent him off alive and breathing, we'd given everything we had for him to live.

I looked at the kids, at their immobile faces, their open mouths, all of them staring off into space. The doctor, too. Spitzer kicked the television cabinet and left the room. I left, too, ran straight for the company commander's office. "Zitlawi's dead?! One of my soldiers is dead and the whole country knows it before us?" I shouted at Furman. I threw chairs around, pulled binders from shelves onto the floor, kicked the telephone. "Has the army lost its mind? That's really the end," I said. "These things destroy the soldiers, crush them. And as usual there's not going to be any retaliation, right? We're not going to march into Arnoun and fuck them good. We'll sit up here on the hill like bitches on the rag and take it all." Furman remained sitting, listening, restrained and expressionless. "I thought you'd grown up" was his response.

13

ZITLAWI WON'T BE ABLE TO FANTASIZE about heaven anymore. "Soldiers don't get sent to hell. Ever." That was something he would always say, and I would admit there was something encouraging in that.

You know this game that everyone plays, right? When a friend of theirs dies, I mean. Zitlawi won't say "Life is beautiful, but I'm *more* beautiful" anymore. He won't whisper to Spitzer "Come on, little monkey, let's make love all night long" anymore, and he won't hear us laughing anymore, and he won't kiss Spitzer on the lips so that Spitzer spits on the floor of the submarine, and he won't roll around with him between the beds anymore and hit his head on the metal legs.

Zitlawi won't make up new words for us anymore, he won't smoke Marlboros through his nose or in the rain, he won't eat the cream from Oreos and throw the cookies away or buy any more Mars bars from the canteen. He won't make fun of the fat non-commissioned education officer who thinks she's a hot babe. He won't shout to her anymore,

"Ilanit, you're like a five-shekel coin: worth something, but not much." He won't need Miri anymore, the ugly bitch he phones when he's sick of jerking off, and he certainly won't need to lie to her and swear that he loves her and call her "my pinecone" the way she insists. Zitlawi won't come in any girl's mouth or on her face. He'd never come on a girl's face but he'd planned to.

Zitlawi won't take Hodaya to a film in Tel Aviv anymore—he promised her he would—and he won't bring Spitzer's dad's jeep and let her drive in the sand at the Gaash beach, and he won't go down on her in the car, just as the sun sets. He said he would, but he didn't. He won't buy her a bathing suit, either, she'll continue to wait forever.

He won't mash our faces in the pitch-dark anymore trying to guess which one of us it is and always getting it right. He won't ask every night, "Hey, did they say about us on the news?" *Say* about us?! And we won't laugh at him anymore, and he won't get offended anymore and ask "Are you making fun of the way I talk?" And he won't stick his special words into every sentence anymore. Wild guy. An arse with a cigarette behind his ear. But as far as *chakras* are concerned, he's the man. Sunbeams came out of the guy and watched out for all of us.

Zitlawi won't play the only song he knew—"London Bridge is Falling Down"—on the electric piano anymore. He won't get tickets to be in the audience of the Dudu Topaz show and he won't get to see Tzvika Pick in the Caesarea amphitheater. He won't buy a black Mercedes, the convertible he swore he'd buy, with the black leather seats and the wooden dashboard and everything electric—the windows, the seats, the steering wheel, the girl. Because he won't be opening a stand in the *shuk* in Tiberias anymore, and he won't be selling watermelon seeds (roasted and unroasted) or olives—lots of them in green and purple, big and small, with and without pits, pickled in vinegar or brine or sugar for that matter. He wanted to so bad.

He won't wake up on Saturday afternoons anymore to the smell of his mother's *khamin* meat stew. He won't spy on his aunt taking a shower anymore. One sweet pussy, that aunt of his. Li-or-a. Sounds like someone who'd play the violin. I'll bet she really does. Now we can fantasize about her whenever we want because Zitlawi isn't around anymore, isn't anywhere anymore, and certainly not with us on ambushes. And when we bring an empty juice bottle to the submarine for pissing into he won't ask his question anymore: "Didn't your mother tell you my dick is too big for that?"

Zitlawi won't tell Herzl the homeless guy anymore "May you live long and prosperate." Holy shit, prosperate! What an idiot. But really good-hearted. He won't buy two *shwarmas* for Herzl anymore, one after the other, both smeared with hot sauce and swimming in pickles. He won't pick his nose at stoplights anymore, he won't run a red light anymore just when there's a traffic cop right behind him. Always had shitty luck, right up to the end. Maybe because of that he won't be an old-timer in the army, or a father, or a grandfather, and he won't learn to skydive. Did you know that fuckup wanted to be a paratrooper? It's true, he actually tried to get in, but he lasted about fifteen minutes. Lucky thing. Or maybe not.

Zitlawi won't know that we weren't even at his funeral because they wouldn't let us. Because it was impossible. They sent other squads from the brigade in our place so there'd be a lot of berets there, all crowded, and the parents would be proud.

Zitlawi won't anymore. That's the way the game is played. Then his name is erased from the duty roster. His bed becomes the submarine's storage area and you try not to talk too much about death. You get back to routine. But at night you fall asleep all curled up, a kind of tense anxiety that comes from the split second that awaits on the other side, when your eyes open and the news hits you again, suddenly, so that morning after morning you have to get used to it all once more. If only we didn't have to sleep, it would all have been much easier.

14

A NEW WORD: "EATEN." The eaten. Eatenness. That's it, in all its conjugations. It replaces the word "a-f-r-a-i-d," which was not allowed to be used at the outpost. Occasionally, an entire squad was eaten, temporarily or chronically. But mostly the eaten ones were individuals—one here, one there—who tried to hide their condition, to blend into the crowd. A guy who's eaten will never, ever say so—it's others who will point him out. If they recognize it.

There are identifying signs. The eaten, for example, wrote wills. At the time, whole squads went around with wills in their vests. They bequeathed the car to Mom, the stereo to River, the dog to their little brother. The eaten either talked about death obsessively or they refused to mention the word at all, going mental if someone turned the conversation in that direction. The eaten attached good luck charms from miracle-working rabbis to their vests or put laminated cards from the Lubavitcher Rebbe under their pillows or carried ancient Chinese coins in their pants pockets or had an angel tattooed on their stomachs or built little altars and danced around them with their buddies before going out under the open skies, to danger. They latched onto signs, to superstitions, to ancient and ornate Iraqi good luck sticks capped with gilded eagles, their expressions cruel and demented.

They kept their distance between one another when their pictures were taken so there would be room for the "death circles," the red ones used by the newspapers with the caption FINAL PHOTOGRAPH. A pornography of grieving. Naturally, they tried to disguise their eatenness as humor. They would laugh with embarrassment. They were only pretending to laugh, the eaten, because in fact they were dead serious. Even reading "The Traveler's Prayer" over the loudspeaker on the internal transmitter was a certain kind of eatenness.

This isn't the time to fall apart, I would tell them. It's a time to be strong. And they all made the effort, apart from a few exceptions. Emilio, for example, announced that he wasn't capable of taking part in guard duty anymore, wasn't willing to go up into a guard post. He became completely cold, blank, stayed away from people, listened to discs in Spanish alone in his bed, went to eat when everyone else had finished. I asked if he wanted to leave the outpost. He refused. "I'll never leave my friends here, just don't put me out in a guard post," he said. I told him that someone would have to guard, and that I myself had no intention of filling in for him for the next few months. He didn't respond. I tried to keep him moving as much as possible, give him tasks to carry out, keep him busy rearranging the storeroom, preparing the duty roster—you can call it a kind of occupational therapy—but there was no talking directly to him. We all tried to sound him out. He kept silent. That's how it is with the eaten: it's all stuck inside them, stuck, stuck, stuck, until suddenly it comes bursting out big-time. I figured the trick was to make it burst out. One night I asked him to guard the door of the computerized surveillance room. No one had ever guarded there: it didn't make any sense to guard it, there was no need for it, and no fear involved because there was no chance of anything dangerous happening. He made a face but agreed. A few minutes after he reported to his post I went up to join him, with two cups of hot tea. I stood next to him but kept quiet, on purpose. Just like that, waiting. He didn't say a word. I muttered at one point that Beaufort had become the pits, and then I fell silent for a long time. I watched him from the side and saw how the wheels in his brain were spinning wildly. Here and there he mumbled a word or two, which I ignored on purpose, as though I wasn't listening, not even paying attention to the fact that he existed. And then it happened.

"That's it! I can't take it anymore!" he shouted suddenly. "I can't take it anymore, I can't take it anymore! I don't get what's going on here: We've got wounded all over the place: at Karkum and Reichan, Ishiye, Galgalit. What the fuck are we doing here?" He fell silent again before erupting once more. "I'm sick of everyone around here pretending they don't think I'm *afraid*." There it was, the forbidden word. He'd managed to say it. "I'm sick of everyone trying to find solutions that are supposed to make it easier for me. I know it, I know all of you think I'm afraid. I know I *am* afraid. I don't need your pity: I'm afraid! But tell me this, please, I want to know: why the fuck are we in this hellhole anyway?"

I tried to explain that there was a certain operational logic to it, but he didn't give me the impression I'd convinced him or even that he was really listening. Then I tried moving the conversation to girls, to home, to his family in Argentina. "Tell me something, would you set me up with your sister, Ariella?" I asked. "I'm serious. Would you? If the answer's no, hey, it's no problem, forget I asked. Mistake! Never mind." I told him lots about myself, got carried away. About the breakup with Lila and trying to decide if I should get back together with her. "No communication," I told him. "Not a word between us. Well, I did go to her house once during the summer. To check. She wasn't there. She'd already been discharged from the army, went down to Eilat, was working in security at the airport there. She never even let me know." I told him about money troubles at home, too, things I never should have talked to him about, but I did. It was a long conversation. He talked a lot, too, kept grabbing my shirt, pulling at it while he talked. "Look what's going on here," he kept saying. It was clear to me the guy was not okay, that he was deeply warped. "You've got to get this fear of yours under control," I told him. "Because fear is catchy. If you don't manage it it'll spread like a plague through the outpost and knock everyone down, every last man. I've been afraid, too, a lot of times. I've almost even fallen apart, but I haven't let myself fall. Listen, Emilio, listen up: you can't be afraid." When I said good-bye he wouldn't let me go. He said, "Stay here with me," even when there was nothing more for us to say.

The next morning at breakfast I found it hard to look straight at him. I was a little embarrassed. I'm an officer, a lieutenant, and he's a kid, and I'd told him things I shouldn't have. He knew I thought the place was a hellhole, too, and how bad matters were between me and Lila. He knew so many personal things about me.

Three days later I saw in his eyes how fear can turn into complete apathy, another known phenomenon. In the beginning he'd been afraid to leave his bed in the secure area, but now we'd find him running around the parking area without a care, exposed. He would say, "Screw it, fuck Hezbollah." His eyes looked more worried than ever, but he didn't pick up on any of the stuff happening around him. Nothing interested him, he wasn't afraid of mortar shells or missiles. He started doing guard duty again.

In the meantime, I declared war on black humor. Humor can also be a vehicle for distress, and nearly the whole squad was guilty of using it. "Okay, man, go get wasted on guard duty. We'll meet in heaven, later. I'll be an hour and a half behind you getting wasted," they'd say and bust up laughing. They'd make jokes about dead people, too, and ghosts, and they'd make up songs. "I've been hearing wisecracks I don't like too well," I informed them. "Some people around here are sensitive and you don't notice it. It has a bad effect on them, weakens them. I don't like the mood around here. Get this bullshit out of your heads." I kept them busy, arranged sports instruction for them in the evenings, workouts, sprints, group competitions. I tried to keep them away from the radio and television, and if they did watch the news I wanted it to be in my presence.

"The surveillance point at the Galgalit outpost took a direct and painful hit," explained the correspondent for military affairs. The kids were mesmerized, didn't open their mouths. "The casualties are Captain Eyal Koppel, twenty-two, from Ashdod, and Staff Sergeant Yair Harari, twenty, from Tivon. Six other soldiers were wounded, one critically. The cabinet will hold a special session this evening to discuss the recent escalation along the Lebanese border. IDF chief of staff Lieutenant General Shaul Mofaz will present the cabinet ministers with plans for withdrawal from Lebanon, which is supposed to take place this coming July." The correspondent for political affairs added that "the government again today approved the seventh of July as the day for IDF withdrawal from Lebanon." The picture skipped and faded, the broadcast was cut short. When the commercials came on the kids' mouths watered. They learned about life on the outside, since this was their connection to the world.

And how about the reporter at the Kiryat Shaul cemetery: "The government is abandoning our best soldiers," a father shouted at one funeral. "Something needs to be done, this can't go on. The best among us are going like sheep to the slaughter. Poor soldiers, they're willing to fight but they can't even look after themselves and keep safe. After all, this isn't really a war. This is absurd and primitive! And how long is it going to last? The people of this country are frayed to the bone."

Then the faces of the fallen soldiers, handsome, with wide smiles, their last photos from their final tours of duty. And a street poll, a wandering microphone, parents relating that they no longer sleep at night.

One day someone hung on the wall of the dining hall an interview that had appeared in the paper with a paratrooper who had refused to attack. And not just any paratrooper but a member of the commando squad. His company commander had been killed, and his squad commander, and an Engineering Corps officer, and five others were wounded, sensitive weaponry had been stolen from them, including night-vision equipment and a transmitter, and he watched it all without storming, stayed behind a boulder, hiding. "I didn't want to just die for no good reason," he explained to the paper. That piece of shit said he was afraid, said it without any embarrassment. The thought that we didn't even need to be in Lebanon had overcome him right in the middle of battle.

Not only was this interview hanging next to the cabinet where our holy books were stored but SUPERSTAR! was scrawled on it with a thick marker. That same evening at a briefing, Furman called on the guy who hung it there to turn himself in. We all looked around to catch sight of who it was that had dared to take that traitor and raise him to the status of a hero and then prove to be a chicken himself and not admit to doing it. No one claimed responsibility. We waited five minutes. Furman asked if there was someone who thought the paratrooper had been right. From every corner of the room the men shouted, "He's scum!" "A guy who doesn't go on the attack is a loser!" The briefing ended. I yanked the interview from the wall and tore it up. Just before dumping the pieces into the garbage that night in the submarine, I had a look.

What the hell would cause a guy not to storm? What makes him lie there doing nothing while he watches his friends dodging bullets, shooting, and taking hits while his commander shouts "After me"? That evening and for every evening after that for the next few weeks, my eyes were constantly on the lookout, checking out the outpost soldiers in search of the ones who could possibly, at a crucial moment, fail to go on the attack with me. If something like that could happen in an elite paratrooper unit—a unit that takes itself very seriously and commands a lot of respect—then it could happen with us, too. I knew which ones would make the sacrifice for me: the arses, the punks, the stupid guys—they'd do it for sure. They may not be smart but they know what friendship is, that's just how they are. Take a guy like that and tell him, "Brother, it's good to bang your head against the wall," and he'll say, "Oh yeah? So let's do it," and he'll bang his head against the wall, he'll split his skull open if he needs to. If he loves you, then he'll take a bullet for you, too. That's how it is with the arses, the punks. The smart ones, on the other hand, they don't always stand behind you and charge when you need them to. The smart ones start wondering each time about the benefit of everything they do, asking themselves if this or that is worth it, or the cost is too high, or wanting to know who'd made the decision, and just generally being preoccupied with all kinds of questions that frankly had no connection to warfare. At the Sujud outpost there were paratroopers like that, so that when a terrorist penetrated and planted a flag there they didn't even chase after him, they let him escape. The chief of staff himself dismissed them, the unit never recovered from their humiliation. They walk down the street and everyone looks at them, the unit that had a flag planted on them. Yeah, that's what happens when you question too much.

Personally, I'm on the side of the fools. I always march at the front of the squad, knowing that the head is where the casualties are. And when, here and there, I'm afraid, I'm glad. I tell myself that it's healthy to be afraid, it makes you do everything by the book.

I put the pieces of the torn-up article on my blanket, I was riveted again. What a disgrace, leaving your friends in the lurch. He hadn't gone on the attack with them, he'd buried himself in a hole. And then, when he'd gotten home, instead of burying himself in a hole, he'd gone on the attack. Sent letters to politicians, put up a fight, wrote that they were sending us out to get killed without a second thought, but they weren't thinking about us, the fighters, or about managing this war. They didn't worry about those things, only about their own campaign wars.

What an arrogant bastard, the homo. What was he trying to say? At Sujud, the paper said, a wounded paratrooper had fought with his bare hands against an armed terrorist who'd infiltrated the outpost, a crazed six-foot-two Hezbollah operative wearing a camouflage uniform and planning to wipe them out with an M-72 LAW missile, a Kalashnikov machine gun, and two hand grenades. The *tznef*—that's what we called the young, green paratroopers—attacked the terrorist, nearly fell captive, but managed to wrestle the gorilla to the ground, get his weapons off him, and chase him away. For a day he was called a hero. Then the chief of staff dismissed him for failing to continue the chase. Why, in fact, hadn't he run after him? "A disgrace," the paper called it. "The soldier went back into his hole." I was hankering for a little action right there at the outpost to get morale up and remind all the soldiers why we were there. We'd come there to fight.

River entered carrying two cups of hot chocolate. When River brought hot chocolate you knew he wanted to talk. I tossed the torn pieces of newspaper in the garbage. "What do you think?" I asked him.

"I don't know," he answered.

"What's there to know?"

"It's complicated."

"It's not complicated at all, believe me, River. I read it. He admits it, the poor fuck. His mother's a leftist activist who drilled the stuff into his brain every weekend he was home. That's what happened. Here, excellent proof in the argument about whether home visits harm your ability to function."

"It's not that simple, Erez."

"Go on," I said, pressing him. "Let it out."

"How can you argue with his claim? He saw that everyone around him who stood up got shot. He understood it was a lost cause, hopeless, that he was in a completely impossible situation and at an insurmountable disadvantage. He knew that if he stuck his head out of his hiding place he was wasted, no doubt about it. What was he supposed to do, commit suicide? Aren't three casualties better than five or six? Was he supposed to die just to be able to say he'd engaged in combat?"

Levanoni jumped down from the upper bunk bed—we'd thought he was sleeping. He was wearing his killer eyes, and he grabbed River around the neck. "You're going rotten, Naor River," he told him, quiet but threatening. "Rotten apples need to be taken out of the barrel." We stood there, stunned; we couldn't understand what the lunatic wanted. River muttered, "Never mind," and ran out of the submarine. I shouted at Levanoni: "What are you, totally out of your fucking mind? Let the guy talk!" I raced after River, found him in the hallway by the stretchers, and pushed him up against the wall. His eyes were red and he had the look of a wounded puppy. "It might just be," he said, "that the IDF prefers its heroes dead."

"We're all here in the same boat," I told him. I was holding him tight, by the arms. "If something happens to me it'll happen to you, too, to all of us, and there won't be anyone to rescue you. If something happens to Bayliss, or to you, or to Spitzer, it's because one of us didn't lend him a hand. You all have to understand that if one of you doesn't go on the attack it'll be selling out your friends. It's no longer a matter of carrying out an operation or defending the settlements along Israel's northern border. It's between all of you, between friends."

River nodded, he understood. I went into the senior staff submarine with him and gathered everyone. "Listen up," I told them. "Engaging in combat, camaraderie, bravery, leadership, personal example. Remember those? That's what we're doing here, and that's what will protect us and how we'll protect each other. I'm giving you one more chance, your second and last—a parachute, an ejector seat that will float you right down out of here to a mediocre life at home. If there's someone here who feels he doesn't have the balls for it, who doesn't love the squad enough, who isn't prepared to sacrifice, let him speak up now. That sort of person doesn't need to be here."

No one made a sound. Silence, again.

"Who here thinks we don't need to be here?" I asked. "Raise your hand." Boaz and Itamar put their hands in the air. A few seconds later Emilio and Koka did, too. It was clear from his eyes that River was dying to raise his hand as well but he was afraid of disappointing me, again, in front of everyone. "So why are you here?" I asked. They said nothing. "Answer me!" I shouted.

"We're being betrayed by Israel," Boaz erupted, agitated. "We're here and nobody could care less about getting us radiators when we're freezing from the cold, and nobody gives a shit about getting supplies here on time or refilling the empty water tanks or giving us a lift when we're standing at an intersection in Kiryat Shmona trying to get home. So what are we doing it for? Nobody in Israel respects us anymore."

"Are you listening to yourself, you big fucking whiner?" I asked, pouncing. I pulled out my Zionist speech about the eyes trained on Nabatiye and the back guarding Metullah: I didn't have any better ideas. "There's a well-known rule of war," I explained. "The line of contact can never be broken. If there's a chain of people and I run at them, they'll repel me the first time, maybe the second, too. But eventually I'll break through. If two of us run at them, then one will manage to jump over their heads. The IDF set up the security zone to ensure that if a terrorist gets past the first outpost he'll run into the second, and if he gets past that one he'll get snagged on the third. The point is that he'll never make it to the border fence itself. And it's a fact that thanks to the security zone there haven't been any infiltrations over the border. Don't listen to a lot of nonsense. The IDF thinks it's crucial for us to be here and so we'll stay."

"Cut the officer-talk now," River interrupted. "You're one of us. Put your hand on your heart and, as a citizen of Israel, you tell me that you believe we should be here."

"Forget it," I said, silencing him. "There's an army order and we have to carry it out."

As a soldier I'd never dared to ask what we were doing in Lebanon. My older brothers, who were in Lebanon before me, never asked. Neither did my father. When I was a common soldier no one questioned the authority of their commanding officers because the prevailing style was completely different. Suddenly, over the last two months, everyone was arguing and asking questions that undermined authority.

"What's the purpose?" they would ask. Every time they were sent outside from under the reinforced concrete roof they said, "You want to send us to our deaths?" I'll admit, it wasn't easy to command soldiers during this wave of funerals and thirty mortar shells a day. That's no way to wage a war. Yes, it was all the fault of that band of old women who didn't understand shit about the army. They were the ones responsible for creating the fucked-up situation in the country. Them and Carmela Menashe from Israel Radio. And the pictures broadcast on television, which weakened morale: of weeping soldiers, of fighters telling everyone they were targets, close-ups of wounded soldiers bleeding while getting medical attention after a battle. The IDF was guilty, too. Guilty for not carrying out a deadly retaliation when the division commander, Brigadier General Erez Gerstein, was killed. None of the soldiers could believe it. "No retaliation?" they asked. "They murder the biggest hero in the IDF, they humiliate us, and we don't even react? We're not even going to raze some village?" All these things plus the public debate were harming our ability to engage in combat. There was frustration hitting us from every angle. It killed the kids to hear on the radio that people didn't believe in what they were doing. Yes, something had changed, had seeped in, you could feel it. Suddenly people in your neighborhood were shouting, "Sucker! You're getting wasted in Lebanon for nothing!" They didn't give you the respect they'd given you once.

And the fear that your friend wouldn't go on the attack for you—it wasn't only me who was worried about the possibility that there were frightened soldiers hiding among us. All of them were suspicious of each other, of their comrades. I actually saw it in their eyes.

And how were they supposed to feel when a caricature of Beaufort appeared in the weekend papers, with guard posts manned by dogs instead of soldiers? That happened, too, right after Zitlawi died. Bayliss saw the picture, held his head in his hands, and ran from room to room shouting, "What is this?! What is this?!" They all walked around completely in the dumps. They came to me wanting answers—I was the establishment, as far as they were concerned—but I could give them no explanation.

15

ONE MORNING WE RECEIVED A SHIPMENT of mannequins. Twenty-five of them, made of wax, the kind you see in store windows with little noses and big ears and a masculine face and broad chest and open mouth, with eyelashes and scalps painted black. They had nice physiques and flexible hands that could turn three hundred and sixty degrees. The only thing missing was their privates. They were unloaded from a military equipment truck driven by a Lebanese, one of our regulars, a guy named Kabuk.

We asked Kabuk, "What are they bringing us these big dolls for now? We haven't heard anything about it from Command."

"What do I know?" he answered, claiming he was only the messenger. He shrugged as if he didn't have a clue. But Kabuk always had a clue, he was always up-to-date on everything. When pressed, he winked and told us, "It's a 'thickening procedure,' but make sure that stays between us, okay?"

"What's a 'thickening procedure'?" I wanted to know.

"It's new, comes from way up high in Command. You

thicken your guard posts," he explained in a whisper. "A mannequin in every guard post, every trench. Confuse those sons of bitches. Someone'll tell you how it's done. Don't worry, the order's on its way."

We laid them out on the tables in the dining hall and dressed them in uniforms, complete with vests, helmets, dog tags—the works. We didn't have enough boots, though, so we gave them our own flip-flops, which we didn't need anyway. When we'd finished making soldiers out of them we dispatched them everywhere. We put them where they'd stick out and the enemy could see them. Every few hours we'd move their arms so the enemy wouldn't catch on. During the day they'd guard from inside the hedgehogs while the real soldiers hid behind sandbags in the trenches—one would watch with a pair of binoculars, scanning the sector, while the other patrolled. At night it was the real soldiers who guarded from inside the hedgehogs with the mannequins between the sandbags. For the time being, that was procedure. Furman would walk around checking to make sure everything was carried out properly, that the arm positions were shifted and the heads moved. We took good care of them, made sure they weren't cold. We gave them names—men's names, African-American names. We wrote their names on their vests and helmets so we could keep them straight since they were all from the same mold: same face, same overly broad shoulders. The kids stood farther back or off to the side on guard duty, watching, better protected. If a missile fell they'd be injured by the blast, but that's all; the mannequins would absorb the direct hits. That was the logic.

From the start, the whole business with the new guys was conducted in English. There were conversations late into the night, pre-duty briefings. The kids would entertain them, get advice from them, bring food for them, make them salute officers and sergeants so they knew who to give respect to, who was senior. They volunteered them for operations, saddled them with heavy loads, sent them on errands. They carried them from place to place so they wouldn't get bored from staring at the same view all the time. Everywhere you looked you'd see a soldier walking around holding a big doll like it was nothing, normal. They'd bring them to bed at night in the submarine, fall asleep with their arms around Snoop Dogg or Magic Brown or both of them together.

Beaufort in those days turned into something different, entrenched. Under the code name *"Shawshank Redemption,"* Christian Lebanese laborers—collaborators from the surrounding villages—took part in a fortification process the likes of which there had never been, in an attempt at dealing with the new missile threat. Fifty cement trucks climbed the hill to the outpost, construction crews erected walls, concrete roofs were strengthened, huge nets were stretched above the guard posts so that incoming missiles would be detonated from contact with the nets and explode in the air rather than on the ground, where they would do more damage. The laborers built and poured and excavated, giant walls of concrete sprang up as though we were never leaving. Secret electronic scrambling devices were installed as well. "Ten million dollars are being spent to reinforce the outposts," Furman informed us. Things went on like that for a month. We already knew that the innovations, the treats, always arrived too late.

16

AND THEN THE MILLENNIUM ARRIVED, on a Friday night. At the exact moment, the first second of the first day of the first month of the year 2000, I was in the kitchen of the Beaufort outpost baking a lemon cake. Chili was sitting next to me giving advice and scarfing down a cheese lasagna while working on a crossword puzzle. "The star of *Gone With the Wind,* eleven letters. What are you talking about, 'Sharon Stone'!? Are you crazy? You're as stupid as a Lebanese whore! Next. The code name the Americans gave to the bombing of Hiroshima. Nagasaki? I don't think so. That's the other city they bombed." Dave dashed in just then, called us, told us not to miss the fireworks from the celebrations at Tibnit, which we did—by choice—and in the end, nothing actually happened at that moment. The gates of heaven did not open and did not spit cascades of fire, the weather didn't go bonkers, the sea didn't rise and flood, the Litani River didn't dry up. Even Hezbollah didn't attack. It was a totally boring moment, the kind that'll be forgotten. When my grandchildren ask about it I won't be able to tell them "I was with Grandma," or "I was dead drunk, drunk with joy," or "I was engaged in momentous events." I heard the kids gathering at the entrance to the secure area, counting backward. Seven, six, five. A shortwave radio was tuned in to a broadcast from Tel Aviv. The broadcaster was shrieking like she was having a fucking orgasm, counting down with people at a big party at the Tel Aviv port where everyone was shouting, "Four, three, two!" I wondered what Lila was doing at that moment. No way to know. I shouldn't have been thinking about it, about her. Then again... maybe she was just coming, at that very moment, in perfect synchronization. Some German guy giving it to her in a five-star hotel. Or a security guard from the airport. I couldn't believe she wasn't with me. "One, zero," everyone was whistling, cheering. Where's Oshri? I thought. I'd have planted a big fat one right on his lips if he'd been there. I even missed his scent. And where was Zitlawi? He would have pulled out a bottle of whiskey from who knows where and gotten everyone going. I put the baking tin in the oven, filled a canteen with strong tea soaked in mountains of sugar, and went out to tour the guard posts.

Two mannequins and Spitzer were guarding Green. I could hear him in the dark practicing *Henry V* inside the hedgehog. *"If we are mark'd to die, we are enow to do our country loss; and if to live, the fewer men, the greater share of honor."* I went in. If he hadn't been blue with cold he would have blushed with embarrassment. I stood next to him, asked him to go on. I told him it was actually interesting, I enjoyed it. *"O, do not wish one more,"* he mumbled, by heart, not glancing at the pages poking from his pants pocket. *"He which hath no stomach to this fight, let him depart; his passport shall be made and crowns for convoy put into his purse: we would not die in that man's company that fears his fellowship to die with us."*

"War, huh?" I said. "There's nothing like a show about war."

"We few, we happy few, we band of brothers," he said, raising his voice as he gained confidence and put on a real performance. *"For he to-day that sheds his blood with me shall be my brother; be he ne'er so vile, this day shall gentle his condition: And gentlemen in England now a-bed shall think themselves accursed they were not here, and hold their manhoods cheap whiles any speaks that fought with us upon Saint Crispin's day."*

"You think they'll make a show about us one day?" I asked.

"A play?" he said, correcting me. "No, I don't think so."

"No? Really? What about Goni, the guy who conquered Beaufort? He was a real hero, every kid knows about him. Don't you think he'd be great for a Hollywood flick?"

"No, I don't," Spitzer answered.

He drank his tea. "They weren't even supposed to conquer this hill, they didn't mean to. Did you know that?" he asked me. "To this very day nobody knows how it happened that they conquered Beaufort. When the war broke out it was a mistake—there was no military significance in conquering Beaufort. IDF convoys had already surrounded the whole range of hills on the first morning of the war and our troops were much deeper in Lebanese territory, on their way to Beirut. They'd left Beaufort behind and the fortress itself didn't bother anyone. It was just a little enclave. The terrorists weren't firing from there, they'd have taken off, disappeared within a day or two out of boredom, since nothing was happening here. Central Command gave the order to call off the operation, told them not to attack, but the order got lost on the way, fell between the cracks somewhere between Command and division officers: someone forgot to pass it on. So the reconnaissance unit came up here. On foot."

"What the fuck are you talking about?" I asked, getting mad. "Who put this bullshit in your head? You're profaning the dead."

"No really, it's the truth," he said. "It was a totally senseless battle, Goni's battle. The next morning Ariel Sharon arrived—he was minister of defense then—and stood right here facing the guard post, on what's known as French Hill, wearing a windbreaker, with a whole entourage and a TV crew. There were still puddles of blood on the ground. He proclaimed it as a historical achievement, boasted about how they'd taken the fortress so smoothly, without any casualties or wounded. One of the young soldiers, a guy named Tamir, corrected him. 'Six men were killed,' he said. 'I saw them, I helped evacuate them. The head of the reconnaissance unit was killed.' But the minister of defense said, 'I think you are mistaken. No one was wounded here. You've had a difficult night, I believe you don't really understand what happened here.' Menachem Begin, the prime minister at the time, didn't get it, either. He was all happy about the air on the mountaintops, proclaimed the place 'godlike' and asked if the terrorists had machine guns."

"Go on, get off it," I said. "You're totally fucking wrong, you pussy."

He persisted. "The radio reported no injuries. They said it was a case of 'supreme heroism and daring enterprise' and that there were no casualties. But in the war room and at Command headquarters nobody could understand how it was that the reconnaissance unit had taken control of Beaufort against orders."

"Somebody's been fucking with you, man, they've been telling you stories."

"Begin was overheard talking to his wife on the phone when the war broke out, told her it would all be over in two days."

"For shit's sake, Spitzer, cut it out."

We were quiet for a few seconds, both of us smiling but for different reasons. "For your information," he said, "I've never had a friend that I loved like Zitlawi. And I won't ever again. I spend hours up here every night and the only thing I can think about all the time is him, nothing else. I try to picture his last few seconds up here, what exactly they were like. I stand here reciting Shakespeare, waiting for him to make fun of me. For him to call me a sperm-sucking piece of shit and whisper in my ear: 'When you win an Oscar you say a big thank-you to Zitlawi into the microphone and tell everybody, "This is for the guy who made me a great actor and loved me to death," and if you don't, I'm going to open up a second hole in your ass.' "

They were that good friends? Even I had no idea.

"Tell me a secret," I said. "Toss me a bone. Something top-secret and sensitive, something personal that nobody else knows about."

He thought, took his time, tried to dodge the question. I wouldn't let him off the hook. I wanted him to feel close to me. "Lana," he said. "She makes me listen to The Cranberries whenever we do it. Exclusively, The Cranberries. That's my only secret, I think."

"Always?" I asked.

"Fifth song on the first disc. Always. She can't do it without it. Same song playing over and over again."

"What the fuck! Makes it hard to concentrate," I said, dead serious. "She's really warped. I mean, cute."

"I'm willing to listen to her Cranberries until I'm a hundred," Spitzer said, all smiles.

River was guarding in the hedgehog guard booth at Blue. "Happy Millennium," I said when I saw him. I shook his hand, held on for a while. At Beaufort we didn't have the luxury of staying mad at someone, especially on a holiday. "Everything okay between us?" I asked him. He nodded. "I'm sending you guys home to squeeze some quality time out of mom next week," I informed him.

"The Sons-Shall-Return-to-Their-Borders Procedure," he said with a grin.

"River, you personally have two extra missions. I think both are waiting for you on the Golan Heights."

"Missions?" he asked, pretending not to know what I was talking about.

"First, the Reconciliation Mission, otherwise known by its code name, 'Bayliss's Boots.' You've got to make up with him. That's an order. It's not open for discussion. Second, the Holy Vagina Mission, whose code name is 'River Grows Up and Goes to Talk to the Girl Who Has Turned His Brain to Mush for an Entire Year.' "

In the introduction to the basic orders of our division—the black Ten Commandments—there was one iron rule that everyone swore to wholeheartedly: never, ever, covet the bereaved girlfriend of a friend who's gotten wasted. Do not drool over her, do not seduce her, do not cop a feel under her shirt. She'll undress when it's not even warm out, she'll ply you with hot coffee, she'll stroke you all over, and you will be seduced. But you will be strong, you will not cheat on your brother. When a fighter goes into battle he must be tranquil and lucid, must focus on the aims without suspecting that if, God forbid, he bites it, his friends will take turns doing his girl. If this kind of suspicion takes hold of him, if he can't be sure they won't make her forget him, he won't be worth shit in battle. Shlomo Artzi screwed a girl like that who was in mourning for her boyfriend and wrote a song about it. That just tore me up when I learned about it. How could he? But that Shlomo, he's a king, so this once I forgave the unforgivable. It made me feel better to know that he tortured himself over it, never got this friend of his out of his head: the guy would visit him in his dreams, crying and afraid and getting hit by a bullet and dying. Shlomo realized what a mistake it was. With us, it couldn't happen. But in River's case, Hodaya was his from the first moment, back at Rabbi Elipaz's cowshed in the Golan Heights. Old Zitlawi had bypassed him, gotten in there first and staked out the territory. River had to go to her.

"No way," he said.

I wasn't giving in. "Somebody has to tell her about Zitlawi," I told him. "She may not know. Or maybe she does—saw it on television, if they even let religious girls watch TV—and hasn't got anybody to talk about it with or anybody she can lean on, and she's a complete mess."

River dismissed the idea.

"I'm giving you three days from the time we land in Israel," I informed him. "If you don't do it, I'm going there myself."

He had a sad smile on his face, or maybe it was resignation. It was hard to tell. The flames that blazed in the eyes of the River I loved were not there. "What's happened to us?" I asked him. "Why have you suddenly given up? You should have been an officer by now, not wasting your time here as a common soldier. What's going on with you? Is it fear that's been eating you up inside and smashing your faith to bits? Is that it?"

"I'm not afraid of the fear," he said. "On the contrary, Erez: the best thing is not to be afraid of the fear."

"Good," I said. "Excellent. Don't be afraid of the fear."

"I'm not afraid to give in sometimes, too," he continued. "It's not going to turn me into a mediocre individual if I give in on occasion. You, either."

"Yes it will," I responded. "And you'll be pissed off with yourself. You won't forgive yourself for years."

Meanwhile, up in White, Emilio was crying. That's what he can tell his grandkids about the first hour of the new millennium: that he spent it crying. He didn't stop, either. It came in waves, came and went, all the way to morning. That's the way his video recorder—which was once his alone, until it became a tour guide for Lana—seared him into all of our memories that morning, biting his lips as if trying to stop, and looking exhausted.

Come on, that's enough. Enough already. Stop filming, Spitzer. Leave me alone. Isn't it enough already that you brought us bad luck with all your bullshit? You and Zitlawi. You shouldn't have started with all this filming, believe me. Now look what's happened to us, everything's gone sour. No, I'm not crying. Come on, already, leave me alone. All of you. It's enough.

Do you feel it, Spitzer? Shut up a minute, turn the camera off, and try to feel it. I'm telling you, I feel it, in the air. Something bad's about to happen. You'd think we've had enough bad stuff already, but no. It's going to get worse. Much. I was beginning to think the bad shit was behind us, but now I don't think so anymore. Do you feel it? My heart's already booming on its own, like exploding missiles. All our drills and exercises aren't worth shit. A big hoax. How can I possibly dodge a missile that takes two and a half seconds to reach here? Why am I standing here guarding right now? I can feel it coming. I'm done for, believe me. Done for.

Enough.

17

WHAT ARE YOU GOING TO DO when you get home? First thing for me: beach. I need to smell the beach, stop there on the way home just to breathe. Next: a bath. A six-hour bath. And then, cruising in the car. Man, you've got to see how many virgins there are walking around this country. Soft, smooth skin, belly shirts, huge tits full of milk—I'd go wild if I weren't so shy. Just drive around for an hour, slip on down to the highway without even planning to, tear it up, alone, quiet music on the radio, no plans, no navigating, no map, going places there's no chance of knowing how to get out of. End of the world. To think. To float. That's what I feel like doing. And I'll blow my money on a strawberry-banana milk shake and lots of beer, get drunk. Really drunk, blind drunk, and then, when my head clears, I'll spend some quality time with my sister, Vicky, make sure none of the guys in the neighborhood have been groping her, God forbid. Elias and Motke, friends from the street, they'll get their hands on a jeep and a camping stove and we'll check out the desert, go crazy, act like juvenile delinquents, nutcases, the kind you'd never in your life trust for a second.

* * *

Good evening. Outpost briefing. New rule: no removing of boots, by order. Not even every two days, or every week for that matter. No discussion. Maybe just three minutes to air the feet, a quickie, in the secure area—but no more than that. No showers, either. From this minute on the showers will be locked shut. They're too dangerous, not a place you can take off your vest and helmet. Bathe at home. Anyway, it's risky to waste the water in the emptying tanks since there's no way of knowing when the supply trucks will come to refill them. In emergency situations you can rinse off in the room behind the kitchen over the drainage hole using gallon jugs, but only with special permission and under the supervision of Furman. That's exclusively for life-and-death rinsing. And, since the sewage system is blocked and the shit has overflowed onto the toilet floors, a sign has been posted saying BY ORDER: CLOSED FOR REPAIRS until a combat plumbing unit can be brought in to fix it. In the meantime we're going to shit into our helmets lined with plastic bags. There's an emergency supply of shit bags, enough for everybody. Anybody who wants to can take antidiarrhea pills to stop you up.

So far is everything clear? Okay. Intelligence update: they have a sharpshooter. That's to say, they have a terrorist cell with an antitank missile sharpshooter. The real thing, imported from Russia. He never misses. He gets IDF guard posts in his sights and hits the bull's-eye every time. Yeah, it's insane, inhuman, Olympian, to have a one hundred percent record, like shooting with a pistol from five hundred yards and hitting somebody between the eyes. What are the chances of that? By the time the fourth missile hit we wised up. The intelligence officers put the maps on the table and figured out their moves: They killed our guys at Rotem in the western sector, then Galgalit, then here at Beaufort and at Dlaat, moving straight across the security zone, very neat, from west to east, outpost to outpost. The next few addresses are already prepared for attack: Sujud, Ishiye, Reichan. They're next in line, if the pattern holds. And what's going to happen when they finish? Will they start a new round? From beginning to end? From end to beginning? In the same order? They're no dummies, Hezbollah. It took them a little while, in the end they figured out that the IDF is barely letting its soldiers stick a big toe out of the outposts, so if you want to mow a few down you've got to get inside. And that's exactly what they're doing. Command has issued orders effective immediately to change operational procedures, security methods, and sentry duty. Note that in the event of mortar shells being fired, fighters are now to close all openings of the hedgehog. On the other hand, if it's missiles being fired, then you need to leave the door open so you can get out and into the trench, take a step backward, and hide behind the concrete walls. You've got to keep your eyes peeled on the sky at all times, use a minimum of lights, never raise your voice. We're talking total concentration. And sprint every time you're outside the secure area even for a second. That's all for now.

A heavy snow, soft and airy and pleasant, covered our hill. It fell slowly, hovering in the air. Long rows of bare, skeletal apple trees stood draped in white in the valley below us, while black and brown cows sank into the ice on the slopes, pawing at the ground but not finding a single speck of green. Everything looked friendlier, with little Arabs building fat *kaffiyeh*-wearing snowmen and the old lady in Arnoun opening the red door to her black stone cottage and stepping out into the alley wrapped in a *galabia* and leaning on her cane. Her eyes peered out from between layers of cloth; she'd spent seventy winters there, maybe more, but I'm sure every year it managed to fascinate her, make her head spin all over again. At the pastoral little kiosk by the Litani River, under the Khardaleh bridge where the oleander stood frozen, members of the UN forces were wrestling like kids, cracking up with laughter, really happy. It's more beautiful there than our own Hatzbani River, I swear it, more beautiful than anywhere else in the world. You can be really happy there until nightfall, because that's when a cold wind makes you moody and depressed. And lonely. Apparently even the old lady. The faraway clusters of light, from home, tickle your imagination and torture you.

Twenty minutes after the winter sun had set on the second day of the first week of the new millennium, a Yasur chopper landed and took us back to Israel. By nine-thirty we—me and my squad and Levanoni—were already at Grandma's, a pub in the town of Katzrin in the Golan Heights. It's a small place, intimate, an old Syrian house, and it's kosher, closed on the Sabbath. We were there for group-building, a kind of off-the-base social activity that was supposed to make us closer. We ate grilled feta cheese sandwiches and drank beer. The whole thing felt pretty forced and strange. We were dying to laugh but couldn't find anything or anyone to laugh at. We spread out across the room: Boaz and Zion tried entertaining the waitresses, Tom took care of the background music on the stereo system over the bar, Spitzer sat at the piano, attempting to keep up with the music. Bayliss was swallowed up by the locals, burly *moshavnik* types in old-style sandals and kibbutz girls with wet hair wearing fleece jackets and dripping with the scent of sweet bath oils. River sat in thoughtful silence, observing us all from the corner of the room. Emilio told him that the fight with Bayliss was a shame. "One of you will suddenly get wasted," he said, "and the other one will feel so bad for not making up that he'll kill himself over it." I leaned over to Emilio and whispered into his ear: "Listen up, buddy. From this moment, no more talk about death, no more whining, no more hysterics. Enough of this bullshit. It just brings us all bad luck and puts us in a shitty mood." Emilio fell silent. River and Koka didn't say anything, either. They were dying to get out of there and go home, praying the evening would end, but they knew it wouldn't be nice to just get up and leave for no good reason.

I went to the bar for a refill. "Can I talk to you for a minute outside?" some girl whispered into my ear. She was small and dark-skinned, with big, puffy, heart-shaped lips and no tits to speak of. I said, "What?" and she persisted: "I wanted to talk to you for a minute outside."

"What about?"

"Are you afraid?" she asked.

So I agreed to step outside with her. When the door slammed behind us she offered me her hand and pulled me along, leading the way. Then she stopped and stood facing me in the parking lot, fixing me with a gaze that said it all.

"So?" I asked.

"Do you have a girlfriend?"

"Yeah," I answered. I don't know why. I still felt like I did.

"Ah," she said. Truth is, she looked the opposite of disappointed. This was confusing.

"Was that your question? That's it?" I asked.

"No," she said.

"It's cold out here. Let's go back inside."

"How about my car?" she asked. "It's parked over there."

"Okay," I said.

We got inside. She sat at the wheel, I sat next to her. She closed the door, pushed the seat backward, and brought her lips close to mine. "Excuse me," she said, and started kissing me. At first the kisses were slow and gentle and then they weren't anymore, and she started opening the belt of my uniform and the buttons on my shirt. She stroked my stomach, it was hot. She drew her hand across my pants.

"How long's it been since he came?" she asked.

Whoa. I was totally disgusted all of a sudden. I grimaced. You slut, you reject, why are you talking about my dick in the third person? What do you want? You want it, you want it here in the car? You're sick in the head! And with my soldiers a few feet away, they can come out at any minute. Who are you, anyway? You don't know me, but the thought that I have a girlfriend makes you all horny, doesn't it? What a nymphomaniac! I opened the door, said, "This isn't for me," and got out of the car. I wasn't even polite about it. On the way back inside to my kids I buttoned myself back into shape, but in the few quiet seconds it took to reach the door I understood that I should be worried—very—because what I'd just done was totally fucked up. It was unnatural behavior. If anyone found out about it they would be disgusted by me, not her. What was going on with me? Was I a homo? Why didn't she make me horny? If I'd had, say, in theory, a good reason not to fuck her, hadn't wanted to "duplicate the key inside her," as Zitlawi called it, then at the very least I should have said, "Baby, you're more than welcome to suck me." I should have pulled her panties down to her feet in one swift motion and sucked the living daylights out of her clit. There were lots of things I should have done, but I didn't even have a hard-on. Now, that's sick. I was tired and didn't care about anything at all when I got out of there. I felt extinguished, and wondered if all of me wasn't still bound to Lila, who'd probably been bound to somebody else for ages already.

Inside I found Levanoni holding forth with everybody gathered around him. "The fear of humiliation is greater than the fear of death," he was saying, explaining his motto and why it was suitable for every situation. What humiliation? The humiliation of the soldier who is afraid, has a panic attack, fails his mission, lets his friends down. And also the humiliation of the wimpy image people are forming of us, all of us, as long as we sit up there on the receiving end, never going out on operations or doing anything useful at all or having a chance to succeed at anything, at killing terrorists. He told them we were good at spouting slogans—"We won't rest until we've made sure they're dead," or "That which does not kill you, strengthens you; that which kills you, strengthens your mother," or "The pencil pusher's prick is a combat soldier, the combat soldier's prick is a pencil pusher"—but I didn't like his slogan about humiliation and I was hearing it at totally the wrong moment. "Get over here, fast," I signaled to him. Levanoni left the guys and followed me to the toilets. "You'd better shut your mouth, I'm warning you," I told him. "One more time I hear something I don't like, I'm going to push your head into the toilet ten times or so."

"You didn't like what I was saying?" he asked in a cynical tone, his eyes squinting at me and his face mocking me. "I'm turning them into fighters. You got a problem with that?"

Without a second of forethought my hands flew forward and pushed him hard in the chest, smashing him into the door. He was all fired up in no time, crazed, and flushed with hatred, a real hothead, the guy, no less than me. A wild beast. But he bit his lips, threw a punch to the air, and stopped himself. "I'd finish you off right here, Erez, I swear it," he whispered. "But I'm not stupid like you. I'm not getting myself tossed in jail." And before I could even digest this or react, he was out the door, back into the main room, while I stayed behind alone, not knowing what to do with myself. Maybe kick the door, maybe ram an elbow into the window or a wall. I'm telling you, I felt completely powerless. I didn't know what was happening to me. I felt like a pear whose insides have been gutted by a worm and there's nothing left of it, but it refuses to fall from the tree and doesn't even understand why. What was happening to me?

Early the next morning, in his older brother's little Fiat,

River made his way back up to the Golan Heights from a suburb of Tel Aviv. He went to the winter pool, Bajurya. Incredible, but a year had passed since they'd stripped there and chased after the ATV, waving their hands like wounded animals and cursing like Palestinian cops. Even the road itself had grown older, its three layers of asphalt were cracked and graying, but at least the smell was the same, a healthy green, and the ground was wet just like back then, when he'd first seen Hodaya's shy smile and stolen her bicycle, and her blonde hair was so smooth that he wanted to reach out and caress it, even then, and ever since he'd tried endlessly to recall the contours of her face, and the smell, and that brief moment when her eyes were scrutinizing him. He didn't know if they'd taken him all in, that is to say, what exactly they saw and how much they focused in on any one part of him, or what exactly they thought of him. It was driving him crazy not to know. Now, a year later, he was resting on a small boulder looking at the pool of water, alone, wearing a white V-neck shirt and a red-beaded choker his brother had brought him from Costa Rica. He hated this place intensely without knowing why—simply hated it. Maybe it was the eucalyptus trees. There was nothing he despised more than cheap eucalyptuses, which reminded him of army bases. And now how the hell was he supposed to find the girl? He wondered if he'd have the balls to talk to her if he did, to tell her everything he'd planned to. He'd even practiced in front of broken mirrors—I'm willing to swear on it—because he wanted to make sure he used the right words to prove he was after her heart, that love was his intention, since maybe she'd lost her faith in guys after what that horny bastard Zitlawi had dragged her into. And what had Zitlawi told her about him, anyway? There was no way of knowing. Maybe he'd made fun of him, filled her head with bullshit about him. River was tormented, but decisive. He would take her up to the wind turbines at Alonei Habashan and hold her in his arms while strong gusts of air swirled around them, making them freeze up there on the hill. If they connected, then they could use the sleeping bags waiting in the trunk of the Fiat. They could go to the Odem Forest and fall asleep among the trees and the anemones, among the deer and the small, ruined Syrian stone buildings. Maybe even on the banks of the Sea of Galilee, at Naftali's beach, where the sunrise would wake them up. Whatever she'd want he'd give her—anything but letting her return to the reign of terror in her religious girls' school. That he couldn't bring himself to do.

River drove the length of the road that led to the cowsheds, toward the fields belonging to Kibbutz Natur: maybe she was there, walking around like she had been a year earlier. He rolled along slowly, scouring the landscape, praying she'd pop into view. Black and brown cows with white faces were walking around there, too, just like they did on our side of the fence, in Lebanon. Carefree, they could fuck each other whenever they felt like it, mounting one another and taking a ride. No pressure, no accountability. She didn't show up. An hour later he parked by the bus stop at the entrance to Nov thinking maybe she'd come out, then after a little while he gave in and drove through the metal gate, parking the Fiat in the center of town, in front of the synagogue, between two idle tractors. He decided not to move from that spot until she turned up. A while later he took off on foot to the playground, which he thought should be checked out. When he failed to find her on one of the swings there, he set out to find the girls' school, going so far as to ask directions from a lady riding a large tricycle along one of the paths. When he found the school he sat down on the wet grass facing the front door and waited for her to walk out, or at least peer through a window. But she didn't, not for two hours. Then out of nowhere, at three in the afternoon, Bayliss turned up. All of a sudden he was there, sitting to his right—he'd come up from behind in silence. He didn't say a word, just sat there on the grass. At first, River was taken aback, averted his eyes, thought for a few moments. In the end he asked, "How did it happen?" and Bayliss squeezed his hand and said, "I'm sorry." "Me, too," River said. And that was the end of their big, stupid, senseless falling-out. It was gone, as though it had never existed, and it left no scars. They didn't even try to argue about the facts or blame one another. They talked for a while, catching up on things and swapping stories.

Bayliss went inside the school to get Hodaya. She came out wearing a blue skirt and a white shirt. Her hair was in a ponytail, and in River's eyes she was more beautiful than ever. He stood there barely breathing. She gave him a shy hello but didn't seem at all surprised to see him. Bayliss left them alone.

"Did you hear about Zitlawi?" River asked.

"Yes," she said.

"Oh. I wanted to know that you'd heard. Who told you?"

"I saw. I mean, in the paper."

"Nobody told us, either, we learned from the news that he was dead," River explained. He asked if it was hard for her.

"I'm sure it's harder for you guys," she said nonchalantly, which came across to River as pretty strange. "I'm sorry," she said in a cold voice that didn't tremble in the least.

River took a few seconds, trying to decide whether to continue. She smiled. "I can tell you're a pretty sensitive guy," she said. He didn't know if that was good or bad, because in any other situation it would be bad but in this one it might just, logically, be good. There was no way of knowing. She laughed, maybe he was making a funny face: tortured, focused, intense. He had so many questions he wanted to ask her, but once again she got there first: "They're waiting for me inside," she said. "Thanks for thinking of me. I'm really all right." What a coldhearted bitch. When he didn't respond—he barely managed a nod—she took a few steps backward and said, "Take care," then she turned her back to him and walked away. So did he, to Bayliss's house. That was how it ended. Like nothing. Stupid. Senseless.

That night they sat at the observation point above the El-Al Creek, Bayliss and River along with a few friends from Nov. They lit glow-in-the-dark stick-lights in four colors from the secret weapons stash of a neighbor. You bend the stick-light in the middle, making a little slit, then you shake it and the stuff inside shines like the sun, like some radioactive pond. Stick-lights last for eight hours, and you can see the night and the world painted in totally different colors. They took advantage of Bayliss's father's mobile phone and got updates from all the squad members about what they were doing. It made no difference that nobody had had any interesting experiences to speak of—nobody had gone to the sea, nobody had been cruising around Israel in search of virgins. But there was always something to tell. Late at night, sprawled out on side-by-side mattresses in Bayliss's bedroom, they tried figuring out what everyone would be like when they were adults, at a reunion—a poolside barbecue party at Eldad the rich boy's private pool, the one he'd own because he'd already be stinking rich by then. He'd take his father's millions and turn them into billions, that slick, manipulative little white boy. Spitzer would be famous, a big-time actor. The whole neighborhood would go crazy whenever he showed up with some fancy car and a babe, maybe even Lana, since he loved stability. Then there was Boaz, who hated stability. He'd come for a short visit to show off for the guys between an operation with guerilla rebels in Angola and commando training in Chile, or maybe even with the Shiites in Iran. If someone was willing to pay, Boaz would sell himself: for excitement, he'd give his all. He'd circle the globe with suitcases full of cash, train assassins, fall in love with local girls, the daughters of off-the-map cannibal chieftains. He'd continue to think of himself as a killer, running around with a khaki-colored piece of cloth protecting his wristwatch and his hair cropped like a marine's. Totally juvenile. He'd wear Timberland mountain-climbing boots and drive around in a slick jeep filled with guys with little pricks: he'd never stop being a member of Erez's squad. In the end, when nobody needed the services of an aging mercenary anymore, he'd rot, alone, but not before trying to set up, say, an anti-auto-theft business. He'd convince himself that car theft was the scourge of Israeli society and he was going to find himself among the rich bastards of the world thanks to some special gadget: a steering wheel that electrocutes the thief, or an air-conditioning system that poisons him. But nobody would buy it. Pathetic. Then there was Pinchuk: he'd be a homo. You could see it in his eyes, the pervert. He'd go teach phys ed to kids, get himself in trouble with some sexual harassment case—suits him—then he'd leave Israel, in fact he wouldn't even make the reunion, they wouldn't manage to find him. Zion, on the other hand, would be there, driving a 1986 red Subaru. He'd bring his wife, a fat nursery school teacher who'd started growing to the size of a gorilla the day after their wedding. She'd shout at him all the time, too, totally disgusting. Girls always kept that guy on a short leash. He'd be employed by Egged, arranging vacation packages for the bus cooperative's employees. Koka would be a lifeguard at a city pool, the first Ethiopian lifeguard. Itamar would be fat. River would be a doctor. Bayliss, a reporter. Barnoy would be a veterinarian, or else he'd own a shoe store in Jaffa. Tom would get special permission to come to the reunion from the psychiatric hospital he'd be living in. They'd take off the strips of brown cloth that normally tied him to his bed and shoot him up with sedatives before they sent him to us. He had the look of a psychotic and the eyes of a murderer, and he wrote poetry, whole lines of it that were disjointed and made no sense. For sure he was going to wind up in a nuthouse. And Emilio? No way of knowing. It was hard to imagine him grown up. And then there was Zitlawi, who wasn't anymore. This group wasn't going to produce a chief of staff like we'd thought once, or a prime minister, either. Weird. How could that be? And me? They figured I'd still be living in Afula, a little guy with a big opinion of himself, a Shin Bet operative who interrogates Arabs and handles agents. A family man and a government man who sometimes takes his kids fishing. They didn't have any doubts when they talked about my future, it was all clear to them.

The next morning we went to Zitlawi's grave, all of us. The military cemetery in Tiberias is very small—two parcels of land, seventy graves, and two huge grassy plots waiting for more bodies. It takes up a lot less space than it sounds. On the path that leads to the non-military cemetery there are old gravestones, farmers from among the early Zionist settlers, and a learned rabbi's wife who died in 1906, back when it was still possible to skinny-dip in the Sea of Galilee in the middle of the day, or walk on the water, and everything was deserted and pristine and there weren't a thousand picnickers grilling meat and choking you to death. On the fence was posted an official IDF black-bordered announcement that Sergeant Tomer Zitlawi, may he rest in peace, son of Abraham and Aliza, had gone to his eternal resting place. From his grave, which was covered with flowers, you could see the Sea of Galilee between the Israeli flag and a tall palm tree. Behind it was a black basalt memorial plaque engraved with a verse from Jeremiah: "For whenever I speak of him, I earnestly remember him still." The Hebrew was hard, though, and none of us—even Bayliss—had any idea what it meant. Three Arab workers were paving the pathway between the graves and watching us with curiosity. We stood there twenty minutes or so. Every once in a while someone would imitate that toy-arse of ours that we'd lost. "Cocksucker!" someone would say in that deep, happy male bass of his. "What's up, cocksucker? Coming to eat, cocksucker?" He'd shout, "Hold your horses!" when he meant "Chill out," all proud of the new expression he'd coined, when we'd inform him, "You jerk, that's a translation from English. You didn't make it up." That would drive him crazy. Birds of every kind gathered there, in the military cemetery.

After that we found a little spot of shade under some cypress trees and we sat down there, on the dirt, in a circle, like some Boy Scouts activity. "What would you be willing to die for?" I asked, opening up the discussion. "This land," Koka answered. I grabbed a handful of earth and tossed it. "For that?" I asked. "Who'd be willing to die for that?" They looked at one another, nobody raised a hand. Even Koka himself was quick to lower his. "So then," I said, "nobody at all?" They all looked to Bayliss, thinking that as the company's right-winger he'd be willing to sacrifice himself for the homeland—even if he had stopped wearing his kippa. He said, "I'd be willing to die for the guys." They all nodded, every one of them, and raised their hands—they'd be willing to die for their friends. "The trouble with dying," I explained, "is the feeling of missing out on something. Most people in the world die with the feeling that they've missed out because they die for no good reason. But if you yourself and the people who love you know that you didn't get wasted for nothing, that you saved someone's life, that you wiped out a terrorist, that you did something that'll go down in the history books, it makes dealing with it a lot easier. Being buried here in this cemetery—in this well-tended plot, with Israeli flags and grass and benches—means the nation salutes you, honors your memory for having given your life in the line of duty. That's not like smashing into a truck and getting thrown in a pit alongside all the people who died in vain without any glory. When you're afraid, ask yourself why you're endangering your life and it gets easier."

Something caught their attention off to the side, and all at once they were all staring at the path, stunned. Nothing could have prepared me for that moment. I turned my head, too, and there was Oshri walking toward us. He was with his mother, an iron rod fixed to his arm. It looked like a spaceship, with metal rings held from the sides by all kinds of nuts and bolts. He saw me and gazed straight in my direction. Eight months without him, and what did I have to say?

The kids raced to him, crowded around him in a circle of hugs and kisses. I stood up, too, walked toward him but not all the way. I took my time. When he'd finished petting them, one by one, with his left hand, he came over to me. His timid Yemenite face had remained soft and smooth like it always was and his skin was like a baby's. But it was thinner than before, more mature, really mature, like he was looking at me from some other world, the world to come, where I hadn't reached yet. I was a memory, one of those guys stuck in the past and not maturing, someone still inside the bubble who hadn't learned all the things that Oshri knew and maybe even had had time to forget. That's what he was thinking. "What are you doing here?" I asked him, idiot that I am.

"River told me you'd be here," he answered. "So I came. I was at the funeral, too."

"You look good," I told him. "Really good, like you've been on vacation. Tanned and shaven." Hemda, his mother, was watching us from the side, pretty emotional—maybe happy for him, but worried, protective, like she was standing by waiting to pounce if he got hurt. Why would he get hurt?

"How are things up there? The usual?" Oshri asked.

"Like always," I said. "It's not like I haven't thought about leaving. I thought it over, before the winter. In the end I decided to stay on, for the time being."

"Of course," he said. "They need you there, right?"

He pulled a black wristband with a red bead from his pocket. "I made it," he said. "Want it?" I put it around my right wrist and tied it. We went down to the benches that look out over the pier. I wanted to ask, but didn't, how exactly that metal thing on his arm worked and what exactly it was there for, and what Oshri couldn't do anymore. He said, "It's easier for you there than at home. At home you'd sit around staring at the ceiling and going over the newspapers again and again."

"Yeah. At least up there they need me," I said.

"But down here they'll need you, too," he said. "When you have the guts to give it up and start something totally new."

"Life in Israel is boring," I told him. "You know me, I'm afraid of being bored. Boredom makes a person do stupid things. It's like a drug, and it makes you depressed."

"I'm your brother," he said. "Still. We'll watch out for you when you come home, when it'll all be over."

18

SPITZER HAD THIS SMILE that winked at you and whispered in your ear, "I've got it all figured out, but I'm not telling you." And I would say to him, "Come on already, out with it," to which he would laugh. He'd say, "It's nothing. Forget about it," and he'd shut up. He was the quiet type.

When I returned to the Soldiers' Hotel at the end of our furlough, his smile was the first to greet me. All Yasur chopper flights had been cancelled and the convoys weren't going out since there was a high alert on possible attacks, so we were staying in Kiryat Shmona, waiting to be called. The entrance to the hotel and the lobby were crawling with reporters on the prowl for clichés, like a soldier who'd say, "I only wanted to make it home safe," and for blood, too. There were microphones, cameras, recording devices, soundmen on cigarette breaks—all ordinary citizens in the territory of the simple soldier, no senior officers to speak with, no representatives of the IDF Spokesman's Office to give briefings. "Don't you feel like cannon fodder?" the reporters clamored. But the combat soldiers, acting like combat soldiers do—finding everything funny—shouted, "Take my picture for the paper!" and smothered every reporter in the vicinity. Spitzer was sitting off to the side, on a couch, surrounded by soldiers I didn't recognize, with Carmela Menashe standing over him. Yup, *the* Carmela from the radio: mouthpiece reporter for the Four Mothers and the whiners and the faggots. I knew it was her, it couldn't have been anyone but her. I came close, recognized the voice from the radio, and all the blood rushed to my head. I wanted to say something, chuck the truth in her face—the damage she was doing to the Israeli army, to all of us. "How do you boys feel?" she asked, sticking a microphone into the face of a burly Golani Brigade sergeant sitting on a table. "Carmela, I'm telling you: after the withdrawal everyone's going to say, 'Wow, too bad we didn't get out of there a few years earlier, what a waste.' I have a message for Prime Minister Barak: man, get us out *now,* what are you waiting till July for? The sooner the better."

"What about you?" she asked, turning to Spitzer. "Why are you so quiet?"

"I don't have anything special to say," he answered with a smile.

"So what is it that you feel? Afraid?"

"If anyone here tells you he's not afraid, he's a liar," he said.

The fat little Golani teddy bear grabbed the microphone back, asking to send a message to the protesters preventing us from getting our tough job done. What exactly was it that he wanted? It was hard to know. I took advantage of the distraction to whisper into Spitzer's ear, "Come on, buy me a cappuccino." He was surprised, really and truly surprised. He followed me out of the room. "Don't get mixed up with them," I told him. "Journalists will fuck with you, believe me." He asked me if he'd made a mistake by answering the question about being afraid and I told him no, he hadn't. "Bro, you were totally cool," I said. "It was fine. Talking straight is important. Just remember to be careful."

Yeah, fear is catchy, you already know that, and when someone admits it, suddenly it's a thing that exists, a legitimate possibility, and it knocks everyone over, one by one. There's nothing more dangerous.

"So what you're saying is that I did blow it," Spitzer said.

"Next time use the word 'tense,' don't talk about being afraid. Save being afraid for the really big stuff, when there's no choice. That's what I do. Just don't spend too much time worrying, that's the most important thing."

The cafeteria was swarming with soldiers waiting in a long line for candy bars and chocolate milk. "We're from Galgalit, the Outpost of Death," three young soldiers told the cashier, all proud of themselves, trying to impress her, shouting, nearly coming to blows. Who the hell had decided they were the Outpost of Death? Who was to say it shouldn't have been Ishiye or Karkum? Everyone wanted to be the Outpost of Death. I asked Spitzer if he'd taken the key to his room yet. "Top floor," he said, "great view of the Katyusha rockets." I suggested we get away from the crowds, and if it was okay with him we'd go to his room until Levanoni came back with the key to mine and the squad returned from bowling at the mall. Again Spitzer looked surprised. He pulled his knapsack from a huge pile in the lobby, along with a new guitar. "I'm going to shower," I informed him, "and when I finish you'll be waiting with a mug of hot coffee with steamed milk, and MTV on the television, but with the volume turned down, just the picture, the way I like it, and you can play me one fucking great solo on your guitar. Go crazy: rip the shit out of the strings, break the wood, make the building shake."

When I came out of the steamy bathroom wrapped in a towel, to the hot mug of coffee waiting for me, Spitzer didn't go wild on the guitar. He strummed quietly, sang soft and pretty, almost in a whisper, a well-known psalm, but to a new, Middle Eastern tune I didn't know: "A Song of Ascents. I will lift up my eyes unto the mountains: from whence shall my help come? My help comes from the Lord, who made heaven and earth. He will not suffer your foot to be moved; He that keeps you will not slumber. Behold, He that keeps Israel does neither slumber nor sleep. The Lord is your keeper; the Lord is the shade upon your right hand. The sun shall not smite thee by day, nor the moon by night. The Lord shall keep you from all evil; He shall keep your soul. The Lord shall guard your going out and your coming in, from this time forth and for ever."

We sat there feeling kind of funny, embarrassed, when he finished. There wasn't much to say. We kept switching channels looking for film clips, especially girls in bikinis, and happened on the news. "It appears that something has changed, a landmark in the history of the war in Lebanon," the correspondent was saying. "Now it is no longer the parents demanding immediate withdrawal, it is the soldiers themselves. 'Bring us home,' that is the new motto spreading from unit to unit. They are saying in a clear, direct voice, 'None of us wants to be the last casualty in Lebanon. None of us wants to die for no reason.'" A young Armored Corps soldier looked at the camera and said, "You have the power to help us. Help us get out of there. Anyone who serves in Lebanon knows we have no way of winning there." And as if that wasn't enough, an Engineering Corps fighter added, "We've gone from being the hunters to the hunted. We're just targets that draw fire and never return it, targets waiting to be hit. Six of our guys were killed in ten days. What are we still doing there?"

But the chief of staff came on to calm things down. "We are defeating Hezbollah," he announced. He was right, I decided: in this war there was no such thing as a knockout, it was all a matter of adding up the points. He'd visited the Reichan outpost and called the fighters who'd opened their mouths "whining rags," and forbade entry to journalists and photographers. It wasn't the time for talk, for the media. What a mess, what a noisy fucking blitz. The commander of an elite unit told a reporter that it was the public at large that needed a psychologist, not the soldiers.

"What do you think?" I asked Spitzer. He told me about some Irish playwright named George Bernard Shaw who once said that commanders never expect their soldiers to think. "Maybe that's the problem," Spitzer said. I didn't even get mad. I was glad that he could talk honestly, that he wasn't afraid of me. "I thought you were the type that never asks questions," I said. He laughed, looked all happy. After all, as always, he had it all figured out.

"You still with the Russian girl?" I asked.

"Yes," he answered, with that innocent look in his eyes.

"Don't worry, she'll drop you soon enough," I said, laughing. "They all do."

He pulled a few lemon-flavored wafers from his knapsack and had trouble opening them, did it like a nice Ashkenazi boy with his delicate hands. I thought how nice the peace and quiet was. We ate. "I'm okay," he said. "Don't worry about me. But Emilio? He's a mess. Can't pull himself out of it, sees war everywhere he looks." He waited for me to react. I kept silent. "What we're going through," he said, "it isn't like a movie, is it? I keep telling myself it's not like a movie, where you know the good guys are going to win. This time the good guys could lose."

How was I supposed to answer that? "The good guys will win," I reassured him. I stood up to get dressed. From the corner of his eye he caught sight of my wallet, with my army ID sitting on top of it, on the dresser. He looked at the picture, read what was written there. "What is it?" I asked him with a smile. I knew.

"Nothing," he answered. "Nothing at all."

"The name?" I asked.

"It says, 'Liraz Liberti,'" he said.

They hadn't known until then, didn't have a clue. Everywhere—signatures, lists, documents—I was Erez. "When I enlisted I was still called Liraz," I told him. He was stunned, I think, but he played it cool, afraid of offending me or asking too many questions. "Yeah, that makes sense," he said. "I have a friend named Jaime, but all the punks in the army couldn't say his name so he changed it to Hebrew: Jimmy." Jimmy? What kind of Hebrew name was that? I didn't get the connection. "Maybe my girlfriend's going to change hers to a Hebrew name, too," Spitzer told me. "She doesn't like her name. Lana. She hardly even has an accent. No shit."

They'd met on a beach at the Sea of Galilee, he told me. "What are you ashamed of, you jerk? She's fucking beautiful, right? You love her, right? She doesn't need to change her name. You convince her to stay as she is. Trust me, it's a great name. And, next furlough, we're all going to meet her. It's time. We're all going to love her, I can tell."

"Can I say one more word about fear, or is it catchy?" he asked.

"Fire away."

"Ever since I've been with her I'm afraid. To die, that is."

"What's that supposed to mean? That before you met her you couldn't care less?" I asked him, idiot that I am.

"I don't remember. I don't think so. Less, for sure. Now I feel it real strong."

A dark-colored plastic bag was sticking out from one of the oversized knapsacks on the floor. He pulled it out, opened it, and took out a black T-shirt. It had our unit's insignia on it, with the words "There is love inside us, and it will conquer." He handed it to me, said he'd had enough of them printed for all of us. "What's going on?" I asked him. "You turning into a fag?" "No," he answered. "It's a man thing. You remember how Zitlawi's favorite soccer team was

Hapoel Jerusalem? Well, their star player said it, and Zitlawi used to quote him. He'd tell us, 'This love is going to send us up to Lebanon safely and bring us back safely.' "

I turned the T-shirt around. A silhouette of Zitlawi in white—smiling, his hair wild—took up the whole back side. "Kind of sick, isn't it?" I said.

"A memorial," Spitzer answered.

On the screen, a mother who had only just lost her son was talking about how the whole thing had slammed her in the face. "I phoned his mobile, I wanted to play the song 'Forever Young' for him, it was his birthday. I left a message. I didn't know he was already dead." Spitzer watched her, mesmerized. There was a tear in his eye. I'm not kidding, what a good guy, so sensitive. One minute he had the resilient look of a real man; the next minute he looked like a kid, tender and fragile. Zitlawi used to call him the Little Prince. He was thin, tall, with huge eyes and tiny ears. And that winning, beautiful smile. The face of a genius, of a rich kid—but the quality kind—the kind who worked in fancy Tel Aviv suburbs as a DJ when he was in the seventh grade, his hair full of gel. He was considered one of the rising stars, right from the time he enlisted, and destined for great things. He was quiet, but a leader, had great stamina and a positive attitude. He was always singing. Everyone knew him. I actually hadn't thought much of him at the beginning. In training, and during the first tour of duty in Lebanon, he hadn't seemed enough of a killer, wasn't hot-blooded enough. He was about as opposite of me as possible. "So tell me," I said to him that evening in the hotel. "What would you think about being sent to officers' academy?"

"Are you serious?" he asked.

"No, the question is, are *you* serious," I answered. "And if you're willing to postpone your acting-school audition for another year or two."

His eyes sparkled. "Why me?" he asked, and then answered immediately: "I think so. I mean," he added, beaming and confused, "sure. Sure I am. I'm willing," and he played some more on his guitar.

The next morning the whole squad had coffee together at Yedidya's Place in the central bus station, then we filled out lottery cards and had an early lunch at Bomba Burger. It was a fun day. Kiryat Shmona was filled with khaki: tank convoys, equipment trucks, and legions of fighters crammed into the town waiting for clearance into Lebanon. There were two doors with long lines outside them: one was a tiny synagogue that hadn't ever had so much business. Or maybe it had, during the 1982 war or one of the big military operations in '93 and '96. The other was a shop called the Blue Dragon, Kiryat Shmona's tattoo mall. A Chinese dragon for luck, angels of death, the black cougar that was Golani's mascot—"A little good luck charm can't hurt," Boaz explained, all worked up and excited after a trip there. "When a missile can fall on your head at any moment, any kind of amulet is welcome," he said. "Piercing, too. People want to feel the pain." When he came back from there I announced a moratorium on the Blue Dragon. "There's even a rule about it," I warned them. "You're desecrating IDF property by burning your skin like that. Next guy caught is going to be sent home."

And they were afraid of being sent home. They didn't want to drop out. It's a fact: everyone showed up when it was time to pull out, just after sunset. During the last furlough, mothers had been more hysterical than ever and fathers begged their sons not to go back and girlfriends threatened to break up; the pressure was intense. Shit, what stupid, hypocritical parents: they convince their kids not to serve with us, then they give them the keys to the car on Friday night to go drinking at a pub, as if twenty times more people didn't get killed on the roads than in the army. Those parents didn't understand that fighting a war is good for their sons, makes them grow up, teaches them, toughens them up, makes them good citizens. And in the end, the guys themselves are happy. You can take my word for it. The kids weren't stupid like their parents, they showed up. Eldad, Boaz, Tom, Itamar. Zion, Koka, River, Bayliss. Pinchuk. Barnoy. Spitzer. It was good for them. Status report, iron numbers for count-off. Where was Emilio? No, Emilio wasn't there. He'd disappeared, vanished. No army officials—the social worker, the adjutant—had heard from him. We phoned his kibbutz, talked to his adoptive parents. They said he'd taken off. They called it a vacation, gone to see his parents in Argentina, but he hadn't left any message or phone number for us. They would tell him we'd been looking for him, would send regards if he called. That was that: he'd stepped onto a plane without a word, and no one's heard from him since. No, the earth didn't swallow him up, but Argentina is a big place, there's no way of finding him. Every once in a while we'd mention his name or imitate him and bust up laughing, all nostalgic. He was a nice guy, kind of out of it. He'd walked out of our lives without even saying good-bye.

This time we didn't fly. Another turning point: according to intelligence reports, the terrorists were planning to knock out a chopper and the arithmetic was simple: one to fifteen casualties sustained during a Hezbollah attack on a convoy going into Lebanon by road was preferable to forty in a downed helicopter. After all, when a chopper is on fire there's no escaping. No miracles, no wounded. So we were back to Safari trucks like the good old days. Iron numbers, count off. Mission confirmed, move out. Everyone was fingering something: with me it was the dog tags with Lila's message inside, and Oshri's wristband; Spitzer had a medallion imprinted with the image of a golden dove that his mother gave him for luck. For Levanoni it was his own face.

He kneaded his cheeks. We rolled along fast enough to get there as quickly as possible and slow enough not to overturn and fall into the dark abyss. Any vehicle parked at the side of the road was liable to blow us to smithereens. I thought about being tense, not afraid. The gate opened and we ran like crazy for the secure area. Everything was a big puddle of mud and water, and like always, the whole place was covered in dirt. When you came back from a furlough it choked you.

Just inside, in the middle of the open area, was a dense pile nearly as tall as the room itself. It was all there: our toaster oven, the French-fry maker, the mini fridge, and the microwave from the war room, the squad's candy cabinet, the senior staff coffee cupboards, all the televisions and videos and the projector—the Miriam and Shushu cinema had been shut down—even the electric kettle. "What's going on?" we asked, stunned. "Folding up shop," the guys at the outpost told us. "New decrees. They want to check out how we'll manage without all this stuff."

I went to Furman's office. "What's the story?" I asked.

"They're starting to move equipment out of the outposts," he answered, "in stages, in preparation for the withdrawal."

"Withdrawal? There's not going to be any withdrawal! What are they fucking with our minds for?"

"They're starting with the personal belongings. They don't want anything to remain here that isn't essential."

"What's the problem with leaving us a television set?"

"Those are the orders," he said.

At two-fifteen in the morning, three empty Mercedes trucks passed through the gate with an armed escort. Painted black and carrying local license plates, they parked with their backs to the entrance of the secure area. The kids loaded the trucks, and twenty minutes later all our refuges of sanity, every connection we had with the outside world, made its way down the hill, back to Israel. We watched with an air of farewell as the trucks grew distant, as though stretchers carrying our friends under blankets were in there. Even Spitzer's guitar was confiscated and sent down. It had only just arrived, hadn't even had time to breathe the Lebanese air. "Orders," Furman insisted. "Explicit and detailed." All we managed to salvage was Spitzer's electric organ and the little video camera, both of which had been stashed under the sofa in the Signal Corps Company Club.

Dave stuck his head out of the war room and called to me. "Good thing you're back," he said, "because I'm not making this list by myself." He pointed to the left-hand column of the duty roster: the Green guard post. "Don't tell me you've started with that bullshit, too!" I shouted. In seconds I had randomly filled in the names one after the other, in whatever order they popped into my head. "Sorry," Dave said, "but I'm not willing to place people there." He watched everything I did and copied it all down, like an old lady on bingo night, onto a big pink poster, and asked me to hang it on the message board next to the kitchen. "Me, I don't want to have anything to do with that!" he wailed. I gave him a resounding slap on the back and asked him when he was going to grow up, then I went to hang the thing. A few seconds later a crowd of curious guys had emerged from their holes to see who'd landed on the highest, most exposed guard post, the one the sharpshooter was familiar with and was expected to visit again. They looked, digested the information, and went back to the company club for a smoke, carrying leftover cartons of juice. They sealed the door closed and threw themselves down on pillows and wicker mats. "Hey, man, who wrote Sherlock Holmes?" A crossword puzzle. "And what's the capital of Vietnam? Five letters." They got stuck. There was no longer a stereo system hooked up there, so Spitzer took over the keyboard, which was kind of a replacement for the stereo, and played a slow dance under the dim lights. River pulled Pinchuk to his feet for a waltz. One, two, three;

one, two, three. They danced gently but it still came out clumsy, and just like in a ballroom, the others joined in one couple at a time, five couples in khaki dancing to love songs. Itamar the gorilla squashed Bayliss, Zion the beast made Tom swoon, grabbed his little ass and swung him around. Yeah, this was in place of the gloomy atmosphere. Who says we didn't have it good? Eldad lit memorial candles he found in the old war room cabinet (scented candles without the scent) and asked where Zitlawi was when we needed him, the yellow, the blue, the green, and the red he'd lit in that very same place when they'd held the séance, on the floor; there were even wax puddles still there that squished under their feet, small cold drops that had turned black with mud. Eldad suggested they hold a séance and bring back Zitlawi himself. Yeah, a group channeling meeting with departed souls. After all, Zitlawi's professional equipment was lying there orphaned in the club. River pulled out the board. For the record, Dave expressed his dissent, but he stayed to watch.

They started with a short meditation ceremony for spiritual cleansing and balancing energies, their eyes closed: the flow of a river, a waterfall, tranquility. A plant was placed in the middle, and a bowl of water. Three middle fingers on the wood waiting to be moved. "I call upon the pure soul of our brother Zitlawi, may he rest in peace," Eldad proclaimed. "Are you with us? Are you here, friend?" The fingers moved, all by themselves, over the words on the board. Yes. Yes, he was with them. Silence. Could it be? "Thank you, thank you for coming," Spitzer said. You have to be polite, remember to say thank you, as Zitlawi had taught them. You had to honor the spirit's will.

"Zitlawi, did you see the missile coming at you?" Tom asked.

"Yes," the fingers answered.

"Did it hurt?" Spitzer asked.

"No."

"Were you afraid?" Koka asked.

"Yes."

"What should we do?" Pinchuk shouted hysterically. "Tell us what we should do!" Eldad grabbed his face, shook him, made him calm down. "He can't answer questions like that, you birdbrain!" he shouted.

"Can you see us from up there?" Bayliss asked.

"No."

"Is there sex in heaven?" Zion asked.

"Yes."

"Are any more of us going to die here?" Barnoy asked.

"Cut it out," Eldad said, angry. "It's not the kind of question to ask him. That's determined by the head honcho of the world. And the prime minister." After all, if some guy was to die, why should they know about it, and why should they put Zitlawi in such an unpleasant position by telling them? It wasn't fair. But Barnoy persisted. "Is anyone else going to die?" he shouted. "Let him answer! It's the only thing that's worth knowing!" And the fingers moved.

"No," the board determined.

At three-fifty a missile landed on the Tziporen outpost. Our kids saw it fly and explode. They waited at the doorway to the war room for updates, for the names of the wounded, because they all had friends there and rumors flew around in the wake of attacks like those. Guys walked around crying. I finally gave up trying to get some shut-eye and went to Furman's office. "How close is he?" I asked.

"The sharpshooter?"

"Yeah. When's our turn?"

"He's back in our sector," Furman told me. "It's Galgalit or Dlaat or us next in line."

I sat down. He offered me chocolates and a bottle of orange soda but I couldn't have swallowed a grain of rice. "What's the plan?" I asked. He pushed a big, thick book at me that was sitting on the desk in front of him. Six hundred pages, more even, smelling freshly printed, the Northern Command insignia on the cover. *Back to the Future* was the title. "Command Deployment." Classified.

"It's for the withdrawal," Furman said. "Procedures for evacuating the outposts."

I leafed through it. Charts, maps, instructions: everything was there.

"They're totally serious," he said.

I opened to one of the pages: "Directions for *shikhluf,"* one of the subheadings read. *"Shikhluf?"* I asked. "What's that?"

"It's a new word," he explained. "There are loads of them."

Slowly, choppily, I read, trying to understand the jumble of words: *"All means for carrying out a quick* shikhluf *must be coordinated upon arrival at the site."*

"Shikhluf is something carried out by the Logistics Corps," Furman said, trying to explain. "It's a procedure for moving equipment between trucks to keep it from getting ruined in all the madness. They give details for the command to take out the screws from the beds and wrap them in plastic."

"I'm sure as hell not going to wrap any screws for them," I said. "You're making this *shikhluf* stuff up!"

"And," Furman continued, "you have to remember whether to unscrew them left to right or right to left. I can't remember."

A small radio transmitter stood on the desk playing Israeli songs. Periodically, the songs would be interrupted when the enemy's Nur station overtook the adjacent frequency. We could hear the news broadcast in poor Hebrew, and the Lebanese jingle we heard all the time and knew by heart: *"You'll go down, you'll go down, get it now: you'll go down. To us war is a dream and peace is a nightmare. That's why we'll win. Get it now: you're going down."*

We looked each other in the eyes, dead serious and worried, for a few seconds; then, with no warning, we both burst out laughing. For no reason, at the same time, we found ourselves roaring, totally out of control. Smiling from ear to ear I said, "Holy shit! This situation is totally fucked!" and smashed my head on the table once or twice. "Completely!" Furman answered, practically choking with laughter. It came in waves, this laughter; when one of us tried to settle down the other would start up all over again. It took us a few long, hard minutes to get back our self-control. We were still smiling, but now we were quieter, more self-conscious. "What the hell was that supposed to be?" I asked. Neither one of us had an answer.

I went back to bed. Levanoni was lying there like a sphinx with his eyes wide open, not moving or breathing. I didn't even try talking to him. There wasn't any point. I prayed I would fall asleep, but it didn't help. Hi, Sweetie, I wrote on my yellow legal pad. The situation here sucks big-time. No, that's not a line from a Shlomo Artzi song; Shlomo doesn't have any songs that fit us anymore. I am so tired. Missiles whiz by my ear, but even that doesn't rouse me. No energy left. You could put the body of a dead terrorist on the ground, between my legs, and I would still be tired. I guess a soldier's body, too, maybe. I'm not so gung ho anymore. No fire in me, no tension, only exhaustion. I met this journalist when we were waiting to be shipped back into Lebanon. Haimovitch is his name, a white-haired guy, very experienced. He got into the base somehow, came up to me when I was sitting alone while Levanoni was handing out the iron numbers for the count-off. He says to me, "Sad?" and offers me a cigarette. Then he sits down next to me in the sand. I tell him everything is fantastic, couldn't be better—and anyway, I don't talk to reporters. I say, "You guys, all you want to do is catch us crying, pushing your cameras into the whites of our eyes when they're wet so you've got shots of us weak, at funerals. And that makes us weaker. Pictures of soldiers crying—that's a disgrace. Brings everyone down, weakens our fighting abilities, our parents." "I've been to a lot of funerals this year," Haimovitch tells me. "Lots of really sad memorial services. I watched your friends hugging each other, kissing, crying, and I learned a few things about myself. I'm an old paratrooper, Class of '65. Your boys dare to do what we saved for the depths of our sleeping bags. Late at night—and only late at night—you could hear the sound of stifled crying in our tents. In our company there was a sign that read: IF YOU DON'T HANG TOGETHER YOU'LL BE HANGED TOGETHER. You guys don't need signs. You believe in tears. So who, exactly, is stronger? Who's more of a paratrooper, more of a fighter? I don't have the answer." That's what he said. I answered, "If you fought in the Six Day War in '67, then I have a lot of respect for you. Really. But I was taught that we're a country of strong people who know how to keep things to themselves. That's how we won. And that's the reason we're going to lose now." I took a cigarette from him.

After that, sweetie, I came back here, leaned on the wall, and looked at my squad and I realized: they're just high school kids at recess. Boys. Standing in front of the message board, horsing around, punching each other for attention, smiling all the time. Not one of them has come through adolescence yet. They're puppies. Human puppies.

What, was I becoming a poet all of a sudden? The pompous, whining, absolutely honest thought that some of these guys were the walking dead was what did it to me. Yeah, I'd started thinking about that recently. I didn't like thinking that way, but that's what was sitting on the tip of my tongue: the walking dead are among us, with death cards in their hands, even though they don't know it. You know what's really sick about this? If one of my soldiers had said that to me, I would have chucked him right out of there, no questions asked, and without a trial. And here was this thought, this realization, and too much knowledge can make you crazy, because without a sophisticated mechanism for suppressing it, how are you supposed to be a fighter? I wasn't who I thought I was anymore, I'd lost my peace of mind. And what incredible peace of mind a fighter or a sharpshooter or a gun-layer needs, no matter how experienced he is, in order to make a direct hit on a soldier standing inside a hedgehog or a trench, barely any part of him sticking out. I don't have that kind of peace of mind anymore.

I can't help myself, baby, but the time is drawing near for me to read your note, the one inside the dog tags. I don't have the strength to wait anymore. I'll try to hold out. Just for you. Love you.

I wrote until sunrise. When the loudspeakers announced morning standby alert I ripped the pages out and destroyed them, then I put on a vest and went upstairs. I stood for an hour and a half like a zombie in the corner of the secure area, along with everyone else, staring at the air and waiting for an attack on the outpost. By a quarter to seven I was back in bed. I read old graffiti drawn on the walls of the submarine in thin colored markers: YOU'LL NEVER WALK ALONE and MEN OF GOLANI, AUGUST '88 and this one, dated March '94:

> Here we are a bunch of jocks
> Hiding out between the Lebanese rocks
> We'll fight this war for Sharon the fox
> And come back home inside a box

Just before seven there was a boom, and shouting: "Missiles! Missiles! Missiles!" Someone broke in over the loudspeakers: "Carmel One to positions"—that's the emergency alert force—then somebody ran through the hall shouting, "Wounded in Green!" I was already on my way, running like a madman up the endless stairs that lead to the guard post, no helmet on my head, winded; all that mattered was getting up there. We're only talking about a hundred-and-fifty-yard climb, but that time I could barely breathe, it seemed like more than I could handle, too much, and I felt so heavy. I told myself it was possible that the guards had done what we'd trained for and managed to jump from the post and broken a shoulder, and we wouldn't even need the lifesaving equipment this morning. But a missile like that—what were the chances of dodging it? It was in the air two and a half seconds, six at the most. How could you possibly jump back behind the reinforced concrete? All the procedures were a crock of shit. But maybe, just maybe, it was only a broken leg, I muttered to myself, or maybe just the mannequins that had been wasted. There was a sharp smell of burnt chicken, really, really strong, nothing like you've ever smelled in your life. Heavy smoke rose from the fighting trench and debris was scattered everywhere. Eldad was lying on the ground, blood covering both eyes. A crescent-shaped piece of shrapnel had sliced open his ankle and more shrapnel was littered across his face, but he appeared to be whole and alive. He'd managed to drag himself to the transmitter, I could see the trail of blood. I went over to him. "I can't see anything," he said. "My eyes, I can't see." "It's okay," I told him. "It's only sand, it's covering your eyes. Just stay calm." I stroked his forehead. His hand was cut wide open, I could see the tendons, the bones.

"Talk to me," I said to him. "Talk to me, I'm here, I'm with you."

"I can't see," he said.

River and the evacuation team opened stretchers, began treatment. "Forget about me," Eldad shouted. "What about Yonatan? What about Yonatan Spitzer?" An axe blow hit my soul, a knockout punch slammed my heart. My whole body got the shivers all at once, and real hard. How had I forgotten? Something had suppressed it, kept me from reviewing in my mind the duty roster, prevented me from asking questions. I ran inside, feeling through that black cloud and trying to find my way down the tunnel. I got down on my hands and knees, groped the air, the ground. I shouted to him: "Spitzer? Yonatan?" but he didn't answer. A few seconds later I saw a body in front of me, through the haze, a pair of legs. He was lying on his back. I leaned toward him, trying to see. I grabbed his vest and pulled with both arms. In a split second the thought entered my mind that he was too light, that there was no counterweight to my pulling, and that that was strange. But before I could begin to grasp why, I saw the terrible thing. His entire head, from shoulder to shoulder, was missing. His arms were dangling there. Everything was scorched inside. There was no blood, it had all been burnt away. I let go, sprang backward. I didn't want to get close to that anymore. Furman was there beside me. "Go back down," he said. "Give a report and prepare the Nakpadon for rescue." But I couldn't move, I felt I was collapsing like a house of cards. River came in, too. Took hold of the body, screamed. He leaned over Spitzer, his forehead on his stomach, and held on tight. Furman and I tried to pull him off, get him outside. It was impossible. I don't remember what we did next, there are a few long moments that have been wiped out of my memory. But we were there, inside, until I decided I'd better start acting like an officer, a professional.

Furman shouted, "Everyone on all fours, crawling, I don't want any part of you sticking out above the tunnel," so we wouldn't get hit by another missile. We got River out of there, then we crawled back inside, me and Furman, to bring Spitzer's body down. I held his upper body, Furman took his legs. We got him to the stairs that way. Two standby alert soldiers were waiting with an open stretcher there. We put him on it and covered him up right away with a blanket.

There was no head to be found. We went back to look for it. From all that stress I was in need of air, lots of it, but inside the cloud it was impossible to breathe. I could feel myself choking, getting dizzy. I shouted, "Where's the head?" The only thing I didn't want was for the kids to find it by accident. We searched for it. "We've got to look around the hedgehog, between the rocks, near the fence," Furman insisted. "Maybe it flew out, hit a boulder, and bounced back."

We made our way through the entire tunnel. Nothing. We came out empty-handed. We didn't find a head, only a mannequin, in one piece, lying on the ground. "Shit, Erez, it must have flown down to the river," Furman said. I told him that couldn't be. "Maybe it just went up in smoke," I suggested. Furman dashed off to the war room to talk to Command, get instructions. On the way there he sent Tom and Barnoy, the next on the list, to man the post.

I went to the stairs. River, Bayliss, Zion, and Koka were waiting there. They asked me where Spitzer's head was. I told them we hadn't found it. Yet. "Maybe it rolled down the slope, there's nothing we can do about it."

"Let's go and look for it," River said with determination. I told him to forget about it, it was too dangerous and against the rules, forbidden by Command: there was no crossing the barbed-wire fence of the outpost. I said we were waiting for instructions. "If we wait, the head will disappear, it'll be carried off in the Litani," River said. "I'm going out to look for it, I don't care." I shouted at him: "Stop!" But he took off at a run, jumped over the trench, climbed the small fence. I saw his hand get cut. I raced after him, to stop him by force, but I didn't make it in time. He kept going. I stopped at the edge. "River! Stop!" I shouted. "Now! You're exposed! Stop!" Bayliss gave me an apologetic look and he jumped over the fence and out, too, followed by Zion and Koka, down the slope. I stood there, powerless, pressed up against the fence, commanding them to come back, shouting about breaking orders. But I wasn't really fighting them, wasn't really threatening them like I know how to do, wasn't blocking them with my body. Then I fell silent. My brain was thinking slowly. I could see them making their way down the slope, then I jumped over and ran after them. I got the war room over my transmitter and said to Dave: "We're looking for the head, send out whoever you can to help." In minutes, they were all there, the whole squad, all the kids. They were running between the boulders, scanning the ground. We worked together as a team—organized and fast.

There were so many times I'd wanted to disobey orders since I'd become an officer. I'd bit my lips on so many operations and facing so many senior officers that talked bullshit when I knew better than they did, because I knew the lay of the land and had the full picture. I swore to myself I wasn't going back to jail, I would be an exemplary military man—so orders had to be obeyed. Never again was I going to have anyone shouting into a transmitter at me, "Erez, you psycho! Stay where you are. That's an order! Erez, you're in violation of an order!" I'd kept my mouth shut so many times, but not again, not now. It wasn't because there was some terrorist on the slope outside the outpost that I was hungering to kill. I was disobeying orders to bring Spitzer's head back to his mother.

Furman showed up, caught sight of us overturning stones on the slope, and joined in. Even he was outside the gate now. He gave me a look that said "You're okay, you took the right action," or maybe even "I'm proud of you." But we didn't find the head. We searched for it until four that afternoon. It was a lost cause. "There's no choice, we've got to go back inside," Furman said, and everyone returned, resigned, to the secure area. He came to me and said, "I've got a real shitty job for you. Go pick up the little bits and pieces left behind. Take a pair of gloves. We don't want the kids to see this." So I went, carrying a black bag. I walked the length of the tunnel collecting burnt clothes, pieces of flesh, his weapon and magazine, everything spattered with blood. The walls were covered with it, too, red and black, and shiny.

Bayliss packed up Spitzer's personal belongings to send to his mother. What could you possibly find in the kit bag of a dead guy? A few books, some underwear, linens and discs and snacks, a toothbrush and shaving cream, and the kind of pajamas only a little rich boy would own, folded neatly and nice-smelling, which he never wore. River took over his video recorder, asked to hang on to it for the time being with the cassette inside, the *Guide for Lana,* his Russian girlfriend. He wanted to finish the film, turn it into a guide with a commemoration, and I approved his request on condition that he write to the family, updating them and explaining. I wanted him to have their permission. At five o'clock, another attack on the outpost began.

Truth is, it wasn't really an attack on the outpost, it was just some nutcase running up the hill and shooting in our direction. Maybe he was on drugs, maybe he was kind of a retard. We watched him dashing back and forth and shooting, out of control. We had a field day: the whole outpost started shooting at him at the same time. Everyone. But not only at him. Grenade launchers, MAG 58s, and M24s, tanks: a real Firebox Procedure. We called for combat choppers, which fired as well. I climbed a rampart and emptied ammo like crazy, like Rambo, another round and another and another. You have no idea who you're shooting at, or where, but you've got your outlet, you can vent. The air is dark and full of dust, there's no visibility, all you care about is shooting. It was a total loss of control, we were running wild, one big, bad party. All the tension that had been in the air just burst at once. The guys in the White guard post kept shouting, "Die, you fucker, die!" It wouldn't bring Spitzer back, but at least we'd killed a terrorist. At last. How long we'd been waiting to do that. We were so trigger-happy, so worked up. All we were praying for was for them to keep coming, more of them, up close. We didn't care if they threw grenades at us as long as they acted like men and came close, we'd kill them with blows. Someone shouted, "Suspicious movement!" and we opened fire again with M24s and 60mm mortar shells, turned everything into fog. I couldn't see a thing. They were firing the MAGs like madmen, not even aiming. Spitzer was dead! If we didn't take down at least three terrorists that night it would turn into another Masada! Suddenly somebody says they heard a noise from one of the unmanned tank positions near Yukhmur. I shouted, "Position Eleven! Position Eleven!" and before I'd even finished the command we were firing two phosphorus bombs and a round of grenades and massive tank fire in that direction. The whole outpost was shooting at the spot. And then it ended. Everything was a blur: you couldn't remember what you were doing there or why you were being attacked or who was attacking or what was even going on. All you knew was that they hated us and we hated them. All you knew was that they killed Spitzer. We waited fifteen minutes and watched as an ambulance entered Yukhmur. It left with casualties. Only then did we close up shop.

A few days passed and I could still feel that sharp burnt smell in the air. It came in waves, every day, like it was never going to go away, and the guard post itself remained black. In the dining room we had to face the table we'd put Eldad on before he was evacuated. Nobody would eat there, only the youngest soldiers during Sabbath meals when the place was full to capacity and there was no choice. In the meantime, the sharpshooter had let up; he'd been silent for two weeks. Surveillance cameras were installed on top of the sandbags lining the trenches, and were operated by joysticks. Soldiers on duty could watch the screen from a seated, protected position without exposing themselves. Cement mixers came up the hill to us every day and made walls of reinforced concrete, and convoys brought protective equipment and took back all unessential items, breaking down the outpost from week to week. And we—we didn't poke our noses out of the place the whole time. Sometimes we got permission to perform a preventive bombardment and our weapons would fill up the nights with noise and we riddled the wadis, those lush hothouses perfect for hiding terrorist cells, with bullets and bombs. Every night I would imagine that the whistling of the wind was actually the sound of propellers coming to take us out of there. But on we stayed, shut inside and waiting. And we played "What Yonatan Spitzer Can't Do Anymore," sometimes for hours: Yonatan won't know the feeling of renting an apartment with his girlfriend. He won't take a piss with us from the highest peak in South America, he won't ski in Chacaltaya, he won't screw the hottest Peruvian chick in Casa Fistuk anymore. He'll never cheat, he'll never be in pain, he'll never understand, he'll never know what's happening with us anymore.

One morning I was standing in the trench, looking through the binoculars. Everything was quiet, when suddenly I spotted two strange civilian trucks, a kind I wasn't familiar with—Mustang something—that looked like huge refrigeration vehicles. They approached Arnoun, then turned onto the road leading up to Beaufort and began their climb. A few minutes later they entered the gate and their doors were opened. I came out to see what was inside. It was totally unexpected: towers of hundreds of land mines piled one on top of the other filled the space. "M15 and M29 antitank land mines," Furman explained. "Nine hundred and eighty of them, six and a half tons." They were round, with a cake of TNT on the top center of each one. "It's our job to take possession of them and store them safely," he announced. "We'll put them in the storeroom next to the fitness room." Dave gathered twenty or thirty soldiers he found lounging in the submarine and had them form a human chain. The goods were taken off the trucks and piled in the storeroom, which filled up entirely, then Furman put a lock on the door and that was the end of that. They were out of sight, as if they didn't exist. From that night onward we slept on top of those land mines, which were a kind of hourglass, and it was like your mind could sense the sand pouring through all the time. We walked back and forth past that locked door all day, every day, knowing, even understanding, but trying not to think about it.

19

EVEN IF WE THOUGHT ABOUT IT we didn't talk about it. There was no withdrawal. None whatsoever. It was business as usual, that was the tactic we'd chosen. Too dangerous to dig around in these matters, the kids would ask too many unhealthy questions. If you mentioned withdrawal once, then it would happen. If you set it out on the table it would hover around forever. Keeping quiet was best. It was hard enough already as a commander to keep them in suspense for such a long period. They were curious, stuck their noses in places they didn't belong, understood even when nothing was explained to them—there was no hiding anything from them. Especially when we started thinning out the place, getting rid of the nonessentials: the fitness room was dismantled and new orders infiltrated the hill every day. So we made an effort to suppress it, to play dumb, and from the time Spitzer was killed the word itself was never mentioned. From our point of view there was no withdrawal.

That is, until Brigadier General Kaplan joined us for the Passover Seder. We read the Haggadah, held the ceremony like usual. We were waiting for someone to shove a chicken leg down the military rabbi's throat for going into such great detail and explaining every ramification of every word of the story of Passover. It seemed like he was going to go on forever, until Furman, thank God, cut him off and asked to speak. He tapped his wineglass and said, "Brigadier General Kaplan, the commander of our division, took part in the historical battle in '82 in which Beaufort was captured. Back then this place was a breeding ground for Palestinian terrorists. They would fire on Israel right from here until a small band of brave, young fighters cleaned out the place and set up our presence here, on the first day of the war. Kaplan commanded those fighters, the reconnaissance unit. He himself was injured."

Holy shit, what a man this General Kaplan was! We gave him a big, noisy round of applause. He smiled, kind of embarrassed, and sank down in his chair. "We've prepared a little surprise for you," Furman said as he produced a framed parchment that had a silhouette of the Beaufort fortress along with the text of the communication log from the big battle. He read out Kaplan's last commands before he was wounded: "Commander here, all armored personnel carriers in a single line. Over. Commander here, shine a light so we can see you. Over." Then he got hit, and when he fell backward a voice came out of the transmitter: "Kaplan, have you been hit? Kaplan, are you wounded?" Then it was quiet. It was quiet, too, in our dining room just then. "Kaplan, you're hit!" Furman said as he turned to him. "I'm sorry I took you by surprise like this, Commander. But we'd like to hear about that battle, especially since the commandment on this holiday is to 'tell the story to your sons.'"

We waited for Kaplan to react.

When he stood up, tears were coming down his face. We all saw it, a brigadier general crying. I figured Zitlawi would have been on the floor laughing if he'd been with us. He'd have bit his lips, tried to stop himself, really made an effort, but in the end his big laugh would have come bursting out and pulled half the room along with him, or at least a fourth of us, spreading through the benches. If he'd been with us. But he wasn't. Good thing. Without him, the place was silent and serious. "I've come full circle this evening," Kaplan said. "Most of my adult life has been connected to this piece of earth, my entire military service has had something to do with it. My friends—my best friends—remained here, most of them, and they'll stay behind when we pull out. Tonight I'm here at Beaufort for the last time. To say good-bye to it. You men will be the ones who evacuate it."

So that was that.

That's when it happened, when it was all over. There was no going back. We'd taken it all in, understood. The IDF was serious about this, we'd really be leaving. That's how it happened that in one matter-of-fact moment the story ended. It was over. Even Kaplan had given up. All I could think about was how I could have been so incredibly stupid. How?! And how a place that was an entire world, that had everything, that was a real city, an empire, our own, our whole lives—how could it suddenly just disappear? How could we abandon it? Blow it up so that it ceased to exist and nobody would live here again, wouldn't sleep here anymore, guard the place? It was our own patch of heaven and we were going to be moved somewhere else? There wasn't a single drop of logic in it.

Kaplan took a look at the parchment, read the words to himself, and looked out over the expectant faces of the crowded rows of soldiers sitting in silence. "No," he said. "I wasn't in command of the battle. I didn't have a chance, I was wounded before it started. While they were being killed, my friends, one after the other, I was lying wounded in a field down below, on the slope. I was doped up with painkillers, sometimes alert and sometimes not, lying there waiting to be evacuated with an injured lung and trying to follow what I was hearing from the transmitter.

"I'd been given this mission back in 1980," he said as he moved away from the head table and crossed the room to squeeze in between two startled Russian soldiers, the youngest among us. "They told us that taking control of Beaufort meant taking control of the entire region. It can be seen from everywhere, and everywhere is visible from it. A fortress, with walls that look out for miles and miles. Even the Syrians used to dispatch observers to Beaufort. Back then I was an operations officer. I took my men up to Kalaat Nimrod, the Crusader fortress on the Golan Heights, to train. After that I took a year off to study, and when I came back—a week before the war—Goni handed over command of the unit to me. His discharge party was planned for Saturday night. Two days earlier terrorists had attacked the Israeli ambassador in London, who sustained severe injuries. All furloughs and leaves were cancelled, we got orders, the party was cancelled, and we were sent up to the launching area, preparing to enter Lebanon.

"We moved out at two o'clock Sunday afternoon. We crossed into Lebanon in armored personnel carriers, passed by Mount Shomriyah and the Akia bridge, and started climbing. The trip took four hours. We watched an evacuation chopper fall, killing five, and there were huge numbers of troops streaming in, and long columns of armored vehicles. We actually made it in without incident, were barely even shot at once. Beaufort was constantly bombarded by IDF artillery, we could see the smoke all along the way. My guys shouted, 'Stop firing! Come on, leave something for us! What are you doing?' They were afraid there'd be nothing left for them to do. They laughed, had a good time.

"It was the sixth of June. We entered the village of Arnoun from the south so we wouldn't pass through the main street.

The attack, with tanks, was supposed to start between three and four in the afternoon so it would be light out, but we got stuck in a long traffic jam and it was getting dark. It was there, in a grove between Arnoun and Beaufort that you men are all familiar with, that we came under fire for the first time. We weren't wearing our bulletproof vests yet and I took a bullet in the upper back. They dragged me to an open field at the edge of the mountain and put me on a stretcher.

"Goni, who could never let himself give up and had volunteered to join the forces at the front, heard what had happened and asked to take my place. He jumped in an armored personnel carrier and raced toward the mountain. On the way up he overturned on one of the curves and was thrown out of the vehicle, injured, but he kept on, on foot. In the meantime, the tanks had stopped running—they were a mechanical mess, they never even reached us. The track on the last of them fell off on its way out of the village. So our backup was nil. Goni ordered the men to storm Beaufort on foot. He came over the transmitter: 'Commander here, all men off vehicles, meet at the house with the arched windows.' He briefed them: 'Okay, men, we're going up to take the Beaufort. We've waited years for this moment and we're going to pull it off as best we can. Erez to the right, Avikam to the left, Yuval in front, Tzvika in back.' And they started up the steep path in the moonlight, figuring the terrorists had bailed out because it was quiet up on top of the hill, and the terrorists always ran off at night—at least that's what we'd been told—and if they didn't always run off, then surely they would when they saw armored convoys and troops coming at them from every direction. They had every reason to run off. I was lying there, listening—the connection was poor—without being able to take in the fact that my men were being mowed down one after the other. Yaron Zamir, my signaler, was killed at a run, at the entrance. Yossi Eliel, on the day of his discharge, was downed by a round of ammunition on the road. The squads continued up there, I heard them as they discovered that the fighting trenches were too narrow because of reinforced concrete, and they couldn't fit inside them. The terrorists were entrenched inside reinforced positions where no grenades could reach them. Gil Ben-Akiva fell, too, and then Avikam Sherf—Abu we called him—whose brother had also fallen in battle. And Razi Guterman. Erez was wounded. Morris, too, who injected himself with morphine. They all lay in puddles of blood and tried taking care of themselves. To tell you the truth, we'd thought we'd get out of there without a single injury. The guys had set up to meet for their concluding lineup in the national stadium in Beirut. And then Goni was hit by a single bullet to the chest, right inside the target, and died. Goni Harnick.

"I've been moving around inside Lebanon for years now," Kaplan continued, "and every time I go from village to village I look up at the hill. I send troops up here, make visits. In the meantime, Beaufort has become famous, every kid in Israel has heard of it. The men who gave their lives to this place have turned into symbols. Goni. Erez, too. You all know that Brigadier General Erez Gerstein, the Erez who was wounded with us, was killed last year. I keep asking myself what Erez would say if he were here, what he would do. And Amir. And Hussein. All the guys I loved. Whenever I brief soldiers before a mission I tell about them and how each one was killed. You men are already experienced, you know how hard it is to lose a friend and also how you have to go on. You bite the bullet and carry on. Personally, I've continued in their path, it's my way of making up for their deaths that helps me cope."

"And was it worth it?" River asked. It came out suddenly, and so loud that no one could miss it. "Do you feel it was worth it?" River persisted. Shit, what courage. I shot him a look that said, "Just you wait, I'm going to rip you to shreds the minute Kaplan's chopper takes off." Kaplan searched the crowd to see who'd spoken up, waited a moment, then pulled himself together and said, "I've always asked that question: was it worth it, or not? I hope it was. I remind myself how many lives we've saved. How we always tried to take a minimal number of risks and protect the sanctity of each and every one of your lives. More than that, I can't answer."

"I'm sorry," River said very quietly, though each and every one of us could hear him. "I've been trying to convince myself that what we lost was worth it. I haven't succeeded." Kaplan stood up. His face had a consoling look to it, and he was smiling thinly, but you could see a deep sadness in his eyes. He said, "Imagine it's the European league basketball championships, one second to the finish. The other team is leading by a point and our own Katash is at the foul line. You know the situation? Well, that's where we are now. All that's left for you men is to be strong, focused, and to make sure that we end this campaign ahead of the other guys."

"Hey, wait a minute," everyone shouted. "A second to the finish? Really? When?" They wanted a date.

"This summer," Kaplan told them. "Three months from now, more or less. There's a lot to get ready. It'll be the biggest battle this division has seen since that war, the battle of two divisions waging a withdrawal. And in this kind of battle you need heroism. There's no room for people to fall apart."

Spitzer wasn't there to sing and Zitlawi wasn't there to play the *darbuka* drum, so we ate. When it was over, Kaplan took Furman for a face-to-face chat in the office. On the way there he caught sight of me leaning on the doorpost of the war room, watching nothing happen out there, a steaming cup of black coffee in my hand. He asked if there was any more where that came from. I offered to make him a cup, and he invited me to join them, so I did. We sat there, the three of us, tired, talking about what had happened in the dining room. "It's a different era," Kaplan said with a smile. "You're a different generation, a generation that asks questions. And we are obligated to give you answers. That's good." I was hoping to hear him say, "Between us, this withdrawal business is bad shit, dangerous, and the country's sick in the head."

"Yes," he said, "I'm one of the squares who thinks that the only way to protect Israel's northern settlements from the growing threat that is Hezbollah is by maintaining a security zone in southern Lebanon. And control of Beaufort, with its topographical superiority, is exactly what makes the difference. We weren't lying to you when we told you we believed our presence here has prevented terrorists from reaching Kiryat Shmona, and we weren't lying when we said that the attacks on Beaufort—instead of on the Good Fence at Metullah—are saving civilian lives. We believe it. Or at least I do. And I'm frightened. I don't know what's going to happen the day after." That's what he said. "But who knows? Maybe afterward, when this whole thing is over, we'll ask ourselves how we didn't think of this withdrawal a few years earlier, why it was that we were sunk deep in tactics, without strategies. It isn't simple. Not at all."

I was a little drunk. I sucked in some coffee. Furman was pretty worked up, you could tell. Kaplan cut us each a piece of cake and handed it to us. "Tell me something," I asked him. "Is there a chance it all happened by accident?" He didn't exactly understand what I was getting at. "This whole mess," I explained. "Is there a chance that you weren't even supposed to conquer Beaufort that day, but you stormed anyway?" Kaplan took a deep breath, and his small, sad smile nearly disappeared. "Yes, there is," he answered. "There was apparently some sort of order like that—not to attack—but it never reached us. To this very day it's not clear where exactly it got stopped."

So it turned out I was the real jerk here: Spitzer had been

telling the truth. "You have to know this: it's the history," Kaplan continued. "Everything began here. Not only the heroes and the symbols but the public rift, too, and the protest demonstrations, and the Peace Now movement. Here, for the first time, was where thoughts of the futility of it all first began. I don't think such thoughts among soldiers have ever been stronger than here and now. It's only natural when you're dealing with withdrawal, and that's our mission at the moment: to clamp down on the torment, not to broadcast it—or the doubts, either—to the outside world. Simply to strengthen the soldiers. That's what we need to do, for the time being."

That was the night of the Passover Seder, the nineteenth of April.

20

FRIDAY NIGHT, THE NINETEENTH OF MAY. Hezbollah likes to strike on Friday nights. Three hundred missiles, shells, and bombs landed on IDF control positions in the security zone during one twenty-four-hour period. The Reichan outpost went up in flames and three soldiers were critically injured before the fire extinguishers could cover the area in a blanket of white. Terrorists tried to capture another outpost, Rotem, on foot—and failed. And at the SLA's Armata outpost, a local minibus loaded with nearly ten pounds of explosives blew the gates open and caused the buildings to tumble one after the other, killing scores of people. The Israeli Air Force responded by shelling Sujud and Yaatar, destroying 122mm and 130mm cannons and vehicles with rocket launchers and a pickup truck carrying heavy machine guns. That hell was the background music to our Friday night prayers and Sabbath meal.

On Saturday night Amos landed at Beaufort. "It's going down faster than we thought," he said as he jumped out of the chopper. "Maybe even within the month. We're closing shop. And from now on everything's going to be tougher, more dangerous." He called the officers together and talked straight, put his cards on the table. "Intelligence has been issuing warnings about what we're likely to be in for on the night of the pullout," he said. "Hezbollah is looking for a bloodbath. They want to make sure this withdrawal is etched on our collective memories as a bloody retreat. The terrorists have been coordinating code names for the 'big surprises' they've got planned for us. They're stashing ammunition and loading the arsenal with new-model explosives and preparing operational plans for attacking our convoys. Not an easy situation." He asked us to believe him when he told us the entire IDF was working day and night on this, and that the army was spending big bucks to thwart enemy plans to the extent that it could and provide as much protection as possible. But as for us, he said, we were going to have to be mentally and physically prepared for what was ahead, because it was about to happen.

"You've got to get out of here tonight," I whispered to Furman. "Go home. It's going to be your last chance before the grand finale. We'll manage." He lifted off with Amos and I settled into his chair and got River to quiz me on withdrawal procedures from *Back to the Future.* With no video and no toaster there was nothing to do at the outpost, only test each other from the book. At the time, all of us were walking around with the thing, learning it by heart and making up quizzes. It became a kind of sport. River made fun of it all. "The most important thing," he said, "is not to let that stupid book fall on your foot, because that's the only dangerous thing that can happen to you in the pullout."

Procedures for burning secret documents, the gathering of equipment for destruction, how to dismantle a generator, when to disconnect the wires to the hotline, which foods from Chili's pantry to pack and which to leave behind, according to the expiration dates. How much ammunition to stock up on, when to open fire, status reports on the area of operation, land and aerial backup forces, main time schedule, dozens of code names. River read out the situations and I gave the responses.

At six-thirty on Sunday morning a convoy carrying limited supplies managed to reach us. There were packages from home, newspapers, uniforms, laundry. A little food. The SLA drivers who unloaded the large plastic containers were in a hurry to take off. We offered them coffee but they just wanted to leave—no laughing, no cigarettes. I went off to get some sleep.

Dave shook me awake at ten-twenty. "The Taibe outpost has fallen!" he shouted. "It's a real mess!" He said that from the Green and Red guard posts, facing south, you could see hundreds of women and children climbing up toward it. The main area of our own outpost was its usual Sunday busy, the way it was at the beginning of every week, with everyone doing outpost chores, disinfecting the kitchen, polishing equipment. At a run we pushed through the crowd until we reached the computerized surveillance room and I grabbed a pair of electronic binoculars and looked to the far left. It was hard to see, but I could just make out a long, long line—endless, in fact—of people heading toward the Christian-held outpost in the south of our district. The imams in the mosques in the village below were urging them to march on the outpost, and they were. "Shit!" I shouted. "Why aren't those fucking SLA soldiers firing on them? They should keep them at bay by shooting at them!"

"The SLA isn't there anymore," I was told by the surveillance officer on duty, a Russian.

"What do you mean?" I asked.

"They abandoned the outpost. It's deserted. At exactly ten o'clock the gate opened and they left: five Mercedes, a jeep, and an old tank. They took off like madmen."

At ten-forty-five we watched as the yellow flag of the enemy was raised on the flagpole. Green flags of Islam covered the guard posts. From that moment, Hezbollah was in possession of an outpost, its first ever, and it was obtained without a battle. Our choppers took off and circled in the air as a deterrent, but it was too late. Fucking bad news, we all said. I sent Dave to redo the guard duty roster, to provide more backup for Blue so that four soldiers would be on duty there at all times. If a procession of marchers headed toward us, too, the guys in Blue would be the first to know it. I ran to the office and contacted Amos on the encrypted transmitter. "We're completely exposed from the south," I told him. He already knew about it. "Not only you guys," he said. "There are processions like that in every district. Listen in to the transmitter. We're trying to block them." What we were hearing on the division's operational transmitter was stuff we'd never heard before: "They're jumping ship from Shayareen, too," came the report from Galgalit. And from Olesh: "Randuriye, too. There's a long line of citizens marching. In another five minutes they'll be across the Litani." A river of people—Lebanese locals, simple folk—flowed to the Kanetra outpost and captured it without warning. It was war. Our allies the Christians had run away without letting Northern Command in on it. The Gamba outpost was about to fall: a country that had been living for years in hiding was suddenly showing its face, by the thousands. It was a populist revolution carried out on a bad morning for populist revolutions, since the visibility on that foggy day was so poor.

Half an hour before lunch, at eleven-fifty-seven, the teleprinter spit out a cable and I told Dave to call everyone to the briefing room immediately. He made the announcement and sounded a siren and the entire outpost squeezed in, abandoning dirty pots and pans and buckets of ammonia and sewing machines where they were working. I didn't even have a chance to get worked up. When you get a cable like this you let your soldiers know about it right away—it's procedure, they teach it in officers' academy. And so I did:

"There's a good chance we're leaving here soon," I told them. "Very. Maybe even tomorrow." For the rest of their lives nobody will ever see the dropped jaws and the popping eyes that anybody there with me saw at that moment. Let's hear some whistling, some applause! Nothing: they were in paralyzed shock. "There's a lot to do and we're starting now, so concentrate," I said. "First stage: strip the submarine bare, empty out the rooms. In the next fifteen minutes I want all personal belongings upstairs. That means knapsacks, sleeping bags, Walkmans, souvenirs, narghiles. Whoever feels the need should take a second to slip on his lucky underwear. Second stage: take down all the maps, collect all the secret documents, fold up the flags, whitewash the graffiti. The kitchen will be closed down, the phone and transmission lines cut. We're not leaving a pin behind when we leave here, not a single can of paint with the IDF logo on it. That's our mission now, and we're all going to help pull it off. Third stage: prepare the buildings for explosion. We have nine hundred and eighty mines to hook up. My squad will start placing them. Furman will be arriving this evening and he'll have more information. He'll let us know exactly how we're going to be carrying this out."

I told them, in short, that we were going to leave Beaufort in the most dignified way possible. Like gung-ho beasts of prey they attacked the outpost, ripping eighteen years from the walls. River put himself in charge of forming a human chain to remove the fat, round cakes of TNT from the storeroom and stacking them like towers at the gathering point for company wounded. Levanoni and I took two wooden crates—the withdrawal kit, which contained equipment necessary for breaking down a base—from the cabinet in the office. We found five nail guns and the outpost construction plan. "We have to scatter the mines," we explained to the crew. "Two mines every two yards or so. The first one will be attached to the wall about two-thirds of the way up from the floor and held in place by three nails, one above and two below the mine. The other will be placed on a chair or stool or box or table; ideally it should be off the ground. Also above and below the beds in the submarine. And of course surrounding the building and inside the trenches, except for the eastern wall because it abuts the ancient fortress."

I phoned Amos. "We don't have enough trucks to carry all the equipment," I informed him. "We'll need at least another five. And we need a crane to load the generator. It's written in the book."

"Listen," he said, cutting me off. "No trucks, no cranes. Whatever you can manage to load into your vehicles, do it. Burn the secret documents. And that's all you can do. Everything else goes up in smoke with the mines. And one more thing: Furman won't make it back into Lebanon before the withdrawal. There's no way of getting anyone in this evening. You guys are on your own. I have full confidence that you'll manage."

Yes, sir. Roger. Over and out.

I went to gather my own personal belongings. I packed my bag, removed the pair of my grandfather's *tefillin* from the small cabinet, and the yellow legal pad filled with letters I never sent, and a photo of me and Oshri, both of us looking so young, arms around each other on our way into Lebanon in the winter of '97. And the big flag of Israel that had been hanging on the wall from our first night at Beaufort. I packed it all in and tossed my knapsack onto the pile that nearly reached the ceiling.

At about twenty-one-hundred hours I was up on the roof with six soldiers preparing to pull down the main antenna, which would leave us without phone contact. No hotline, no civilian phone. Only the wireless encrypted transmitter was left. We pushed the iron rods one way while they tugged from the other side using a rope, and Itamar stood ready to saw off the metal legs. We started the countdown. "Hold on,"

I shouted. "Wait for me, just two minutes." I ran to the ladder, climbed halfway down, then jumped the rest of the way. I ran to the war room and phoned Israel from the hotline. "What's up?" I asked Furman. He happened to be in the division's command room at the time, just back from a brief visit home, and he told me how the whole country was flooded with rumors, people were talking in the streets, word was spreading from person to person.

"How about you?" Furman asked. "Stressed-out?"

"No, not at all. We're pulling it off, no big problems."

"It'll be fine," he told me.

I hesitated for a moment. I didn't answer.

"What's the matter, little girl? Are you afraid?" he asked. He was making fun of me. After all, that stupid question about being afraid was stolen from my own repertoire. I didn't laugh.

"Furman," I said. "Get your hands on a Nakpadon and get yourself up here, on the double."

"I wish I could," he answered. "Border's closed. They're not letting anyone in. We're on high alert for incoming missiles."

"Listen," I said, gaining a few seconds. I swallowed. "I'm being serious now. I need you here for this thing. There's no way you can leave me here alone with the kids. I don't care how—grab a motor scooter and get yourself here."

"No chance," he said, making himself clear. "I'm sorry."

Minutes later the antenna came down. We spent the whole night like a conveyor belt, sticking mines to the walls. Every once in a while I'd send some of the guys off for a quick sleep on their cold mattresses, and I passed through the submarines turning off the lights. "Tomorrow's going to be a really tough day," I told them. But within seconds they'd slip outside again. Anyway, who could possibly sleep at a time like that?

An order came over the transmitter suspending all ambushes being carried out by special and elite units across the various sectors, and the squads were told to return to their home bases in Israel immediately. All operations were halted at once, the fighters gathered up the newspapers they'd been shitting into and the bottles they'd been filling with piss and moved back to base in the dark. Meanwhile, River, Bayliss, and I placed mines in the kennel and on top of the generator and the diesel oil tank.

"Can I ask you a totally unrelated question?" River said. "Well, actually, two questions. A kind of a test."

"General knowledge?" I asked. "What, you want to humiliate me at a time like this?"

"After you're wasted, who would you want to be remembered like? Give a name. Somebody, you know, famous. Say it fast, don't think first."

"I don't know. Nobody. I'm not interested in that kind of bullshit."

"Try anyway," he pleaded. "Who would it be?"

"How about you? You go first," I insisted.

"Buddha, I suppose," River answered. "A little Indian prince, fed up with life, bored, sitting under a tree and suddenly he attains enlightenment. Or maybe like Gandhi."

"So what's the second question?" I asked him.

"If you had only two weeks left to live," River said, "what would you do?"

"How about you?" I asked.

"I'd fly to Fiji," he answered.

"Shit, River, cut it out already," I said. "What's with all these stupid questions?" He explained that it was the gap, the chasm between the life you want to live and the life you want to be remembered for. People live, mistakenly, the life they want to be remembered for, he said. They live the wrong life instead of the life that would make them feel good. The smaller the gap between the two, the happier the person. Because wanting to be remembered like Ariel Sharon, for example, or David Ben-Gurion, or even Bill Gates the billionaire just doesn't go together with dreaming of spending the final two weeks of your life tangled up all happy with someone you love on a Red Sea beach. They don't fit. Then, when River pushed me to tell him the truth about what my choice would be, my mind went blank. I couldn't think of anything. Like who would I want to be remembered as? A decorated soldier? A famous general? That would be too obvious, under the circumstances. It would be a letdown for the guys. Maybe Michael Jordan? Everyone says he's a god, a really great guy. And a good businessman, too. Not a bad way to be remembered. But kind of juvenile on my part. No ideas, none at all. And what would I do with the last two weeks of my life? Nothing. Nada. Home? Friends? A trek? It all seemed to miss the point.

"I would sit and write," Bayliss said. "I would spend the last two weeks of my life writing."

"What good would that do?" River lashed out at him. "A waste of time. Barely even enough to remember you by."

I still hadn't come up with anything. I was empty of ideas. What did that mean, anyway? By four-thirty in the morning we could barely see straight. I fell asleep on Dave's mattress beneath the mines I'd hung. I figured I'd catch fifteen minutes to relax the muscles. In a fraction of a second I was already dreaming, a dream I can remember: It was a geometry lesson, we were learning about triangles for a matriculation exam and I didn't know a thing. My friends started whistling from outside; Jojo was there with a car, calling me to come out for a spin, shouting that they'd leave without me. The teacher, a real bitch, was staring at me like she hated me, I swear it. A second later I found myself back on my feet at Beaufort, with huge explosions shaking the cement floor and a fresh round of mortar shells pounding us. From that time on they didn't let up: half an hour of bombing followed by fifteen minutes of quiet. Again and again and again. The terrorists had figured out that something big was going down. River came in just as I was waking up, with tears streaming down my face. "It's just fatigue," I told him when he looked at me, all suspicious. "I swear it, I'm just tired." I pulled myself to my feet with difficulty.

"We've got visitors on their way up here," he said.

"Who?" I asked.

"A Nakpadon and a Safari," he answered. "They're on their way. But how the hell are we going to get them in, with all this shelling?"

We went to the entrance of the secure area and looked outside, trying to count the seconds of quiet between one explosion and the next to learn the rhythm. When we thought we'd figured it out we took a deep breath and River shouted, "Run for it!" and we hightailed it to the computerized surveillance room. We stood there in front of the display screens watching as two vehicles roared along the dark, narrow road not far from Manzurieh. They were driving like madmen. I told the tank to fire in all directions and from Israel I requested 155mm explosive artillery to be aimed at the sources of the launches in the villages, in the hopes of keeping the enemy busy for a while. I asked for a smokescreen, too, on the road leading up to Beaufort. And so it was that they navigated the curves through a thick, gray cloud of smoke, hidden from Hezbollah observers.

At about five-thirty they entered the compound and stopped. The back of the Safari was empty, and Furman popped out of the Nakpadon. "You missed me, huh?" he whispered into my ear. The commander of an Engineering Corps company—Meir Koffler, the "bomb doctor"—had come with him. "Hezbollah's placed seven huge, dormant explosive devices along our access road," Furman reported. "They're waiting for us, for the pullout. That's what

Intelligence is saying." I brought him up to date with our work in progress, and then he divided up assignments between us.

"What's happening with the SLA?" I asked him.

"The collapse has been stopped," he answered. "Their brigade commanders have informed us that everything is under control, that they'll keep fighting for a long time, as long as it takes. Division command wants us to calm everyone down here, keep everybody from believing all the rumors. Especially the radio headlines."

By nine-fifteen Monday morning, two SLA battalions in the western sector had laid down their arms, and in their wake, the Druze battalion had deserted. At ten-fifteen in the tiny stronghold of Arnoun, directly below us, the old T55 tank aimed its barrel toward the gate and stood waiting. Lined up behind it stood a diesel-operated half-track, a black Mercedes, and a few military jeeps. The SLA soldiers jumped into the vehicles and came hurtling out in a crazy race to reach the border with Israel. In Manzurieh the cannons were abandoned. We heard via transmitter that everyone there had taken off at a run. From Tibnit, too. Hezbollah had captured the security zone without firing a single shot. By noon the territory still under control of our good Christian partners commanded by General Antoine Lahad had been reduced to a single enclave near Marjayoun and two small outposts near us at Beaufort, on the mountain range. An entire army had disappeared.

At ten-thirty-five we were, for the first time, in the sights of the mob. The surveillance officer for the entire range reported dozens of vehicles with Hezbollah flags making their way toward the central square of Tibnit, just a mile and a half from us, as well as a huge procession of local residents heading in our direction. Furman asked Israel to begin preps for artillery fire but his request was denied. He was informed that smoke would be provided when the procession got close and that there was still time for that. The loudspeaker announced a drill against incoming terrorists. The sharpshooters took their positions. I watched from the White guard post, with Bayliss and Itamar. An orange van suddenly appeared out of nowhere on the road and stopped less than a mile from our gates. "If they get any closer we're opening fire," I told Bayliss. He positioned a bullet. The van moved forward at a crawl, just a few yards, then stopped. Bayliss was waiting for me to give the word. I waited. The van lurched forward again, braked again. We didn't shoot. The van zigzagged in spurts on our winding road as if testing the limits of our patience. The driver came as close as seven hundred yards away from the gates to Beaufort.

"Maybe we should ask Israel?" Bayliss said.

"No," I answered. "There's no question here. Another step and we pump them with bullets."

After a few long moments of suspense, the doors of the van opened. What the fuck was he doing? Out came a woman, a kid, and a young guy on crutches, in the middle of a closed military zone.

"Should I shoot?" Bayliss asked.

"Wait," I answered.

"Let me shoot," he said. "We'll take one down and they'll get out of here."

"Wait," I insisted.

"It's a ruse!" he shouted. "In another second they'll pull a shoulder-launched missile out of the van and send us all sky-high. Let me finish them off!"

They stood erect in a row in front of the van, looking toward us. They did not move. "What are they planning?" Itamar asked, worried. Truth is, I didn't know what to answer. I got on the transmitter. "Cheetah to Deputy One," I said, calling Furman. I asked him to join us at White. "How old do you think the kid is?" Itamar asked. Bayliss pulled his eye away from the viewfinder and took a good look at the pudgy little redheaded Arab boy standing there in a khaki shirt and blue tie that looked like a Boy Scout uniform.

"Eight," he said.

"No way," Itamar insisted. "I have an eight-year-old cousin who's twice as big as this kid."

"Arabs develop slower," Bayliss answered. "This kid is eight. Seven at the very least."

They argued about the kid's age, about the color of Boy Scout ties, and whether they were international or not, but I could only hear them dully. I wasn't listening. I was trying to gather my thoughts together, situations and responses, thinking how Furman would react. When he showed up he issued an order for every guard post to open fire. "Shoot two hundred yards away from them," he instructed. He was holding a weapon, too. Three thousand bullets were fired all around. "You have to show them you're aggressive enough," he explained. We fired shells and rounds of ammunition and the kid looked scared. But he was disciplined, and the three of them stood without moving. A few seconds later they began marching forward together, up toward us. This was fucking unbelievable. "Sharpshooter," Furman called out to Bayliss, "push them back. We're done playing around." Bayliss took a deep breath and said, "These people have no limits, they're not afraid of anything." A few more long seconds passed. We waited. "At least eight years old," he whispered and then he fired, hitting the passenger seat and shattering the front windshield. Before he could even fire another bullet at one of the headlights, the van turned around and the three of them jumped inside and disappeared. The whole scene was totally surreal. The mortar shells began exploding on us in greater force again and we had to find shelter. And that was how the day passed: once an hour or so a few citizens would approach—sometimes riding motorbikes, sometimes driving vans or ice cream trucks—and Bayliss would shoot at them until they turned around and went back, and then the shelling would increase. Furman and I went running between the guard posts with earphones and mikes on our heads waiting for instructions from Israel and trying to buy time.

At fifteen hundred thirty hours we dragged four five-gallon jerry cans of diesel fuel and gasoline outside. Crates of ammunition, too. Everything had to go up in a huge flame. Dave told us about soldiers from the Golani brigade who'd abandoned an outpost close to the border with Israel. They'd gone home on their own, on foot. He also said Hezbollah was plundering equipment and uniforms in each place that had already been evacuated. No way, guys walked around saying, it must just be rumors. Couldn't be true. Over the transistor radio we could hear a military correspondent broadcasting from Narkis. "The Beaufort is behind enemy lines," he announced. "Hezbollah has the outpost surrounded. At present, IDF soldiers cannot leave there. Beaufort has been cut off." All our parents were probably shitting bricks.

Furman gave the command and the squads began unraveling white detonating cords between the mines. This kind of fuse is composed of TNT and lead covered in burlap cloth and is wrapped in white plastic. Each fuse is only about four hundred feet long, which means we had to set up dozens of them and knot them one to the other if we wanted to cover the entire outpost. It was a job that would take at least four hours, since we needed to proceed from one mine to the next, pulling tripwires out, inserting detonating cords into the hole, filling them with TNT, and, in order to overcome possible disconnections, adding backup connections and security. From that moment on we understood we were in danger of blowing ourselves up. We couldn't tell what the chances were, but it was a chance we had to take. We realized we might all go up in smoke, because a detonating cord like this would explode if it took a hit, and since this fuse ignited at ten thousand feet a second, it would take everything with it.

At nineteen hundred hours we held a briefing. Furman spoke to the point—no speechifying, no play for emotions. "In exactly one hour from now we're sending out two Safari trucks, an equipment truck, and an APC," he informed them. "Nearly all of you will return to Israel with this convoy. You'll be taking all the remaining equipment and the soldiers' personal belongings. Anything we don't manage to load will be destroyed here. The only people staying on with me here will be Erez and Levanoni, thirteen fighters, the tank squad, and Meir Koffler, the Engineering Corps officer. We'll hook up the fuses, make a secured double-loop fuse, and then we'll turn out the lights. Three hours after the rest of you have left we'll blow the place up and get out of here, fast. We'll meet up in Israel at midnight."

That night there were something like eighty guys at the outpost: fighters, surveillance officers, soldiers from the Signal Corps, the Ordnance Corps, the Armored Corps, and two D9 bulldozer operators. Furman read out the list of who was assigned to which vehicle. "These are the fighters who will be here to the end," he announced. "Erez's squad: Tom, Itamar, Zion, Koka, Boaz, Pinchuk, Barnoy, River, and Bayliss. And four more from the first-tour group: Murphy, Koby, Shauly, and Sela." He didn't wait for questions, took off immediately, and left everyone to go nuts without him. All the guys scheduled to leave in the first group went mental, threw furniture around. "No way we're not taking part in the big pullout," they hollered. "No way, it can't be!" It was such a historic operation, who wouldn't want to be part of it? "I'm not leaving!" was the cry heard from several soldiers. I tried to calm them down: "You're all part of the pullout. It's only a three-hour difference."

When I left them, Dave ran after me. He was among the

first-wave evacuees. "It's important to me," he said. "I've got to stay here with you. Got to be here to the end." I told him there was nothing I could do about it, it was a matter of priorities and professional considerations. He removed the black kippa from his thick, red hair and crumpled it in his hand, waving it in front of my face. "You've got to understand how important it is to me," he pleaded. "Tell Furman he has to let me stay."

"What's the kippa got to do with anything?" Levanoni said with a mean laugh as he came up from behind. "You think God gave you an assignment in the withdrawal? Or maybe you think we need, like, divine protection? A miracle?"

"Erez understands," he said. "Erez understands."

"No chance," I told him coldly. This wasn't the time for drama. "You've got to go. And that's an order." I'm not kidding, he started crying. When he turned to walk away I called after him, "Wait for me at the fence, okay?"

Running quickly back and forth under the open sky, exposed, we loaded the trucks with sensitive equipment, special surveillance apparatus, transmitters, and even missiles, along with all the personal belongings of all the soldiers, even those of us staying on to the end. Everything but the little video camera, because Furman wanted to film the mushroom cloud from the explosion. We wrapped up operations in a kind of pandemonium, everything happening at a run, and then, under the tall flagpole at the fortress, River and Boaz and Pinchuk and a bunch of younger soldiers pushed and cursed each other and nearly got into a brawl over who was going to climb up to lower the flag and fold it. There was only room for one on the flagpole. "Chili!" I shouted from the parking area. "Everyone take a step back," I commanded them. "Let Chili do it." So, with calls of encouragement from below, our cook climbed to the top and undid the knots and slipped back down wrapped in the old, stained, and faded cloth.

At five minutes before eight o'clock the first-wave evacuees stood in two long lines in the secure area facing the exit like paratroopers preparing to jump. The first truck had backed up to the exit. Furman passed among the soldiers and gave them iron numbers for the count-off and a tap on the shoulder. The rest of us—the select few staying on to the end—made the rounds for farewell hugs. "Don't worry, we'll meet at midnight," we said. "Watch our bags for us." Then the order came and they were sent out. There was heavy shelling all around. The Armored Corps outpost below Marjayoun tried to hit the sources of their launches and cripple them, and the sky glowed like a lightning storm. The gates were opened and the convoy left, and, just before slamming the iron door shut, we managed to get a glimpse of the yellow trail of dust from the trucks that lit up the darkness. With the door closed we had left the storm outside. We stood there in reduced numbers, trying to get used to the unaccustomed silence. We looked around at each other.

"Kind of alone, aren't we?" River said. A barrage of mortar shells fell on the roof but there was no one to announce "Hit! Hit!" since there was no longer a war room. There were only six guys manning the guard posts and without the use of electronic monitors or digital binoculars, so they were half blind out there. I joined Bayliss, who had lit a fire in a large metal rubbish bin in the corner of the room and was burning classified documents. "Kind of sick, don't you think?" he asked. "Everybody wanted so bad to stay on even though they knew there could be a slaughter here. What people won't do for glory. So they can walk around their neighborhood like big shots."

"Action, that's what people love," I told him. "Action. And fear. Fear's pretty addictive."

"The whole time you serve here," Bayliss said, "your survival instinct gets more and more messed up, dulled. It seeps in, really affects you. They tell you that carrying out your mission at all costs is at the top of the eleven IDF basic principles, even before the preservation of human life. The mission before human life. Does that make sense to you?"

I was ripping pages from *Back to the Future,* the withdrawal guide, and slowly dropping them in bunches into the bin so the flames would remain under control and wouldn't set the building on fire. All of a sudden, in a flash, fire leapt from the bin and took hold of me. Maybe I'd put my hand too far in, because it started to burn. My right hand. Bayliss jumped on me, knocked me to the ground, and sprayed me with an extinguisher that was standing by. I lay there on my arm, then I ran to stick it in cold water. River showed up with the medic's kit. "These burns look pretty deep," he said. But there wasn't any chance of being evacuated. There were no choppers. He would have to treat me right there with wet bandages and some morphine for the pain. "There you go," Bayliss whispered to me. "At the very last moment you managed to get yourself a scar from this place. It's actually pretty strange you never had one before." In fact, I did. Two. Once I'd split my head open fighting with a guy named Twina while waiting in line to lift weights. Another time I fell on a piece of rusty metal during an ambush, when we stormed the Abu-Jabai terrorist cell. There was still a line running from my calf to my foot where they'd sewed up the deep gash. After River finished with me I went back to work with everyone else.

Another few minutes and the whole thing should have been over, the end of Beaufort. According to our watches, it was thirty-five minutes past twenty-two hundred hours. Bayliss was already sitting in the seat of the Nakpadon and had asked River for his small, laminated copy of "The Traveler's Prayer." He attached it to the front compartment, the spot where in a normal car you'd find the rearview mirror. Pinchuk, who'd tucked his shirt into his pants and primped himself, was standing in the doorway with his helmet and his vest and his gun slung from his shoulder, waiting for a green light. It was then that a female voice came over the transmitter with a brief message: "Mission postponed," she announced. "We'll get back to you with more information later." Postponed? Till when? "No way of knowing," the voice answered.

Furman went off at a run to the White guard post, near the bunker. He pulled a mobile phone he'd brought from home out of his pants pocket. It was only there, at one certain angle between the third and fourth sandbags, that there was mobile-phone reception at the outpost, and only sporadically and with luck. No soldier would ever dare phone, even though generations of fighters were in on the secret. Furman phoned Amos. "We can't postpone," he said. Amos apologized, told Furman everything was chaotic and he couldn't get answers. It turned out there were still a few differences of opinion, something to do with the prime minister, so we'd have to stay on in Lebanon another few days. They were stalling while political negotiations could be completed. But it was still likely the withdrawal would take place that week, he guessed, because the politicians understood the situation was dire. "Hang on," Amos concluded, and the line went dead.

21

ON TUESDAY MORNING, a few minutes before sunrise, River started shouting that the flagpole was bare. There was no flag on it! Shit! We'd taken it down when we thought we were on our way out, but now we were staying and Hezbollah would soon be rolling out of bed and looking up at Beaufort, where they would see a bare flagpole and conclude that we'd abandoned the place—and up they'd come to capture it. A huge wave of people would make their way here with pickaxes while a group of armed terrorists in black commando uniforms would provide cover for them. And what exactly would we do in the face of all this? We had to get the flag back up there, and fast, because in just a few minutes, when the skies lightened, it would be too dangerous to send a soldier on a ladder up the wall of the fortress, and from there up the flagpole, exposed.

I was lying on the kitchen floor wrapped in one of the blue tablecloths Chili saved for special occasions, trying to relax my muscles. River and Furman ran in, kicked me, and pulled me to my feet. Where was the flag? We went hunting for it, looking everywhere: the office, the gathering place for wounded soldiers, inside crates, under beds. Where could Chili have tossed it before he caught his ride home? Wait a minute. Was it possible...? Sure. Likely, even: the flag was probably back in Israel. Chili could have wrapped himself in it in the Safari. Yeah, it had to be. We were seriously fucked. In that whole goddamned outpost there wasn't a single flag, not one of the little ones from Independence Day, not the plastic kind lined up on a string that until the night before had been draped over breasts and bikinis on the wall and around the framed pledge to defend Israel's northern border, not even a single piece of cloth a flag could be drawn on. What were we supposed to do? Draw a flag on a piece of cardboard? Wood? Bayliss suggested that someone—especially someone fat, like Itamar—should take off his white T-shirt for us to use. And that's when it hit me. I ran to the senior officers' submarine and overturned the rusted iron cabinet in the corner. I was right, it was still there, stuffed behind the cabinet. Unbelievable. An entire year of cleaning duty and they hadn't once moved the cabinet and pulled it out. I myself had stuffed it in there. It was gray and covered in dust, but it was still there, Ziv Farran's Four Mothers T-shirt. I cut the cloth with a penknife. Furman found a tube of green camouflage paint and squirted out two stripes, added a lopsided Star of David, and we ran outside with it. Bayliss, the skinniest and fastest of us, climbed the pole and hung it. "This is totally surreal," he called down from above. "Totally fucking surreal," I answered him. The sky was already orange. River was humming the national anthem and busting up laughing. Furman filmed us saluting.

A new day was starting. A tough one. The soldiers spent it doing nonstop guard duty. Furman and I went from one post to the next, oblivious to the mortar shells falling like crazy all around us. A little after nine in the morning the SLA soldiers at Hadar and Valencia waved good-bye to the nearby Dlaat outpost, which they were supposed to be guarding, and took off. We watched as their half-track stalled about two hundred yards from the gate and they jumped out of it—two of them barefoot even—and ran away on the hot asphalt. A few minutes later, while dozens of local citizens were climbing on top of the half-track, a tow truck showed up and the mechanic started to fix the engine and do a little bodywork. Kids were fighting over the steering wheel, and suddenly the thing started moving. "It's all over," I said to Furman. "There's no such thing as the Ali Taher range battalion anymore." We were surrounded by terrorists. There were three combat choppers circling over our heads, keeping us safe from above by driving off anyone who came near. By this time there were processions streaming out of every village—with flags, without weapons—that were marching slowly in our direction. I watched them from Blue, trying to make out their faces through the binoculars and waiting for them to reach our shooting zone. Each time someone got there the choppers would open fire and push them back. That morning word had also come from Israel that they could use the artillery, live ammunition. They fired two hundred shells at our request in order to scare off everyone coming near on all fronts and to convince Hezbollah to stay in their foxholes. "Don't trust anyone in situations like these," Furman said. "Anyone coming close gets shot." He ordered the tank outside the gates to shoot at Arnoun so they'd get the message down there. If Hezbollah entered the village and settled in there, at the foot of Beaufort, we wouldn't be able to get out. They'd be waiting for us around the bend.

At fourteen hundred hours the order came: we'd pull out that night at twenty-three hundred hours. Supposedly. Bayliss climbed onto the bulldozer and we went out and tore up the asphalt, pulled down the sheds, and crushed the rubbish bins. Hezbollah wasn't going to get anything from us.

We whitewashed the unit insignias that were painted on a concrete wall. Just before nightfall we started laying the detonating cords outside, in the trenches and at the guard posts, to be sure they would burn down, too. From then on, a direct hit by a shell would kill us all on the spot. We'd be vaporized, because the mines would blow up in a chain reaction. There wouldn't even be any remains of bodies left behind. We understood this, but nobody complained. There was no choice.

At twenty-one hundred hours we received bad news that was really hard to swallow: Amos explained to us that the Lebanese government had registered an urgent complaint with the UN that Israel was planning to blow up a historic site. "Dismantle the mines," he told us. "You're going to hand over the outpost undamaged to the UN." "We don't have time," Furman told him over the transmitter. "There's no way we can manage it. And we can't leave behind six and a half tons of TNT as a gift for the terrorists, which will come back at us in the form of bombings along the northern border towns. All the fuses are already attached and in place. We spent three days setting it up, a real work of art. And what about the equipment we didn't manage to load onto the trucks? What are we supposed to do with that? We've got TOW missiles that didn't make it back to Israel. How can we leave those behind? I can't bear to watch the Lebanese messing around with our uniforms, and the missiles, on television tomorrow. And what am I supposed to tell the soldiers? That we did all this work for nothing?" Over the earphones the fighters could hear Amos, powerless, and Furman exploding, barely in control, his voice trembling. When he understood it was a lost cause he ripped the earphone from his ear, went into his office, and slammed the door.

The kids roared, released all their built-up tension. I did, too, swore like a maniac. All of a sudden they're playing dumb? I mean, it never bothered those bastards before—the

UN, the Lebanese government—that Hezbollah was bombarding the fortress with mortar shells day and night. Damaging the landscape? Destroying historical ruins? My ass! They'd never shown the slightest interest, so what was all this playacting now for, this pretending to be bleeding hearts?

I opened the door and went in to talk to Furman. "This is fucked, isn't it?" I said as I sat down on his desk.

"Royally," he answered.

"So tell them we're not leaving," I said in a voice full of confidence.

"What?" he said, grimacing.

"Let's inform them that we're not leaving this outpost without blowing it up," I suggested. "We blow it up or we don't leave. We stay here."

"You're really crazy, aren't you?"

"What do you have to lose?" I asked. "You believe it's the right thing to do, don't you? We're right, aren't we? So do the right thing and go all the way with it."

"You want us to disobey an order? In the middle of the withdrawal?"

"You did it before, when we went looking for Spitzer's head. You'll get used to it little by little. It'll turn you into a nice guy."

"It's actually been a while since you've disobeyed an order," he said with a smile.

"I've never stopped missing those days," I told him.

"It'll be the end for both of us, you know that," he said.

"Short prison term, nothing too bad. After that I'm inviting you to Fiji. The trip's on me!"

He put on his headset and contacted Command center. We were happy. It gave us great satisfaction to do something important, to make a brave decision. "We cannot carry out this mission," he told them. The operations sergeant on the other side didn't understand, she asked him to repeat himself three times. Then she got off the line. Everything was quiet. We sat and waited. "Tell me about prison," Furman said. He didn't even look especially tense. I mean, less tense than at any other time during the last day. I told him that officers' prison was a country club, a Garden of Eden without the swimming pool and the girls. Make sure you bring suntan lotion and sunglasses and you'll be fine.

We spent a long time alone in the room together. In the meantime, Levanoni, on his own initiative, was keeping the kids busy with pre-op vehicle maintenance before pullout time. We joined them, sat with them in the dirt. Zion handed out cigarettes, River gave us the last of the apple juice. And we waited. At twenty-two hundred hours and twenty minutes Barnoy, who was guarding at the farthest guard post, White, suddenly thought it was too quiet. If it was that quiet, he reasoned, we must have left already without calling him. He figured we might have forgotten him in all the craziness. After all, the count-offs don't always work, there are screwups. He thought that in another second or two he was going to be blown up with the outpost and started making weird animal noises and shouting "hello" to see if anyone could hear him. Nobody answered. He came running to the computerized monitoring station and found no guards, only mines and detonating cords. That's when he really started panicking. He felt a really strong need to run down and look for us but he knew that if we hadn't left and we caught him running around and abandoning his post he'd be court-martialed and tossed in jail (and this was no officers' prison we're talking about). It was dangerous, too, to abandon the guard post like that. He climbed back up, continued to guard. But fear was eating him up inside. Five minutes later he took his chances and made a mad dash to the secure area. The entrance, which was usually as busy as a shopping mall on a Saturday night, was dead quiet. Barnoy was sure it was all over for him, that we were already back in Israel. He figured maybe it was better for him to get away from the explosion on foot and spend the rest of his life under a new identity with some Lebanese woman in the village below. He started running again, this time in the direction of the front gate. It was only then that he saw the Nakpadons, and Levanoni. And us. He calmed down. And then he panicked again, because he realized that the White guard post was standing empty. He grimaced and sprinted back up to his post. It took him three months to tell us the whole chain of events because he was afraid he'd be court-martialed, or worse—that he'd be a laughingstock for generations of soldiers to come, until his dying day. In fact, we were completely sympathetic, because even I had the thought that we might forget somebody up there on the hill, some spacey young soldier. It wasn't such a crazy idea, and it was scarier than the threat of being attacked by terrorists or sustaining a direct missile hit on one of the mines.

At twenty-two hundred thirty-five hours we heard Kaplan's warm voice over the headset. He was looking for Furman. I quieted the guys down so we could hear. "You are authorized to detonate," Kaplan said, and we cheered, threw our arms around each other. You wouldn't believe it, it was at least as emotional as when the hostages were freed at Entebbe. "Go on, get out of there," Kaplan ordered. "You have clearance to leave."

From then on, everything happened in a whirlwind. Levanoni ran from guard post to guard post, relieving the last guards of their duty. Just like that you were allowed to abandon your post, desert the holy of holies. The hedgehogs were empty and yet the sky didn't fall. Furman and Meir Koffler checked the mines to make sure no wires had come loose, and they secured the backup systems. I gave an order to "man your vehicles like you're going to war, because there's going to be combat involved. I want four MAGs on each Nakpadon." At twenty-three hundred hours we stood ready at the gate for our last briefing.

In officers' academy you learn to prepare yourself for briefings that last an hour and include maps, maneuvers, and diagrams. But here was Furman holding one crumpled sheet of paper and making the shortest speech we'd ever heard about the biggest mission we'd ever carry out, the mission of a lifetime. "You know what to do," he said. "There's no time. Just operate the way you did today and good luck." Someone from division headquarters was shouting at us down the transmitter: "Get out of there already, get out as fast as you can." We got the kids into the two Nakpadons. The tank and the bulldozer were first in line.

"River," I said, "adjust the frequencies in the Nakpadon."

"I'm not a signaler," he answered.

"You won't believe this but you just got certified. You're the signaler for the withdrawal."

I asked Furman to wait sixty seconds for me. "There's no time," he shouted from behind. "You fuckup! *Now* you need to take a piss?" I didn't answer. I went back into the secure area for one last look, to sear it into my memory. The kitchen, for example, an image that will stay with me for the rest of my life: a tray of schnitzels pulled out of the oven that no one took a single bite of, and the salads and French fries that Chili left on the aluminum counter before he left. We hadn't had time to eat any of it, hadn't had the inclination, either, so it was all being left behind, those schnitzels all lined up and waiting to be exploded. I went to the Signal Corps Company Club, too, and stood in front of the memorial wall and read what was written there: IN MEMORY OF OUR FRIENDS IN THE ALON SQUAD—THE BEST AND BRIGHTEST—WHO FELL IN THE HELICOPTER TRAGEDY, FEBRUARY 1997. Who were we, anyway, compared to them? Who were we to cry over what we'd lost, when they'd lost twenty comrades in a single blow? One minute they were here, twenty men, the next they were no longer alive. How do you lose dozens of men in a moment and keep on going, surviving, like nothing happened? When all of a sudden you don't have anyone to fight with or sleep with mattress-to-mattress anymore. This guy's laugh and that one's eyes, they all hound your memory, and all you want to do is forget, and sometimes all you want to do is *not* forget. Thirty-three men bound for Beaufort died that night, including the district commander, Lieutenant Colonel Moshe Muallem. And the squad leader, Lieutenant Alon Babiyan. I wondered in what ways the guy was like me. And who I was compared to him, a man who'd given his all.

I didn't notice Furman come in behind me until he put his hand on my shoulder. I thought about saying something about how emotional this was but I was afraid of sounding pompous. Neither of us said a word. All of a sudden the guy pulls me close and plants a hug on me. "You little shithead," he said. "Come on, let's get you home to Mom."

We turned off the main light switch and left the building. "Command to Cheetah," Kaplan came in over the transmitter, "take my friends out of there with you, will you?" We raced over to the low whitewashed wall and set to work on taking down the metal plaque hanging from it by chains. THE BEAUFORT WAS CAPTURED BY THE SOLDIERS AND COMMANDERS OF THE GOLANI RECONNAISSANCE UNIT. . . . WHERE DO YOU FIND MEN LIKE THE . . . This was just where Menachem Begin had stood in his windbreaker. When Ariel Sharon bragged about it being one of our greatest achievements, Begin said, "It was an open wound. An open wound."

"Did you fight the whole night long?" Begin asked Tamir, a soldier. "What kind of resistance had they set up there?"

"There weren't a lot of them," Tamir explained, "but they were really entrenched."

"Were there a lot who surrendered?" Begin asked.

"No, sir, no one," Tamir told him. "Everyone was killed."

At Beaufort, no one surrenders. There's no gray area, only

black and white, for the past many hundreds of years. This time it was us. I wondered who the next boys to be sent up here would be, and what reason there would be to spill their blood. We pulled the plaque free and loaded it onto the Nakpadon. We pronounced the outpost empty.

At the gate, Meir Koffler connected the electric detonator to the detonating cord and, using a double-wire cable, spooled it all the way to the Nakpadon, which was parked thirty yards down the hill. The tank had already set out down the road and stopped at the J-curve, where they could maintain eye contact. "Come on, Meir, sweetheart," I shouted. "Enough pussyfooting. Blow that baby sky-high already." At that very moment another huge round of mortar shells began falling, dozens of them one after another, from every direction, from all the surrounding villages and towns. We could see the launches, it was like a hailstorm on the hill. "Take off!" they shouted at us from division headquarters. "Go, now, leave everything, don't even blow the place up if it's not working."

Thirteen flares went up in the air and night turned into day: Hezbollah knew something was up and they were trying to light the darkness. When the enemy uses flares the procedure is to get out of the place immediately, as fast as possible, like a blue streak, and not in a straight line. But we had nowhere to escape to for the moment. Furman ordered explosives and a smoke screen, the tank fired, and Bayliss never stopped screaming, "Missiles! Missiles! Missiles!" A huge flame surged over the Dlaat outpost. That was our friends closing shop, on their way out. Over the transmitter they kept yelling at us. "We're fine, don't worry," Furman told them, and asked for several more minutes as he went off to help with the wires and connections. "We feel great. Give us a little time, be a little patient, it's about to happen." In fact it took another seventeen minutes, which felt to us a lot longer than eternity. The kids sat hunched up and crowded in the belly of the armored cars. Nobody said a word. There was only the sound of the engines, and the exploding shells. "Get out of there," Kaplan said. "And that's an order. Now."

Meir Koffler finished his work. "Thirty seconds to explosion," he shouted. "Thirty seconds to explosion," Furman repeated into the transmitter. "Give a last look around for me," Kaplan responded. "You're cleared to detonate."

River pressed the little PTT button and cut in to the transmitter, just like when we came up for the kids' first tour of duty, only happy. He was just as scared as then, but strong: " 'May it be your will, our God and God of our forefathers, that You head us toward peace, guide our feet toward peace, lead us to peace . . .' " Bayliss flashed him a look, a look only the two of them understood, and River left off, just like that, in the middle of the prayer. Everything was quiet for a few moments, then Bayliss took over: " 'And make us reach,' " he recited, so that everyone could hear him, even at headquarters back in Israel, " 'and make us reach our desired destination for life, gladness, and peace. May You rescue us.' " We all said, "Amen." Furman came over and handed me the wires, the fuse that would set off the explosion. "All yours," he said simply, passing up on doing the honors himself. "Good luck," he said. To everyone he shouted, "Close all hatches!" and he climbed into a nearby Nakpadon. They all battened down: there were only thirty yards between us and the gate, according to the rules barely a safe distance even for detonating a half-pound explosive brick, while we were about to ignite six and a half tons of dynamite, and not a single one of us—including the professor from the Engineering Corps—had any idea what the force of the flames and the blast would be, or whether the fortress would collapse, and what would happen to us. We knew there was a chance we'd go up in flames, too. But there's this moment when you don't care, you're indifferent. You say to yourself, Maybe I'll die, turn into ashes, and maybe not, let's just get it over with.

You're so exhausted, so full of emotions. Meir Koffler sat down next to me. He nodded, waiting for me to activate it. My hands were paralyzed. I relaxed my fingers a bit, took a deep breath. "Come on, bro, set it off," he said to me, going through the motions with his hands. "Do it. Do it."

"You do it," I said, handing it over to him. "I'll watch."

22

AND SO, WE WERE THE ONES who pressed the button to make the Beaufort outpost go up in smoke. Actually, it was Meir Koffler who pressed the button while the rest of us covered our ears tight. Everyone was closed up inside the vehicles; only I couldn't stand it, I had to stick my head out to watch nine hundred and eighty mines blow Beaufort to smithereens. Holy shit, what an explosion that was! There was a huge red flame in the sky, an orange mushroom cloud, a wave of fire, light and bright as day, and then everything just fell apart, crumbled, and the earth shook. We were jolted five yards forward by the force of the blast, sixty-three tons of Nakpadon tossed into the air. I fell inside the vehicle. "Done! Exploded!" I shouted into the transmitter. All around us, mortar shells continued falling. "Move out. Over!" Furman shouted over the transmitter. "Move out. Over!" We could barely hear him, the explosions continued to come in waves. "Eighty-two, forward!" he commanded the tank. "Aim, adjust, and shoot while moving in the direction of Tibnit." "Come on, sweetheart," I said to the soldiers, "let's get the engines rolling. We're taking you home," and off we went. It must have been really shitty for the guys hearing this back in Israel, at Command headquarters on the other side of the fence, and not here with us. And for all those people drinking lemonade through a straw at a café on Sheinkin Street. I stuck my head out again. Our air force was striking at a distance. On the darkened horizon I could see the Reichan outpost going up in flames. Christ, what a wild night. Slabs of cement were flying in every direction, pieces of the outpost were falling from the clouds, concrete was coming down like rain. BOOM! A concrete wall had fallen on our vehicle, nearly crushing it. "Eighty-two, get your heads inside!" It was Furman shouting over the transmitter, but I couldn't do it, I kept watching. All of a sudden I noticed him, Furman, behind me, his body also half exposed as he stared, too. His Nakpadon slowed down and mine did as well, and we watched, blinded, lit up in yellow, wanting to make sure with our own eyes that nothing would be left intact. Huge, shocked smiles were drawn across our faces. And no, you'll be surprised to hear that you don't think about home at a time like that, and you don't think about your mother, or girls, and you don't see your life flashing before your eyes like in the movies. All I could think about was uncertainty, about the seven explosive devices awaiting us on our trip home, how maybe they'd be set off and maybe not, about the operation. And about the strength inside me—I suddenly had so much strength in me—and how I felt revived, and focused.

Four whistling bombs landed right in front of us, to the right of the tank. The tank was quick to fire white phosphorus shells, the kind that are supposed to misguide missiles and prevent them from reaching their targets. But the shells hit us instead, and we rolled around coughing, practically puking our lungs out because we couldn't breathe. "Don't shoot any more of those!" Furman ordered over the transmitter. "Even if they're firing missiles at you, don't shoot. It just hits us." In the meantime, an unmanned aerial vehicle circling overhead sent thermal photos back to Israel showing the damage done by the white phosphorus shells. In the division war room they figured we were goners. "Chill out," we told them. From Israel, more shots were being fired in order to set up a smoke screen for us. "Not so close!" I shouted. "We can't see a thing." But we weren't afraid, I swear. We crossed the J-curve, where Ziv had fallen, and we got our last look at Beaufort while Cobra choppers flew in formation above us, escorting us home. "Okay," I shouted to River. "Make a sharp left here," and we popped the Nakpadon onto the main road.

Like magic, everything suddenly cleared up. On the road we seemed to be inside a ring of peace and quiet. Off in the distance everything was still burning, and an orange storm lit up the sky like some virtual war, and here and there the transmitter clicked to life and gave worrying reports about a lone tank stuck way off near Hatzbiyeh with ten soldiers inside, or about an overturned armored personnel carrier. But with us, it was like we were in a tunnel, on a yellow brick road, and everything was quiet and calm. Near the Khardaleh bridge, ten minutes before one o'clock, we met up with convoys on their way down from Ishiye and Reichan. A group of Golani troops laid tracks and we crossed. We saw the convoy from Dlaat, too, moving along ahead of us. I sat down, it was pretty cold. Pinchuk pulled our homemade flag from his pants pocket, the one we'd made out of Ziv's torn shirt. "When did you guys manage to lower that thing?" I asked with a smile. He handed it to me, put it around my neck. And that's how I remained for the next forty minutes: wrapped inside it, silent like everyone else, trying to think about what I should be thinking about and actually thinking about nothing at all. I could hear Furman shouting, "Guys, the Beaufort is burning! Beaufort is burning!"

At one-forty-three in the morning Gate 93 was opened for us. We entered Israel, and nobody said anything like "The nightmare's over," and nobody shouted that we'd "run away." We left with dignity, with pride. We climbed out of our vehicles, everyone was hugging everyone else, including Kaplan and Amos. They were saying what a great thing it had been, historic, a glorious event. People were kissing and slapping each other's backs and handing out compliments about a job well done. Furman was telling everyone he loved them all, and tears of joy were flowing, and they all piled on top of each other in a huge human heap. They danced and went crazy with happiness. But not me. I went off to the side, took off my vest and equipment, removed my helmet, and sat down on a rock. Alone. I believe that then and there was the saddest moment of my life.

We stayed there, next to the fence, until sunrise. Soldiers from the Northern Command prepared a lousy breakfast for us and a doctor and medic treated my hand, changed the bandages. When Bayliss took off his helmet there was a kippa on his head. Everyone asked him about it, and he told them he'd gone back to being religious, and that's the way he was going to stay. Turns out he really still did want to be part of the clan. A person has to believe in something, hold on to something, he explained with a smile. And when the sun rose we looked toward Lebanon together, at the pillars of smoke still climbing skyward. I heard Amos telling about the guys from the Ishiye outpost, how they'd gotten into trouble on their way down, and something strong inside me wanted to go up to him and request to go back in to help rescue them. I felt I needed another short, quick breath of that piece of earth. Of that action. But I didn't have the strength to get up. At six-forty-two the town of Kiryat Shmona was still under curfew, on high alert due to the threat of Katyusha rocket attacks. The gate to Lebanon was sealed off. "And so it has ended," the military correspondent reported. "Eighteen years after they crossed the border into Lebanon, IDF troops moved last night in the opposite direction—inbound. One after the other they blew up the outposts: Shani and Karkum, Ishiye and Reichan, Dlaat and Galgalit, names we've learned that have now been wiped from the map. And Beaufort, the most recognizable symbol of southern Lebanon." The guys stood behind him, arms around each other, waving to the cameras, shouting and singing. *"Mother, Mother, embrace me/We'll never be separated."* I just sat there, still on my rock. I didn't even phone home, never thought that my family might be worried or that the whole country was going nuts. It never occurred to me that at six in the morning everybody was preoccupied with us. Just then a red Mazda stopped on the road and the door opened. Out came Oshri, and his mother, and an officer from the Adjutancy Corps, and that space-age metal pole of an arm he had—all that suffering in store for him because of it, all of it avoidable, I thought. He came up to me and held me firm, while tears flowed from my eyes. I didn't try to hide them. "If we'd only gotten out earlier..." I started to say, but he cut me off. "No," he said, kissing my forehead, his eyes shining, "what's important is that it's over," he said. "Everything's going to be fine, now that it's over."

23

GAZA, 2001. It's not over. Is that possible? Again? It doesn't make any sense. We've lost enough, while there are others who haven't lost a single man. What shitty luck. "Live hammer!" the transmitter calls out. That's the code name for an explosive device. There's a thick, black cloud of smoke and small flames and they're inside it, on the ground, unconscious. Two guys. There's muffled crying—I don't know who it is—and a cry for help, and a few shouts and some coughing. A little mumbling and then everything goes silent, even the muezzin in the mosque at the refugee camp. All that's left is a ringing in the ears and the sound of burning, like a huge popcorn popper gone berserk. There's a strong smell of burnt rubber, like a basketball that slams you in the face, knocks you down, and makes you dizzy. Burnt rubber and charred flesh, a fatal and asphyxiating mix of smells. I lose my balance.

I check myself out. The body's whole, no blood, and I run over to them, bend down, grab hold of each of them in turn. Above the right hand there's a black wristband with a red bead that is meant to be removed only on discharge day. Our squad's good luck charm. Oshri made them for all of us as gifts. I search for a pulse, verify death. These days I don't insist on pumping on the chest, going mental, screaming at the body like I used to: "Breathe, you motherfucker, please breathe," or "Hang in there, man, don't die on me now." Even when they were dead I was convinced they wanted to tell me something, their dying words. Not anymore. Dead is dead. Like now. And in the paper they'll call us the COMPANY OF DEATH once again. Only a little while longer to discharge.

That's the way it is here, man. It's only routine. In the first second a dark screen covers your eyes and puts out your breath. You go blind for a few moments, you freeze in your tracks, ball your fists. You don't breathe. In a flash your mind empties out of all thoughts, erases, like it's making space, and that's scary. Then the dam breaks, and within a second or two, thousands of confused fragments of thought pump through you like crazy. And the words echo again and again in your brain: they're dead, they're dead, they're dead. You haven't even had a chance to take it all in, but grief washes through you from the inside like someone's pumping gallons of it into your veins—you can feel it that hard. Like the end of the world. I personally have gotten used to experiencing the end of the world on a regular basis, gotten used to crumbling at first, then pulling myself together within a matter of minutes and kissing a bloody forehead, a farewell of sorts. A last look into eyes that remain open as I put an end to the matter. And then I go back to the barracks.

I'm used to going back to the barracks, to pairs of flip-flops next to army cots, and sunglasses lying on top of blankets. The book lying open on the pillow, with a title like *His Whole Life Ahead of Him*: that's irony pissing in our faces. The pastries Zion bought to get him through the Sabbath, the bag of potato chips we didn't finish, it's all still there. Pinchuk's green and white checked towel, the tattered one that's been unraveling in every hellhole we've served in, hanging to dry on the rusted metal rack. A memory from the first week at the training base: that towel was there, faded and knobby, so that it already felt like sandpaper. Zitlawi said, "What gives? That's the best your mother can do for you, you stinking rich boy? She couldn't have made a little effort for her baby?" I remember how Pinchuk didn't say a word. You could see in his eyes that it hurt him, a lot, that he was a sensitive kid, a mama's boy. Wait a minute, his mother! Holy shit, she still doesn't know! They haven't gotten to her yet. She's probably smiling right now, calling a cinemaphone to order tickets to a movie this evening, has friends over sitting in the garden. Pretty soon her life is going to end, devastation. Unlike us, she's not used to it. It's her first time. What a waste. If she'd only known that somebody had teased him that night at the training base she would definitely have bought the most exclusive, the fanciest, the most glamorous towel ever for her little angel. He's the one who probably insisted on hanging on to that ratty piece of sandpaper because he didn't want to make his mom feel bad. Poor guy. I sit on one of the beds holding tight to the blanket and trying to put the brakes on the confusion that's sucking me under. My head's banging around, going nuts, but I'm used to it. Used to folding up personal belongings and packing them into knapsacks that aren't mine. The white T-shirt still has his smell. Hello, and welcome to the suppression stage. Because in our squad if somebody stands still he gets two slaps in the face, then he pulls himself together and snaps out of his shock.

Am I a crybaby? Absolutely not. Not a pansy, either, or a pussy. I'm not the type that cries at funerals. I hug sometimes, real solid-like, only to give support to others, hold them tight when the coffin is brought out, tuck their heads into my shoulder while the eulogy's being read. Sometimes, when the situation is critical, I'll pat someone, stroke him. But I never cry. I go on. Two days later I'll be cracking jokes like anyone else, laughing about the situation. The usual.

When Barnoy was killed, Palestinian protesters crowded around the front gate of our outpost, put pictures of him cut from the morning papers on the ground, and pissed on them. It was all still really raw, only twenty-four hours after it had happened, and there they were, pissing on Barnoy. I don't know how I managed not to open fire on them, put the gun on automatic and pump them full of holes. I was ready to perforate every last one of them, I swear it. I watched my own guys looking at them as these assholes pissed on their friend. How did they manage not to fall apart then. How? I felt the need to boost their morale, so that afternoon, when we went out again to open up the roads, I was even more hotheaded than usual and I shot up the boilers on the rooftops as we passed by, firing rounds at three hundred and sixty degrees into the refugee camp, into the filth. I got my hands on a local wagon driver, grabbed hold of his ears real hard, and spit a big goober right between his eyes. I shouted at him like a maniac. I had the feeling it was making my guys feel better, especially the younger ones. Part getting it off my chest, part hanging on to our dignity. Afterward I felt bad about it, but I'm used to that.

It's fucking Saigon here, believe me, brother. Real fucking Saigon. Not as green, but the same shit. You enter Gaza through the Karni crossing, go to Garbage Road, turn at Death Bend, continue straight till you get to the bridge where the paratroopers were killed, then on to Suicide Bomber Curve, and in another four minutes you reach us, at the Netzarim junction. Mounds of metal junk line the road, the head of a dead donkey sticks out from a concrete slab, flies and mosquitoes fill the air like a plague of locusts that darken the skies. And the stench, the stench. This place is an endless garbage dump. When you're used to the standard of Beaufort, the Gaza landscape isn't going to win you over.

Our outpost at the Netzarim junction is called Samba, otherwise known as Magen Three. It's got thick barbed wire, rusted guard towers, and a shed where the toilets are. Sometimes Palestinian police trucks show up outside the gate and unload dozens of kids and a supply of large bricks. Local ambulances give rides to groups of teenagers carrying Molotov cocktails, and in the end a slightly older crowd of men comes on the scene, armed Fatah members. They have a wild time out there. On bad days, at least a thousand people gather outside the gates of Samba. Inside there's only a handful of soldiers, about twenty more or less, and they're besieged and worried about the day when the animals outside, the ones with murder in their eyes, will break the rules of the game without warning and storm the gate, overrunning us. Palestinian policemen wave wire cutters in the air shouting, "Here we come, here we come," like they're about to cut into the fence at any minute. They shout "You're not a soldier, you're a lady" at me, promising to fuck me up my ass, slit my throat, in just another moment, really just a minute from now, but in the meantime they haven't forced their way in. Maybe in the end they actually prefer to live.

On the horizon, there's a slow convoy crawling along the Gaza coastal road. Dozens of trucks and cars and donkeys, the flags of Hamas and Palestine, Islamic songs over the loudspeakers, Arab grandmothers with megaphones. Ten or twenty people are crowded onto the roof of every truck. The procession continues for an hour, coming from nowhere and leading nowhere. Where are they headed? It's the middle of a workday, a weekday, there's no funeral. What's with them? We don't even bother to ask, we're too exhausted for that. Crazy place, this Gaza.

All of a sudden two rounds are fired into the air. A Tanzim activist is firing from the east. We ready our guns while a battery of foreign photojournalists records us, Israeli soldiers with loaded weapons facing kids who have come to protest a cruel occupation. Looks bad. The wounded and battered guy lying on a Red Cross stretcher with a cigarette hanging from his mouth takes a drag, women shriek and moan all around us, and it doesn't let up for a minute. Great stuff for a newspaper. That's the way it is here, normal, what we're used to.

So what do you say, bro? How do you explain that on these black nights in Gaza I'm still dreaming about Lebanon? And that the sadness I carry around inside me always connects to Lebanon? I think that's the only place I've ever been afraid. How can it be, it doesn't make sense, that I'm lying here in an ambush in the mud, or falling off my feet from fatigue on guard duty, or riding in an APC, or approaching an Arab vehicle that might blow me all the way to hell with the press of a single button, and it's only Lebanon I've got on my mind all the time? When it's calm and when it's not, I can feel the Beaufort, smell its smells, sometimes get the shivers from it. And how do you explain that it's strongest when I'm enjoying myself? I'll be sitting with friends over a cold beer, having a great time, there's no mention of anything to do with Lebanon or the army, and then suddenly somebody laughs, and I laugh, and someone tells about some babe he's hooked up with, some new love interest, or a great party he was at. And right then, at that very moment, it hits me without warning, and it hurts, the worst hurt there is. I can see green and it makes me feel bad. I think about the tulips and the poppies, the peanut fields, the laundry flapping in the gardens of the homes in Arnoun, and I'm all choked up. Nature doesn't calm me down, and quiet hurts my ears. The slamming of a door can send me flying. I'll be dancing and dead soldiers will be there, dancing along with me in my heart.

Remember the feeling of holding a dead man in your arms and his body is completely slack? And he's warm from all the pooling blood? Sometimes I feel just that feeling in my fingers, all of a sudden, when I'm having a good time. I hear explosions from far away even when there aren't any, but they make me jump like launches from Tibnit used to. I hear a lot of things, a lot of voices.

I'm sane, don't worry. I'm not shell-shocked. In our country I'm certainly not the only twenty-one-year-old who's held the body of a friend missing a head. You could almost say it's normal around here. And with a lot of pain and my hand on my heart, I've got to share my thought with you—and it's not exactly the most popular one at the moment: if peace doesn't come in the meantime, I want my own kid to go through what I did. The challenges, the pain, the fear. They made me look at the world in a different way, find myself and what's important to me. My love for my family and the love of my life, and how fragile they are. That's how it is when you're surrounded by people who have lost friends. Suddenly you're a lot more careful on the road, for example. Sounds stupid? That's how it is with me. I grew up in Lebanon, for better or worse, and I even had it good there sometimes.

Sometimes, when we'd be lying in an ambush—Spitzer, Zitlawi, Eldad, all the guys—I would try and imagine what the last few moments would feel like: packing the bags, closing the gate, catching a ride home. Life without Beaufort. Then I'd think about returning there, and there would be peace, and exactly where our outpost had stood there'd be a fancy hotel. A hotel in that spot would rake in big bucks, the whole world would be talking about it. And Lila would be there with me, we'd walk hand in hand, and stone by stone I'd show her. "Here, baby, this is exactly where it happened." That's the way I picture it, and I'm afraid I'll have tears in my eyes and she'll laugh at me and say, "What's the big deal? This is the place where you broke down?" and she won't understand.

The truth is, I personally believe we'll return there, to Lebanon. There won't be a hotel on the hill, there'll be a Hezbollah command post we have to capture. What, you don't think we'll have to go back there? You don't think there will be another attack on Misgav Am, another attack in

Maalot? You don't think Kiryat Shmona will be bombarded again? Or that we'll get slaughtered along the way? That's my opinion: it's all going to come back again, and if it's quiet up there for the time being that's only because the terrorists are gathering strength and weapons. They have lots of patience, it's a kind of tactic of theirs, and we're going to be in deep shit. They'll take a soldier hostage, commandeer a jeep at the border fence, bombard some northern settlement with mortar shells—little by little they'll let up on the reins. And when it comes, anyone who thinks a flock of IAF fighter jets is capable of taking care of the job from the air is going to learn there's no replacing foot soldiers. We'll march in there, clean the place up, pass from house to house, overturn every stone. That's because for the time being, we're the losers in that war. We're the losers big-time, exclamation point, no doubt about it. We didn't come away with a peace agreement, we didn't crush the terrorists before we left. We ran away, we left weapons behind, we left our partners—the SLA—high and dry. And that year, that last action-packed year the kids and I spent inside Lebanon, did it contribute anything to anyone? Did it help something, move something forward, change anything? I don't understand why our army waited, what they got out of that. Why didn't they pull us out a long time earlier, when we weren't so weak? Why not a year earlier, when they'd decided to withdraw? Why were we there at all?

Yeah, brother, my main man: it was all for nothing.

I WILL STILL

Autumn 2005. I'm still going to find Oshri. He's hiding from all of us. Maybe that's what he needs, to hide out, but I'm going to pull him out of his hiding place and we'll tear up Africa on motorcycles. We'll find some sexy babe who'd like to engage in hand-to-hand with us and we'll do it with her, the two of us. We'll go all the way to the end and look back. I'll still say to him, "Yeah, man, it's fucking scary, no doubt about it." Out loud, I mean. And I won't be afraid of the fear, and I won't be afraid to leave or to have things end and then start something new. And I won't scare myself with stuff like "If you give in now, you'll always give in." I'll still give in a lot, and I'll disengage loads of times.

I'll still see all of us growing ugly. We'll never be this handsome again, Spitzer was right. I'll still sit naked on the banks of the river, freezing, and I'll write. Lila wants me to write. All that stuff I destroyed, the stuff I was afraid to send, she wants it. And Bitter will wag his tail—the lion king—and I'll eat a flower and drink the stem. Save me a bush or two, my friend, or at least a leaf. The time has come to rest.

I'll still wake up to my mother's meat stew, and I'll stick out my hands in the pitch-black to feel faces and guess who's who, and I'll get it right every time. I won't get addicted, either. Even mourning is addictive, not only fear, and it drips in like poison. I'll still talk less about death, I'll try, because compared to an atmosphere of gloom, my situation is fantastic.

Five years have passed, so how could we not heal? A few things have changed since those times, when we were such jerks. There's no more purple rain. Tapuz stations don't say "Over and out" anymore, or "Diesel, in order; Kfir, in order; Puma, in order; Venus, waiting for confirmation." There's so much to make time for, and at the same time no pressure to finish anything. I'll still watch Hapoel bring home the trophy, I'll still take one of my little nephews to a movie, and my son, too, and maybe even my grandson, and we'll sit just the two of us on the grass. He'll be chakras and sunbeams, he'll smile that smile of his that winks at you and whispers in your ear, "I've got it all figured out, but I'm not telling you." And he'll love me.

It seems like just yesterday we were dancing a waltz in a cold cave and lighting candles and we were glad to be there, together. "Oshri won't anymore..." River said to me when he saw me off to the side, gloomy and alone, on one of those sad days I remember only too well, when we couldn't see the end from up there. "Oshri won't anymore..." he said, waiting for me to continue the thought. But I remained silent. Oshri won't be jacking off anymore? Or maybe he can do it with his left hand, with effort? How about saluting? Playing an instrument? Changing the world? Oshri and I are still going to storm, to rebel. We'll still believe and dream, and dream and remember, and we'll ask questions, and we'll fall, together. We'll suck down vodka sours and drown ourselves in everything wet and hot and salty. And we'll make Mom proud, we'll piss from the highest mountaintop, maybe I'll still cheat on my woman and maybe I'll be sorry I did. Bottom line: I'm totally lucky.

And in the garden of our new little house, on a hill that looks southward, toward the Sea of Galilee, I gave Lila a ring this fall. I have room for her now, lots of it, in my life and in my heart. And when I leave for work each morning, with my camera and my motorcycle, I ask her if maybe she'll let me open the pouch with the dog tags and read her note. She laughs, flustered, and says, "No, not yet. Only at the end." And of course I'm a jerk. I never learned to say no to her.

AFTERWORD: BETWEEN TRUTH AND IMAGINATION

No, I wasn't familiar with the game that everyone plays when a friend is killed, "What He Can't Do Anymore." How could I, when no friends of mine have been killed? I wasn't there, I didn't know what they were doing. On the radio there would be reports on exchanges of fire, even heavy ones, and for eighteen years people came and went and talked about outposts and ambushes. But I stayed in Israel.

I first met up with Lebanon in the heart of the Gaza Strip in the fall of 2000. That was when David Biri, a combat medic in the Givati Brigade Engineering Corps, was wounded by an explosion on the access road to the Netzarim settlement, and died. He was the first IDF soldier to be killed in that war. At the time a young reporter on the news desk at the *Yediot Ahronot* daily paper, I was assigned to the company in mourning. A Tel Aviv pencil pusher, I wasn't accustomed to the smells in the field, but there I was taking down every curse and swear word in my notepad and trying, in vain, to peel back the armor of the company commander, who was tormented at having the media around.

Outside the mess hall, completely by accident, I met Rotem.

Rotem Yair. Everyone called him Ronen, though, because Rotem was a babe's name. And there are no babes in the Givati Brigade. He was the gung-ho type, but worn-out, and sad. He was as dusty as if he'd been plucked right out of a chimney, but his spiked hair was shiny with gel.

"You know what?" he said to me. "Wait an hour, I'm going out on an escort mission, I'll set off a bomb, lose a leg, come back and shower with you and tell you everything." Later, he made me a cup of coffee and wondered what a newspaper could possibly want to write about them.

There's nothing interesting here, he insisted. It's all the usual stuff, and everybody back home knows it all, and if they don't, then they don't want to. Toward morning, after we'd gotten carried away with questions, he told me—on the grass, beneath the thunder of explosions and machine-gun fire from a nearby Palestinian town—about Lebanon.

We spent four days together. During daylight hours he would go out on the white dunes accompanying settlers who wished to cross the death road. When Gaza fell asleep and the lights went out, he would return to the barracks in the tiny enclave, lie down next to me, and get blasted with my questions. He would compare Gaza to Beaufort, brag about and miss it.

Three months later, on the day of his discharge, I was waiting for him at the gate of Givati headquarters. I offered him a ride. On the way we stopped off for a late lunch and I started asking him about the Land of Cedars. I asked if he'd be willing to hole up with me in a hotel on the beach and cut himself off from life for a little while to sift through the details, fill in the gaps. He was hard put to understand my reason for wanting to hear his tale, was not convinced, but eventually gave in to my insistence and agreed to come away with me and tell his story.

With time I came to know the others: Uri Glickman, signaler and Nakpadon driver. Idan Koris, medic. Eran Tzabari, sergeant. Guy Pozitzky, squad leader. At Beaufort they lost a fighter from the bomb removal unit, Noam Barnea, and their squad member Tzakhi Itakh, who was the last IDF soldier killed in southern Lebanon. Tzakhi's good friend Roi Cohen, who was with him in his final moments, was severely injured. He managed to call for help, and when it arrived he insisted that Tzakhi be looked after, worrying only about his friend until the moment he lost consciousness. Roi lost sight in one of his eyes and underwent a number of operations. Today he works in business and is planning a trip to India. For the most part, he's happy.

I met Shai Khingali, too, the commander of Tzakhi and Roi's squad, who was the first one to reach the scorched guard post that had been hit by a missile. He looked at Tzakhi lying there, at peace, kissed him farewell, and loaded his body onto a helicopter. Days later he received a citation for evacuating wounded soldiers under fire that morning. He never stops thinking about Tzakhi and Roi, even today, and about the terrible things he saw there. They keep coming back to him, especially when he is happy.

The popular company sergeant major, Ran Yurman, was seriously injured when a piece of shrapnel hit his arm during a barrage of mortar shells that fell on the outpost. He's been rehabilitated and now lives in an agricultural village in the coastal region of Israel. He studied business administration, but he's pursuing a different dream now, in the kitchen, and rumor has it he's a promising chef.

Two months before the IDF withdrawal from Lebanon, the Givati Brigade Engineering Corps completed a tour of duty and returned to Israel. They were replaced by an engineering unit from the Nahal Brigade. At twenty-five, the company commander, Avi Dohan, became the last commander of the Beaufort outpost. His final mission was to peel eighteen years off the walls, blow the outpost up with nine hundred and eighty mines, and leave the hill. Today he is a lieutenant colonel and the commander of a Nahal battalion, alternating with his troops between Samaria and the outposts spread along Israel's northern border. He moves around with them and with the flag, the one he took down from the flagpole at Beaufort and which now hangs behind him in his office. He is troubled by the company's long list of bereaved families, a squad of which was killed in the helicopter disaster in February 1997. He makes himself available to them in his free time—on weekends and holidays and for late-night phone conversations.

How many commanders in history have had the privilege of giving a speech like the one Avi gave minutes before the hill was blown up, or like the one Goni Harnick gave minutes before the hill was captured? An exceedingly short speech that contains no pathos and no prophecy, only an ending and a beginning.

There are two more people I would like to mention from among the commanders of the outpost in that period: Gal Tamir and Boni Mazar.

Also the commanders of the Ali Taher mountain range battalion, Oren Ebman—who remained on the hill to the very last moments—and Lior Lifshitz.

In the meantime, last year Rotem married Lipaz Azoulai, his girlfriend from the age of fourteen. She has never read the dozens of letters he wrote her from the hill because he destroyed them, afraid to send them, fearing she'd be disgusted and alarmed and that she'd leave him.

The plot of this novel was woven from the events that characterized the last years of the IDF presence in Lebanon, but it is not a work of historical documentation. Liraz (Erez) Liberti is not Rotem Yair. He's an invention. The soldiers he commands are also not based on real people. They are all creations of my imagination, and every last one of them, from the lowliest soldier to the highest brigade and battalion commanders, the live ones as well as the dead ones, though inspired by real people, are the children of my invention. Only the commander of the division at the time, Major General Moshe Kaplinski (Kaplan), today the IDF's second in command, has been named among the story's heroes.

I originally published the diary of an officer at Beaufort in a much shorter version in *Seven Days* magazine in May 2001. Since then the story has been hounding me, following me everywhere: the feeling of futility etched onto each of the victims, and the scars, the powerlessness in the knowledge that I knew nothing, the deep, personal feeling of having missed something by not having been there and experiencing it, and the will, through the characters, to sear the force of their experience onto myself, and to understand—all these together are what brought me to write this book.

During the first week of the Lebanon War, June 10, 1982, my mother's brother, Colonel Haim Sela, was killed. Although from then on we became "members" of the military cemetery at Kiryat Shaul, I remained—as a child and as a soldier—oblivious to what was going on on the other side of the border. The characters in the book opened the gate to Lebanon for me.

ACKNOWLEDGMENTS

I am grateful to all those who assisted me in researching this book, who read the manuscript, commented, and gave advice.

With regard to the pain in dealing with this subject, I am indebted to the Itakh and Barnea families, and to Moran Khizki, Tzakhi's girlfriend for the last two years of his life. These people opened their doors and their hearts to me, as well as the depths of their pain.

I was never for a moment alone with the torments of this story, and I wish to thank from the bottom of my heart all those who were my partners in this endeavor:

Oren Ganor and Aviram Elad, who pored over the manuscript at every stage and gave so much advice that they seeped into it. Their voices can be heard in these pages.

Oren Griffin, Hanan Furman, and Elad Katz, who made up words and created thoughts that no one else could have.

Nir Baram, who forced me to get to know my characters for real.

Joseph Cedar, who has been living Beaufort with me now for four years.

Professor Avi Oz, who, from afar, provided me with a wonderful stash of translated quotes from Shakespeare's *Henry V.*

Noa Mannheim, the editor of this book and my refuge of sanity, who orchestrated this journey gently and firmly and made all the difference.

Shahar Alterman, Ruthie Yuval, and the team at *Seven Days,* who first helped bring the story to life and courageously took it as far as possible. It never would have been without them.

Amnon Dankner, editor in chief of *Yediot Ahronot,* who made me write and refused to be disappointed, and who continues to believe in me and instruct me and keep watch over me.

And finally, to Anat and to my parents, who are all that, and more.

RON LESHEM is the former deputy director in charge of programming at Channel Two, Israel's most watched television network. Prior to moving into television, Leshem was deputy chief editor of *Maariv* newspaper and head of its news division. *Beaufort* won the Sapir Prize—Israel's top literary award—in 2006, and has been translated into more than ten languages. Leshem is also the coscreenwriter for the film version of *Beaufort,* which was nominated for the 2008 Academy Award for Best Foreign Language Film. Leshem lives in Tel Aviv and is at work on his second novel.

ABOUT THE TRANSLATOR

EVAN FALLENBERG has translated books by Meir Shalev, Alon Hilu, and Batya Gur. He teaches creative writing at Bar Ilan University in Israel, where he lives, and is the author of *Light Fell*, a novel.